I0664396

A River Of Orange

by

Roberta C. M. DeCaprio

This is a work of fiction. Names, characters, places, and incidents are either the product of the author's imagination or are used fictitiously, and any resemblance to actual persons living or dead, business establishments, events, or locales, is entirely coincidental.

A River Of Orange

COPYRIGHT © 2007 by Roberta C. M. DeCaprio

All rights reserved. No part of this book may be used or reproduced in any manner whatsoever without written permission of the author or The Wild Rose Press except in the case of brief quotations embodied in critical articles or reviews.
Contact Information: info@thewildrosepress.com

Cover Art by *Tamra Westberry*

The Wild Rose Press
PO Box 708
Adams Basin, NY 14410-0706
Visit us at www.thewildrosepress.com

Publishing History
First Faery Rose Edition, 2007
Print ISBN 1-60154-161-9

Published in the United States of America

Dedication

I dedicate this book to my children, William and Tammy;
and my granddaughters, Fiona and Mia. The years of
telling them all fairytales has inspired me to write this
one for adults.

Meav felt her spirit rise from her body. She looked down at the stone slab and saw herself lying peaceful, deep in sleep. Neteru stood beside the stone altar, chanting and singing words Meav could not understand. The melody had a tranquil effect on her, as she floated to the chamber ceiling. 'Twas from that vantage point she spotted the large, black cat. He entered the room slowly, his amber eyes rising to meet hers. Meav floated down...down...until her bare feet touched the stone floor. Then she climbed upon the panther's back. With each feline step his muscles moved sensuously between Meav's bare thighs. She gripped the fur at his powerful shoulders and rode his sleek, shiny body out of the chamber.

He took her to his cave, carefully setting her onto the pile of animal pelts. Then he sat before her, opened his large mouth to reveal long, sharp fangs and looked into her eyes, growling ferociously.

Meav was not frightened...oh, she should be, but she was not. She reached out and stroked the cat's chest. "You do not scare me, so you can stop trying. I will not be that easily dealt with. 'Tis time you let another help you."

The cat's eyes bathed Meav in adoration, searching each and every facet of her face. Slowly he backed away to the far corner of the cave and stood on his hind legs.

"Come to me, Rule," Meav gently coaxed, extending her hand. "I am here now."

In a blink of an eye the man replaced the animal, standing before her in nothing but a green loin cloth.

"'Tis really you, then?" Rule muttered.

Meav stood. "Aye, 'twas always me, it just took some time for me to understand." She smiled warmly. "I am not afraid or repulsed by you, milord."

Rule stepped closer. "*Sute*...how could you not be? I repulse myself." He looked away, his words clipping into silence.

Meav inched her way toward him. "Look at me, milord."

He brought his gaze to meet hers, regarding her for a long moment.

Meav saw the hurt and longing lying naked in his eyes. "I choose to see the man first, and marvel over how he has handled his plight instead of condemn him for it."

Wings Press best selling author, Mariah LeGrand, (Reiver's Passion and The Gypsy Witch) has classified Roberta C.M. DeCaprio's writing as riveting and captivating. "Ms. DeCaprio is an excellent writer who knows how to create believable characters, putting together page turning plots and storylines that definitely keep the reader's interest."

Chapter One

Atlantic Ocean, July, 1830

Meav sat in the bowels of hell, grieving the death of her family; dirty and sick, scared and tormented. The old wooden vessel creaked with the waves that crashed its side. Meav curled her knees to her chin, and covered her bare feet with the hem of her skirt. Closing her eyes she buried her face in the palms of her hands. Somewhere in the darkness rodents scampered, looking for a morsel to feed on. Her stomach churned at the mere thought of eating another raw potato, and she swallowed hard.

She had stowed away in the dead of night, leaving her homeland and the disease, famine, waste and death that littered the streets of Dublin.

She wiped the grime from her hands down the side of her dirty and tattered skirt. The dampness seeped into the cracks of the old ship, down upon where she slept, and into her young bones. Meav felt achy and older than her twenty years. With fear in her heart she worried she would die of consumption in the dank slime of the floating dungeon.

"'Tis not consumption, but the lack of water that will be the death of me for sure," she groaned.

Her frail body would be found, eaten away by the rats, amongst the potatoes the thieving Brits took from her country. How Meav despised them, and yet she had been forced to take refuge on the *Sea Dragon,* one of their vessels. Would it have been better then, to have stayed put in Ireland, and die with the rest of her family, rather than in the belly of the enemy's ship?

"Nay," she whispered. "I do not want to die at all."

She had no idea of the ship's destiny, only that it carried her as far away from Ireland as it could; leaving behind, not only the destruction of her land, but the lecherous Hollister McGreary as well.

1

The scraping of the hatch being pulled aside and the sound of men's voices forced Meav to gather her will and move behind a large piece of mahogany furniture. The elegant wardrobe, no doubt on its way to adorn some mansion owner's bed chamber, hid her petite frame from view. Like the vermin, her own flesh foul and displeasing to her nose, Meav blended into the shadows.

Heaven help her! What would her dear grandmamma say if she could see her now? The auburn curls that bounced with the shine of an Irish morn were matted to her scalp. And the cotton peasant blouse, once crisp and white, was pasted to Meav's flesh; grime embedded into every soft fiber.

"Blimey, Mate, methinks the crate of rum is by the gentlemen's cupboard," one of the men bellowed. Meav peeked around the armoir and caught a glimpse of him, stout and menacing, holding the lantern high above his head.

The sailor's steps neared the wardrobe. Meav crouched lower, her face nearly touching the musty floorboards, not daring to breathe.

The ship tossed, and a small crate slammed into Meav's back. The pain brought tears to her eyes. Clamping a dirty hand across her mouth, she stifled the moan that threatened to escape from her throat.

The younger man lost his footing, and fell against a crate. "Bloody hell!"

"Hey, Grissom, be watchin' your step there. I cannot be havin' the cargo damaged. The Captain would have me bloody head for sure."

"If the rockin' of this blasted ship 'tain't jarrin' it, me measly hide 'tain't gonna." Grissom inhaled sharply. "The stench down here is drawin' from me belly the meal I just ate, Denton," he complained. "Grab whacha gotta grab, and be done with it."

"Get use to it, Mate." Denton threw the light of the lantern Grissom's way, and laughed heartily as the younger sailor tried to stand. "Seems ya forgot ya sea legs."

Grissom braced his feet and stood erect. "Who the bloody hell ya think ya laughin' at?"

Denton laughed again and shone the light behind the

younger man. "There it be, the crate of rum the Captain's wantin'. Been only out to sea four days, he has, and already made his way through one crate," Grissom complained. "Least hope this last one will be gettin' the bastard through the stretch ahead." He handed the lantern to Grissom. "Now hold steady. Do not be droppin' the light, or ya will be settin' this hell hole on fire." Denton made his way to the crate. "And keep it shinin' on me," he shouted back to Grissom."

"Doin' me best, Mate," Grissom snapped. "'Tain't all that easy."

A sharp, high pitched scream echoed through the hold. The haunting screech seemed to paralyze the two sailors.

The shrill reverberation set Meav's ears ringing.

Grissom's voice trembled. "What the bloody hell was that?"

Denton stumbled to the hatch. "Get up the ladder, and be quick about it, Mate."

Again the penetrating noise filled the hold.

Meav covered her ears with her hands.

Grissom hurried to follow Denton up the ladder. "Will ya tell me what the bloody hell that sound is?"

"'Tis the water folk, the cry of the mer-people," Denton explained, reaching down to take the lantern from Grissom.

"Mermaids?"

"Aye, mermaids," Denton said. "Sirens of the sea. Their song is deadly."

Crouched and trembling in her hiding place Meav swallowed hard. She had heard stories of the half women, half fish creatures that lived beneath the ocean. Their bewitching voices lured ships onto the rocks and men to their death.

"Saints preserve us," she whispered. "Me end has come."

****

Mcav licked her dry lips, tasting particles of sand in her mouth. She spat the grit from her tongue and slowly rolled onto her back. Every bone in her body cried out in pain. She opened her eyes slowly, shielding them from the sun's light. Intense heat burned her alabaster flesh.

3

Slowly she sat up and looked around, blinking into focus the ship's cargo strewn across the white sand, pieces of crate and wood scattered everywhere.

Her head began to swim. Squeezing her temples, Meav tried to relieve the pain that throbbed within. She watched a small crab walk across her lap and make its way over her tattered skirt. It scampered down her leg and disappeared behind a rock.

She inhaled the salty air, trying to clear her mind. What did she remember last?

"The cry of the mermaids," she whispered.

In an instant it all came flooding back to her. The ship had struck a rock; the wooden frame had been ripped apart. Water had gushed into the hold, and she had been swept away. Meav remembered she had sunk down, into the deep, black waters. Her lungs had been ready to explode; her heart pounded within her ears.

Then suddenly a pair of hands had reached for her and with great speed pulled her to the surface. Meav had been placed on the beach. The water she inhaled had gushed from her lungs. She had choked and gasped for air. And then she had felt nothing, until now, waking on a warm bed of sand.

Meav brushed the earth from her face and pushed aside the strands of hair that fell across her forehead. Slowly she stood. Her legs, too weak to hold her, brought her quickly to her knees. She gathered her bearings for a moment before crawling to a nearby rock and pulling herself upon it.

Her gaze wandered about the land. The trees were green. A rich, deep green; greener then any tree she had seen in Dublin. Huge blue and purple flowers adorned the bushes, their petals so vivid with color it took her breath away. Casting her glance out to sea, Meav marveled at the crystal clarity of the blue water. She rubbed her fingers along the rock where she sat. It felt smooth and polished. She dug her toes into the warm, white beach. The sugary dirt shimmered in the sun. Slowly Meav reached down and scooped up a handful of sand, watching it sift between her fingers.

"Where am I?" she whispered, awed by the brilliant colors, and the peaceful beauty that surrounded her.

4

Meav's rumbling stomach broke the serenity. *When had she eaten last?* Again she tried to stand. Her legs, though wobbly, held her. Slowly she took tiny steps over to a bush that sprouted berries. She plucked one free and held it between the tip of her thumb and forefinger. Hesitantly, she brought the tiny red orb to her mouth. *Did she dare take the chance it wouldn't be poisonous?* Slowly she stuck out her tongue, and lightly licked the fruit. It left a sweet aftertaste. Her temptation overcame caution, and quickly she popped the berry past her lips, its juice moistening her dry mouth, the flavor a welcome treat to her palate.

"Have mercy on me soul, should I keel over and die where I stand," she prayed, filling her hands with the delicious outgrowth and shoving them into her mouth.

Meav devoured the entire crop from where she could reach then circled around to consume what grew on the opposite side. From that point she noticed a plantain plant. A few had fallen to the ground. Meav fell to her knees and grabbed a large, fat one. She pealed its greenish skin with trembling fingers, and hungrily sunk her teeth into the soft produce.

It practically melted in her mouth. She rolled her eyes heavenward. "'Tis paradise that I have landed upon," she muttered; her cheeks full of the luscious food. But it left Meav's mouth gummy.

Water, I need water.

She pushed herself to her feet, and walked into the tropical forest.

Meav had no idea where she was headed. She just knew she was in dire need to quench her thirst, and began to make her way through the thick foliage hanging from trees and sprouting from bushes. The large, leafy obstructions hampered her greatly.

"Ah me," she groaned, pushing aside the branches that whipped about her legs, caught on her skirt and tangled in her hair. The thorns cut through her flesh, leaving stinging wounds.

Stopping to catch her breath she inhaled the intoxicating aroma of the flowered plants that scented the air with their beautiful floral mix. The heady fragrance would have normally lifted her spirits, but the sweltering heat had left her agitated. She continued on in her quest for water.

Just when she thought she could bear no more, she came upon a clearing. The sight of the scene before her nearly took her breath away. Beautiful floral bushes and large, crystalline rocks lined the path of a river. A river of orange.

"Orange water," Meav mused, moving toward the edge.

How could that be? Would it be suitable for drinking?

Slowly she dipped one big toe into the colored stream. Its tranquil flow instantly refreshed her flesh. She sunk her foot deeper, the revitalized feeling traveled up her leg. Quickly she knelt, scooped the water into her palms and brought it to her mouth. Eagerly she drank the cool liquid. It was sweet and energizing, quenching more than her thirst. Meav suddenly felt everything inside of her tingle. All sensations were magnified; her wet hands, the breeze playing with the auburn curls that framed her face, the aroma of the Tiger Lily and Snap Dragons nearby; all of it was heightened.

"Oh, Lordy be...'tis not just water."

She stood, again taking in her surroundings, marveling over the colors, now more extraordinary than before. The scenery around her and its magnificence wasn't all that left her awed. Meav herself felt rejuvenated, and suddenly extremely aware of her own body.

It was then that from the depths of the serene pool a creature emerged and slid upon a pearled rock. Meav instantly crouched to her knees and crawled behind a large bush. There she hid, scarcely able to breath, and peered through the branches at the incredible sight before her.

The beautiful water nymph's long, golden curls fell around tanned shoulders. Meav watched the mer-woman push aside the ringlets, exposing rosy nipples that stood erect in the sun's heat. Naked and content the creature reclined, playing, pinching and teasing the peaks; oblivious to the fact that another watched her every move.

Meav gasped as her own nipples hardened beneath her blouse. Slowly she began to rub her fingers back and forth over the firm nubs.

The mermaid then stretched her long tail. The silver scales began to slip from her waist, down her hips and past her thighs. Slowly she brought her hand down to her flat belly, and gently massaged herself.

Meav felt the muscles in her own belly quiver. She rubbed herself as she saw the mermaid do.

The water woman's hand roamed down past her hips. She slipped her fingers between her thighs and stroked herself, back and forth, until her tail curled with pleasure and her beautiful face smiled with contentment.

Meav grew moist between her legs and felt a strong urge to touch herself. The thought of her grandmamma's conservative ways suddenly made her feel guilty at taking such pleasure in her own body. The heat rose to Meav's cheeks. It would have meant a trip to the wood shed for sure, and a switch to Meav's bared bottom. A woman's parts should be kept sacred, covered. Meav had been taught that only when conceiving a wee one does a woman let those private areas be touched, and then, only by her husband. No God fearing woman would ever take pleasure in the deed, least she be considered impure. And watching this water creature doing sinful things would truly send Meav's soul to hell upon departing this life.

Silently she chastised herself. *Turn away; crawl from this hiding place and go back to the beach.*

But Meav's senses were too stirred to move, too engrossed in watching what the mermaid was going to do next.

The sea woman rolled onto her belly, threw back her head, and arched her spine like a feline animal; warming both ends of her slinky form beneath the sun's rays. Curling the tip of her tail, she stroked herself with the fin, up and down the center of her bare behind. Her smile grew as deeper and deeper she inserted the tail, taking much delight in how she fondled herself.

Meav felt her posterior muscles tighten, and longed to strip off her dirty, tattered clothes; allowing her own nakedness to drink in the warmth of the sun. She yearned to explore the forbidden areas of her body—to rub and caress the parts that were now begging for her attention. And the strange, yet wonderful sensation she was having in the inner most depth of her womb was so gloriously intense, she groaned aloud.

****

Rule had been hiding in a nearby copse of trees, admiring the slim, wild beauty as she drank from the mineral spring and took in her surroundings. Her jutting breasts and narrow waist were well proportioned to her delicate frame, yet there was strength about her, a force that did not lessen her femininity. Her head was capped by a mass of amber curls. The long, fiery strands tumbled carelessly down her back and brushed back and forth over firm, rounded hips.

Rule had been prowling his usual haunt to do a bit of *quin furena*, good hunting, when she had taken him by surprise, standing at the edge of the river, the sun gleaming on the deep copper strands of her hair. *Monca!* Where had this enchanting character come from?

He had remained hidden, watching her sneak peeks between the bushes at the sensuous Loreli performing her afternoon pleasures. Rule had enjoyed observing the mermaid's ritual many times as well, but now, the seductive young woman touching herself in places he would love to experience for himself mesmerized his thoughts.

Rule swept his thick, coarse tongue across his jowl, waiting in anticipation for the shapely maiden to shed the tattered garments that covered her splendor. He growled deep in his throat as the beautiful young woman's skirt rose high over her supple thighs. She was just about to touch herself, when the blissful mood was broken by the snorting that emerged from the trees beyond the sea nymph's rock.

****

In an instant a wild boar pounced forth from the vegetation and with fast, stubby legs ran toward the beautiful sunbather. Just as the ugly animal neared the mermaid, she expanded her fin, shimmered into the water and swam away.

Meav sighed, relieved that the water woman had escaped safely. But her relief was soon replaced by sheer fright. The nasty animal was now running straight for the bush where Meav hid. Before she could think on her own behalf the boar was beside her; his pig nose dripping with yellow discharge, and the sharp, protruding teeth ready to rip her to shreds.

"Lord be merciful," she choked, backing slowly away from the beast.

The ugly creature moved closer, salivating and making guttural noises.

Meav's foot hit a rock and she fell backward.

The boar leaped forward.

Rule felt the hairs on his spine bristle. In an instant he pounced forth and in mid-air gripped the boar by the throat. The ugly hog squealed as Rule sunk his fangs into its tough hide. The boar's blood darkened the earth; its screams of horror dying away as he made his kill. Then there was silence.

Dropping the bore's lifeless body, Rule slowly turned his attention toward the young maiden. With a swipe of his tongue he licked away the pig's blood dripping from his mouth. On sleek, long legs he made his way to her, his outsized paws sinking into the soft sand.

The panther's amber eyes locked with hers as it moved closer, so near, that Meav could feel the warmth of its breath. The cat growled, exposing sharp, massive teeth. She stayed riveted to where she sat. Her heart beat rapidly against the walls of her chest. Deeper he peered into her eyes then searched her face, his large jaws looming over her neck. Would he now rip her throat as he had the boar's?

Rule thought her azure eyes were as blue as the sea. Her peach-tinted skin was flawless except for the soft pattern of freckles that dotted her straight, charming nose. Slowly his eyes roamed over the nubile curves beneath her clothes. He could feel his loins tighten; his blood ran hot through his veins.

Slowly, he lowered his mouth to the hollow of her neck. Gently he licked her with his rough, bloody tongue, tasting her flesh.

Mcav suddenly felt very tired, a peace washed through her, that she had only known in deep sleep. She felt every muscle in her body go limp, and her eyelids grew heavy. The beast's golden eyes were the last thing she saw before darkness flooded the edges of her world.

****

The elderly woman looked down at the enchanting, young female before her. Rule had brought the tattered individual to her humble cottage and arrogantly expected her to help. Slowly the old crone knelt down on her sore, boney knees beside the bed, wet a cloth from a basin of water on the wooden stand, and began to wash the younger girl's sullied face. The auburn haired beauty did not stir; Wysteria's touch was not enough to raise her from the deep sleep spell Rule had cast. As she cleaned the girl's cuts and scraps, Wysteria thought back to the intrusion of an hour ago.

Rule had unexpectedly marched into her abode, carrying a woman in his muscular arms.

"She is in need of healing, Wysteria," he had snapped, lying the maiden upon Wysteria's bed. "And wash the putrid smell from her body," he had added, wrinkling his nose from the stench. "Do what needs to be done, *seda!*" he had demanded, stalking to the door.

"*Seda, seda*...always now with you," she had retorted sharply. "But how...*sute*...am I to care for this waif without knowing her birth sign?" she grumbled, putting her sewing aside.

"I do not care *sute*, just do it *seda*," Rule had shouted over his shoulder.

"Each of the twelve houses of the birth chart governs a definite part of the body, its weaknesses and strengths. 'Tis my duty as a healer to know the exact compound of herbs in respect of planetary laws, or else the active principal of one will counteract the active principal of another," Wysteria had explained.

His massive frame had halted at the dwelling's opening, blocking the sunlight from entering the small house. Slowly he turned around. "And will not knowing her birth sign be injurious?"

"Nay, but 'tis a waste of time, of herbs, of..."

Rule's amber eyes fixed harshly on Wysteria. "I care not for any of these things," he had bellowed. "You will do as you are told, ancient one, else I'll have your old bones hung to dry and bleach in the hot sun."

Wysteria stood abruptly from her chair and waved her hand dramatically above her head, dismissing his threat. "Much wind pours from your mouth, Rule." She had matched his glare, thrusting out a defiant chin. "You can go kiss an *orkly* for all your threats, it matters not to me." She had looked over at the young woman asleep in her bed, and her heart softened. "Should I choose to help her, 'tis because her inner spirit beckons to me, and not because you demand it."

Rule's wide shoulders had tensed. "I have no time for your insubordination, old woman. Just care for the girl, *seda!*" his deep voice had grated.

Now Wysteria slowly rose to her feet. With gnarled hands she emptied the basin and refilled it with clean water from a cistern. Before returning to her new charge she closed her eyes and mentally summoned Merrow, Chieftain of the Elwins.

Merrow's deep, soothing voice filled her thoughts. *"What is it you need, dear healer?"*

"The help of two of your women," Wysteria mentally replied.

"Which two do you request?"

"Twila and Raika," she quickly answered.

"Say no more," Merrow responded.

Within a matter of moments the two albino women entered the cottage.

"Vedela," Twila chirped.

Wysteria nodded tautly at the first Elwin woman. "Greetings to you too, Twila. I thank you for coming to my aid so quickly."

"Why are you in need of us, Wysteria?" Raika questioned.

Wysteria pointed to Meav sleeping on the bed. "The mere wisp of a girl there is in bad need of a bath. I need help in undressing and washing her." She smiled warmly at the second Elwin woman. "I know your daughter Aliki is almost ready to give birth, so I will not keep you long."

Raika's soft, pale, pink eyes filled with curiosity. "Who is she?"

Wysteria shrugged. "I have not the slightest notion. Rule brought her to me only an hour ago, demanding she be cared for."

Twila moved to stand beside Raika, and peered down at the sleeping maiden. Gently she picked up one of

Meav's hands. "Dainty bones, do you not agree, Raika?"

Raika gently pushed aside a rich auburn curl from the girl's forehead. "Aye, she is sweet faced, in spite of all the dirt." She smiled mischievously. "No doubt Rule has seen this as well."

Twila giggled lightly. "I am sure you are right, sister."

Wysteria moved to stand at the foot of the bed, crossing her arms over her boney chest. "Are you ladies finished discussing her attributes?"

Both the Elwin women nodded.

"Then help me strip her of these horrid garments and get her into a tub of water."

In her sleepy haze, Meav felt the gentle administering to her body. Oh how glorious the tiny hands felt that scrubbed her head, making her scalp tingle. Another pair of hands washed her breasts, belly, parted her thighs and cleansed her sex. Each stroke of the soft cloth was tender, refreshing to her abused flesh. The heather scent pleased her senses, and clung to her dreams, as she pictured herself lying in a field of the sweet smelling blooms. She thought to rise from her sleep, but the care she was receiving felt superior, so wonderfully delicious, that to halt it would be foolish.

Meav could feel the caring hands wipe her dry and rub soothing salve gently into the parts of her that ached; her back, her shoulders, her thighs, the cuts and scraps along her feet and ankles. *Was this heaven? Were these the hands of angels preparing her for eternity?* She struggled to open her eyes, but a gentle influence coaxed her to remain slumbering.

"Questa ven...rest well little one."

The voice was sweet to Meav's ears, like a beautiful song, lilting and light. *What could it hurt to let the caresses, the care, continue?* She felt safe and loved, totally relaxed. Her body was finally free from the rancid stench. Ah, 'tis a glorious state for sure that she now experienced, and as long as she did not wonder how or why, she imagined she could easily enjoy it for just a wee bit longer.

Wysteria conjured up a salve made from *TusSilahgo farfara*, which binds toxins in the system and removes them; and *Symphytum officinale*, which serves as a demulcent, expectorant, and emollient. The leaves from this herb were a great poultice for cuts and wounds, and possessed pain relieving properties.

She rubbed the mixture along the young woman's spine; working in circular motions around the firm, rounded buttocks, down to her thighs, calves, and ankles. It was there she stopped short, examining the crescent shaped mark on the bottom of the young girl's right heel. She traced the form with her finger, over and over. *Could it be her old eyes were deceiving her?* Was, after all these years, after all these centuries, she to be the one privileged to witness what those before her foretold?

Slowly Wysteria made her way to the table, setting her old bones down on the *jinni*, a stool her father had carved from a single piece of hardwood. She reached for her medicine book. The cover, made of cornhusks and palm leaves, was inscribed with mysterious hand-sculpted symbols. It bound the pages of the spells, the recipes for her healing herbs, and the Prophecy of the isle of Keronia, made by Wysteria's grandfather a half a century ago. She reached for the bronze lantern by one of its dragon shaped handles and brought it closer to the book. Carefully she turned each yellowed leaf, until she found what she searched for.

Twila came beside her. "What is it you look for, dear healer?"

Wysteria pointed toward the maiden without raising her eyes from the book. "Look on the bottom of her right heel and tell me what you see?"

Both the Elwin women examined Meav's foot.

"'Tis the crescent of Keronia," Raika gasped.

Twila nodded slowly, looking somewhat stunned. "I have actually lived to see this day," she muttered and turned toward Wysteria. "Is she the one, then?"

Raika covered Meav's naked body with a clean linen sheet. "Thank our Divine Maker," she whispered.

Twila moved toward the table. "Is she the one, dear healer?" she repeated anxiously.

Wysteria looked up from her reading, the translucent depths of her topaz eyes misty with hope. "Aye, she is the one, she is Meridith's child." She pointed to the page. "The one the Prophecy speaks of."

The two Elwin women clapped their hands with joy.

"Read to us what the Prophecy says," Raika asked.

Wysteria cleared the emotion from her throat and returned her old eyes to the page before her. *"Constellia Lo glowena timenta coupla*...a star shall shine on the hour of this meeting, for all is not doomed, dear Keronians," she read aloud. "The one who steps upon the crescent moon, with hair like fire and eyes like the sea, will arrive in the night; tattered and worn, hungry and scared. She will be innocent of her own powers; of the blood that runs through her veins. Only she...with the same blood as the evil one...can undo what the evil one has done. Only she...with love of her own accord and that of a true heart...can save the Highest Son. Only His Majesty's love from his own accord in return, will then break the curse and Keronia will be rid of the one with the evil heart. Elders of the isle, teach the fire-haired maiden well how to use the gifts of her ancestors. In turn, she will save your rule."

Tears filled Twila's pale eyes. *"Yaluna*...at last we will be set free."

Raika brought a small, chubby hand over her heart. "Gone will be Devora's reign."

Wysteria looked up sharply from the book. "Hush, Raika, lest she hear you."

Raika quickly slapped her hand over her mouth and looked around the room in fear. "I am sorry, dear healer," she apologized. "I got carried away with hope."

Twila put a comforting arm around her sister's shoulders and drew her close, then spoke to Wysteria, "That Prophecy was foretold by your grandfather. Devora's grandfather as well...would she not already know of things to come?"

"Nay," Wysteria whispered. "My dear grandfather only allowed the eldest child of each generation to learn how to read the symbols. Because your Chieftain's ancestors and mine were the original knights of Keronia, only you Elwins and I know what these pages hold. Devora knows nothing about the Prophecy and we must keep it that way."

Raika nodded in agreement. "My lips are sealed."

"We must be very cautious, Raika. Devora's henchmen are everywhere. One never knows where they lurk, what they hear, or how quickly they bring her what they have learned," Wysteria warned.

She closed the book and stood, moving to the window and looking out over the field. "Devora was not always evil," Wysteria said softly. "I remember fondly the days my younger sister and I had laughed and played in the very fields I am gazing at now, collecting herbs and flowers for mixtures we would use in the healing of injured animals." Devora's sweet smile, the way she had brought joy to all she met suddenly filled Wysteria's memory. "In my mind's eye, I can almost reach out and touch Devora's beautiful ebony curls, see her violet eyes crinkle with her laughter."

Wysteria wiped the lone tear slipping down her thin cheeks before turning to face the Elwin women. "I am sorry; I meant not to frighten you." She forced a smile. "Thank you for your help. You may go now to your homes."

Both the tiny women nodded and made their way to the door.

"And, I beg of you," Wysteria called after them. "Breathe not a word of this to anyone."

****

Slowly Meav opened her eyes. Sunshine from the small window divided the room, tiny powdery flakes gliding through the beam of light danced around her. She rubbed the sleep from her eyes, and blinked them into focus. *Were the particles fragments of dust or tiny bugs?* Nay, they were...were...miniature naked, winged women.

Meav sat abruptly, the linen sheet falling to her waist. "Ah me, have I lost me mind?"

One of the tiny fairies giggled lightly.

Meav shook her head in disbelief. "Saints preserve us."

"Preserve you, not me. I am perfectly fine," the little imp answered, her large blue eyes twinkling with merriment.

"Who...what...are you?" Meav stammered.

"I am Gyla," the little cherub offered, landing on Meav's knee.

15

"And I am Titiana," the other one chimed in, setting down upon Meav's other knee.

Meav brought her hands to her forehead and squeezed her temples. "Lord have mercy on me soul, I have lost me mind."

"Where have you lost it?" Titiana questioned.

"We would be glad to help you look for it, if you could tell us when you last had it," Gyla added.

"I lost it the moment I woke up in this strange land," Meav groaned. "Truth be told, me mind is a complete blank."

"Then 'twas gone long before you arrived here," Gyla concluded.

"How *did* I get here?" Meav asked, looking around.

The tiny cottage was simple and clean. A stone fireplace stood to the far end of the room, an oak table, a small stool and two chairs beside it. A cupboard with a washbasin on it, along with various cooking implements occupied the opposite side of room. An apothecary chest rested against another wall, with several candles upon it. The small windows were framed with wooden shutters, opened slightly to bring in the afternoon's light. Wooden floors gleamed clean, the worn boards covered here and there by animal skin rugs.

"And *where* is here?" Meav added.

"Here is where you are," Titiana beamed.

"And where might *here* be?" Meav was becoming slightly annoyed.

"You ask a lot of silly questions," Titiana snapped.

Meav frowned. "Perhaps 'tis because you are not giving smart answers."

Titiana stood with her hands on her hips. "My answers have been truthful, and you are a silly, stupid girl if you cannot understand them."

"Quiet your tongue, Titiana," Gyla warned.

"I will not!" Titiana snapped.

"Then you force me once again to make you do as you are told," Gyla said, grabbing Titiana by the arm. She threw the impish fairie across her knee and began to spank her.

"Stop!" Titiana cried. "I have done nothing wrong."

"You have been rude," Gyla retorted, continuing to

redden Titiana's bare bottom, each slap harder than the last.

Though Meav had not appreciated Titiana's attitude, Gyla seemed to be getting a wee bit carried away with administering the punishment.

Meav cleared her throat nervously. "Perhaps she has learned her lesson, Gyla."

"She never learns her lesson," Gyla said. "I have to spank her at least ten times in a day."

Meav gasped. "Surely no one can be that naughty?"

"Well she is," Gyla replied, angrily pinching Titiana's raw backside.

"Stop, please!" Titiana screamed. "'Tis enough!"

"I agree, 'tis enough," Meav added.

Gyla looked up at Meav. "Perhaps you are right." She threw Titiana off her lap. "That should hold her for at least an hour."

Titiana stood slowly, her wings drooping, tears streaming down her little cheeks. Quickly she scampered to the foot of the bed, and burrowed beneath the quilt folded there.

Meav stretched her neck to see her. "Do you think she is all right?"

Gyla waved her hand casually above her blonde curls. "She is fine, just embarrassed that you saw her getting a spanking." She sighed, as though she had done a strenuous days work. "She always sulks after a punishment, pay her no mind."

Meav watched Gyla settle herself back down, her little legs spreading shamelessly apart, showing all she was about.

Meav reached over and gently pushed the tiny limbs together. "That really is not the most lady-like way to sit, especially without your clothes."

Gyla tilted her golden head sideways. "Pixies don't wear clothes."

Meav frowned. "Well you should. 'Tis shameful for your little womanly parts to be showing for all to see."

Gyla pointed to Meav's chest. "Yours are showing, and they are much bigger and can be seen much better than mine."

Meav looked down at herself, and gasped. Quickly

she brought the sheet up to cover her bare breasts. "What happened to me clothes?"

"Perhaps they are where you left your mind?" Gyla suggested.

Meav brought her hands over her eyes. "Ah, me," she groaned.

****

Wysteria sat on a rock, waiting for the pale, pink dress to dry in the gentle breeze. The delicate, white lace that framed the neckline had yellowed with age.

Wysteria grunted. "'Tis a wonder it has not rotted," she whispered to herself.

The dress had been hers, the one she'd donned over a once shapely form. She had worn it while dancing to the music, the hem tickling her ankles with each step, and her handsome beau looking down into her eyes.

Wysteria smiled at the memories that flooded her thoughts; scenes of a love that had died before his time, the tears and years of her youth that had been stashed away for decades, like the dress. They had never been forgotten, just too sad to recall.

Her smile deepened. "Until *now*," Wysteria said aloud.

"Until, now...what?" a deep, male voice interrupted the serenity.

Wysteria turned to find Rule standing behind her, hands on hips, legs spread apart. His usual stance...the one he used to intimidate all on the island; and it worked on all but her.

"Have you nothing better to do than sit upon this boulder and watch your clothes dry?" he bellowed.

Wysteria tucked a gray strand of hair behind her ear. "And have you no other octave to your voice than one laced with anger?"

Rule frowned and made his way to stand before her. Leaning against the trunk of a nearby tree, he crossed his arms over his chest. "Was it not you, my dear nanny crone that taught me not to answer a question with a question?"

Wysteria arched a gray, bushy brow. "Yet you have."

Rule's jaw tightened. "And yet you still treat me as though I was in your charge."

Wysteria pointed a boney finger at Rule. "I can say

this with honesty, lad, I liked you much better when I was cleaning your messy bottom and feeding you your meals." She stood. "And it appears I coddled you way too much, gave you your own way to a fault." Wysteria placed her hands on her hips. "I should have turned you over my knee more, made you feel the switch of consequence across your bare backside. Perhaps you would have respect for your elders, if I had."

Rule moved closer to the elderly woman. "You dare to talk to me of such things?"

Wysteria looked up into his amber eyes. His massive build towered over her slight frame, mouth curled into a sneer, his brows furrowed. She raised a defiant chin. "Aye." Squaring her thin shoulders, Wysteria challenged him. "What will you do about it?"

"I will...I will..."

Wysteria waved her hand casually in the air. "You will do nothing."

Rule roughly grabbed the elder by the shoulders. "Why do you continue to bate me, rile the very nerves from my body, old woman?"

Wysteria pulled away. "You have much to learn, Rule." Again she admonished him with a wagging finger. "Just because you are heir to the throne..."

Rule quickly cut her off. "That is truly rich coming from your old lips." He laughed sardonically. "Thanks to the spell your darling sister placed upon me, I am no longer considered the heir...instead I am destined to forever roam these jungles; to leave my confines would mean certain death." Hatred blazed in his eyes. "Maybe death would be better...better than my man's form changing to that of a panther every time my stomach hungers." His lips thinned. "I disgust myself, the way I have been made to hunt for food...like a savage beast...ripping apart my meal with animal fangs and large, clawed paws, blood dripping from my jowls, and forced to live in a cave. But for all my shame, at least I will be revered here in the jungle...the last domain that sees me as ruler...which I am...I am Rule," he snarled.

Wysteria's face saddened. "I am deeply sorry for what my sister has done to you. Devora's greed for riches and power has turned her to the dark side, and I have not forgotten the way she destroyed your family. 'Tis etched in my memory, the way she had wheedled herself into the castle and deceived King Stefan; taking a position as nursemaid and devoted servant to his dying Queen."

Rule smirked. "When my mother finally succumbed to the illness that riddled her body, Devora was there to pick up the pieces, comforting my grieving father. But her intentions were not genuine."

Wysteria nodded in agreement. "'Tis the truth...she wasted no time in mesmerizing Stefan with her exotic beauty and black magic to gain the seat of queen for herself. And her manipulation turned the king against you...his own son. Devora persuaded Stefan to leave all to her in the event of his death...which mysteriously happened within a few months time after the decree was signed."

"And when I challenged the document my father signed and the circumstances surrounding his death, Devora cast a spell on me."

A second time Wysteria apologized. "Again, I am sorry for all you have endured at the hands of my sister."

Rule's tone was thick with bitter sarcasm. "Forgive me if I do not accept your apology."

Wysteria turned and reached for the dress drying on a branch. "I did not expect you to." She made her way up the path. "Now, if you will excuse me," she called over her shoulder. "I have a very lovely young woman in my cottage that is in need of clothing."

"The dress...'tis for her?" Rule questioned.

Wysteria stopped walking and turned to face him. Her tone held a tinge of amusement. "Aye...certainly I can no longer wear it."

"Did she speak her name...tell you from where she comes?" Rule probed.

"Nay, she still sleeps. Your slumber spell has relaxed her thoroughly." Wysteria smiled. "Shall I come for you when she wakes?"

Rule nodded. "Aye. 'Tis best to be cautious. She could be a spy, one of Devora's tricks."

Wysteria remembered the crescent shaped birth mark beneath the girl's right heel and quickly cast that notion from her mind. Meridith's child had returned and the Prophecy said she would undo all the evil that was done. But to tell Rule of what she knew would not be wise. "I suppose 'tis best," Wysteria agreed, turning to make her way back up the path to her cottage.

****

Meav was growing restless...and hungry. She decided to search the tiny cottage for a morsel of food. Surely there had to be something, a crust of bread, a homemade biscuit or two, in one of the cupboards? Meav swung her legs out of the bed and wrapped the sheet around her nakedness. Slowly she made her way to the cabinet and opened the door. She spotted a bowl filled with apples. Just as she was about to reach for the fruit, the cottage door opened.

"I see you have awakened," Wysteria said.

Meav turned to find an elderly woman standing in the doorway. Her hair, saturated with gray, was coiled into a braid that hung over her shoulder. Slight of frame, the crone's watery topaz hued eyes twinkled as she smiled.

Meav's face reddened, embarrassed to be caught rummaging around in someone's home. She modestly adjusted the sheet and cast her gaze to the floor. "I...I...was hungry," she stammered in a wee voice.

Titiana finally poked her head out from beneath the quilt, and fluttered over to Wysteria. "She has lost her mind, as well."

Wysteria opened her hand for the pixie to land upon. "Has she now?"

"Aye," Titiana said, pulling back her wings and sitting down on the boney palm. "And she is clueless as to where she is or how she got here." She tipped her head slightly. "Not all that smart, I would say."

"Titiana!" Gyla shouted, flying across the room. "What have I told you about being rude?"

Wysteria chuckled lightly. "Careful little one or else you will be getting that bottom reddened."

Titiana pouted. "I am sorry, sister."

Gyla landed on Wysteria's arm and pointed to Meav. "Who is she, dear healer?"

Wysteria looked over at Meav. "Who are you, child?"

Meav cleared her throat nervously. "I am Meav

21

O'Shay, from Dublin, Ireland."

"And where is Dublin, Ireland?" Wysteria questioned.

Meav shrugged. "I know not how to explain the where about of me homeland, only that me journey on that ship was for many days." She clutched the sheet to her breasts. "And who might you be?"

"They call me Wysteria...healer and wise crone of these here isles of Keronia," Wysteria explained, placing each pixie gently on the mantel and moving closer to Meav.

"And how have I come to be here?" Meav asked.

Wysteria smiled warmly. "Suppose you tell me what you remember."

Meav licked her dry lips. "When the *Sea Dragon*, the ship I had stowed away on, sunk to her doom, I was washed upon your shores."

"Aye," Wysteria said. "Many ships meet their fate in these waters. 'Tis the siren's song that lures them to their death."

"Aye...'tis what happened," Meav admitted quickly. "Exactly that way...the mer-woman's screech...the ship being tossed...and then..." Meav's voice trailed off, as she remembered the way she plunged into the depth of the black sea, her lungs filling with water till they would burst. She shivered. "Then a hand gripped mine; pulled me from the deepness and placed me on the beach."

"'Twas Loreli who saved you," Gyla chirped.

Meav frowned. "Who is Loreli?"

"She is the mermaid that lives in the river...a river of orange," Gyla explained.

Meav's face brightened. "Aye, I have seen her...I remember waking on the beach, searching for food, and coming upon the orange waters. Loreli sat sunbathing on a rock. She is a magnificent creature, so beautiful...so...so free," again her voice faded, as she pictured Loreli upon the rock, touching and fondling herself. Suddenly Meav remembered how the sea nymph had awakened strange feelings within her own body. Nervously she cleared her throat. "And then there was a boar, rushing from the bushes...he came after me...and...and then..." Meav sighed. "I can remember nothing more from that point on."

Wysteria gave Meav's arm an affectionate pat. "What matters is that you are alive and safe." She handed Meav the garment. "And after you get dressed, and I fill your belly with a thick slice of homemade bread and a bowl of eggplant soup, you can tell me why 'tis you stowed away on the *Sea Dragon*."

Meav's mouth watered at the thought of *real* food. She quickly took the dress Wysteria held out to her. "Where can I change?"

Wysteria arched a brow. "Right where you stand, child."

Again Meav felt her cheeks grow hot.

Wysteria chuckled lightly. "There is no reason for your shame. I was the one who undressed you and bathed the dirt from your body. So, you hide nothing beneath that sheet."

Meav reluctantly dropped the sheet to the floor, and quickly slipped the dress on over her head.

Wysteria helped the young woman to smooth down the flared skirt. "Aye, it suits you well," she said. "You have brought the old garment to life once again.

"'Tis beautiful," Meav whispered.

"Aye, 'tis," Wysteria agreed. "I remember feeling the same way whenever I wore it. Her eyes softened. "I once filled it the same as well."

Meav smiled lovingly. "Thank you so much for giving me something that obviously was very special to you." She looked around the tiny cottage. "And for opening your home to me."

Wysteria felt the kindred spirit of the sweet-faced maiden. "Sit," she said, motioning to a chair at the table. "And let me make you that meal." Wysteria began to prepare the food. "Now tell me, lass, why did you steal away on the ship."

Meav sighed heavily. "'Twas because of Hollister McGreary. When I refused his marriage proposal, he had me home burned to the ground and murdered me family."

Wysteria gasped. "Mercy me...and how did you escape?"

"I had slept at the Connor home on that eve, to help Maggie Connor birth her child. If not for that, I would have perished along with me folks," Meav explained.

"Timothy Connor, sweet Maggie's husband, had somehow learned of McGreary's plan to destroy me home and family. Come midnight Timothy had helped me sneak out his back door, to the pier and into the hold of the *Sea Dragon*, the only ship leaving the docks the next morn." Meav shivered. "There I slept with the rats in the stench and the cargo." She sighed again. "So, I am an orphan now."

Wysteria placed the bowl of soup before her guest. "You have a place here, with me," she offered. "Though 'tis humble, 'tis also clean, warm, and a happy place."

Titiana flew to the table and broke off a tiny piece of Meav's bread. With a smile she popped it into her mouth. "'Tis true, Meav O'Shay. You will be happy here."

Meav smiled down at the little pixie woman, who was lying on her back with her legs spread wide apart, boldly displaying all she was about, and enjoying the sun that shone from the window above the table.

Wysteria reached over and rubbed the fairie's belly with the tip of her finger. "I am pleased you agree."

Titiana giggled. "I do wholeheartedly," she said, stretching her naked form, thoroughly enjoying the attention Wysteria was bestowing upon her.

Meav shook her head in disgust. "You truly have no shame, little one." She pursed her lips together. "I must sew you clothes."

Titiana giggled again. "Gyla told you before, pixies don't wear clothes."

Wysteria gently picked the tiny woman up by a sheer wing. "Off with you now, so I might get acquainted with Meav." She released Titiana and the little fairie flew out the window.

Gyla sat down upon the table. "I thought she'd never leave." She smiled at Wysteria, then at Meav. "Now, ladies, let us chat."

Wysteria chuckled. "Off with you as well."

Gyla's smile drooped. "Surely you jest."

Wisteria faked a stern face. "Surely, I do not." She gave Gyla a gentle push. "Go *seda*, back to your tree and the Treogs that dwell with you."

"Very well," Gyla mumbled. "'Tis a safe bet Titiana is in need of another spanking anyway."

Once they were alone, Meav talked through mouthfuls of soup about the potato famine in Ireland, the disease and death that ravaged the land, about the British and how they treated her people.

Wisteria cleverly moved the conversation around to family. "Tell me more about your folks."

Meav broke off a piece of bread and savored its flavor. "I have..." she paused. Her face saddened. "Before McGreary's rage I had," she corrected, "two younger sisters, a grandmother and a father."

Wysteria arched a brow. "What of your mother?"

"She died when I was only five...after giving life to me younger siblings, twin sisters, Sinead and Shawna," she added softly. "I have been told I favor her, with me fiery head of hair and the blue eyes."

"Then she must have been a beautiful woman," Wysteria commented.

Meav smiled at the compliment. "She was...always laughing, singing, dancing...me Papa would say she had a dancing heart."

"Aye, I know the type well," Wysteria whispered, seeing Meridith's spirit in the young woman who sat before her.

"Me mama was not from Ireland...never spoke of her homeland or her family. She just showed up in Dublin one day and me Papa fell head over heels in love with her."

"Then I can only imagine how hard and long he grieved when she passed," Wysteria sympathized, feeling the sadness of Meridith's death as well.

Meav nodded in agreement. "I do not believe he ever got over her death, and though he was a good and loving father, there was something lacking in his spirit...his joy disappeared. He went through the motions of living, did right by his family, never failed to do his best, but his heart was not in it. Grandmamma came to live with us a few weeks after Mama died. And Papa just left the rearing of us girls up to her." Meav sighed. "Out of the three of us, I am most like me Mama, not just me coloring, but the fact that we both have the same birthmark under the right heel of our foot."

Wysteria's heart suddenly began to beat rapidly. She leaned forward in her chair. "Tell me your mother's name,

Meav." She needed to hear it from the maiden's own lips.

"Meridith," Meav said. "Her name was Meridith O'Shay."

Chapter Two

Queen Devora rang the summons bell. Quickly, Zailia rushed to assist the queen before the bell rang a second time. From experience, Zailia knew being prompt was what kept Devora happy. And when the queen was happy, it made everyone else's life in the castle that much easier to bear.

Zailia opened the bath chamber door, and stood obediently beside the huge tub, the scent of jasmine oil filling her senses. Slightly, she bowed her head. "At your service, Your Majesty."

Devora held up her hand. "The tips of my fingers are shriveled like prunes and the bath water has grown tepid." Slowly Devora stood, proudly displaying her naked form before the maid. "You pathetic creature," she snapped. "You are a disgrace to my eyes...your hair tied back in that ratty bun, and your complexion looks gray."

Zailia held back the words she would have loved to rain down on the selfish, arrogant woman. How was she to take a moment for herself, when Zailia was at Devora's beck and call, even at the wee hours of the night? "I am sorry, Your Majesty. I will try to present myself better."

"See to it you do," Devora spat.

Zailia draped a plush towel over the queen's shoulders and reached for the scented oil. For the next hour Zailia would be expected to pamper every nerve and muscle of Devora's female form. Zailia silently cringed at the task at hand. Serving the witch was bad enough, but to have to touch her naked body brought her disgust.

Devora walked over to the full-length mirror, and stood before it. Removing the towel, she took a few moments to admire her naked reflection. She loved the sight of herself, the way her hair hung shiny and black to her well-rounded hips; the deep violet of her eyes. People said she had an exotic look, a timeless beauty.

Devora turned sideways and ran her hand over her

full, rounded breasts, tweaking the nipples. "I am quite a woman, do you not agree, Zailia?"

Zailia bowed her head in submission. "Aye, my queen; that you are." If Devora knew the real context in which those words were meant, Zailia would be whipped.

Devora reached for the strand of carnelian and turquoise beads hanging on the mirror's hook and slipped them over her head. "Aye, quite a woman," she marveled again, stroking the smooth gems that lay between her cleavage.

Zailia watched Devora make her way to the bed. The queen's slow, sleek strides announced the confidence and obsession she had with herself. The woman was anything but modest, parading around the castle's upper chambers stark naked. And Devora cared not who walked in on the premises at the time. She took satisfaction in exhibiting her endowment.

Devora lay face up upon the satin sheets, spun from the silk brought to the island by ocean traders, and fingered the beads around her neck. She fully enjoyed using Zailia to appease her desires. "I want you to massage my flesh till it glows."

An unwelcome blush crept into Zailia's cheeks. "Aye, Your Majesty."

Devora looked deep into the young woman's large, brown eyes. "I want my nipples to look inviting beneath my white, sheer robe."

Zailia grew increasingly uneasy under the queen's scrutiny. Awkwardly she cleared her throat. "Aye, Your Majesty."

Devora laughed wickedly. "I must look positively delicious." She rested her head back against a satin pillow. "I am entertaining Shell tonight, and I want his mouth to water for my charms." Zailia would prepare Devora for the handsome sentry that later would pay a visit to the queen's bedchamber. "Though I can have my pick of any of the men that guard this castle," she boasted, "I favor Shell; he's a burly lad, hung amply between his thighs." Devora smiled iniquitously. "And he has no problem bestowing his services...over and over again."

Zailia's embarrassment quickly turned to

annoyance...in her self mostly, for accepting and allowing another's disrespect.

"He becomes so hard...so hot...he knows just what to touch, and just what to rub, at just the right time," Devora elaborated intentionally, knowing Zailia's discomfort at such bold words. She continued. "He loves my mouth upon him, moans with pleasure when I draw him to the back of my throat." Devora sighed. "I almost have trouble consuming his entirety."

Zailia could not imagine why, the woman's mouth was certainly big enough.

Devora studied Zailia's face. "Why, Zailia, am I embarrassing you? Or could it be you had Shell in mind for yourself?"

"Nay, Your Majesty," Zailia quickly corrected.

"Not that any man would look at the likes of you," Devora added.

Zailia almost dropped the bottle of oil she held.

Devora sat up and with one swipe of her well-manicured hand, slapped Zailia hard across the face. "You little twit," she shouted. "You could have spilt oil all over the bed." She grabbed the edge of the cover sheet. "Oil can stain satin permanently."

Zailia held her emotions in check. "I am sorry, Your Majesty."

Devora slowly rested back against the pillows, again fingering the beads around her neck. "Why I must put up with such incompetence is beyond me," she complained.

"I will do better, my queen," Zailia whispered.

"See to it that you do," Devora spat.

Zailia swallowed the tears that stung her throat.

Devora drew satisfaction from Zailia's crushed expression. "*Seda*...get to work, girl," she demanded, stretching her naked form. "Pour the oil onto your fingers this time and massage them over each and every inch of my glorious body."

****

Rule watched the peacock strut past him; its plumage rendered in stunning detail, the delicate pattern an array of color. "'Tis a good thing for you, my rainbowed fellow, that I am not in the mood for foul this evening," Rule teased.

"Are you in the mood to meet Wysteria's guest?" a jolly voice said from behind.

Rule turned to find his good friend Ibrehem leaning against the trunk of a tree. His face brightened. *"Vedela."*

"Greetings to you as well," Ibrehem responded cheerfully.

"The lass is awake, then?"

Ibrehem nodded slowly. "And Wysteria told me to tell you she has washed the putrid smell from her body." He raised a brow. "That was what you had ordered her to do, was it not?"

Rule's face reddened. "Aye, 'twas."

Ibrehem frowned. "As brash as that, my lord?"

Rule arched a brow. "Afraid so, my friend."

Ibrehem chuckled lightly. "Then I see nothing has changed with you, much wind still pours from your mouth."

There was a faint glint of humor in Rule's eyes. "And you can go kiss an *orkly*."

Ibrehem threw his head back and laughed heartedly. He had kissed many arses in his time, some for self gain; some for sheer pleasure.

"Did you talk to the lass?" Rule probed.

"Nay, she was not with Wysteria when I came upon her on the path to your dwelling."

Rule appreciated Ibrehem referring to the cave as a dwelling; somehow it sounded less demeaning. He went to his friend and embraced him. *"Neva sa lume*...it has been too long."

"Aye," Ibrehem quickly agreed, returning his friend's welcome. "Way too long."

Rule pulled back and looked Ibrehem over, head to toe. "You are well, then?"

"Aye, as well as can be," Ibrehem said.

"And the battle at Jabari Valley...did you free the Humblers?"

"Aye, but at a great cost. We lost four men." Ibrehem clenched his jaw muscles. "'Twas not easy to come home without so many comrades. I grieve their loss and feel guilty for walking and talking while they are rotting in their graves."

Rule's heart suddenly burned with anger. "I should

have been with you, led the charge, 'tis my place, not yours."

Ibrehem's expression was tight with strain. "Your men understand 'twould mean your death if you left the jungle. And not one among them thinks ill of you, only—"

"Only pity for my plight," Rule interjected harshly.

"Nay, my lord, never would any of them pity you," Ibrehem quickly corrected.

"Then *sute*, Ibrehem...how do the men feel?" Rule demanded.

Ibrehem drew a deep breath. "They are at a loss, my lord."

Rule frowned. "I do not understand...you are the most feared army in the isles, what are you all at a loss for?" The original band of soldiers was eighty men strong, trained by Tobiah, the late king's best warrior.

Ibrehem faltered in the long silence that engulfed them.

"I demand an answer, my friend," Rule snapped.

"We are at a loss to help you," Ibrehem finally blurted out. "We can conquer lands, win battles, and yet we are no match for Devora's magic, cannot release our king from...the curse that..."

Rule put up a hand. "Enough!"

Ibrehem bowed his head in silence.

Rule turned away, walked to the edge of the river and watched the sun set. He inhaled the aroma of magnolias in the air, the heady scent bringing him back to the days when he was a lad. His thoughts were suddenly filled with the times he sat on the river's edge with his mother, watching the shadows across the rocks, and marveling over the remarkable hues of rose in the sky.

"'Tis here, on the banks of this river my mother, Queen Oneida would tell me stories about the knights in shining armor, gallant men in their garb fighting for victory and freedom. And 'twas then that I knew what I wanted to do as a man. My goal was to lead an army, bring freedom to those oppressed," Rule said. "But, my friend, all those ambitions were not to be." A cruel joke was to be played on him instead. Just twenty-one, and at the height of his military career, his dream had been ripped from him by his step-mother. "Devora robbed me of not only my life's goal, but dignity as well. Now when I hunger I am forced to eat like an animal. My legacy and the hope as the next to sit on the throne have all been taken from me. I am a king only in my imagination."

Ibrehem stayed silent.

Hiding his emotions, Rule straightened his shoulders, captured his pride and turned around to face Ibrehem. "Are you still with me, my friend?"

Ibrehem smiled. "Aye, my lord...forever and always."

Rule forced a smile. "Then let us be off to Wysteria's cottage, before it grows too late."

Ibrehem nodded in agreement. "The old crone never did like us to keep her waiting." He walked in step beside Rule up the path to Wysteria's home. "Does she still have the switch she threatened to use on our backsides?"

Rule chuckled lightly. "Aye, that she does...and at times she still believes she can use it."

****

Zailia ran through the forest to the tiny cottage she once called home. She had an evening's reprieve from Devora's ringing bell. As long as the queen had Shell between her thighs, she would not need Zailia's services...not until the noon hour on the morrow, when Devora would wake, demanding to be bathed and pampered once again.

Zailia pushed open the wooden door to the quaint cottage, forcing a calm she did not feel. Never would she want her father to know what she endured by the queen's evil nature.

"Is that you, Zailia?" Tobiah called from his bed.

"Aye, Papa," Zailia responded, trying to make her voice light and cheery. Her father had gone through enough in the last ten years; losing an arm and a son in battle, then a wife to consumption. He was frail and hanging on to his own life by a thread. Zailia would not add to his pain and suffering.

Zailia faked a smile as she walked through the bedroom door. Quickly she glanced over at the bedside table. "You have not touched a morsel of the bread and cheese I left for you to eat."

Tobiah studied his daughter's delicate face. "Ah, my

daughter...those deep, brown eyes look tired; your coloring, pale." He sighed. "You must take care of yourself and stop worrying about me. I am fine, and know how to tend to my own needs."

Zailia sat down on the edge of the bed and took her father's hand in hers. "If that were true you would have eaten the food."

Tobiah pushed a tendril of hair from her forehead. "You look as though you are ready to collapse where you stand."

Zailia wished she could tell her father how exhausted she was, how much she hated working in the castle at Devora's beck and call. Instead, she stifled the agony that welled up to choke her, desperately trying to forget the jobs she performed and the verbal abuse that demeaned her very existence. She was at the mercy of one who knew no mercy, all so she could maintain caring for her father.

"I am fine," Zailia lied.

"I hate you being in the service of that witch," Tobiah said, lovingly kissing his daughter's hand.

"For now 'tis how it has to be, Papa. My position at the castle is needed to pay the steep tax of our land."

"King Stefan would turn over in his grave if he ever knew what that woman has done to his son, to the kingdom," Tobiah hissed.

"Hush, Papa, before you begin to lose your breath again," Zailia warned.

Tobiah laid his head back on the pillow and inhaled sharply. "I am good for nothing, daughter."

"'Tisn't so, Papa," Zailia said. She gently released her hand from her father's grip and caressed his bearded face. "Rest while I fix you dinner."

Tobiah again reached for Zailia's hand. "I pray our Divine Maker has not forsaken the people of Keronia. We need help, Zailia, and we need it soon...very, very soon."

****

Wysteria's tiny cottage smelled of her cooking; mouthwatering meals that kept Rule hungering for the food she once prepared for him. Now days he could only take his nourishment in the form of an animal, his feast consisting of whatever he could ferociously hunt down and rip apart. While he was in the altered state he would dine

33

on the raw flesh of boar, dragging the bloody carcass to his cave to eat in the shadows. When he had his fill, Rule would then lay down to sleep, only to wake in his man's skin, naked and covered with his meal's blood; the aftertaste of raw animal flesh still in his mouth. How he disgusted himself. It was then he would run to the waterfall and wash until his flesh burned. To have any trace left of what he had become, turned his own stomach to such a degree that the thought of his next meal drove his sanity nearly to the breaking point.

Wysteria's door was open, no doubt to cool the dwelling from all the cooking going on within. Rule hesitated, calming the appetite growing in his belly.

Wysteria looked up from her boiling pot of possum stew and smiled at the two men who stood at her door. "'Tis about time you two lads arrived. Much later and 'twould have been tomorrow."

"And am I too late for a bit of what you have cooking in that pot, dear healer?" Ibrehem's mouth salivated.

She chuckled lightly. "Is the aroma getting to you?"

Ibrehem placed a large hand over his heart. "Aye, and ever so strongly."

She chuckled again and filled a bowl with the hot, meaty broth. Placing it upon the table, she motioned Ibrehem to sit. "Dig in, while 'tis hot."

Ibrehem hesitated. Quickly he glanced over at Rule. "I am sorry...I meant not to be rude."

"Eat your meal," Rule interrupted gruffly. "'My affliction is my own hell." He anxiously looked around the cottage. "My purpose here is to speak to the maiden." Rule frowned. "And where might the lass be?"

Wysteria motioned to the back door. "Yonder, in the garden."

Rule arched a brow. "Has she spoken of where she comes?"

"Aye," she said, filling a bowl for herself and joining Ibrehem at the table. "She came by ship from Dublin, Ireland."

Rule's frown deepened. "I do not know of this Dublin, Ireland." He glanced at Ibrehem spooning the stew into his mouth. For an instant he could almost taste the humble banquet. Rule swallowed hard and cast his gaze out the back window. "What of you, Ibrehem? Does her homeland strike a note to your knowledge?"

"Nay," Ibrehem quickly answered; his mouth too full of the stew to say anything more.

Rule suddenly became agitated. "Nay...a worldly soldier such as you...has never heard of Dublin, Ireland?"

Ibrehem's spoon stopped in midstream to the path it made to his mouth. Looking annoyed he slowly placed the utensil down on the table. "I am a worldly soldier upon land, my lord," he grounded the words out patiently. "Not a navigator by sea."

Rule grunted. "Why do you not hurry with that meal?"

"Why do you not go out to the garden and speak to the girl?" Wysteria challenged. "'Tis why you are here." She waved her hand in the air. "Go...go to her before we all die of old age," she demanded in a shrill voice.

Rule sighed in exasperation. "Why, old woman, do you continually nag me?"

"Someone has to," she snapped. "You have not a lick of sense on your own."

Rule's tone was cold and exact. "Who do you think you are talking to?"

Ibrehem shook his head. "Rule, will you never learn?"

Wysteria jumped from her seat. In a heartbeat she was beside Rule, looking defiantly up into his eyes. "The disrespect you hold for your elders, lad, is disgraceful. No man can be a leader with an attitude like that. 'Tis honor that makes a king...a king." She shook her finger at him. "You are not too big to take a switch to; remember that."

Rule's mouth twisted with anger. "Must we again go through this nonsense, crone?"

Wysteria grabbed hold of the flesh upon his arm and twisted it.

Rule quickly pulled his arm away. "Keep your bony fingers to yourself, old woman," he replied sharply. "Or else I will—"

Wysteria's eyes widened. "You will do nothing!" she interrupted.

Ibrehem choked on his food while trying to stifle a laugh.

Rule turned to look at his friend, giving him a hostile

glare. "I am glad you find the crone amusing."

"'Tis you I find amusing," Ibrehem retorted.

Rule's lips thinned in anger. "I fail to see the humor in any of this conversation. Or in the way she treats me."

Ibrehem chuckled lightly. "But humorous it is, my lord. And how Wysteria treats you is a reflection of how you treat her." He pushed his empty bowl aside and rubbing his full stomach with satisfaction, looked over at the old woman. "Wysteria, love, you are a gem of a cook."

Wysteria smiled and made her way back to her own meal. "I thank you, lad." She reached forward and gave Ibrehem's hand a gentle pat. "You are always welcome at my table."

"You see, I have no problem with the woman," Ibrehem gloated.

"You are the son of a scoundrel," Rule spat. "Who charms every woman you set your eyes on, old or young."

"At least I am not afraid to speak to them, as you are to the one beyond that door," Ibrehem teased.

Rule laughed sardonically. "I assure you my friend, I am not afraid."

Ibrehem arched a brow. "Nay?" He stood and made his way toward Rule. "Then why have you lingered this long?"

Rule's features hardened. "Because I am made to deal with the foolish antics of this old woman," he said, motioning toward Wysteria.

"You are going around in circles, my lord." Ibrehem grinned. "And stalling for time."

"She's just a slip of a girl," Wysteria commented. "Nothing to fear."

Rule glowered at her. "I fear nothing."

"Then go," challenged Ibrehem. "The fair maiden waits."

Rule straightened his shoulders and made his way to the back door. "I fear nothing," he mumbled to himself and turned the knob.

Chapter Three

Meav watched the sunset cast a veil over the day. The fiery, red ball set low in the sky and lit the horizon as she had never seen before. Then again, this island held colors and smells, and strange sights that Meav was sure she would only encounter in a dream. Yet it was all real, she had pinched herself several times and could clearly vouch for the fact that she was awake. But all of it was so incredible; from a river of orange, to the mermaid that sunned herself upon a rock, to the naked pixies that fluttered about the cottage.

Meav, lifted her waist length, copper curls from her neck, allowing the gentle breeze to brush across her nape. She stretched and swayed with the breeze, dancing around in tiny circles, feeling relaxed and free.

****

Rule walked onto the cobblestone terrace quietly, enchanted with the scene before him. He watched the beautiful female at one with the nature that surrounded her. Rule did not know when he had viewed such a magnificent sight.

He watched as she inhaled the magnolia scented air. "Ah me, 'tis all so magnificent," she said aloud to herself.

"Aye, indeed 'tis," Rule's voice cracked. Why was he suddenly unable to speak correctly?

Meav quickly spun around to find a man—a large man—standing behind her. The muslin tunic he wore did little to conceal the muscles bulging beneath. His jet, black hair, shiny and thick, fell to his powerful set of shoulders. His bronzed flesh pulled taut over the elegant ridge of his cheekbones and complimented the amber eyes that now surveyed her quite intensely. Meav was momentarily rendered speechless. Nervously, she licked her dry lips. She was at a loss for words and became acutely conscious of his athletic physique, and the way his dark, brown breeches hugged his muscular thighs. She

37

cleared her throat, and her wandering thoughts, quickly realizing she couldn't remain here just standing like a mute and staring. Her grandmamma had taught her better manners then this.

"And who might you be, sir?" she said in a shaky voice.

Rule moved closer, his eyes roaming the length of her. She was enthralling in the dress she wore. The light fabric clung to every shapely curve of her body. He moved to the stone wall and set a foot upon it, pleased by the way the neckline of the dress dipped just low enough to reveal the tops of her full breasts. He wanted to trace the valley of her cleavage with his tongue.

"I am Rule Thornton," he said. "I am the—" he almost announced to her that he was the *king*, but that would only be half true. "I am the protector, keeper and lord of the jungle," he admitted instead.

She walked toward him and extended her hand. "Me name is Meav O'Shay."

Rule almost reached out to take her tiny hand, lift it to his lips and bestow a kiss. But instead he stepped back, contributing his desire to the fact she must have bewitched him. That thought irked him. Hadn't he been tricked enough by a woman's magic? Quickly he moved to the other side of the terrace.

Meav felt a blush shadow over her cheeks as she was left with her hand in mid-air. Never had she felt so humiliated. All she wanted now was to distance herself from the handsome brute. She made her way to a bench at the far end of the cobblestone and sat down.

Rule cleared his throat, crossing his arms over his chest. His tone was gruff. "Wysteria tells me you come from Dublin, Ireland."

"Aye, Dublin is me home...was me home," she corrected, her heart filling with sadness for the family she lost.

"And where might Ireland be, lass?"

"Far, far from here, milord." She looked deep into the tawny color of his eyes, familiar to her...but how could that be? "I know not where 'tis, in accordance to this island, only that I traveled many days aboard that dank ship before it crashed upon your shores."

Rule searched her exquisite and dainty features; her complexion was an illusive pink. If he did not keep himself from floating on the softness of her voice, he would never be able to conduct this interrogation properly. "And what were you doing on the ship, lass?"

"Escaping," Meav answered.

The sudden sadness that clouded her blue eyes disturbed him. He softened his tone. "Escaping from what?"

"Hollister McGreary," she said softly.

He moved closer to the bench. A disquieting chill ran down Rule's spine. Why was he suddenly feeling protective of her? "Tell me why you needed to leave your home, lass. And who is Hollister McGreary?"

Hatred glowered in Meav's eyes. "He is the rogue who proposed marriage to me, milord. When I refused, he had me home and land scorched and me family killed."

Rule's shock yielded quickly to fury. Had he the chance to meet this Hollister McGreary he would strip him of his clothing, and have him tarred, feathered, and quartered.

Meav swallowed the tears burning her throat. "A dear friend's husband helped me board the *Sea Dragon* and to hide below without being noticed." She cast her gaze to the hands she held clenched in her lap. "For several days I lay on the damp floor of the hull, hungry and cold." Meav shivered now with the memory of the rats and mice scampering over her feet, the foul odor, and the fear of being caught by the British sailors. "Then the mermaid's song lured the vessel, and it crashed." She sighed heavily. "I am the only survivor."

Rule wanted to place his hand over the two small ones she held so tightly clasped together; give them a reassuring squeeze. Just the thought sent a stimulating sensation coursing through him. But instead all he could do was look down at her. "You are safe now."

Quickly she raised her eyes to lock with his. They were compelling, drawing her in. Her heartbeat quickened; again she felt she had seen those eyes before, but surely that could not be...she had just met him.

"I give you my word, Meav O'Shay, that I will allow no one to hurt you."

The sound of his deep voice saying her name suddenly made Meav believe his words. Just having him near elicited a feeling of being safe, though his manners could use some improvement.

"I believe you, milord," she whispered...and she did.

****

After Wysteria had sent Ibrehem off to Tobiah's home with a pot of possum stew, Raika paid her a visit.

The Elwin woman entered the cottage smiling from ear to ear. "It has happened, dear healer. My dear daughter Aliki has given birth to a beautiful woman child. We are calling her Saje."

Wysteria clapped her hands together in delight. "I am so pleased for your family. And Aliki had no trouble during the birthing?"

Raika shook her head. "Not anymore than most."

"Then she is blessed and will have many years mothering the babe in good health."

Raika smile broadened. "Aye; this I believe as well...but a blessing from you, dear healer now is in order."

Wysteria nodded. "I will come on the morrow, as of this moment I wait to see how the meeting of Rule and Meav turns out."

Raika frowned. "Meav?"

"Aye, the young maiden you and Twila helped to bathe."

Raika's eyes brightened. "Aye, I remember." She folded her small arms across her ample bosom. "So, she is called Meav?"

"Aye, Meav O'Shay from Dublin, Ireland...and I have no idea where Ireland sets in this vast universe," Wysteria added.

Raika walked over to the kettle and helped herself to a cup of tea. "Perhaps Merrow would know. I shall ask him when I return to the glen." She placed the cup on the table and hoisted herself upon a chair. "And where is the maiden now?"

"Out in the garden with Rule. 'Tis their first meeting...eye to eye. I am hoping all goes well."

Raika slipped off the chair and crept to the window, staying hidden behind a shutter. She peered out at Rule and Meav in the garden.

Wysteria followed on tiptoe. For a moment she was captivated by the beautiful sunset. "Ah, look Raika at the setting sun. The heavenly display reminds me of just such a night, many years ago."

Raika turned to Wysteria. "I remember how in love with Morgan you were."

The sound of his name filled Wysteria with warmth. She looked down at her friend. "I still am," she softly admitted. "Though he has gone from this earth he will never leave my heart."

Raika smiled and cast her gaze back out the window. "Look, Meav has extended her hand to Rule. 'Twould have been a perfect opportunity for him to bestow a kiss."

Wysteria smiled. "I remember the times Morgan kissed my hand. I felt so cherished, so beautiful."

"Ah, youth, young notions and love," Raika muttered.

"Where has my youth gone, Raika? It seemed to slip by so quickly. One day I had hair of gold flying behind me in the wind, and the next strands of gray falling in my eyes."

Raika nodded slowly. "I remember those days as well. Now we are both old crones."

"A crone was not what I sought to be, certainly not what I had hoped to become," Wysteria said.

Raika turned her attention again to Wysteria. "But the crone stage of life has definite benefits. It has given you the opportunity to help those around you. Now, others seek your wisdom. Truly, you have a sense of just being yourself, able to express what you know and feel. 'Tis the crowning inner achievement of the third stage of your life."

"'Tis true, Raika. I am finally able to take action when need be...like now, with the task I have ahead of me to save Keronia and those that dwell on the isle."

"And what is your plan of action?" Raika said softly.

"First, I must swallow the urge to whine over all I have to do. Whining is an attitude that will only block spiritual growth; squelch the positive light that will make me wise and strong and effective in accomplishing what I must." Wysteria placed a hand on her forehead. "Then, I must take the time to be still enough to listen to the quiet of my own mind and spirit; pay attention to all I perceive, to my instincts and intuitions...then act upon them."

"'Tis wise of you, dear healer."

"Oh...but what an undertaking there is ahead of me, Raika. The Prophecy clearly states both Rule and Meav need to come by love through *their own accord.*"

Raika frowned. "And you do not think that can happen?"

Wysteria groaned. "Nay...look how he acts. He has positioned himself opposite her."

Raika looked back out the window. She frowned. "He is walking away from her."

"None of this will be possible unless that buffoon opens his heart, begins to trust her," Wysteria whispered, feeling negatives nagging her within. She instantly set her mind to stifling them, knowing full well she would not be able to live in the present or be good company to anyone, especially herself, if she gave in to them. "Nay, there is no time for negatives," she said aloud.

"That is so true, dear healer...nor is there time for worries...'tis a time only for nurturing the young maiden, fostering her growth. She needs you to teach her of the powers she is gifted with. You must be her mentor, protect the girl's vulnerability, and help her to bloom into the warrior the Prophecy has destined for her life."

Wysteria gave Raika a gentle pat on the shoulder. "'Tis fortunate my skills have improved with much practice. Now I draw patience in knowing there is a season for all things. I have learned many things from my experiences."

"Then you must apply those past lessons to present choices and situations." Raika left the window as silently as she had come and returned to her seat by the table. Slowly she sipped her tea. "I trust you will do what is needed of you."

"I appreciate that, Raika." Wysteria walked to the fireplace, becoming mesmerized by the flames. For a moment she watched them dance before her, than she fixed herself a cup of herbal tea and joined Raika at the table.

Taking a moment to sit and sip the brew, Wysteria contemplated the task before her to alter the present situation. Slowly she organized her thoughts, as she savored the mint flavor of the tea.

"What are you thinking, Wysteria?"

"That I must remain strong, clear my mind and renew my spirit."

Raika leaned forward in her seat. "Why not bring Meav to the blessing ceremony tomorrow? Perhaps after you could take her to the river and perform the ritual bath."

Wysteria nodded in agreement. "Aye, I think she would enjoy the blessing ceremony, and after would be a good time for her own cleansing."

"Then what?"

Wysteria thought for a moment. "I think 'tis best I *not* work the problem through Rule, but through Meav. I will teach her how to use her gifts, slowly at first, not to frighten her, and make her aware of what she was sent here to do."

"Not through the angle of the angry young man...but instead through the soft, beautiful maiden," Raika plotted. "I can see that working well." She took another sip of the warm brew.

"And I will stay steadfast in my decisions," Wysteria said, taking a sip of her own tea. "I cannot let Rule interfere, or find cause to manipulate me."

"As he so often did as a lad in your care," Raika reminded her.

Wysteria set the cup down on the table, closed her eyes and took a deep breath. "I expect there will come some ugly moments, Raika."

Raika frowned. "Like what?"

"Fear, misunderstanding," Wysteria replied, contemplating her words before she spoke further. "But from the agony comes experience and a means to learn. I see forgiveness, humility and courage being a part of the healing path as well."

"And what of love?" Raika whispered.

"Ah, love," Wysteria reflected. "Without love none of the struggles and hardships of life would be bearable, Raika. 'Tis a given love must be at the heart of the solution, I just need to find a way to help the cause. Meav and Rule need to discover each other of *their own accord*."

Raika nodded in agreement. "As well as the plan the universe has mapped out for them."

Wysteria sighed. "Aye, Raika, we cannot forget the plan."

****

Ibrehem walked carefully up the path to Tobiah's house; not wanting to spill the possum stew Wysteria had sent for the old soldier and his daughter, Zailia.

Ibrehem smiled when he thought of Zailia; hair of gold, eyes round and dark beneath hooded lashes. And though she filled his thoughts with sweet incantations, Ibrehem's heart also went out to the young woman, admiring her courage and tenacity. Zailia was devoted to the care of her father, and served Queen Devora in order to save the land that had been in her father's family for generations.

Ibrehem had offered many times to lighten her load by paying the taxes on the property with what he had managed to save. He worried for Zailia's safety and did not want her subjected to the queen's evil ways. He wanted Zailia as far away from the witch as possible.

But Zailia's pride would have none of what Ibrehem had offered. She refused his generosity time and time again with her chin raised defiantly, shoulders squared. Ibrehem had to stifle a smile, finding her most charming when she stood up to him. It took all he could do to keep from sweeping her into his arms and smothering her luscious lips with kisses. If he ever appeased the impulse, there was no doubt it would gain him a hard slap across his face.

Zailia was a feisty one and Ibrehem knew she was determined to take care of her own affairs. She did not want his pity and believed she could handle the care of her sick, aging father, and still work the demanding schedule at the castle. Truth be told, Zailia looked tired and worn and Ibrehem was concerned.

Why was it so hard for this beautiful woman to believe he did not pity her, but instead wanted to help her...because he cared for her? Then there was the honor he held for Tobiah, who had been like a father to him. Through Tobiah's skill Ibrehem had learned how to survive in the wilds and to master the fight. Now it was

Ibrehem's turn to repay his mentor for all he had done for him and to protect and love his daughter.

****

Zailia was washing the dinner plates in a pan of soapy water when she heard the knock. Wiping her hands on the apron tied around her waist, she made her way to the door and opened it wide. There stood Ibrehem Chancelor holding a large pot. The warrior was strong and handsome...dark eyes framing a face bronzed by the wind and sun; dark hair tapering neatly to his collar.

Ibrehem smiled warmly. "*Vedela.*"

Zailia returned his smile. "Greetings to you as well." She looked down at the pot he held. "And have you left your post in the military to be a peddler?"

Ibrehem held out the container and made a comical face at her teasing remark. "Nay, I bring you a meal sent by Wysteria."

Zailia beckoned him in and took the food. "Ah, the good and loving healer is always looking out for me and father." She placed the pot on the hook over the fire. "I have not been to see her in over a week. How does she fair?"

Ibrehem closed the door behind him. "Quite well, I would say. She is kept busy by a house guest at the moment."

Zailia removed a cloth from the raisin bread she had just baked and cut off a large piece. Placing the bread on a plate, she set it down on the table and motioned for Ibrehem to take a seat. "Whom has she taken in this time?"

Ibrehem quickly went to the table. "A young woman that washed up on shore after her ship had been wrecked." He nodded thankfully as he took a bite of the bread.

Zailia gasped. "Poor soul, only she survived?"

"Aye, seems to be the case."

Zailia leaned forward. "What is she like, what is her name, where is she from?"

Ibrehem held up a hand and swallowed a mouthful of bread. "Patience, my dear lass."

Zailia made a face. "Am I to grow old waiting?"

"Her name is Meav O'Shay," he began.

Zailia's eyes brightened. "Ah, such a beautiful name. Is she beautiful?"

"I have only had a glimpse of her from Wysteria's back window. The maiden was in the garden at the time, and Rule was on his way to speak with her. I lingered in the cottage, not wanting to interrupt."

Zailia frowned. "Rule...why he will scare the poor lass to death."

Ibrehem chuckled lightly. "He has much to learn when it comes to charming a lady."

Zailia arched a brow. "Perhaps you should teach him, since you are so schooled in such matters. There simply is *not* a lass around that you have not enchanted." She folded her arms across her chest. "Of course, I must admit they were all twits, no girl with a lick of sense would listen to your smooth talk."

Ibrehem put his hand over his heart. "Why, Zailia, you cut me to the quick. I have never been anything but a gentleman."

"Do not give me that, Ibrehem Chancelor." She wagged a finger at him. "You forget I have known you since you were a lad."

He gave her a devilish smile. "And you were smaller, lass. If I remember things right, 'twas I who picked you up when you fell and scraped your knee, carrying you home."

Zailia leaned forward. "And 'twas you who tried to sneak a peak when mother raised my skirt to administer the salve."

Ibrehem threw his head back and laughed heartily. "'Tis your spunk, woman, that sends my heart a racing."

"Huh, anything in a skirt would do the trick," Zailia spat.

"Are you two bickering again?" Tobiah called out from the bedroom.

"Aye," Ibrehem answered, making his way to the old man's door. "Some things never change."

Tobiah nodded slowly. "'Tis a comfort to know, especially when so much *has* changed."

Zailia walked passed Ibrehem, her chin raised defiantly, and sat at the edge of her father's bed. "He is incorrigible."

Ibrehem frowned. "I am not."

"You are too," Zailia countered.

"Enough," Tobiah snapped. "You two sound like you are still in bloomers and knickers." He adjusted the quilt around his thin waist. "What is this about Wysteria having a house guest?"

"So, those old ears are still as sharp as the day is long," Ibrehem teased.

Tobiah looked over at Ibrehem. "Do you know where she is from?"

"I understand from Wysteria the young woman's homeland is Dublin, Ireland." Ibrehem frowned. "Have you ever heard of such a place, Tobiah?"

"Aye, I have."

Ibrehem moved closer to the bed. "Do tell."

Zailia's eyes widened. "Aye, Papa, please tell us what you know."

Tobiah scratched his bearded chin. "Well, let me see...I seem to remember my great-grandfather speaking of Ireland when I was just a wee lad. Gramps Finnley called it the Emerald Isle. To reach it one must travel down the Coast of Demons and days upon the sea." Tobiah looked over at his daughter. "'Tis a place the old timers rarely spoke of."

"Why, Papa?" Zailia questioned. As a child she was always intrigued by one of her father's stories.

"Because of the legend," Tobiah said.

"And what legend is this?" Ibrehem asked. "My curiosity builds."

"The one that tells of the flight of the leprechauns," Tobiah said.

Zailia frowned. "And what are leprechauns?"

"They are the wee folk of Ireland," Tobiah explained.

"They left Ireland to come here?" Ibrehem probed.

Tobiah nodded. "The poor souls had no choice. They were being sought after by the Irish for their pots of gold."

A soft gasp escaped Zailia. "They owned pots of gold?"

Tobiah nodded again. "They kept them at the end of the rainbow. The Irish folks got wind of the fact that if one of these wee fellows were caught; he had to turn over his pot of gold for his release."

"So it became open season on leprechauns," Ibrehem

47

concluded.

Tobiah leaned back against the pillow. "Aye, and many times the little men were not released after their captors were paid, but tortured and killed."

Zailia's hand went to her throat. "How awful."

"'Twas awful, daughter." Tobiah pulled the quilt up around his shoulders. "To finish my story, I will say that most of them fled to the hills of Ireland, never to be seen again, but a handful of them boarded a boat and with their families paddled away; letting the sea take them where ever it would." He sighed, his strength waning. "'Twas on Keronia they landed, many sick and dying. The Elwins took them in, saved some of the men, but the women were too weak to survive."

"And without their women they could not keep their kind going," Zailia added.

"True enough," Tobiah agreed. "But they left two things behind."

Ibrehem frowned. "Like what?"

"Their language for one; the elder Elwins speak their tongue and many words we speak are from their lingo." Tobiah smiled. "And they left the *Promise*."

Ibrehem lightly leaned his shoulder against the bedpost. "What was the promise?"

"They promised the Elwins that if Keronia were ever to be in trouble, one from their land would arrive to help."

"A leprechaun would come to help us?" Zailia asked.

"The promise was only that one from Ireland would arrive to help," Tobiah corrected.

Zailia looked over at Ibrehem. "And one from Ireland has arrived."

Ibrehem sneered. "Certainly you cannot believe the slip of a woman in Wysteria's care can save Keronia?"

Zailia stood, shoulders straight and chin raised. "Do you think because she is a woman she cannot help us?"

"Well...I just do not think that..."

"You are a pig head, Ibrehem Chancelor," Zailia interjected. "You think only brawny men with bad manners and sharp knives can be heroes."

Ibrehem's mouth opened to defend himself, but Zailia drowned out any thought of him speaking.

"I am so tired of males thinking females can do

nothing but cook, clean and bear the babies," Zailia raved on.

"But Zailia...I..." Ibrehem stammered.

"I am through with this nonsense. This subject is not open for further discussion," Zailia snapped, and stormed out of the room.

Ibrehem stood stunned. He looked after her with his mouth open and lost for words.

Tobiah chuckled. "She has a point, lad."

Ibrehem turned back to look at Tobiah. "What just happened here?"

Tobiah chuckled lightly. "You have ruffled her feathers."

Ibrehem frowned, feeling a mixture of confusion and annoyance. "I seem to do a lot of that lately."

"She has her mother's spunk."

Ibrehem crossed his arms over his chest. "And what did you do to smooth your wife's feathers?"

Tobiah's eyes sparkled mischievously. "I took her to bed."

Ibrehem arched a brow. "Though that remedy would be one I would not mind, I doubt Zailia is willing."

"Marry her, then," Tobiah said flatly.

Ibrehem smiled. "The thought has crossed my mind."

Tobiah yawned. "Well, do not let it linger there long, lad. 'Tis the first hunter each season that snares the choicest meat."

"Aye, 'tis at that," Ibrehem agreed.

"I have taught you to be a fighter, but no one can teach you to love someone; that you must do on your own accord." Tobiah waved his hand in the air. "Now off with you, Ibrehem...go make amends with her before 'tis too late...and leave me to my nap."

In their conversation, not one of those in the cottage heard the intruder that listened beneath the window, nor did they see him scamper off through the bushes and head toward the castle.

Chapter Four

Rule could not release Meav from his mind's eye. Lying in the corner of his cave on a pile of animal skins for comfort, he saw over and over the young maiden twirling before him on the cobblestone veranda; her skirt flaring just enough for him to get a look at her slender ankles.

Of course the scene in his head played out much different then it did on Wysteria's terrace the night before. Rule's version had him slipping Meav's dress off her shoulders and circling her nipples with the tip of his tongue. His vision had him slowly laying her across the bench, raising her skirt to her thighs, spreading her legs wide and tasting her sex.

He swallowed hard and turned onto his side. He could almost feel her soft nub against his tongue. That vivid image caused him an erection that painfully throbbed between his legs. He closed his eyes and groaned. All he desired would only ever be something he could experience in a dream. No woman would want to make love to him in the hideous state he was in.

"Nay," he whispered to himself. "What I am would only frighten her." Hell and damnation, he frightened himself!

Rule was disgusted with what he had become. Yet he had not the courage to go past the perimeter of the jungle and end his misery. What was he hoping for? There was no cure for the curse upon him, no antidote, and no herbal remedy. Why did he linger or even want to see another day?

Perhaps 'twas the inbred hope in him, the challenge not besting him; or just instinct, but Rule wanted to live. So he answered the pains of hunger that had begun in his belly and worked up to his throat; stood and stripped off all his clothes. With a sigh, Rule was ready once more for the kill.

The change began...first the pains down the backbone, then the arms and legs. Rule felt his head and neck become larger; the stretching of every muscle was excruciating.

He got down on all fours and arched his spine. His hands turned to paws, claws sharp and drawn, ready for action. Shiny, black fur replaced his flesh. Rule opened his mouth and a fierce growl escaped from his throat. The transformation was complete. Now he would hunt for breakfast.

****

While Wysteria prepared the porridge she glanced sideways at Meav, who had already begun setting the table for the morning meal. "What month were you born, child?"

"In August, I am told," Meav said.

"Within the first or second part of the month?" Wysteria questioned as she poured the hot gruel into the bowls Meav had ready.

"Why, the very first day, I believe," Meav announced.

"Then your sign is the Lion," Wysteria said.

Meav frowned. "I do not understand what you mean by me *sign*."

"Leo, the Lion is the fifth house of the Zodiac," Wysteria explained. She caught the confused look on Meav's face and it made her chuckle. "You do not know about the stars in accordance to the months?"

Meav shook her head.

"Then I shall have to teach you, but for now let me continue with the horoscope sign that you were born under, which is Leo." Wysteria grabbed for the bowl of blueberries and an apple on the cupboard shelf. While she talked, she cut up the apple. "This house governs the heart, pleasure, and children...Leos love children. 'Tis a fierce spirit that Leos acquire. They are always speculating what might happen next. The lion sign is brave and loyal, will move headstrong into whatever challenge lies ahead." Wysteria added the fruit to Meav's bowl of porridge and handed it to her. "Leos do well eating apples and blueberries."

Meav nodded in agreement and took the food. "The headstrong part is me for sure. I received many a punishment by the hand of me grandmamma...a switch across me bared bottom for some of me willful ways."

"Then you knew the walls of the woodshed well?" Wysteria probed.

Meav arched a brow. "Aye, a wee bit too well. Once Papa suggested I should move me cot to the shed, since I spent more time in there then I did in the house."

"Were you born in the morning or evening?" Wysteria probed further.

"The morning, I have been told, very early...the dew was still upon the land when I took me first breath," Meav said.

Wysteria blew on her porridge to cool it. "Then the sun is your planetary ruler, and the characteristics you display are that of faith, optimism and the desire to rule and lead. This is important for you to keep in mind, child."

Meav did the same to her breakfast before putting a spoonful into her mouth, "Why so, Wysteria?"

"Because you will need to know you have the strength to carry out all you must do."

Meav frowned and put down her spoon. "What is there for me to do?"

"'Tisn't for discussion now, I will explain all that you need to know in time." Wysteria motioned to the bowl. "Eat now, lest your breakfast grows cold."

Meav suddenly felt the speculation Wysteria had spoken about. She slowly reached for her spoon. "Is there a reason I have washed up on the shores of Keronia?"

"Aye, child, there is." Wysteria gave her a gentle smile. "There is a reason and a season for all things. Everyone has a path that they are destined to travel."

Meav swallowed the uncertainty that formed in her throat. "Will I know mine when I see it?"

"Aye, you will...and I will help you to see it clearly," Wysteria assured her.

Meav frowned. "How can you help me?"

Wysteria put aside her own spoon and leaned forward in her seat. "After you eat every morsel of your porridge I will boil marigold, fennel, comfrey, chamomile and St. John's wort together in a cauldron, and apply the herbs with a soft cloth to your eyes. Then your eyes will be bright...you will see what needs to be seen."

Meav began to feel apprehensive. "And then what happens...after I have seen what is meant for me to see?"

Wysteria bent her head and began to eat her porridge.

"What happens then, Wysteria?" Meav repeated, her voice rising with her uncertainty.

"One step at a time, child...one step at a time."

****

Meav walked beside Wysteria, golden places shining in the morning sun. The journey through the glen to the Elwin's village was a pleasant one, affording Meav the time to take in her surroundings and to admire further the island that would now become her home.

She put aside the conversation she had over breakfast with Wysteria; rehashing it only made her uneasy. Instead Meav focused her thoughts on what the day would bring. She was anxious to meet Wysteria's good friends, especially the two women, Raika and Twila that helped care for her.

"I am so honored you have invited me to the baby's blessing, Wysteria. But are you sure the Elwins will not mind a new face among the old?"

"Nay, they welcome all." Wysteria smiled warmly at her new charge. "'Tis a beautiful ceremony, I know you will be pleased with it, and 'twill give you a chance to make new friends." Wysteria repositioned the satchel she carried over her shoulder. "Raika's daughter Aliki is about your age."

Meav reached for the heavy pack. "Let me carry that for you."

Wysteria smiled thankfully and passed the satchel to the young maiden by her side. "Be careful not to let it touch the ground. There are sacred items in there that I will use for the blessing."

"I cannot wait to see the wee one." Meav's face brightened. "Do you think Aliki might let me hold the babe?"

Wisteria chuckled lightly. "I am sure she will."

"I have always loved holding the wee ones. Their skin is so soft, and they have such a sweet smell."

Wysteria cast a glance Meav's way. "'Tis this way for

you because 'tis your calling. As I told you earlier, Leo's love children."

"In Dublin I helped with the births of many in me town. In fact, helping with a birth is what saved me life. If I had not been by Maggie Connor's bedside the night Hollister McGreary murdered me family, I would be dead too." She felt her heart break for the agony her family must have endured before their souls departed from this world.

Wysteria's voice softened. "'Tis a known fact, lass, that all those who hurt others get their own due. Hollister McGreary will be held accountable for his actions." She reached out and took Meav's arm. "But now you must move on. Our Divine Maker had a reason for sparing you."

Meav sighed. "'Tis hard to pull away from what has been me life...leave all of it behind." She looked deep into Wysteria's eyes. "Will the hurt every go away?"

Wysteria smiled encouragingly. "'Twill hurt less in time, and 'tis expected that you will grieve. Go have a good cry, shake your fists to the heavens if you must...but then, lass, 'tis time to thicken your hide, and become strong enough to face your destiny."

Meav bit her bottom lip. There it was again, the apprehensive feeling from this morning creeping up to swallow her. "Promise me you will not leave me side, Wysteria."

"I can promise you that by the time you know what you have been brought here to do, you will not need me," Wysteria confirmed. She gave Meav's arm an affectionate squeeze. "No more talk of this now. 'Tis a morning to welcome a new life into the world, and I must center my thoughts on the ceremony to be preformed."

Meav nodded in agreement and walked the rest of the way to the Elwin's village in silence.

****

Wysteria led them through an archway of trees and stopped at the clearing. "We are here, lass...before us is the Elwin's village."

Meav looked around confused. Nothing but green grass lay ahead. She frowned. "I see no homes, no one about."

Wysteria chuckled lightly. "That is because you are

looking with your eyes."

Meav's frown deepened. "What else am I suppose to look with?"

"Look with your heart and your spirit," Wysteria advised.

"How?" Meav asked meekly.

Wysteria knelt and brought Meav down with her. "Feel the earth; lass...let it slip through your fingers."

Meav obeyed, reaching for a handful of sand. Slowly she let it sift through her fingers.

"Now, close your eyes and bring a bit of the soil up to your nose...take a good whiff and think of all the good Mother Earth has given to her children," Wysteria continued.

Meav scooped up another handful of dirt and brought it to her nose. With eyes shut she inhaled the scent of the land and thought of how the earth nourished life around her; giving way for homes to be built and nurturing the seeds that are planted. Meav was suddenly filled with appreciation and awe.

"Now, child, open your eyes," Wysteria instructed.

The heavy lashes that shadowed Meav's cheeks drew up. A soft gasp escaped and her eyes widened at the discovery of the scene before her. There, in place of the empty field of just a moment ago, stood an entire village. "I see it," she whispered.

"Aye, 'tis magnificent," Wysteria marveled.

"Aye, more than that even," Meav added amazed. Quickly she glanced at Wysteria. "And 'twas here all the time?"

There was a trace of laughter in Wysteria's voice. "Aye, lass, 'twas. You just could not see past the obvious." Slowly she stood, placing a hand on Meav's shoulder. "Come, Raika and Aliki wait."

Meav followed Wysteria down the path. She stared wordlessly at each tiny cottage she passed, their window boxes brimming with colorful flowers; their chimneys puffing continuously. Cozy and quaint, the soft shades welcomed her and reminded her of home, giving her a feeling of peace and contentment...and a dash of curiosity as well.

Wysteria halted at a small pink home, framed with

white lattice work and picket fence. "We are here, lass." She smiled warmly. "This is Aliki and Jubez's dwelling."

Meav watched Wysteria open the gate. She hesitated before following, suddenly feeling a bit nervous at meeting the new friends. "You sure they will not mind me being along?"

Before Wysteria could answer, Raika's words carried on the breeze. "*Vedela.*"

Wysteria turned her attention to Raika and smiled warmly. "Greetings to you as well, my friend."

Raika looked up at Meav. "And to you...greetings."

Meav was too surprised to do more than nod at the tiny woman with hair the color of cotton.

Raika giggled. "Ah, I see Wysteria has not prepared you for our meeting."

Meav swallowed hard. The shock caused the words to wedge in her throat. She stared into Raika's pink eyes.

Raika turned her gaze on Wysteria. "Shame on you, dear healer, for not telling the lass more about the Elwins."

Wysteria shrugged. "Sometimes too much said is not wise. 'Tis best she learns for herself."

Raika looked over at Meav, concern edging her voice. "But we have dazed her to the point of rendering her mute."

Wysteria removed the satchel from Meav's shoulder. "Snap out of it, lass."

"I am...sorry..." Meav's voice broke off in mid-sentence.

Raika extended her hand and smiled encouragingly. "Come, lass, my daughter, Aliki is waiting. She is so anxious to meet you."

Meav allowed the little woman to lead her into the cottage. Suddenly she felt embarrassed at her awkward behavior, and worried she would offend Raika and bring shame upon Wysteria. After all, 'twas an honor to be invited to a baby's blessing, and she was acting rude. Her grandmamma would never approve.

Meav quickly cleared her throat. "I feel the same."

Though Meav was not very tall herself, upon entering the cottage she had to duck down to get through the door frame. She was met by a circle of wee folks.

Twila came forward and greeted her with a grin. "Last I saw you 'twas when you were fast asleep."

Meav smiled. "I thank you for your care."

"Aye, 'twas nothing," Twila chirped. She turned toward the hearth. "This is my husband, Gorg."

Gorg smiled and bowed slightly.

Meav politely curtsied.

Raika introduced the other two men gathered in the tiny room, calling out each name. "This is Hun, my husband and the proud grandfather." She turned to indicate the Elwin man across the room. "And that is Merrow, our beloved leader."

All of them sprouted thick, cotton like curls and had wide, pink eyes; a porcelain complexion and large, toothy smiles.

The men were clean shaven and the women all wore their hair with flowers entwined within the long braid that hung past their well rounded hips. They were a friendly bunch for sure and each one welcomed Meav warmly.

Merrow, the leader, was the only one that stood out from the rest. His hair was silver and his eyes were smoky. A downy beard fell from his chin to his round belly, and his stubby fingers were adorned with gold rings, various stones inlaid in the settings. He did not speak a word to Meav, just nodded and smiled, sizing her up from across the small room, sparsely furnished with miniature chairs and a table.

Meav felt herself blush under his scrutiny. Shyly she cast her gaze to the fireplace. A kettle of water hung from a hook over the flames, and the aroma of freshly baked bread filled her senses. There were also two other wee folks, both females, tending to the boiling pot. They were completely opposite from the Elwins. These tiny women had brown hair pulled into a bun atop their heads and their eyes were as dark as night.

Raika followed Meav's gaze. "And this is Opina and her daughter, Lupa. They are not Elwins, but Brownies who live by the hearth and perform domestic tasks."

Meav could not imagine so many people, wee or otherwise, all living in one tiny cottage. "All of you live here?" she blurted out, then cringed at her outburst.

All the Elwins laughed.

"Nay, nay," Twila said. "Gorg and I live a few cottages away, and Raika and Hun, across the path. Merrow lives on the hill and the Brownies only live by the hearth by day; at night they dwell in log huts beneath the giant trees at the end of the village."

Raika reached for Meav's hand. "Come and meet my daughter," she said, leading Meav into the next room.

This room had flowered curtains at the windows and was furnished with a table, a chair, a wooden framed bed, a large trunk, and a baby's cradle. A handsome Elwin man with a muscular build sat at the edge of the bed. He looked adoringly at the young woman lying propped up on pillows in the bed. She wore a yellow dressing gown, and her long, white hair was unbraided, flowing down over her right shoulder. She held a babe wrapped in a white, linen blanket.

"This is Jubez and Aliki." Raika walked toward the bed and took the baby from her mother's arms. "And this is Saje, my granddaughter."

The pride in Raika's eyes made Meav think of her own father's adoration toward his daughters. Her eyes misted at the thought. She leaned down and pushed the blanket aside from the babe's face. Meav admired the tiny cherub, pink and plump, and sound asleep.

Aliki's soft, small voice broke the silence. "Forgive me for not rising to welcome you, but I am still wobbly from giving birth."

Meav looked over at the cheery, fair skinned woman and smiled. "Your baby is beautiful."

"Like her mama," Jubez boasted, taking Aliki's hand and bringing it to his lips. He bestowed a gentle kiss upon it.

Aliki blushed. "We have guests, Jubez."

Jubez smiled. "And let them all see how much I love my wife."

Watching the two love birds made Meav's own heart skip a beat. Would a man ever love her so deeply and with so much pride?

"Shall we have the blessing?" Wysteria said.

"Aye, carry on, dear healer," Aliki agreed, motioning for her husband to leave the room.

He nodded, rose from the bed, and quietly shut the door behind him.

Meav frowned. "Jubez will not be present for the blessing?"

"Aye, he will," Raika said, caressing Saje's soft cheek. "He just must leave during the concentration ritual."

Meav was baffled. "What is the concentration ritual?"

"'Tis when I bring myself in accordance to what blessings I bestow upon the babe," Wysteria said, as she pulled from her satchel a white robe. Gently she placed it on the chair. Then she reached for a bag filled with rosemary, a candle holder and a white candle. She sprinkled the herb on the table and rolled the candle in it. Then she placed the candle in the holder and lit it.

"Hush, now and watch, lass," Raika advised.

Meav saw Wysteria strip off all her clothes and stand naked before the candle. It became clear to her now why Jubez was asked to leave the room. She watched Wysteria turn away from the candle, toward the three of them, with her eyes shut. Wysteria stretched her arms out to her sides and then above her head; her sagging breasts jiggled with the movement, her wrinkled stomach was less firm, drooping low and heavy over her womanhood. Meav was instantly reminded of her grandmother's aging body. There Wysteria boldly stood in full view of all in the room. Meav cast her eyes to the floor, out of respect.

Raika caught the young woman's action, and quietly moved closer to her. "You must look at her," she whispered.

Meav could feel an unwelcome blush creep into her cheeks, but did as she was told. Just as she raised her gaze, Wysteria opened her eyes. Meav met the twinkling, topaz orbs and in an instant felt the elder's generous heart. She inhaled sharply as Wysteria's mind spoke to Meav's thoughts.

"It matters not that my breasts sag or my belly is wrinkled...to feel ashamed of oneself is to be oppressed. Because my body has aged I need not feel invisible, inadequate. Listen for the underlying message between your feelings and your body. Spontaneous laughter, a genuine smile, and a pure and loving heart are the things that make a woman desirable and unforgettable; as well

as being resourceful, having the ability to grow and have an adventuresome, spirit filled life. Savor each experience and give it your full attention. Truly take it all in, have gratitude for the moment, embrace your existence, bless all that you are and look ahead with confidence for all that you can be."

Meav stood very still; afraid she would faint if she moved even one muscle. How was it she could hear what Wysteria was thinking?

Wysteria spoke aloud. "Be self-revealing...truth liberates. When you speak the truth, you begin to free yourself from the past holding you captive. This is the first blessing I bestow upon Saje this day." She dropped her hands to her sides. "'Tisn't what happens in life, but how you respond to what happens that matters." Wysteria then turned her back to the three other women in the room and slipped on the robe; tying the gold chord around her waist. Then she sat down on the chair before the candle.

Wysteria held an image in her mind of the babe she was about to bless and excluded her surroundings, banishing all thought of the day's happenings. She centered her focus on the blue around the lower part of the wick instead of the bright upper flame. Staring at a burning candle in this fashion was easier on the eyes.

After a few moments, Wysteria shut her eyes and looked for the flame against her closed eyelids. Quickly it appeared, burning in her mind's view. "I am ready to begin."

Raika laid the baby on the bed and removed the blanket. Gently she undressed the sleeping child and brought her over to Wysteria, placing the naked babe tenderly in the crone's arms.

Wysteria opened her eyes and looked down at the child. Her heart glowed with love for the sleeping infant. Gently she ran her hand over the top of the child's head, down her round face, and stopped at the baby's heart. "From this day you will have a joyous heart and a cheerful spirit," she whispered. She then looked over at Raika. "Summon the others."

Raika opened the bedroom door and motioned for the others to join them.

Merrow entered first, then Jubez and Hun; followed by Twila and Gorg. The Brownies, Opina and Lupa, took up the rear carrying a cauldron of hot water. They placed it carefully on the table before leaving the room.

Merrow walked over to Wysteria and took the child. Gently he spread the babe's chubby legs, exposing her genitalia, and turned to face those gathered. "Witness this babe as a woman child. One day she will give birth to her own. Her breasts will be suckled, her heart will love, and her wisdom will be passed down."

Everyone nodded in agreement.

Merrow walked over to the bed and handed the baby to Aliki.

With loving arms Aliki took her child, kissed her soft cheek, and handed Saje to Jubez.

Jubez did the same, and there it went, as the baby was passed to each person in the room.

It was Meav who was the last to receive the baby. She gently kissed Saje and handed her once more to Merrow.

Merrow silently held the baby while Wysteria prepared the magic circle of protection.

Wysteria pulled from her satchel the bag of stones and a black, velvet cloth. She spread the cloth on the table and placed a stone in each direction. "I place rose quartz, the stone of love, to the west; amber, the stone of change and perception, to the south. I place carnelian, the stone of inspiration, to the east, and amethyst, the stone of prosperity, to the north."

Merrow then placed Saje in the center of the circle.

Wysteria laid her hands over the child and chanted. "Stones of power, strong stones of lore; join with me, I do implore. Bless this babe for all her years; give her courage to face her fears."

Wysteria then picked out a sprig of rue from the bag of herbs and burnt it in the candle's flame. "I purify your soul, Saje, routing out negatives and bestow the blessing of healing and a defense against the spells of dark magic."

Merrow took bits of carnation, cypress, frankincense, lotus, elder and the rue and threw them into the boiling water of the cauldron. He dipped the edge of a linen cloth into the mixture and handed it to Wysteria.

Wysteria took the cloth and brought it to her own face to make sure it was not too hot. Once satisfied with the temperature, she began to wash Saje's face.

The baby woke and began to cry and kick.

Wysteria ignored the fuss, and continued to wash the child. As she cleansed the baby's arms and chest, she chanted. "Pure you are for all to see." She began to wash Saje's legs and feet. "To walk upright, just and free."

Merrow dipped a clean linen square into the cauldron and handed it to Wysteria.

Wysteria again tested the temperature of the cloth, then spread the babe's chubby thighs and washed her sex. "And from her womb life will come."

Gently Wysteria turned the screaming baby onto her belly and took yet another clean cloth from Merrow. This time she gently washed the child's back. "A strong spine to muster a day's work well heeded," she recited. Then with the last clean cloth she washed the baby's behind. Carefully she spread the chubby cheeks and cleansed the area. "And to expel what is not needed."

Wysteria handed the screaming child to Merrow.

He held the baby high above his head. "Let the blessings now of loved ones be called out and bestowed under the watchful eye of our Divine Maker."

Each Elwin bequeathed Saje love, joy, wisdom, prosperity, health, and many more wonderful things for a full and happy life.

Meav was the last to speak. All she could remember was the Irish blessing her Papa recited to her and her sisters before bed. "May the road rise to meet you; may the wind be always at your back. May the sun shine warm upon your face; the rains fall softly upon your fields. And until we meet again; may God fold you in the palm of His hand."

Aliki's face brightened. "That is so beautiful, Meav. Thank you."

Merrow handed the hysterical baby to her mother and replied in a booming voice. "'Tis done! Now feed the child."

Jubez looked around the room, his handsome face shining with pride. "Now, dear visitors, 'tis time for us to eat as well."

One by one the guests filed out of the bedroom.
Raika closed the door behind them.
Wysteria slipped off the robe and donned her clothes.
Aliki bared her breasts and fed the hungry baby.
Meav looked out the window and thought of home.

Chapter Five

Titiana loved the large ledge outside the queen's bedchamber window. It always got the morning sun and a nice breeze as well. But it was her secret place and would always remain a secret. If Gyla ever found out where Titiana spent her time, she would thrash her bottom hard. Titiana had been warned by her older sister to stay far away from the castle and the evil Devora. So whatever Titiana heard or saw while she spied on the queen was hidden away to the deepest part of her being, and could never be spoken aloud.

Titiana watched now as Devora stood before her floor length mirror. The queen admired the smooth flesh of her swan like neck. Devora had taken the potion only moments ago, and already her youthfulness had returned. Titiana knew all about the potion, what it was made from and its effect on the beautiful witch.

Devora smiled with satisfaction and pride at her reflection. As long as she continued to drink the elixir, she would forever be as young looking and attractive as she was this very moment.

She ran a slender finger down her décolletage, to the creamy mounds that lusciously swelled from the scant neckline of her gown. With a long, red nail she caressed herself, pleased with her handiwork.

"I am a clever sorceress for sure," she softly boasted.

Ah, clever indeed, as well as gifted, resourceful, and in possession of a very powerful secret.

The brew was concocted from a plant she had found growing in a corner of the castle's dungeon. The discovery came a score of years ago, when she had been forced to oversee the beating of an employee in need of discipline. While one of the sentries had stripped and whipped the disobedient servant, Devora occupied herself by looking around at the stonework of the dank and musty cell. It was then her eyes had settled upon a flower growing in a corner of the chamber, creeping up through the stone slabs.

The plant's beautiful blue petals and large green leaves were so unusual that it had caught her interest. And how it thrived, with no light, and with so little space to grow, was an even bigger mystery to Devora...one that got the best of her curiosity.

She had plucked the foliage from the chamber floor, and went about to the other cells to find more. Its heady aroma had enticed her to experiment into creating a signature perfume. She had simmered the herbal treasure in a cauldron, chanted a few of her prose, and dabbed a bit of the tincture on her wrist. To her surprise, a small scratch she had there from her cat, Gotham, healed before her very eyes.

'Twas then an idea struck Devora. She poured a bit of the serum into Gotham's bowl, and had watched him drink. In a matter of moments, the old, fat cat turned into a sinewy, lively kitten. Without hesitation, Devora did the same, and had transformed herself into a younger, more vibrant version.

After two days, Gotham had not only returned to his original state, but had aged rapidly and died a few days later. Horror had filled Devora, as her feet took to the dungeon stairs two at a time. If she could not find more of the blue miracle, she would succumb to the same fate.

Relief had flooded her when she spotted a new crop of the youth-inducing herb growing in the same place as those she had previously picked, but in much more abundance. She became hilarious with joy—stripped off all her clothes like a mad woman and rolled around in the flowers.

From that time on, the east side of the dungeon was locked, off limits to anyone but Devora. The potion had been religiously brewed every two days and drank, assuring her eternal youth. She smiled at her reflection again.

"Aye, you are clever indeed," Devora repeated softly.

"And what makes you so clever, my queen?" came a deep voice.

Titiana knew that voice well. She smiled when she spotted Shell the sentry standing in the door. Shell was handsome and strong. Titiana especially liked to watch when he removed all of his clothes for the queen's pleasure. The meaty staff between his thighs would grow and grow, until it stood erect. It made Devora giggle and purr like a cat. Titiana watched intrigued while Shell inserted the rigid rod inside Devora. First Shell would open Devora's legs wide and poke her there, then flip the queen onto to her belly and insert himself there. Titiana believed it must be a magic wand Shell had connected to his body. It certainly wove a spell on Devora.

Devora spun around to find Shell standing in the archway. "You should have had Zailia announce you," she grumbled.

Shell smirked. "Only this morning you were spread upon the bed naked and moist to my touch."

Devora was irked by his cool, aloof manner. "What pleasures I bestow upon your pathetic body gives you no cause to think your attitude toward me is casual," she spat. "Never for a moment forget that I am your queen, and should be treated with due respect for the title."

Shell stiffened as though she had struck him. "Am I not due for a bit of respect as well?" He moved closer. "Do I not give you pleasure?"

"'Twill do you no good to challenge me, Shell."

He gave her a curt nod. "Forgive me, Your Majesty."

Devora turned back toward the mirror and deliberately arranged her full bosom to blossom further from her neckline. She knew Shell was watching, drooling, wanting to suck the rosy nipples. The mere thought of his warm lips encompassing the tender peaks made her wet. Her annoyance increased at how quickly he excited her.

Devora frowned. "Why are you here?"

Shell locked his hands behind his back and stood with legs astride. This stance always brought her down before him, her fingers ready, and mouth searching for what was hidden beneath his breeches. "Hobbs has news that will interest you."

Devora was irritated at the thrilling current moving through her. The sentry's muscular legs spread wide drove her imagination wild. Annoyed with herself for feeling the way she did, Devora waved a hand over her head. "Who the hell is Hobbs?"

"He is one of your gardeners, Your Majesty."

Devora frowned. "And what sort of news could a grounds man have that would be of interest to me?"

Shell arched a brow. "He stands just beyond your chamber door, why not invite him in and hear for yourself."

"You have brought a commoner to the second floor?" Devora screeched. "Have you no sense, no respect?" She wrung her hands nervously. "How can he be trusted?" It was no secret that most of the kingdom hated her, wished her an ill fate. Because of this, Devora had to be cautious at every turn. "He could be in possession of a dagger, planning my demise as we speak."

Shell chuckled lightly. "I doubt such is true, my queen."

Devora's lips puckered with annoyance. "Has he been searched?"

Shell nodded. "That he has, with and without his clothes." He chuckled again. "The little toad squealed like a pig when Carson bent him over and searched him thoroughly with his fingers."

Devora's full red lips curled into a sly smile. "It does my peace of mind good to know Carson takes his position seriously."

Shell returned the grin. "And he takes such pleasure in what he does, as well."

They both began to laugh.

Shell's shoulders relaxed. "Should I show Hobbs in, my queen?"

Devora sighed. "Aye, the quicker he tells his news, the sooner he will leave."

Shell went to the door and opened it wide.

In walked Hobbs, visibly embarrassed and shaking in his skin. His weather worn hands held tightly to the white sheet wrapped around his waist. Upon seeing Devora, he dropped to his knees.

Behind him entered Carson, spear in hand. Politely he bowed.

Devora crossed her arms in front of her. "You have not allowed him his clothes?"

"Nay, Your Majesty," Carson said. "Not until he

leaves the castle." He chuckled wickedly. "And maybe not even then."

Devora sneered. "I like how you think, Carson."

Carson bowed his head. "Thank you, my queen."

Devora looked down at the pathetic little man. "What have you come to tell me?"

Hobbs reluctantly rose from the floor. "Was makin' me way home, me was, and took me a short cut by way of old Tobiah's yard."

Devora glared at him. "Why would your journey home interest me, peasant?"

Hobbs swallowed hard. "'Twas what me ears heard ye'd be interested in, me queen."

Devora moved closer, purposely allowing the gardener a closer view of her heaving cleavage. "And what did you hear?"

Hobbs stared at the scene before him.

Shell kicked Hobbs in the arse. "Keep your eyes in your head before I have them plucked out."

Devora felt immense satisfaction at Shell's jealousy. She stood very near to Hobbs, hoping Shell would become even more disturbed. "I am waiting."

Hobbs quickly cast his gaze to the floor. "Me heard a young woman washed ashore a day or so ago, seems she came from a land called Ireland."

Devora looked over at Shell. "Have you heard of this news...ever heard of Ireland?"

Shell frowned. "Nay, Your Majesty on both accounts."

Devora looked back at the gardener. "What else did you hear?"

Hobbs went on to relay word for word Tobiah's leprechaun legend, how it might pertain to the maiden's presence, and that the young castaway was staying with Wysteria.

Devora felt a momentary panic as her mind jumped on the possibility that Wysteria's new guest could be more than a marooned traveler. She would put nothing passed her dear sister, especially if Wysteria could foil Devora's plans and dethrone her.

"It that all you have come to say?" Devora snapped at the messenger.

"Aye, me queen," Hobbs said, falling again to his

knees.

Devora looked over at Carson. "Take him away, and for good measure, I believe it might be wise if you search him again."

"Nay, please, Your Majesty," Hobbs pleaded.

Devora looked deep into Carson's round, black eyes. "We never can be too sure, now can we?"

Carson smiled. "Aye, that we cannot, Your Majesty." He grabbed Hobbs by the arm and dragged him out the door.

Shell shut the heavy portal behind them. "'Twould be wise for me to find out all I can about Ireland and this maiden your sister houses."

A wave of trepidation swept through Devora. "Do so immediately," she snapped, making her way back to the mirror. "But discreetly."

Shell bowed politely. "Aye my queen," he said and left the room.

Devora continued to admire her reflection, all the while her mind working on how she could obtain more information about the girl. Certainly if she tried to be hospitable, gain the young woman's confidence, Wysteria would warn her against Devora and thwart the attempt. But someone no one would expect of any ulterior motives would be of no suspicion.

Devora tapped her forefinger lightly at her temple. "Think, who would be appropriate for the job?" she whispered to herself. In an instant the perfect candidate popped into her mind. She rang the bell for her handmaiden, Zailia.

****

Zailia had been washing the second corridor's stone floor when the bell of doom pealed loudly. Quickly she rose from her knees, dropped the rag into the bucket of murky water and made her way to the queen's chamber.

Out of breath, she opened the door, and bowed before her evil employer. "Aye, Your Majesty."

"Rise, shut the door, and sit in the chair by the window," Devora commanded.

Zailia obeyed, a wave of apprehension washing over her. She had never been allowed to sit upon any of the chairs in the room.

Devora took a seat opposite Zailia and gazed casually out the large window. "I hear a young woman has been washed ashore this isle."

Zailia swallowed hard, fear gripping her heart. "I know nothing of the maiden."

"Nay, of course you do not, which is exactly why very soon you will," Devora said, turning to look deep into Zailia's eyes.

Zailia clasped her moist, chapped hands in her lap. "I have not the time for socializing, my queen. My duties here take precedence."

Devora twirled a lock of hair that fell down one shoulder. "And who said you would not be doing your duty?"

Zailia frowned. "I do not understand, Your Majesty."

Devora sighed. "Nay, that pea you have for a brain probably understands very little." She leaned forward in her seat. "So I will make crystal clear, my plans for you and this guest my sister harbors."

Zailia felt her heart lurch up to her throat. "Plans?"

Devora smiled. "Aye, Zailia...the ones you will make with our newest dweller. And while you are befriending her, you will find out everything you can about her."

Zailia's mouth went dry. "Why is she so important to you?"

Devora's smile fell. "That is none of your business. All that concerns you is to gain her confidence, become her friend, draw information from her and bring it back to me."

Knowing Devora's black heart, Zailia did not believe it would end there. "Then what, my queen? What happens after I do all what you have asked?"

Devora's smile returned. "Then you poison her."

Zailia gasped. "I cannot do such a thing.

Devora's face twisted. "Oh, but you will, Zailia dear. If you want that old man of yours to remain alive, you will do exactly as I say on this matter." She stood and walked over to an apothecary chest, opened a drawer and pulled from it a small vial. Slowly she caressed the tiny bottle. Devora spun around to face Zailia. "This is the poison you will use."

Tears stung the back of Zailia's throat. "But she is

just a young girl, Your Majesty. What possible harm can she bring down upon you?"

Devora held up a hand. "Silence!" She made her way to Zailia and seized her by the arm, pulling her to her feet. "You will do as you are told, or your father dies."

Tears streamed down Zailia's cheeks. "Please, I beg of you, Your Majesty, do not do this horrible thing to the maiden."

Devora grabbed a fist full of Zailia's hair and yanked it hard.

Zailia cried out as Devora dragged her to the door.

Fear for Zailia gripped Titiana and she almost lost her balance on the window's ledge. Quickly, she repositioned herself. Pity swelled in her heart for the pretty and kind young handmaiden. It took great effort on Titiana's part to stifle the urge to fly from her perch,, into the witch's room, and bite Devora on the nose, which was most affective for inflicting pain.

Devora threw open the portal. "You...Sentry," she called out to a guard standing watch at the top of the staircase.

Quickly the young man left his post and came to his queen's aid. He bowed before Devora. "Wesley, at your service, Your Majesty."

Devora threw Zailia at the young man's feet. "Well then, Wesley, take this peasant to Carson with my orders to strip her and give her ten lashes."

Titiana gasped, fearful and humiliating images quickly building in her mind.

Zailia began to shake as the young sentry lowered his gaze, a look of pity for the beautiful young servant filled his eyes.

"You wish this done for certain, my queen?"

Devora's lips thinned. "I would not have ordered it, Sentry, if I was not certain. And if you do not obey these orders, Carson can do the same to you." She smirked. "And you know of Carson's fancy for men, his punishment would not end with a beating."

Wesley bowed respectively and pulled Zailia to her feet. "As you wish, Your Majesty."

Devora's eyes narrowed. "This will be your fate every day at this hour, for three days. On the fourth day your father will join you and you will watch him die."

Titiana cringed at the thought.

Zailia tried to jerk her arm free from the guard's hold. "Nay...please!"

"Then do you agree to what I have asked of you?" Devora spat.

Tears fell in torrents down Zailia's flushed cheeks. "Aye, I agree."

Titiana cried too, feeling for Zailia's predicament, but also quite relieved there would be no beating.

Devora smiled. "Good." She turned her attention toward the young guard. "Release her and return to your post."

He bowed and left Zailia to face Devora alone.

"Now go...put on something clean, comb your hair, wash your face," Devora demanded. She chuckled wickedly, dropping the vial into Zailia's apron pocket. "And make yourself a new friend."

Titiana watched Zailia flee from the queen's chamber. Spreading her tiny wings, Titiana did the same.

Chapter Six

Meav bid the Elwins goodbye and followed Wysteria out of the cottage. She was thankful for the long walk ahead. She had eaten way too much...not being able to resist all the delicious food offered her, and now her belly felt as though it would burst.

Once down the path, Meav turned left...the way she had come. But Wysteria's hand upon her arm stopped her.

Wysteria smiled warmly. "We have another stop, lass, before we go back home."

Home...the word conjured up visions of the farm in Dublin and nights around the fire with her family, not Wysteria's tiny cottage on this strange island. Yet, that was the only home Meav had now. Silently she followed the elder woman through the glen and into the jungle.

Wysteria glanced sideways at her young charge. "Not a word of curiosity as to our next stop?"

"I trust you, Wysteria, and respect you enough to wait until you are ready to tell me," Meav said.

Wysteria's heart melted. She remembered such devotion from Meridith, and now the daughter was the same. "You honor me, child."

Meav shrugged. "I have no reason to doubt you, dear healer. If 'twasn't for you and your hospitality, me sorry flesh would still be hungry and dirty." She frowned. "There is one thing I do wonder about, though."

"Speak your mind, lass," Wysteria encouraged.

"How did I get to your cottage?"

"Rule," Wysteria said softly.

Meav halted shocked. "Why did he not tell me?"

Wysteria hesitated.

"Why did he not tell me, Wysteria?" Meav repeated.

"'Tis not like Rule to call attention to his good deeds," Wysteria explained, taking Meav's arm and continuing their walk.

Meav regarded Wysteria quizzically for a moment.

"'Twas him then, that saved me from the panther?"

Wysteria clamped her lips tight, guarding Rule's secret.

Meav sighed. "Should I see him again, I will be sure to thank him for saving me life."

"What is most important is that you are safe and no one will ever harm you again," Wysteria promised.

Meav frowned. "'Tis what Rule said as well."

"Then you can believe him," Wysteria said. "Rule is a man of his word."

****

The waterfall was breathtaking. Meav stared in awe at the magical way the water cascaded over the smoothened rocks, ending its journey into the pool of orange below.

"'Tis magnificent," Meav exclaimed. "The water is so bright."

"Aye, 'tis at that," Wysteria responded with a lilt to her voice. "I remember the days as a young girl swimming naked in this sweet channel."

Meav had come upon the strange colored water when she first arrived on the island...but obviously that was from another end of the river, for she would have truly remembered the waterfall. "What makes it orange?"

Wysteria sat down upon a large rock. "The blood of a hero, mixed with the yellow of the sun."

Meav sat down at her feet, dropping Wysteria's satchel and looking up at the elderly woman like a little child eager to hear the tale. "Tell me, dear healer."

Wysteria raised her face to the sky and closed her eyes. "'Tis said that Hugo Pierre Quinn, a mighty warrior-god, came upon this river centuries ago. He found a young maiden sitting where you are sitting now, crying and cradling her dying man in her arms."

Meav gasped, bringing her hand to her throat. "Nay, how awful for her."

Wysteria looked down at the girl. "I am pleased to see the compassion upon your face, child."

"The young woman must have been crushed," Meav whispered.

Wysteria sighed. "Aye, for sure, and her sorrowed heart lay broken."

74

Tears filled Meav's eyes. "I can understand why...she loved him."

"With all that was in her," Wysteria added.

Meav sighed. "Aye, with all that was in her," she repeated softly. A lone tear slipped down her cheek. "Why was he dying?"

Wysteria arched a craggy brow. "He tried to slay the hydra."

"Ah me, what is a hydra?" Meav questioned, feeling slightly fearful of the answer.

"A hydra is a dragon, and this hydra guarded the glass case that held the crystal crown of wisdom," Wysteria explained. "He breathed fire and had deadly venom; just a look from his eyes could kill. His body was that of a snake, the claws of a lion, and the wings of an eagle."

Meav swallowed hard. "And the young man saved his love from the monster?"

"Nay, he wanted to slay the dragon and burn his carcass, whereby the ashes when rubbed together turns into gold. He also wanted the crown of wisdom. With two such treasures he believed he could win the heart of his one true love."

Meav frowned. "Did he not know she would love him for rich or poor?"

"Nay, he did not."

Meav's frown deepened. "He could have simply asked her."

Wysteria chuckled lightly. "You have much to learn about the egos of men, my child." Wysteria lovingly pushed aside a tendril from Meav's forehead. "Our young man believed knowledge beyond all others and riches would win him the maiden's hand"

"How sad he did not trust her enough to love him for who he was," Meav concluded.

"Dragons are not meant to be slain. They are meant to be controlled as a force to empower you," Wysteria went on. "They are the epitome of power, their eyes the gateway to the soul. 'Tis said a hydra knows the true heart of an individual just by looking into their eyes."

"And the hydra saw the young man's greed?" Meav asked.

"Aye, and his quest for power instead of his trust in true love," Wysteria added.

"So it wounded him," Meav said.

"Aye, and his young woman sat weeping with him in her arms."

"But what of the warrior-god?" Meav asked eagerly. "You said he came along and found her crying. Surely he would have the power to help?"

Wysteria smiled. "Aye, Hugo Pierre Quinn felt sorry for the young woman's grief, and he offered her a chance to save her man."

Meav's face brightened. "What was his offer?"

"That she take his place," Wysteria said softly.

Meav inhaled sharply. "And did she?"

"Aye, she did...agreeing without hesitation and before her very eyes, her young man's wound healed and she became afflicted instead. When water is bombarded by negatives, like the spilt blood of a hero, the crystals tend to store the sorrow. As she lay dying, her blood flowed into the river and mixed with the yellow of the sun...thus coloring the water. A river of orange was left."

"So the hero's blood was hers not his," Meav concluded.

"Aye, lass...no where is it written that only men can be heroes."

Meav's eyes saddened. "So the young woman died?"

Wysteria shook her head. "Hugo Pierre Quinn was so taken with the young woman's unselfish act; he blessed the river and instructed her man to place her into it. Her wound was cleansed, healed by the orange water, and she lived."

Meav smiled through her tears. "And they lived happily ever after."

Wysteria smiled, her own eyes welling with tears. "'Tis what I am told."

Meav looked over at the waterfall, its rush filling the river, changing from clear to orange as it accumulated below. Beams of sunlight flickered across the blanket of water like tiny fireflies. "Why have you taken me here, Wysteria?"

"All things have a reason, child," Wysteria said.

"What is the reason we are here?" Meav inquired

again.

"Keronia has been waiting for a hero, lass."

Meav quickly turned to look at Wysteria, her brows arching with surprise. "And you think I am this hero?"

Wysteria placed a loving hand on Meav's shoulder. "I *know* you are, child."

Meav stood quickly, arms straight down by her side, fists clenched. "Nay, I am no hero." She stamped her foot like a child having a tantrum "I am just a scared, homeless girl who fled in the dead of night instead of facing me fate and left me family to die because of me selfish way."

"Your family did not die because you fled," Wysteria corrected gently.

"Aye, they did. Had I accepted Hollister McGreary's proposal all of them would be alive now. 'Tis me fault they are all dead," Meav sobbed. "I am no hero, I am a coward." She fell to her knees. "I let them all die." Covering her face with her hands, Meav poured out all that had been in her heart.

Wysteria slid off the rock and sat beside her on the bank of the river. Gently she reached out and embraced the young woman. "Shush now, child," she comforted. "You place far too much blame on your innocent shoulders. The man that murdered your family was ruthless and heartless...your marriage to him would not have stopped his evil plan, nor spared your family. Scoundrels like that are wicked through and through. Trust me on this...I know of one like McGreary...maybe even worse. Nothing you did or did not do would have stopped him. Your family would have all been murdered in their beds eventually, only you would have been McGreary's wife and made to sleep beside your enemy."

The thought made Meav shudder. "Oh, saints preserve me," she moaned.

"Aye, that they did," Wysteria whispered. "And if you carried on so with your grandmamma, as you did just now, 'tisn't a wonder why you spent a lot of time in the woodshed."

Meav giggled in spite of the sadness she felt. "She was never one to take me guff."

Wysteria pulled away and looked deep into Meav's

eyes. "I have to warn you, lass, I am of the same stock as your grandmamma. If you ever spit and sputter like that again, I will introduce my hand to your bare bottom...over my knee you will go...no matter how big or how old you are. If you act like a child; I will spank you like a child. Do you understand?"

Meav wiped her eyes with the backs of her hands. "Aye, I do."

Wysteria forced a stern face. "See to it you remember it."

Meav nodded slowly.

"Now remove your dress and get into the water," Wysteria ordered.

Meav's eyes widened. "Here, in the open." She looked around her. "Someone could come by and..."

Wysteria interrupted. "No one will come, trust me on this." She slowly stood, her old knees creaking. "Come now, up you go and off with the dress."

Meav reluctantly stood and slipped the dress over her head. Standing naked out of doors made her blush with embarrassment. She modestly covered her womanhood with the palm of her hand and placed her other arm across her chest.

"Into the water with you," Wysteria ordered. "There is much to do."

Slowly Meav entered the river, dipping one toe in first. A tingling sensation crept up her ankle, to her knee, up to her thigh, and settled between her legs. The sensation pleased her, and she suddenly felt unashamed of her nakedness. "What is happening?" she muttered.

Wysteria smiled. "You are experiencing the true potential and natural fulfillment of your woman's body."

Meav lowered herself into the water, feeling its coolness penetrate her. Inside her the water turned warm, easing all her muscles and bones, making every nerve come alive. She lay back and spread her legs, enjoying the sense of peace and joy, pleasure and satisfaction that bathed her insides. "Do you think 'tis shameful to feel this good?"

"Nay, 'tis not shameful in the least, lass." Wysteria rummaged through her satchel for the herbs she needed. "'Tis never bad to feel at one with your body, to know

78

what it likes...to give it what it craves."

Meav's breasts prickled, her nipples hardened. Gently she caressed herself and smiled.

From his perch atop a tree, Rule smiled too. His eyes followed Meav's hands, caressing her full breasts along with her; drooling with hunger. Not the kind one craved to fill the belly. Nay...this was a different kind of hunger...a hunger for human contact and warmth. Rule's phallus grew thick and hard between his hind legs. He felt himself ooze with excitement when she spread her thighs wide...the triangular patch of fiery hair being her only cover.

He watched enthralled as she rolled onto her belly, luxuriated in the water's power. Slowly she pushed her creamy buttocks up, spreading her legs again, and causing all sorts of wonderful havoc within Rule's body.

He licked his jowls, almost tasting her flavor. The thought of jumping down from his hiding place to run his tongue over her flesh became his instant obsession. He knew it would savor sweet; expected it would please him greatly. A purr rumbled deep in his throat, as he fought for control to stay put...quiet...and alone.

Rule cast his gaze to the waterfall, its gurgle passing over the rocks, its song singing a lyric of peace and contentment. At this very moment this was what he knew Meav was experiencing; oneness with life, energy carried through her body by the water she bathed in. The orange liquid was divine, life-giving. It had the power to heal, cleanse and renew; it was a living being all on its own. Rule heard in tales of some life forms way at the bottom of the sea that could live without light, but no life can survive without water.

Rule looked back at Meav. She had turned onto her back, stroking her arms and legs back and forth.

"I read a passage in me Papa's Bible...it read...God created the heaven and earth. The earth was without form and void, and darkness was upon the face of the deep; and the spirit of God was moving over the face of the waters," Meav recited. "Do you think His face has moved over this water, Wysteria?"

Wysteria lined the herbs she would use on a rock. "Our Divine Maker's face is in all we come upon, child. He orchestrates life to a perfect harmony; 'tis man that destroys the plan. Every detail, each and all things have an origin."

Meav frowned. "Like what, for example?"

Wysteria placed her hands on her hips. "The role water plays in our lives, for one. It rids us of negativity, it refreshes and calms. Water is the balance of our lives in many instances." She tilted her head sideways. "Did you ever realize the fluid in your mother's womb was your first bath?"

Meav sat up, water droplets falling from her nipples. "'Tis true, as I think of it."

"Life began in the vast waters," Wysteria said. "It represents time without end, the celestial deep from which all life spiraled. Eventually, into which it must also dissolve and resume."

"'Tis the nectar of the earth's womb," Meav reflected.

Wysteria sat down on a rock. "Aye, lass, and a human hand can reach out and feel the power of the Divine if they are in tune to the earth's spirit."

Meav stared at Wysteria baffled. "How does one become in tune to the earth's spirit?"

For the first time in a long time Wysteria's knowledge was being called upon. Being able to mentor again had made her feel needed. And the young woman before her was such a joy to know and guide. "By praying, chanting, singing medicine songs; all of these things open the portal to grace, and the presence of our Divine Maker, and what He has placed in earth's hands for us to nourish ourselves with, to thrive, live, and even die by. When prayers are offered over water, they are soaked up, their patterns vibrate healing thoughts, negatives are washed away, and a path for spiritual clarity is set." Wysteria began to sprinkle rosemary into the water. "Plants and herbs, like the rosemary I have added to your bath, cleanse the spiritual body."

Meav moved closer to the sprigs, allowing the fragments to wash over her flesh. "Is me body a spiritual one?"

"'Twill be by the time you leave the river," Wysteria promised. "Now, lass, I want you to immerge yourself fully under the water."

Meav nodded and obeyed, dunking herself quickly under the water.

Wysteria waited until Meav's head popped above the water before she spoke again. "I want you now to take a deep, slow breath and feel the water around you...let it caress you, stimulate you, cleanse every part of you. Let it carry away all regrets, hurts, and sorrows of the past. Let Mother Earth's womb hold you, protect you, nurture you as though you were a wee babe again. Trust her, allow her to let her healing juices float away all your concerns and misgivings."

Meav sighed.

"You are comforted," Wysteria said softly. "You are reborn. Feel the sense of your well being and all the parts of your body...your toes, your legs, your buttocks, your genitals...the belly where one day you will nurture life. Let the water soothe your back, feel the wetness on your shoulders, your neck; your face and in your hair. Feel this very moment, the life force in your body, feel the living waters merge with you...connecting you now to this place, the universe, and eternity."

Meav listened to the soft, pronounced words Wysteria spoke. Within her she began to feel the strength, the power of her own body. "I understand what me body is asking of me."

"And what is it saying, child?"

"It needs me forgiveness, it wants to grow and heal." Meav stretched, and breathed, and for the first time in a long time thought of the future. Hope filled her, as did desire. "The water's spiritual tide is washing me with love, contentment, joy of life and the presence of the Divine." She could actually envision the possibilities that awaited her, instead of fearing and dreading each day as she had done in Dublin. "'Tis working, Wysteria. I am reaching out, becoming in tune...one with the earth's spirit."

"And with your own, lass," Wysteria added.

Meav sighed. "Aye...with me own."

Wysteria pulled from her satchel a clay bowl. Filling it with water, she dropped a handful of rosemary into it, along with a bit of rue and lemon balm. Then her shaky voice brought forth a song. "New moon...rebirth...the sliver of the crescent beneath her foot..." Wysteria added a sprinkle of motherwort, hyssop, marigold and basil to the mixture in the bowl. "Lead her down the right path...strength...conviction...she is our hero."

Meav listened to the words closely, but had a hard time understanding their meaning.

Wysteria held the bowl up to the heavens. The sun warmed the mixture, soaking it with renewal and energy. Placing the bowl beside her on the rock, Wysteria reached again into her satchel and brought out a strip of muslin. She soaked it in the bowl of water. "Come here to me, child."

Meav stood slowly.

Rule, watching the ritual from his hiding place, felt his loins tighten as Meav immerged from the water like a goddess from the deep. Her natural beauty left him enthralled.

Wysteria stood and began to wash Meav.

Meav held her arms out to her side while Wysteria spread the mixture over her shoulders, elbows and to her hands, washing each finger.

Again Wysteria dipped the cloth into the bowl.

Meav felt the healer's soft brush of the fabric against her breasts, down her belly, and between her thighs.

"Now turn around," Wysteria instructed.

Meav obeyed, feeling the gentle hands of her mentor run the material down her neck, to her back, around her buttocks and down her legs. One by one, Meav lifted each foot and Wysteria washed her there as well.

"Gaze into the water, Meav," Wysteria whispered.

Meav cast her glance to the sparkling flow, light from the sun playing on the moving water.

Wysteria massaged the young maiden's back with gentle swirls. "Empty your thoughts, lass. Concentrate on the beauty and the meaning of the water, the light dancing upon it, the air filling your senses, and the earth around you."

Rule closed his eyes, wishing Wysteria's words could free him from his horror.

Meav inhaled deeply, feeling connected to every living thing on earth. It was at that moment...the very moment Meav released all of her sorrows that the water around her ankles began to ripple. Before she knew what was happening, a gush of water flew into her face, a flash of silver blinded her.

Loreli sprung from the depth of her world and wrapped her arms around Meav. "I saved her...so now I will claim her." And with that she captured Meav.

"Nay!" Wysteria screamed, reaching forward to hang on to Meav as best she could, but her frail arms were no match for the quick, liquid movements of the mermaid. In an instant Loreli had taken Meav with her, beneath the water.

Meav tried desperately to wiggle free from the mer-woman's hold, but she couldn't release herself. Loreli held Meav tightly, breast to breast. Meav looked into the translucent opals of Loreli's eyes and instantly became hypnotized. The golden locks fanning out from her head framed the water nymph's face like a feather headdress or a halo...like paintings Meav had seen of the saints...and instantly imagined the scene before her as a heavenly vision. It was with that thought that Meav felt her panic being replaced by an unexplainable sense of calm...an unnatural calm...in the face of being drowned.

Loreli felt her captive relax in her arms, and in turn lessened the intensity of her grip, as deeper and deeper she swam. Loreli would now take her beautiful maiden to the caves far beneath the sea's floor, where the air and atmosphere was suitable for a human, and make Meav her companion. The mermaid's heart leaped with anticipation. She had gotten what she had come for, but now she must make haste in securing her prize before it was too late.

Just as Meav felt the last ounce of breath seep from her lungs, a large force plowed into them, breaking Loreli's hold.

The large, black cat clutched Meav by the hair with his teeth, ripping her away from Loreli. With a swipe of his powerful paw, he sent the mermaid spinning in the opposite direction.

Loreli cried out.

The mermaid's piercing screech vibrated through Meav's bones. The high pitched scream reminded her of the night the *Sea Dragon* was lured to its fate.

Loreli had been maimed by the panther's sharp claws. Her pain sounded as though it ran deep and realizing she was no match to fight the animal for Meav, she fishtailed away to safety.

The beast then turned Meav around, holding her close to his chest and swam quickly to the surface.

Meav's terror returned, stark and vivid. But as consumed as she was with fear, she was too weak to struggle. She lay limp in the animal's embrace; the amber eyes the last thing she saw before everything went black.

Chapter Seven

Zailia ran through the corridor, down the large flight of stairs, and out the castle door; not stopping until she was away...far, far away from Devora's evil, cold eyes. The witch had a heart of stone and its malevolence would now penetrate Zailia's soul. Her fear turned her blood to ice, her thoughts to mush, and her hopes for a better life was dashed.

Into the jungle she ran, hoping the large, heavily wooded closure would shield her from the terror, the sick and twisted world of Queen Devora. The things that took place in the castle were too despicable to repeat. Zailia knew the goings on in the dungeon, heard the screams from the torture chamber...even in the queen's own boudoir depraved and sinful acts transpired. The vile woman took her enjoyment in the way others suffered. Their humiliation, their pain, and their degradation brought Devora thrills.

"Heaven help us all for being her pawns," Zailia sobbed, throwing herself down upon a layer of fallen palm branches. There in the lush, green foliage she wept for the task she had ahead. "I care not for myself," she wailed aloud. If it had only been her hide in jeopardy she would have sooner died than agree to Devora's plan. But her aging, sick father would be made to suffer the consequences if she did not obey the witch queen.

Zailia ran her fingers through her snarled hair, yanking at the roots in her agony. Her mission was to befriend the maiden castaway, then betray her. "Nay...I cannot...I cannot." How could Zailia take someone's life?

Her sobs caught in her throat as the sound of heavy footsteps neared. Quickly, she wiped her eyes with the backs of her hands and turned to find Ibrehem standing behind her.

He rushed to her aid and knelt down beside her. "Zailia, lass, what ails you? What is hurt...tell me and I shall do my best to ease your pain."

Zailia cast her glance away, "I am just tired, my friend," she lied. It would do no good to tell Ibrehem the truth. Why get another involved in her plight? If she confided in him the reason she was so distraught, he would definitely interfere, and Devora would have him killed as well. She sighed. "Just very, very tired."

Ibrehem placed a finger beneath her chin and lifted her face so her gaze met his, "Please let me help you, lass." His voice cracked with emotion. "The castle is no place for a young, innocent girl to work...to reside." He chuckled lightly. "Hell, 'tis no place for even me to be." He looked deep into her eyes. "You belong home, with your father, and I can make that possible."

Zailia sat up. "I cannot take your money."

Ibrehem frowned. "Why the hell not, Zailia?"

"Because 'tis all you have, Ibrehem."

"And what good is having it if I cannot help those I care about?"

Zailia's lips thinned. "You mustn't care for me." For Ibrehem's sake she must push him as far away from her as she could. Her life was no longer her own, she would not subject him to the same fate.

Ibrehem reached out and took Zailia's hand. "Why, lass?"

His touch sent excited shivers through her body; his soft, charcoal eyes held kindness and pity. Zailia did not want his pity. "I can take care of myself, Ibrehem.

"Why are you so afraid to be happy?"

Defiantly she raised her chin. "And what makes you so sure you can make me happy, Ibrehem Chancelor?"

He folded his arms across his chest. "What makes you so sure I cannot?"

Zailia stood up and stomped a foot. "You infuriate me. Your head is as big as your ego."

Ibrehem stood. "Why do you always pick a fight when I am trying to be nice?"

"Because...because..." Zailia sputtered.

He smiled widely. "Because you like me...and you know it."

"I do not!" Zailia protested.

Ibrehem's eyes twinkled mischievously. "Aye, lass,

you do...and if you give in to it..."

"Shut your mouth, Ibrehem! I am in no mood for your cocky ways. Your charming wiles will not work on me."

He threw his head back and laughed. "Ah, you admit then, that I am charming."

Zailia stomped her foot again. "I admitted nothing of the kind."

Ibrehem moved closer to her. "You are even more beautiful when you are angry."

Zailia rolled her eyes. "Listen now to the lies you are speaking." She looked down at her soiled, tattered clothes. "'Tis a gown fit for a ball that I wear," she snapped sarcastically, trying desperately to hold back the tears that stung her throat. She pulled at her hair. "And my curls are just so lovely, brushed till they shine."

Ibrehem frowned. "Stop it, Zailia."

Zailia bit her bottom lip, the ache in her heart, the hurt in her soul, nearly too much to hold back. "I am anything but beautiful, Ibrehem."

Ibrehem gently stroked Zailia's cheek. "That is far from the truth, lass. In all your worn garments you are still more beautiful than any lady of the court dressed in all her finery."

Zailia pulled away quickly, afraid his gesture of affection would break her entirely. Her heart cried out for his strong embrace, to be pulled tightly against his muscular chest and feel the safety she so badly needed. But it would put him in danger. "I must get to the cottage to check on father."

Ibrehem reached out for her hand. "Zailia, wait."

She stiffened. Another touch of affection and she would truly fall to pieces before his very eyes.

Ibrehem quickly stepped away. "I am sorry; I know you wish to spend all the time you can with Tobiah."

"Aye, I am not granted much chance to visit home, and when I am allowed away from the castle, I want every precious moment to be spent with Papa."

Ibrehem gave a taut nod. "I understand fully, and I will detain you no further."

Zailia smiled and turned to leave.

"Would you mind if I walked with you?" Ibrehem called after her.

Zailia turned to face him and smiled warmly. "Nay, I would not mind."

Ibrehem offered her his arm. "Then let us be on our way."

Sitting cross-legged on a nearby branch, Titiana watched the two make their way to Tobiah's cottage. How could she help Zailia, and how would she be able to save Meav without revealing her secret place?

****

Rule carefully carried Meav in his mouth, back to his cave. Placing her gently down on a bed of animal skins, he gazed at the pure beauty of her naked form. Every inch of her was perfect. He nudged his nose against her cheek. It was soft, smelled sweet, as he knew it would.

Tenderly Rule licked a nipple, round and round he twirled his tongue over the rosy peak. Her flavor melted in his mouth, longing mounted in his loins.

He watched her intensely. She slept on, not so much as an eyelid fluttered. Rule feared he had lost her. Quickly he brought his ear to her chest and listened for a heartbeat. To his relief it thumped strong.

He sniffed her taut, smooth belly, and then circled her navel with his tongue. Slowly he neared his nose to between her thighs. Her scent was intoxicating. Drawing closer he inhaled deeply; taking in all that was her and let it penetrate his senses. It left him drunk with desire.

His phallus became engorged, hanging heavy between his hind legs. He wanted her, needed her. Ah, to implant himself in her warmth, to take pleasure from the contact, the release.

Gently he stroked her with his large, rough tongue. She quivered. He smiled to himself. Again he tasted her, desiring now to spread her wide and lick her till she woke, or he climaxed, which ever occurred first. But Rule could not take the chance of her seeing him as he was.

He stifled his urges, and did what he thought was best for Meav. Reluctantly he backed away, but for a long moment stared hungrily at the woman in his bed. When she shivered, Rule gripped a fur pallet with his teeth and covered her with it. Then he went to an opposite corner of the cave and willed his transformation to come quickly.

Meav felt so warm and cozy, she almost hated to

open her eyes. But when she did, she almost regretted she had.

She found herself lying on a pile of animal skins in a cave, torches lit and hung from brackets mounted on the wall. The light cast an eerie shadow to the nightmare that was happening in the corner of the grotto.

With its back to Meav, the biggest, blackest panther stood on its hind legs...front paws outstretched upon the wall, back arched, and its large head thrown back as it wreathed in pain.

Meav swallowed hard, and watched paralyzed in her makeshift bed.

The large cat growled, its tail bent upward, and slowly its fur turned to flesh.

Meav watched the beast transform itself into a man...a very large, muscular man...a stark naked man. Meav sat up quickly, the animal covering slipping from her shoulders.

Rule heard the gasp, and quickly spun around to find Meav staring at him with large, frightened eyes; her bare breasts rising and falling with her rapid breathing. *Damn*, he had hoped he would have been done with the ordeal before she woke. Now she was staring with those beautiful blue orbs in disgust, or was it in total panic, either way Rule could not blame her for her reaction.

Meav's mouth fell open as she looked deep into his eyes. "I know you...the amber eyes...the ones of the cat belong to the man."

Rule nodded slowly. "Aye, they are one in the same."

Meav gasped again. "How...how can this be?"

Rule stepped closer. "Please, do not be frightened. I will not hurt you."

Meav scooted away, her eyes wandering down to his broad shoulders, muscular chest, taut stomach, and then to...to...

She inhaled sharply. "Saints preserve me." She continued to gape at the large phallus hanging between his legs.

Rule felt a thrill of pleasure mount with her curiosity, and remained in her full view, allowing her to observe his endowment thoroughly. He suddenly pictured himself walking to her, reaching for her hand and placing it on him. The thought of her fingers folding over his manhood excited him. He began to grow.

Meav's eyes widened as Rule's male member grew hard and erect before her eyes. "Mercy," she choked out. "I have never seen a naked man."

It was then that Rule became embarrassed for his boldness. The maiden was just that...a maiden, innocent of knowing a man. How stupid he had been, of course this would all be a shock to her young, pure eyes. He quickly turned his back to Meav and reached for his breeches. "I am sorry...so very sorry, Meav." His face burned with humiliation. "You should have never seen any of what you have."

Meav liked looking at the other side of him as well...his backside round and tightly formed atop of two muscular thighs. She watched while he slipped on his bottoms, tunic, and sandals.

While Rule buckled his knife holster around his waist, Meav cast a glance down at her own nakedness and screamed.

Rule spun around. "What...what now?"

Quickly she brought the animal skin up to cover her breasts. Her own cheeks burned with embarrassment. "Where are me clothes?"

Rule moved closer and squat down on his haunches. "You were not wearing any clothes."

Meav scooted farther away; her bare back scraping against the cold, cavern wall. "I do not understand any of this. What has happened...why am I here, lying naked in this cave?"

"You do not remember?"

Meav shook her head, swallowing the tears she felt rising to choke her.

Rule sat in a cross-legged fashion in front of her and began to explain.

Meav held the animal covering up to her chin...tightly, as she listened. "I thank you then, milord, for saving me life."

Rule smiled. "I promised no one would harm you, lass."

"Aye, that you did." Suddenly Meav realized, as the events of the day came back to her, that Rule had seen her naked...in the river, wantonly displaying herself. No man had ever seen her without her clothes. And then he carried her here...without a stitch on. She colored fiercely. If there were a hole for her to fall into, she would welcome the chance. She cast her gaze shyly away. "What happens now?"

"I would say the next thing is the problem of your clothes, or lack there of."

Keeping her eyes down, Meav only nodded. For a silly moment she almost thought if she did not look at him, he could not see her.

Rule stood. "I believe I have a remedy for the situation."

Slowly Meav looked up. "You do?"

"Aye, I do," he said, making his way to another corner of the cave and pulling out a large, brown trunk. "In this chest I have all the things a lady's heart desires in the way of fashion."

Meav strained her neck to see from where she sat, her grip never lessening on the pallet that covered her. "How is that?"

Rule snapped the lock and opened the lid. "My mother was a lady all admired, wore the most beautiful dresses; made from the most expensive cloth." He pulled out a blue dress, white lace bordering the collar, cuffs, and hem. He held it up for her to see. "What do you think of this one?"

Meav's face brightened. "Ah, me. 'Tis fit for a queen."

"And that she was, till the day she died," Rule said sadly.

Meav's eyes widened. "Your mother was a queen?"

Rule nodded and reached inside the trunk for a pair of slippers, stockings, bloomers, a petticoat and a camisole. "I believe these are the things you ladies wear along with the dress." He handed everything to Meav.

With a trembling hand Meav reached for the items. "And your father, he has passed as well?"

"Aye."

Meav brought the clothes to her chest, inhaling the scent of jasmine that faintly clung to the garments. "Then that would mean now you are the king."

Rule remained silent.

Meav searched his handsome face. "You live in this cave because of...because you are..." The words caught in her throat.

Rule's lips thinned. Angrily he closed the trunk's lid and made his way to the cave's opening. "I will give you some privacy in order to dress."

Meav swallowed hard. "How could anyone become what you are?"

Rule turned around quickly to face her.

Meav gasped at the sudden hate that filled his amber eyes, the anger that was etched on his face. Again, the man had changed before her very eyes.

Rule's voice grated hoarsely. "Never speak of it again, lass, do you hear me?"

Meav nodded.

"Now hurry and get dressed so that I can return you to Wysteria," Rule snapped. "Knowing the old woman as I do, she is probably sick with grief and lays mourning on her cot," he added before stalking out of the cave.

Chapter Eight

Meav did not know when she had gotten dressed in so many clothes, in such little time. And trying to quickly fasten each tiny, pearl button of the beautiful dress with trembling hands made the task all that much harder to accomplish.

All she knew was that she wanted to be gone from the musty smelling cave, and away from the half man, half beast that brought her here.

Rule called into the door opening. "Have you finished dressing, lass?"

Meav's voice was shakier than she liked. "Aye, I am ready, milord."

When Rule entered the cave, he just stared at Meav. "The dress fits you perfectly."

Meav smoothed the puffy skirt down and backed away from him, wanting to keep as much distance as possible between them in case he turned angry again.

Her actions riled him. "Do you really think I would harm you?" he snapped. "If I was going to do anything to you, I would have already. I certainly had the chance." He stomped over to the trunk, grabbed it by the handle and dragged it to the door. "I have no use for these things. You might as well bring them along to Wysteria's with you." He hoisted the trunk to his shoulder and walked out of the cave.

Meav was momentarily taken back by his strength. He lifted the heavy chest like it weighed no more than a loaf of bread.

"Are you coming, lass?" he called back to her.

"Aye, I am right behind you," she said as pleasantly as the situation would allow. There was no sense in getting him irritated again.

Meav had trouble keeping up with Rule's long strides. Even toting a trunk upon his shoulder, he was swifter than she. She was a farm girl, and not use to

93

wearing the many clothes of a grand lady. Even her Sunday best was not as elaborate as what she now wore. The island's heat made the mounds of fabric that wrapped her flesh that much more unbearable to withstand, and Meav's throbbing feet made the trek to Wysteria's cottage seem endless.

She looked past her billowing skirt, down to her slippers. Her toes were being murdered. The beautiful shoes were made for dancing, not hiking up and down hills. 'Twas Meav who was feeling irritated now. She did not care how angry Rule became; she could not go another step without freeing herself of the cumbersome petticoat and giving her feet a rest.

In exasperation she sat down on a rock. The stiff undergarment puffed the skirt out and up, knocking her off balance. Meav fell backward, the skirt and petticoat flipping up and over her head. No matter how hard she tried, she could not stand.

"Help, help me," she cried out.

Rule stopped walking when he heard her calling. He looked around. Where the hell had she gone off to now? Quickly he back-tracked his steps, and found her toppled over backward, legs kicking the air and the sun bouncing off the stark, white bloomers. Rule lowered the trunk to the ground and took in the comical scene before him, then threw his head back with hearty laughter.

Meav tried to push the full skirt off her face. "'Tisn't a wee bit funny. I could have cracked me head open on a rock."

Rule's voice held a trace of humor. "And did you?"

"Did I what?" Meav snapped.

"Crack your head open on a rock."

"Nay...but I could have for all you care," Meav snapped again.

Rule made his way to the distressed damsel and gently wrapped his large hands around her waist. Effortlessly, as if she was a doll, he lifted her up and placed her squarely onto her feet. Then he reached up beneath her skirt for the waistline of the petticoat, and with one yank, pulled it down to her ankles. "There, now you should be able to navigate freely."

Meav gasped. "How dare you, sir."

Rule continued to help Meav out of the bulky garment. "I have seen you with much less on, lass. Slipping down your petticoat should not have you even batting an eye."

Before Meav could respond to his remark, he sat her down on the rock and began to slip off her stocking.

"What are you doing now?"

He continued to peal the fancy footwear off her leg. "You look warm."

Meav placed her hands on her hips. "I am warm, extremely warm, and me foot is killing me...but I am perfectly capable of doing this for meself. I am not a child needing help in undressing."

Ignoring her words he removed the right shoe. A tiny pebble fell out. "Ah, the culprit for all your discomfort, no doubt." He slipped off the stocking and lifted her foot. "Let me check for a wound." When he inspected the delicate heel, he spotted the crescent shape. He stared at the mark, bewildered at first; then suddenly disturbed. He knew this sign, he had seen it before; but where?

Meav became increasingly uneasy with his scrutiny, and pulled her foot away. She quickly retrieved the shoe and slipped it on. After removing the stocking from the left leg and replacing the shoe, she boldly met his gaze. "'Tis done, now let us be on our way."

Rule stood and extended a helping hand to Meav.

Meav placed her tiny hand in the center of Rule's large palm, looking up into his eyes. Her anger suddenly faded.

His gaze traveled over her face and searched her eyes. Who was this beautiful woman and why did he feel such a connection with her?

Nervously Meav cleared her throat. "I am ready when you are."

Rule nodded, retrieved the discarded garments, and after placing them into the trunk, hoisted it upon a shoulder. Once again he led the way.

Meav followed in silence, watching the muscles beneath his tight breeches work with each step he took. Her cheeks burned in remembrance of the way his maleness hung between his legs, the way it grew, and the smooth flesh of his bare bottom. Up until now, Meav had only seen male babies naked. Oh how much more there was to the grown man. An artist's sculpture did little to depict the real thing. The more Meav thought of Rule without his clothes, the more it pleased her.

If her grandmamma knew her thoughts..."Ah, me," she softly moaned.

Rule turned around. "Is there something more that ails you, lass?"

"Nay," she answered quickly, her cheeks reddening. Even though she was learning from Wysteria that the body's needs were natural and not shameful, Meav still worried her bold thoughts might have her headed for hell.

****

Wysteria sat on the cottage step, weeping. Her Meav...Meridith's Meav, had been claimed by Loreli and taken down to the bottom of the sea. Rule had jumped from the tree, and to Meav's rescue, but Wysteria had not seen him surface either. He probably drowned as well. Wysteria was now without them both...the boy she had once cared for and the girl she had hoped would save him from Devora's curse. All was lost.

"Wysteria," a soft voice called.

Wysteria hung her head and blocked her ears with her hands. Now she would suffer the haunting of sweet Meav. She could hear the young girl's call from her watery grave.

"Wysteria, I am home," the voice called again.

Wysteria looked up to see Meav and Rule walking up the path to her cottage. Without hesitation she sprang from the step and ran to meet them. First she hugged and kissed Meav, and then she reached up and planted a kiss upon Rule's cheek. "Thank our Devine Maker for your lives."

"'Twas Rule who saved me," Meav said, looking over at him and smiling.

Rule grunted and walked past the two women, who were still hugging and crying. He walked into the cottage and dropped the trunk next to the fireplace. When he returned to the path, Meav and Wysteria were still commiserating over what had happened. He walked past them and to the end of the path.

"Wait," Wysteria called out to him. "Will you take no

rest before you leave?"

"Nay," he called back. He looked up at the noon sky...time for some *quin* furena...good hunting.

Meav followed his gaze. "'Tis time for the mid-day meal. Your journey home will go better on a full stomach." She walked toward him. "Stay and eat with us."

Rule wished it were possible to accept the invite, but he could only eat in privacy. "Nay, I cannot." He inclined his head politely to Meav. "*Namakria,*" he said, then turned to walk down the path.

"Farewell to you as well, Rule," Wysteria called after him. "And thank you."

****

Meav watched the sun set from Wysteria's cobblestone terrace. It was here that she first met Rule. He was angry then, as he was several times today. But why was he so angry? Obviously he had great powers, could change himself into a panther at will, truly he must be proud of that. She supposed that was how he protected the jungle. And he was the king, he should be proud of that as well.

Meav frowned. But Rule did not dress or live like a king. He dwelled in a cold, damp cave instead of a royal palace. Somehow his ability to change into a cat had something to do with him not being able to sit on the throne...but what?

Wysteria made her way out to where Meav stood. "You are in deep thought, child. Care to share with me?"

Meav turned to look into the kind, smoky eyes of the woman who was now her only family. "I saw Rule change..." She bit her tongue. Rule had asked her never to speak of his ability.

Wysteria sat down on a bench. "...into a panther," she finished the sentence.

Meav's eye widened. "You know his secret?"

"Aye." Wysteria tilted her head sideways. "You must have been very frightened."

Meav sat down beside her. "I was...and then I realized if he wanted to harm me he had already had the chance."

"Aye, that he did."

"He cautioned me not to speak of it," Meav said.

Wysteria's eyes saddened. "'Tis not something Rule is proud of."

"Why not? Obviously he has been gifted."

"Nay," Wysteria said sadly. "'Tis not a gift."

"What then...and who else knows?" Meav probed.

Wysteria sighed. "All on the island know his plight."

"And he is still respected and liked?"

"Aye, lass, he is," Wysteria said.

Meav frowned. "Then what stops him from sitting on the throne?"

"Devora," Wysteria muttered.

Meav's frown deepened. "Who is Devora?"

Wysteria sighed again. "Devora is my sister, the evil sorceress who put a spell on Rule. Whenever he hungers he is transformed into a panther, to stalk and kill his prey."

"Is that why he declined my invite to share a meal?"

Wysteria nodded in agreement. "And if he leaves the jungle he will die." Wysteria pushed a gray tendril off her forehead. "Devora did this so Rule could never harm her in the castle."

Meav frowned. "What is she doing in the castle?"

"Devora posed as a concerned maiden, willing to nurse Rule's mother when she fell ill. After the Queen died, Devora married the king."

Meav's eyes narrowed. "And so now she is queen."

Wysteria nodded sadly. "After the king's death, Devora became soul ruler, to all Keronia's displeasure. And when Rule tried to reclaim the throne, she cast the spell on him."

Meav shifted uneasily in her seat. "Is this why I am to be a hero, Wysteria...to help Rule be king?"

"Aye lass, 'tis."

Meav stood and went to the stone wall, looking up at the pink clouds in the sky. "But how...how can I help him?"

Wysteria stood. "Come into the cottage, child, and I will explain it all."

Meav followed.

Wysteria lit the lamps and reached for her grandfather's medicine book. She made her way to the table and sat down before opening the worn cover made of cornhusk and palm leaves. "In this book lie recipes and spells, and the Prophecy of Keronia."

Meav sat down on a stool beside her, staring at the foreign hand scrawled across a page. "What does it say?"

Wysteria read the Prophecy aloud to Meav.

Meav frowned. "I do not understand what any of this has to do with me. The one to help Rule and Keronia must have the same blood as the evil one to break her spell." She chuckled nervously. "And both of us know I do not."

Wysteria looked deep into Meav's eyes. "Oh, but lass, you do."

Meav brought her hand to her throat. "That is impossible! I am from Dublin...never known Keronia existed until the *Sea Dragon* crashed upon her shores."

Wysteria sat back in her chair. "Your mother, Meridith, was my sister."

Meav felt the blood drain from her head. "How can that be?"

Wysteria gently reached for Meav's hand. "Your Mama was only your age when she was banished from Keronia."

"Banished...banished for what...why...by whom?"

Wysteria held up a finger. "Have patience, Meav, and I will tell you all."

Meav nodded, her heart beating rapidly.

Wysteria gently stroked Meav's hair. "Looking at you right now makes me think I am looking at Meridith. The resemblance is so striking, so wonderful for these old eyes of mine to finally see again."

Meav shifted anxiously in her seat. "Please, Wysteria; keep me in suspense no longer," she begged.

Wysteria cleared her throat. "Your Mama worked for Queen Oneida, she was her handmaiden. After the Queen gave birth to Rule she was left weak and took to her bed more than not. I was called by King Stefan to care for Rule." Wysteria's eyes grew moist with her memories. "I had just given birth to my own son. Morgan, my dear, loving husband, and I were so happy. But our happiness was short lived. Within a month of his coming, my precious boy baby died in his sleep, and I was left carrying the milk in my breast. When Queen Oneida could no longer feed her son, I was summoned to do the job."

Meav curled her legs beneath her. "Then you were Rule's wet nurse and nanny?"

Wysteria nodded. "And your Mama tended the queen." She paused, wiping a tear that slipped down her cheek. "Both of my parents died within the same year. Since I was the eldest child, married and a responsible adult, 'twas my duty to take my two younger sisters in and gave them a home. But when Meridith and I were called to serve the crown, Devora was left home to do all the chores herself. This irked her, and she became resentful and jealous...especially of Meridith. Because Queen Oneida needed constant care, Meridith lived at the castle." Wysteria sighed heavily. "As Rule grew, he became a handful, and my hours at the castle were long. Many nights I stayed as well. Morgan and I had less and less time together."

Wysteria closed the medicine book and rose to pour two cups of tea. Returning to her seat she handed a cup to Meav. "By the time Rule had turned a decade old, I was permanently living in the palace."

Meav took a sip of her tea. "Morgan too?"

"He would come now and then to spend a night with me, but we had a chicken farm and he was needed to stay on the property to run it. 'Twas during that time that Devora began to feel as though she was Morgan's wife, and in many ways she was; doing all the cooking, cleaning, and mending for him."

"Did he feel the same?" Meav probed.

"Nay, Morgan was true to our vows." Wysteria took a long sip of her tea. "But one day...'twas a very hot day as I remember, Meridith arrived home for a visit unannounced. When she walked into the cottage, she found Devora preparing Morgan's mid-day meal, stark naked."

Meav gasped. "She was hoping for your husband's attention."

Wysteria nodded. "That she was."

"What did Mama do?"

"Meridith argued with Devora, slapped her across the face and called her some names I would rather not repeat. Then Meridith marched out to the barn and told Morgan what had happened."

Meav leaned forward in her chair. "What did Morgan do?"

"He gave Devora two days to find somewhere else to live. In the meantime, the queen was becoming worse, barely able to open her eyes. Meridith was at her beck and call, feeding her and washing her like an infant...even sleeping nights at the foot of Oneida's bed."

"Poor woman."

Wysteria nodded. "Oneida was a good woman too, did not deserve such suffering." She took another sip of tea before continuing. "Devora was desperate now for a place to live, and came to the castle...begging for my forgiveness."

Meav frowned. "I hope you sent her on her way for good."

"Ah, if only I had everything would have been different. But I felt sorry for her; she is my sister, of my flesh and blood." Wysteria shook her head regretfully. "And 'twas then all of our hell began." She folded her hands in her lap. "Devora posed as a medicine woman to the king, promising him the queen would do better if she cared for her instead of Meridith. She convinced King Stefan that Meridith was evil, and that she had cast a death spell on the queen. Then Devora spread the rumor that Meridith and Morgan were carrying on behind my back."

Meav's lips thinned with anger.

Wysteria arched a brow. "No one really realized then what Devora was capable of."

Meav almost dreaded what Wysteria's next words would be.

"King Stefan feared for his wife's life and dismissed Meridith from her duties, then he imprisoned her in the dungeon."

Meav inhaled sharply.

"I was beside myself with grief, knowing full well none of Devora's accusations were true. I tried to go to the king with the real facts, but Devora's charms had bewitched him, blinded him to the truth." Wysteria shuddered at what followed. "Meridith was stripped and beaten for her sins, and set afloat upon a raft." Tears again welled in her eyes. "Meridith sat on that raft with her face twisted in agony and humiliation, trying to cover her nakedness with her hands. She cried out in pain and sorrow, her red, swollen eyes meeting mine for one last time. I watched her form grow smaller and smaller as the raft drifted out to sea." Wysteria hung her head. "I never saw her again."

Meav felt her stomach tighten. "Me poor Mama."

Wysteria raised her gaze to Meav. "And my Morgan was found dead in the barn, a spear pierced through his heart."

Meav brushed a tear from her eye. "Wysteria, I am so sorry."

"'Twasn't long after that Queen Oneida died and King Stefan took a new wife."

"Devora," Meav muttered.

Wysteria nodded. "She then convinced the king his son no longer needed a nurse maid now that he had a mother who could care for him. The king heeded all of her words and I was ousted from the castle. Rule protested wildly, and was sent away to a boy's school in the mountains where he learned to be a soldier under Tobiah's skills. 'Twas then Devora had free reign to devise her plan. Rule was twenty and one when King Stefan fell suddenly ill and died. When Rule heard of his father's death, he returned to the island to claim his rightful place on the throne. But Devora would not be defeated. She cast a spell on Rule, cursing him to forever be a savage animal, and Devora has continued to rule Keronia."

Meav sat silent, a mixture of sadness and hate coursing through her veins.

Wysteria searched the young woman's face. "I am so happy Meridith found her way to another land, and did not die sick and alone on the water. I am blessed to finally learn she made a new life, found love, had a family, and knew happiness again."

Meav stood and looked out the window at the last shards of light sinking beneath the horizon. "And you believe I have been sent here to avenge me Mama and undo what has been done?"

"Aye. 'Twas your destiny, child," Wysteria said. "And has been prophesied."

Meav turned around to face Wysteria. "I am sick to

think I have the same blood in my veins as that evil woman."

"You have the good blood as well, lass...that of your Mama and of me."

Meav smiled warmly. "Aye, 'tis true...and to know you are my aunt...that I still have family."

Wysteria rose from her chair and embraced Meav. "I will always be here for you, child."

Meav pulled back to look deep into Wysteria's smoky eyes. "How...how do I undo what has been done?"

"Soon I will take you to the Temple of Silah. 'Tis there you will find the answer written upon the walls...in a vision quest," Wysteria explained. "'Tis then you will know what has to be done."

Chapter Nine

Zailia wore her best dress, and carried a plate of homemade raspberry tarts to Wysteria's cottage. Any other time the thought of such a visit would have been fun. To meet a new friend and enjoy an afternoon over tea and sweets would have been heaven, under normal conditions. But there was nothing normal about this circumstance, nor was it an ordinary call welcoming someone to the island.

Zailia bit her bottom lip and nervously smoothed back the tendrils escaping the bun she wore high atop her head. She wanted to run back home and gather her father, leave Keronia and the evil Devora. To hell with the land! 'Tis but a patch of worn out dirt anyway. Ah, to live free and far from fear. Zailia knew by staying on the island, and doing what Devora asked, she would then be just as evil as the one she despised.

"Nay, I choose not to be evil," she whispered and turned away from Wysteria's path. But Zailia thought again. Knowing Devora the way she did, the witch probably had her spies out watching Zailia's every move. How then would she be able to leave Keronia? She looked down at the plate of tarts she held...then back at Wysteria's cottage and swallowed hard. With reluctant steps Zailia made her way back up the path. It was essential for her to look as though she was following through as planned, not to spark any suspicion Devora's way. She had not the slightest idea what her own plan of action would be, but for now it had to appear as though she was making friends with the young maiden.

"Take each step as it comes," Zailia whispered to herself, then squared her shoulders and knocked on Wysteria's door.

Wysteria welcomed Zailia warmly, motioning for her to come in. "My, my, what a pleasant surprise." She hugged Zailia and led her to the terrace. "You are just in time for tea."

Zailia forced a smile. "I had hoped I was, 'tis why I have brought the tarts."

"Blueberry?" Wysteria probed, taking the plate.

"Raspberry," Zailia corrected.

Wysteria shrugged. "Just as good."

Zailia stepped onto the cobblestone and stopped short. A beautiful young woman sat at the table by the garden wall. Her copper curls hung to her waist and her large, blue eyes crinkled at the corners when she smiled. Zailia smiled back.

Wysteria introduced the two. "Zailia, this is Meav."

Meav stood and made her way to greet Zailia. "I am so happy to meet you."

"And I you," Zailia said, dipping into a tiny curtsey.

Meav did the same and they both giggled. Taking Zailia by the hand, Meav led her to the table. "We were just about to have afternoon tea." She looked deep into Zailia's eyes. "You do like tea, I hope?"

"Aye, I love tea," Zailia said, taking a seat beside Meav. "I made raspberry tarts...do you like tarts."

Meav licked her lips. "I love eating all sweets, but especially tarts."

Zailia nodded in agreement and rubbed her belly. "But I should not, 'tis sure to make my dress size grow."

"Aye, but only one should not hurt," Meav said.

"Can you only eat one?" Zailia countered.

"Nay, never," Meav said.

Both girls giggled again.

Wysteria smiled in her seat across from Meav. "'Tis good to see two young lasses having fun, and with a little time I believe both of you will grow to be good friends as well.

Titiana also watched Zailia and Meav, but she was not smiling. From her position on the branch of a nearby tree, Titiana was thinking of a way she could stop Devora's evil plan and the terrible fate of these two young women.

****

Shell knocked on the Queen's bedchamber door.

"Enter," Devora snapped.

Slowly Shell made his way to the exotic beauty

105

reclining on the chaise, sheer black robe draped loosely over a beautifully formed body. He eyed her nipples through the material.

Devora stood, her robe flying open. She made no move to cover her nakedness. "Did you follow her?"

Shell bowed his head slightly, not taking his eyes from the view before him. "Aye, my queen. At this moment Zailia is visiting Wysteria and her new house guest."

A slow smile curved Devora's lips. "Good." She threw her head back and laughed. "All of them enjoying their afternoon tea, no doubt." She sauntered over to the table and poured brandy from a crystal decanter into two goblets. Turning around, she handed a goblet to Shell. "I prefer something stronger than tea to drink in the afternoon."

Shell tipped his head graciously and took the goblet. "What else do you prefer in the afternoon, Your Majesty?"

Devora smiled, stroking her belly. Slowly she moved her hand lower, lower, to massage herself between her thighs. "Do you know what the sign of a loyal sentry is, Shell?"

Shell's loins grew thick beneath his breeches. "That he pleases his queen, satisfying all her needs."

Devora tilted her head to one side, offering him her neck. "And how can you do that for me, Shell?"

Shell threw the brandy down his throat, its warmth adding to his anticipation. He placed the goblet on the table. "By spreading you wide, my queen." He moved closer, taking her goblet and also placing it aside. "And licking, sucking and tasting every royal part of your beautiful body, Your Majesty."

Devora moved into his embrace. "Where would you start?"

"Here," he said, bringing his mouth down around a full breast. Gently he bit her nipple, than soothed the hard peak with a twirl of his tongue.

Devora arched her back so he could take her fully. "And then what, Sentry?"

He lifted his mouth and moved his lips to her belly. "And here," he whispered, kissing her soft, jasmine scented flesh.

Devora entwined her fingers in his hair.

Shell raised his gaze and smiled, then stood and lifted her, carrying her over to the bed. Gently he lowered her onto the satin sheets.

Devora lay on her back looking up at him. Shell's swollen phallus strained against his breeches.

Slowly she spread her legs. "Continue, Sentry."

Shell dropped to his knees and with his fingers spread the lips of her womb. "And here," he said softly, exposing her labia.

With soft flicks of his tongue he tasted her; tenderly teased her moist petal.

She wreathed with pleasure. "Aye, this is much...much better than tea."

****

Rule had filled his belly, now he needed to rest. The coolness of the cave was a welcomed shelter from the sweltering heat of the noonday sun. He lay upon the pile of animal skins and allowed sleep to come. In a matter of seconds the dream enfolded him, pulling him from the present and into a time he once knew.

'Twas late...very late. The wall sconces were lit and the long corridor silent. Rule looked down at his bare feet. They were smaller. He looked at his hands, they were smaller too. He smiled. He was home again, roaming the castle he knew and loved so well.

Quietly he came upon his mother's bedchamber door. Putting his ear to the oak portal he could hear two women talking. One voice he recognized as Meridith's, his mother's handmaiden. The other was the agonized words of the queen.

Rule slowly turned the knob and gently pushed the door open a crack. Peering into the room, he saw his mother's body exposed to the waist. Meridith was washing the queen's pale bosom, being careful not to hurt the fragile woman lying listless in the bed.

"Does not this feel refreshing on such a hot night as this, Your Majesty?" Meridith said, brushing the moistened fabric over the queen's bared breasts and down her belly.

Queen Oneida nodded weakly. "You take such good care of me, Meridith. What would I ever do without you?"

107

Meridith dipped the cloth into the basin and rung it out before returning to swab the Queen's flesh. "You shall never have to worry, my queen. I will not leave you. In fact I will never be very far away."

Rule watched as Meridith gently dried and redressed his mother.

Meridith lovingly brushed aside the thick, black curls from the queen's forehead. "I will sleep here, at the foot of the bed."

Rule then saw the caring handmaiden climb upon the bed and curl at his mother's feet. Meridith slipped off her slippers and crossed her ankles. Rule could see the crescent shape on the bottom of her right foot.

Rule snapped awake and sat straight up, finding himself once again in his cave. He inhaled sharply with the memory of his dream. Now he knew where he had seen the crescent shaped birthmark before...on the heel of Meridith's right foot. And Meav...Meav had one just like it!

Chapter Ten

Meav had been too excited to fall asleep. Zailia's visit yesterday played over and over in her mind. They had talked of so many things that 'twas way into the dinner hour when they parted. Their lives in many ways were the same. Zailia had lost her mother at a young age as well, and a brother later on in years. Meav was no stranger to the grief of losing a loved one and knew first hand the emptiness of not having a mother.

Zailia was forced to work at the castle in order to save her family's land from the evil Devora. Meav wished now she had been as sacrificing as Zailia, instead of escaping the terrible fate of marrying Hollister McGreary at her family's expense. 'Twas at that point in the conversation Meav had lowered her head in shame for her cowardly retreat.

But Zailia had not condemned Meav...quite the contrary. She thought Meav was very brave. Zailia's acceptance meant everything to Meav, and 'twas then she knew Zailia would become a dear and trusted friend. She had already been invited to Zailia's cottage for tea on the morrow.

Meav stretched and yawned, feeling content. She would face this new day a bit groggy but still with eagerness. Today Wysteria was taking her to the Temple of Silah. 'Twas there Meav hoped to learn the answers to all her questions.

****

Reluctantly Zailia knocked on the queen's bedchamber door, hoping the information she cared to divulge about Meav would be enough to appease Devora. Zailia had carefully rehearsed what she would say so Devora would not become suspicious in any way that Zailia was not earnest in doing her job.

Devora's voice held a grudging tone. "Enter."

Zailia flinched, knowing full well the queen's

agitation stemmed from Shell having to leave at the crack of dawn to witness the changing of the guards. 'Twas the mornings that Shell still slept in Devora's bed when Zailia arrived that the day went well. Zailia sighed. 'Twouldn't be today.

Devora spoke with authority. "I want a bath...now! My flesh is hot and sticky from the intolerable night's heat and if I am not bathed soon everyone will feel my wrath."

Zailia bowed her head. "I have taken the liberty of having a tub ready and waiting for you, my queen."

"'Tis about time you did something right." Devora yanked the satin coverlet off her body and strode naked to the adjoining room. Climbing into the warm water, Devora looked up at Zailia. "What have you learned about the maiden living at my sister's house?"

Zailia forced her hands to stay calm as she washed Devora's back. "Her name is Meav O'Shay and she comes from Dublin, Ireland."

"Where is Dublin, Ireland?" Devora probed.

"When I asked her that she merely shook her head, then said...far from here."

"How did it happen that she was sailing?"

Zailia chose her words carefully. "She was fleeing from the man who killed her family...stowed away in the hull of the *Sea Dragon* to escape."

Devora pulled her knees to her chest. "Hmm, quite interesting, do you not think?"

Zailia began to wash Devora's arms. "Quite frightening, I would say."

Devora relaxed. "Then she is here rather by accident."

"Aye, my queen...'tis completely by chance she washed up on Keronia's shores."

Devora glared at Zailia. "What is your next move?"

Zailia tried to keep her emotions at bay. "I figured there would not be a need for a next move, since she poses no threat to anyone."

Devora's eyes blazed. "You let me do the figuring. Now...what is your next move?"

Zailia sighed. "I have invited her to my cottage on the morrow for tea."

Devora's lips curled over even white teeth. "Excellent, Zailia. Make her grow to like and trust you."

Devora's wicked laugh reverberated down Zailia's spine. "That will not be hard; she is a very trusting girl."

Devora's voice was cold and exact. "Good, 'tis always easier to kill a person who trusts you."

Zailia's insides shuddered. Touching this evil woman made her skin crawl. Even just playing along at Devora's evil plan made Zailia nauseous.

Devora leaned back in the tub. "Wash me here, Zailia," she said, parting her legs.

Zailia felt her cheeks turn crimson as she brought the cloth down to cleanse between Devora's thighs.

"Faster, harder, Zailia." Devora's wicked laugh echoed the room. "You know how much I enjoy a good scrub."

****

Wysteria watched Meav's lithe form walking beside her. Like Meridith, Meav was willowy, her height in proportion to her weight. Wysteria marveled at Meav's resemblance to her dead sister. If she did not know better, Wysteria could swear Meridith had come home.

"Your Mama loved going to the Temple of Silah...even had thoughts about studying to be a priestess."

Meav tipped her face to the sun. "The temple would have been fortunate to have her loyalties."

"Aye, 'tis true, child. Your Mama was a pure and giving lass. She deserved better than what she got."

Meav looked over at the elder. "I intend to avenge her good name, as soon as I learn how."

Wysteria pointed a crooked finger at Meav. "'Tis not wise to rush ahead, child. If you do as the high priestess advises, all will go as planned."

Meav nodded in agreement and walked silently beside Wysteria the rest of the way to the temple.

Meav recognized the beach...'twas the one she had washed up on. About fifty feet from where she had first opencd her eyes, Meav and Wysteria entered the opening of a cave...carefully concealed by bushes.

Wysteria reached for the lit torch ensconced on the wall and led the way down a winding staircase.

At first the salt of the sea tinged Meav's nose, but as

she followed Wysteria farther into the cavern, the aroma of sandalwood and myrrh incense burning filled her senses. Could they be nearing the temple...at the bottom of a cave? "I envisioned it to be a grand structure of stone and marble."

"The power of enchantment never comes from idyllic conditions or complex settings. It can only come from deep within the sorcerer herself, powered by belief and a pure need," Wysteria explained.

"And there is no purer need than mine," Meav commented.

"Nay, lass, there is not."

When Meav stepped off the last stair she hesitated. "I am scared, Wysteria. Everything on this island is so strange...mermaids, elf folks, little winged women, a river of orange, and a witch who puts a spell on the heir to the throne...can make a man turn into an animal. How can I match these things?"

The elder turned to look at her niece. "You listen to me, Meav O'Shay. Mortal man contains within himself the seed of the divine. If he nourishes this seed, he can accomplish anything. And if he is successful he is rewarded with eternal life and will one day reunite with his divine origin." Wysteria moved closer to Meav. "Lying deep within you is such divinities, and with the help of those who know how to activate the grand cosmic scheme, your seed too will accomplish a specific role. Your actions, though supernatural to the majority, will be in concurrence with natural harmony and you will be able to match all you have witnessed on this island."

Meav's eyes widened. "Are you trying to tell me that the fantastic things I have seen on Keronia are in harmony to a natural life?"

"Aye, that is exactly my point, child. All the powers, the wonders that surround you now have a practical purpose in our civilization. It has eased life for the Keronians, relieved physical and emotional pain and most times benefited society."

"Until one turns to the dark side, then it can be crippling," Meav reflected.

"Aye, 'tis true, but only one among us has strayed from the pure course and the natural harmony," Wysteria said.

"But it only took one, dear healer, to make a shamble of it all...to destroy the balance and terrify this island into submission." Meav placed her hands on her hips. "Was there not one among you that could stand up to Devora? Certainly good magic should outweigh the bad."

"Devora has found a way to hinder the good. Her creative force...the black magic she practices...has bound spirit and matter together and drawn from their energy. No longer can the good find a way past the evil," Wysteria explained.

Meav bit her bottom lip nervously. "And here I be, just a farm girl running from me own horror, and suddenly 'tis up to me to straighten out the situation here."

"Do not resent the mission, lass...but embrace the challenge," Wysteria said softly. "You should feel honored. 'Tis an adventure that lies ahead."

"Not one I readily would have chosen," Meav muttered.

"The pain a woman endures giving life to her child is not one she would have chosen, yet the end result is a babe...far worth the ordeal."

Meav frowned. "'Tis an endearing example...but..."

Wysteria took Meav by the hand. "Come, let me show you something."

Meav was pulled into a room lit by candles burning in translucent alabaster hurricane lanterns. The stone walls absorbed the heat of the flame and spread its luminary warmth throughout the tiny cubical.

Wysteria stopped in front of a stone figure. "This is the female chief, Iolita. Her broad hips and full thighs symbolize fertility and abundance." Wysteria took Meav's hand and placed it on the statue's round belly. "Her cupped hand signifies the womb and the feminine principle through which all enter into life." Wysteria pointed to the goddess's head. "Her jewel encrusted crown represents intelligence and higher consciousness."

Meav's frown deepened. "What does she have to do with me?"

Wysteria smiled. "She emanates the hope and power of women...and you are a woman, Meav."

Meav's response held a note of impatience. "But what directly has she to do with me...why I am here, what must I do?"

Wysteria hesitated, measuring Meav for a moment. "Do you not find the miracle of birth spectacular, yet natural?"

"Aye, I have always been in awe over the way a woman can conceive, nurture and bring forth life," Meav said. "And yet 'tis the way of things, how 'tis meant to be."

"You feel that way because you have knowledge of the properties that produce the element. You accept the sun, the earth, water, fire, and fearsome animals, like the snake, crocodile...and the panther...because you know why and how they exist. And when you learn the elements and properties of why and how magic comes into play, then the mermaids, and pixies will be natural to you as well."

Meav raised a brow. "I will learn all that here?"

"When you understand your part in the things to come, you will feel a connection. And like a mother who understands what her newborn asks for even though no words are spoken, you will understand and accept your surroundings as natural." Wysteria brought Meav's hand up to caress the cloak that hung around Iolita's shoulders. "This cloak is red for a reason...red is the color that stands for life. Blood is red...when it flows within us we live. But red also stands for anger. When you mix life with anger you have conflict and pain. 'Tis what Devora has done to her own life, and to the lives of others."

Meav pointed to the white and black curtain hanging behind Iolita. "What do those colors mean?"

"White means purity and sanctity; 'tis the color of joy. Together red and white symbolize wholeness and perfection. Black is death, yet it also means the seeds of rebirth." Wysteria looped her arm through Meav's. "Come now, child. The high priestess Neteru waits for us. With her help and infinite wisdom you will know the answers to all your questions."

Meav sighed. She was not all that sure, but then again what did she know? She was just a farm girl.

Chapter Eleven

Rule needed an answer to the question that had plagued him since his afternoon dream of a day ago...why do Meridith and Meav share the same birthmark?

Though Wysteria was a wise healer, Rule had the distinct feeling he would find the answer if he went to the Temple of Silah. There he could talk to the high priestess, Neteru. The holy woman's power of the vision quest would render the truth.

Rule could journey to the temple through the winding corridors of his cave. Neteru, when she had learned of Devora's spell, offered Rule the far end of the underground sanctuary as refuge. The high priestess believed cats; big and small, were to be honored because they protected their domain from all kinds of evil, both natural and supernatural. Neteru had made Rule protector of the jungle and kept him close by the temple for safety.

At night Rule could hear the apprentices chanting, their beautiful voices carrying their way gently into his chamber, soothing the wild fury within him. The women sang while they did all their tasks, turning the mundane of everyday living into something sacred. Many times their songs had been the only thing that had relaxed Rule enough to fall asleep.

He fixed his eyes on the east wall of the cave. The logic was that the longer you looked...the more noticeable was the opening. Rule sat cross-legged, hands lightly folded in his lap, eyes ready to see what they usually could not. As soon as he concentrated on the passage, the wall vanished. Rule stood and made his way into the temple.

He only had to travel a few feet when he walked into the light. Lamps were lit with eternal flames throughout the corridor and in every room. Light was a symbol of purity and goodness; the lamps had the power to dispel

115

spiritual darkness and evil forces. Because of this belief, Rule knew he would have to be cleansed before Neteru would grant him an audience.

Rule made his way to the sacred pool. There, in each corner of the room a woven mat covered the stone floor. On top of each mat a holy table was placed. There was an altar for wind, rain, fire and air. Bouquets of flowers in crystal vases adorned the small alters, representing life.

Rule went to the north end of the room and stood before the table of the wind. 'Twas there he had found the comfort and strength to endure Devora's spell. So, 'twas here he was drawn again to stand.

Two apprentices appeared suddenly beside Rule, their bodies completely covered by long, blue robes. They wore blue because 'tis a healing color, one that symbolized the constant flow of infinity. Their faces were also covered. All that peered out at Rule was the glint of their eyes. Rule bowed his head respectfully to each.

Silently they stripped him naked and leading him over to the shallow pool of water, began to rub the essential oil of cassia and sandalwood into his flesh with their gentle hands. Rule's senses were awakened and he thought of Meav. He envisioned her full lips fusing with his, the scent, the sweet taste of her left him desiring her hands upon him; stroking his chest, his buttocks and genitals. His phallus grew hard and erect with his reflection. Awkwardly he brought his hands over his maleness and hung his head in shame. Would the robed women think he was being disrespectful?

The apprentice to his right reached down and removed his hands.

Rule looked over at the woman...searching deep into her eyes, and caught the understanding in them. She nodded her head and began to rub his thighs with the precious oil. Rule knew she read his heart; his passion and she was not appalled by his feelings.

He relaxed as both the women cleansed him, dipping him three times into the pool before they gave him a green loin cloth to wear. Rule was then led into another room, where he was bid to lay upon a raised, stone slap. After lighting incense to cleanse the ritual area, the apprentices left the room.

Neteru walked into the cubicle moments later wearing a flowing white robe, the lace hem gracing her ankles swirled around sandal-clad feet. The hood of the robe loosely framed her delicate face, the ivory complexion flawless. A long, golden braid draped over her right shoulder, cascading down one breast and to her waist.

As she neared the stone bed, Rule sat up and gazed into her aqua eyes. "You know why I have come?" His voice was shakier than he would have liked.

"Aye, I know," Neteru whispered. She placed her hand on Rule's heart. "All your answers are here, my lord. 'Tis when you decide to open the walled chamber that the truth will flow."

Rule could feel his throat tighten. "My heart has been so cold for so long...*seda*...how do I do that, holy one?"

Neteru placed a finger over Rule's lips. "Say nothing...just listen...listen to your spirit and allow the man you are to emerge. He waits unwearyingly for you to permit him to thrive once again."

Rule watched her walk to a table at the far corner of the room. From a crystal decanter she poured a golden colored liquid into a silver goblet. Returning to Rule, she handed him the drink.

"Let it coat your throat," Neteru instructed.

Rule took the goblet. The nectar's sweet flavor blanketed his gullet, spreading down through his stomach. The warmth of the brew circulated through his system, branching out to each of his extremities. He handed the empty vessel to Neteru and lay back down.

"Sleep now," Neteru softly advised. "Let the vision quest take you."

****

Wysteria led Meav to a room, lit with candles. In each corner stood tables on mats, in the center of the chamber was a shallow pool.

"You must be cleansed," Wysteria said. "Go now and stand before an altar."

Meav was spontaneously drawn to the table at the north corner of the room.

"'Tis the altar of the wind you have chosen," Wysteria explained. "Soon the apprentices will appear beside you, undress and cleanse you, then clad you in a green robe.

117

The color green symbolizes nature, growing things, and new life."

"And where will you be?" Meav called out nervously.

"I will be waiting by the figure of Iolita. One of the apprentices will bring you to me when your vision quest is done."

Meav swallowed hard. "Wysteria...I..."

"Hush, child, there is nothing to fear," Wysteria comforted.

Meav watched the elder shuffle across the stone floor to the door.

Within moments two women appeared wearing blue gowns from head to toe. Only their eyes and hands could be seen.

Gently they stripped Meav and led her over to the shallow pool. Their tender strokes messaged oil into her flesh. The woman to Meav's left paid special attention to her bosom, cupping each full breast in the palm of her hand and circling the nipples with the tip of her finger. Meav instantly imagined Rule's hands touching her, pleasing her.

The woman to the right rubbed the oil on Meav's buttocks and between her thighs. Again Meav visualized Rule adoring her body with tender caresses; the thought of him inside of her made Meav blush.

Meav was then dipped into the water three times, dried and dressed in a green robe. She was led to another room, where she was placed on a raised, stone slab. Before the apprentices left the chamber they lit incense.

Meav listened...the silence was suffocating; the candlelight cast eerie shadows on the granite walls. Fear gripped her heart; she wanted to run as fast as her legs could carry her, find Wysteria and leave this subterranean catacomb. Just as Meav sat up, Neteru appeared. Meav watched as the holy woman approached the stone slab. When Meav looked upon Neteru's face, she was awestruck at the high priestess's perfect beauty. Neteru wore a large cat's eye amulet around her neck hanging from a thick, gold chain. Meav looked deep into the swirling amber of the oval gem and thought again of Rule.

Neteru smiled warmly at Meav, and reached out to

touch a curl. "Ah, so much like Meridith you are that it brings me to tears." She gently stroked Meav's cheek. "I loved your mother dearly, treated her as my own."

Meav's eyes met Neteru's as she spoke in a rush of words. "Why did you not save her then from Devora...spare her the pain and humiliation she endured?"

Neteru sighed heavily. "Oh, you have no idea how I wanted to, how it broke my heart to watch it all...but I could not. If I had, then Meridith would not have washed up on Ireland's shores, fallen in love and had a child. The Prophecy would not have been fulfilled."

The shock of discovery hit Meav full force. "You knew what would happen to her?"

Neteru nodded. "As painful as 'twas, all events had to run their course for the sake of the result."

A shadow of annoyance crossed Meav's face. "Me mother was sacrificed then, for the good of...of...what?"

"For the good of Keronia, Meav," Neteru said softly. "And was her life so bad? Did she not love your father; give birth to a lovely daughter?"

"Aye, she did...three lovely daughters to be exact. And even though she died too young...in childbirth, I believe in many ways she was better off in Dublin than here...but how did you know I would come?" Meav asked, searching Neteru's serene face.

"I have always known, in fact I have been waiting for you," Neteru said.

Meav looked around the enchanted room. "What part do I play in all of this?"

"Play is hardly the word, Meav," Neteru corrected. "'Tis more like you will right a wrong."

Meav could feel her frustration rise. "How...how can I fix anything? I have no supernatural powers."

Neteru affectionately squeezed Meav's hand. "You have the greatest power of all, my dear one."

Meav's voice rose in surprise. "What...what power do I have?"

"You will know soon enough," Neteru whispered and turned away.

Meav watched the high priestess walk over to a table in the corner of the room. On top of the table sat a crystal decanter and a silver chalice. Neteru poured the honey colored liquid from the carafe into the goblet. Raising the cup to the heavens, Meav listened to the holy woman chant a prayer in an unknown tongue.

Neteru returned to Meav and handed her the chalice. "Drink," was her single command.

Meav obeyed, feeling the strange tasting liquid layer her throat in warmth; instantly channeling through her entire body. Her eyelids grew heavy, her body relaxed.

Neteru helped Meav lay down. She gently pushed aside a lock from Meav's forehead. "Go now to where you belong."

Meav felt her spirit rise from her body. She looked down at the stone slab and saw herself lying peaceful, deep in sleep. Neteru stood beside the stone altar, chanting and singing words Meav could not understand. The melody had a tranquil effect on her, as she floated to the chamber ceiling. 'Twas from that vantage point she spotted the large, black cat. He entered the room slowly, his amber eyes rising to meet hers. Meav floated down...down...until her bare feet touched the stone floor. Then she climbed upon the panther's back. With each feline step his muscles moved sensuously between Meav's bare thighs. She gripped the fur at his powerful shoulders and rode his sleek, shiny body out of the chamber.

He took her to his cave, carefully setting her onto the pile of animal pelts. Then he sat before her, opened his large mouth to reveal long, sharp fangs and looked into her eyes, growling ferociously.

Meav was not frightened...oh, she should be, but she was not. She reached out and stroked the cat's chest. "You do not scare me, so you can stop trying. I will not be that easily dealt with. 'Tis time you let another help you."

The cat's eyes bathed Meav in adoration, searching each and every facet of her face. Slowly he backed away to the far corner of the cave and stood on his hind legs.

"Come to me, Rule," Meav gently coaxed, extending her hand. "I am here now."

In a blink of an eye the man replaced the animal, standing before her in nothing but a green loin cloth.

"'Tis really you, then?" Rule muttered.

Meav stood. "Aye, 'twas always me, it just took some

time for me to understand." She smiled warmly. "I am not afraid or repulsed by you, milord."

Rule stepped closer. "*Sute*...how could you not be? I repulse myself." He looked away, his words clipping into silence.

Meav inched her way toward him. "Look at me, milord."

He brought his gaze to meet hers, regarding her for a long moment.

Meav saw the hurt and longing lying naked in his eyes. "I choose to see the man first, and marvel over how he has handled his plight instead of condemn him for it."

Rule could feel his insides quake, the ice around his heart beginning to melt. How could a warrior feel such vulnerability? "Tell me *sute*...how can you do this, my lady?"

Meav placed her hand over her own heart. "Here tells me 'tis right."

Rule placed his hand over her heart. "What else does your heart say?"

"That you are the reason I am here, the reason I have been born," Meav whispered.

"Nay, you were born to brighten this world, to love and make the man of your heart happy," Rule said.

Meav swallowed and drew a steadying breath. "Could not that man be you, milord?"

Her simple question filled Rule with hope he had long lost, and a simple hunger he needed to satisfy. "Aye," he whispered.

Meav gently touched Rule's cheek. "You would have me then, milord?"

Rule pulled her tight to his chest. She was soft and yielding. "Aye...in a heartbeat."

She smiled up at him. "Whose, milord? Yours or mine?"

He returned the smile. "Both," he said before lowering his head and capturing her mouth with his.

His lips floated over Meav's gently, their warmth weakening his resolve. She fell against him, and in that moment he was unable to resist her very essence.

He caught her up into his embrace, deepening the kiss, his tongue exploring the soft folds of her mouth.

Rule's groan of pleasure echoed through the cave.

Meav's hand drifted up around his neck, her fingers playing with the curls at his nape.

Her touch sent shivers of passion through his body, through his bones, swelling his loins beneath the skimpy green covering. He broke away and looked down at her. "My lady, you do not know what you are doing."

She stared up with longing at him. "Rule...oh, Rule, but I do."

His name, just a whisper upon her lips, melted the bitterness within. He suddenly sought solace in the silken oak of her voice. Overwhelmed by longing and sadness, Rule fought back his tears. "I have waited so long for you."

Meav's eyes softened with his response. "I am here now, to stay if 'tis what you wish."

Rule unlocked his heart and soul. Gently he traced her full lips with the tip of his finger. "'Tis, my lady."

A small smile curved her mouth, her large, round eyes fluttered bashfully.

Rule chuckled softly. "Ah, my little seductress is just a shy lass at heart."

"I am an inexperienced lass, milord." She tipped her head sideways. "But perhaps...slowly...you might educate me?"

Rule's heart danced with excitement. "The best things are done slowly."

Meav's hand drifted toward his. "Will you teach me now?"

The rich, soft sound of her voice affected him intensely and a delightful shiver of wanting ran through him. He felt her dainty fingers interlace with his, her touch sending explosive currents running through him. "Are you sure 'tis what you want, my lady?"

"Aye, milord...without me knowing it, I have been ready for this moment all me life."

He pulled her to him, his skin sliding against her, his embrace growing more fevered. In one fluid motion he swept her, weightless, into his arms and carried her to the bed of pelts. Gently he placed her down upon the soft skins. Her eyes watched flirtatiously through the tendrils of fire that graced her forehead. "Ah, dear lady, you have not a clue what havoc you are causing deep within my flesh."

Meav cast a quick glance at the bulge between his thighs. She was glad for the semi-darkness that hid the flush of her cheeks. "I believe I do, milord."

Rule followed her gaze. "Would you like to see?"

Meav nervously cleared her throat, her heart was thundering. "Aye," she whispered.

Rule untied the string holding the loin cloth and dropped the material to the floor. He lifted his eyes to meet hers and knelt before her. "Touch me, Meav."

Meav's hand trembled as it reached out toward him. Slowly she wrapped her fingers around his hardened shaft. The heat of his flesh permeated the palm of her hand. Gently she tightened her grip.

Rule inhaled sharply.

Meav moved her fingers to explore the two sacks between his legs. Tenderly her fingers enclosed around the soft pouches, weighing them as she fondled.

Rule strained to keep from exploding, wanting to experience her touch for as long as his hungry flesh would allow. Taking a deep breath he slowly removed her hand, his long fingers encompassing her tiny wrist. He reached for the other wrist and quietly laid her back onto the hides, nuzzling his face into the rich, glowing auburn of her hair. The thick mane fanned in long, graceful curls across the animal skins. Rule inhaled her scent, than moved his lips softly over hers.

Meav gave herself freely to the passion of his kiss; her warm lips sent new spirals of ecstasy through him.

Rule left the heat of her mouth to nibble at her earlobe, then to sear a path down her neck. Lower he traveled, till he came to the V neckline of the robe. With his teeth he pulled at the string lacing. The material opened wide, revealing two creamy orbs.

Meav gasped when his urgent tongue explored one globe, its rosy peak marble hard. Her breast surged at the intimacy of his touch.

Rule drew the swollen nipple into his mouth, sucking and tasting. Then his lips slid down her silken belly, where he gently outlined her navel with the tip of his tongue, the musky scent of her flesh lingering in his nostrils.

Rule put his head between her shapely legs and buried his mouth deep into her crevice. With feather like licks he teased the hidden petal.

Meav spread her thighs wider for him.

Rule left the moist valley under the tip of her triangle and moved his kisses down to the inner part of her knees.

Meav breathlessly protested his departure. "Nay, stay where you were."

Between each word he planted kisses down her leg. "I will return, my lady."

"Sooner rather than later, please, milord," she whispered.

He smiled to himself and made his way to her right foot, kissing each toe.

She began to giggle when he roamed down her arch and to her heel. 'Twas then he pulled back and looked at the bottom of her foot.

"This mark," he said, tracing the crescent shape with the tip of a finger. "'Tis the same as the one my mother's handmaiden had at the bottom of her foot."

Meav sat up. "You mean, Meridith."

Rule lifted his gaze to her. "Aye, Meridith." He frowned. "Has Wysteria spoken of her?"

"Aye, but I knew her long before I met Wysteria," Meav said, pulling her foot away and closing the front of her robe.

Rule stood. "*Sute*...how?"

Meav took a deep breath. "She is me mother."

Rule stared at her in disbelief. "But she was set out to sea to die."

"And she did not die. Instead her raft found Ireland's shores where she fell in love and had three daughters...me being the eldest."

His shock turned quickly to fury. "Then she is alive and well?"

Meav's voice broke slightly. "Nay, she died after the birth of my twin sisters."

The silence lengthened between them. Meav shifted uncomfortably.

Rule felt like a volcano on the verge of erupting. "Did you know Meridith tried to kill my mother?"

"Nay, 'twas not her," Meav objected quickly.

Rule's nostrils flared with ferocity. "And now you have come to kill me."

Meav shot to her feet. "Nay, milord...you have it all wrong."

Rule's expression darkened. "Ah, my lady, for the first time I think I have it right. You thought you could bewitch me, as your Aunt Devora has done...as Meridith did to my mother, and then finish what each of them has started."

Meav's lips thinned. "None of what you say is true."

He glowered at her. "Nay?" His lip curled. "I beg to differ."

She threw the words at him like stones. "I do not hold any loyalty to Devora; have not even met the woman."

Rule threw his head back and laughed sardonically. "Oh, this is rich, my lady. You lie with such sincerity."

Meav stomped her foot. "I am not lying!"

Rule spat the words out contemptuously. "You are nothing but a little witch, and I want you gone from Keronia. I will see to it that you are banished like your mother." He retrieved the loin cloth from the floor, wrapped it around himself, and looked fiercely back at Meav. "If I have to put you on a raft myself!"

Rancor sharpened Meav's voice. "I am not a witch...I am just a girl from Dublin who has come to..."

Rule interrupted her vehemently. "*Deona*...be silent!"

Meav suddenly stepped away from the heat of his rage. "Will you not allow me to explain?"

He replied with disdain that forbade any further argument. "Banished...do you hear? From this time on you are banished!"

Chapter Twelve

Titiana sat cross-legged on a branch overlooking the sea. She had a big decision to make. She wanted to help Meav and Zailia but she could not do it alone. Titiana needed to gather the other pixies and enlist their aid as well. If she did this, of course, she would have to divulge her secret...the fact she had been visiting the castle, even after being forbidden. There was a chance Titiana's disobedience would win her the spanking of her life from her sister Gyla.

Titiana sighed. "What am I to do?"

As she thought on it further she came to the conclusion that another spanking, no matter how painful or humiliating, was not as horrific as what would happen to Meav and Zailia.

Squaring her tiny, bared shoulders Titiana spread her wings and flew to the meal assembly. 'Twas at the campfire the pixies were gathered, eating their dinner and chatting about the day's events; the only time of the day Titiana knew she would be able to talk with the entire clan at one time.

Titiana landed near Gyla, who sat on a rock eating her dinner. "*Vedela.*"

"You are late," Gyla snapped.

Titiana smiled nervously. "Sorry." She inhaled deeply. "I need to talk with the clan about an urgent matter."

Gyla frowned. "You need to sit and eat."

Titiana nodded in agreement. The last thing she wanted to do was rile Gyla. Making her way to the unity table, Titiana filled her leaf sack with food and rejoined her sister. For a moment the two quietly munched on their meal.

'Twas Gyla that broke the silence. "What is this urgent matter?"

Titiana placed aside her meal leaf and cleared her

throat. "You are not going to like what I have done, sister..."

"I never like what you do, Titiana," Gyla interjected sharply. She put her leaf sack down and folded her arms across her chest. "Well, what now?"

Titiana sighed heavily. "I have been visiting the castle."

Gyla's large, blue eyes widened in horror. "Have you lost your senses?"

"Nay, my senses are still with me," Titiana mumbled.

"I think not, sister," Gyla snapped. "What have I told you about nearing the castle?"

Titiana scooted away from Gyla, who now had the face of a thunder cloud. "That 'tis an evil place and I could be killed should I venture near its walls."

Gyla's lips thinned in anger. "And yet you still did as you pleased."

Titiana nodded slowly and hung her head.

Gyla grabbed Titiana by the arm and swung her over her knee. "I am sick and tired of having to keep you in line," she griped, spanking Titiana's bare backside severely.

"Stop, Gyla," Titiana cried; the cheeks of her bottom stinging with every slap of Gyla's hand.

Gyla halted. "Aye, I will stop." She pushed Titiana to the ground and stood. "Only long enough to finish your punishment in front of the entire clan." She reached for Titiana's hand and pulled her to her feet. "All will laugh and point their fingers at you and call you names. Perhaps that will teach you to stay away from the castle and to mind your own business."

Titiana pulled her hand away. "Nay, you will not humiliate me further!"

Gyla's eyes widened again this time with anger. "You dare to answer back your older sister?"

"Aye, I do," Titiana said flatly. "This time you must listen to me."

"Why, Titiana...why should I listen to you?"

"Because lives depend on it," Titiana blurted out.

Gyla folded her arms in front of her. "Whose lives?"

Titiana took a deep, calming breath and explained to Gyla the plan she had overheard between the queen and

Zailia, and the youth brew that Devora had concocted from the blue flowers that grew in the dungeon. "I think I have discovered a way to help Keronia be rid of Devora...and in turn help Meav and Zailia," Titiana concluded.

Gyla screamed in frustration. "How can you possibly do any of what you boast?"

"Well, I cannot by myself, but with the rest of the pixies we can..."

Gyla gave Titiana a hostile glare. "I have not the time to listen to nonsense; to a pixie who thinks she can do something when she cannot."

Titiana stomped her foot. "But I can...I have found a way to help, to stop Devora's plan and to put an end to her...but I cannot do it by myself."

Gyla impatiently grabbed Titiana's arm. "Come, time for an arrogant pixie to get a spanking she will never forget nor live down."

Titiana dug her heels into the earth. "Nay, no more spankings, Gyla." She looked deep into her sister's eyes. "Please, I beg of you to just hear me out."

Gyla countered icily. "You have only a moment to speak."

Titiana swallowed hard. "One afternoon, while Devora and Shell lay entwined in each other's arms, I was able to fly into the castle and squeeze through an opening in the door. Once out into the great hall, I stayed to the ceiling, in order not to get caught. When I came upon the dungeon door, I slipped through another hole and made my way to where the blue flowers grow."

Gyla rolled her eyes. "Mercy me, the chance you took."

"I plucked one from the earth," Titiana continued. "But in an instant two grew in its place."

Gyla placed her hands on her hips. "There, you see...'tis a hopeless venture."

"Nay, 'tisn't," Titiana said.

Gyla narrowed her eyes. "'Tis if you pluck one and two comes back."

Titiana's voice held a rasp of excitement. "Not if you wet instead of pluck."

Gyla gasped. "You wet on one?"

"Aye, 'twas an accident really...I had drunk lots of coconut nectar earlier and while I hovered over a flower I suddenly got the urge to go. Before I knew it I had saturated the blossom. Within moments it shriveled and died. I waited for another to grow in its place, but none did."

There was a tinge of wonder in Gyla's voice. "And without this herb Devora has no brew?"

Titiana nodded. "Without the brew the queen will turn old."

Gyla smiled. "And die."

"Aye, sister, she will die." Titiana bit her bottom lip. "Unfortunately I have not that much moisture in me to wet on every one of the flowers." She looked over at the other Pixies still enjoying their meal. "But with the help of the clan..."

Gyla finished the sentence. "All the flowers can be destroyed."

Titiana's heart was overjoyed that her sister finally understood. "Aye, all of them."

Gyla reached for her sister's hand. "Come, let us talk with the others...there is not one moment to waste."

****

Zailia did not welcome the morning. 'Twould be just another day spent trying to survive Devora's control. Zailia sighed and made her way to the window, looking out at the few remaining flowers that grew. She wondered how the hardy blooms survived the weeds of an unkempt garden. 'Twas Zailia's mother that had the green thumb, growing herbs for Wysteria's healing potions, and bringing forth each year an abundance of crops that graced their table at every meal.

Though she too was blessed with a green thumb, Zailia's hours were spent differently. With an ailing father to tend, and working at the castle, Zailia had not the time or the energy to follow in her mother's ways.

She sighed heavily and stuck her hands deep into her pockets. 'Twas then her fingers touched upon the vial of poison. She flinched and pulled the tiny glass tube from the apron's pouch, holding it up to the light. "There has to be another way to save my father," she mumbled aloud.

"What nonsense do you speak, daughter?" came a

gruff voice.

Zailia spun around to find Tobiah standing behind her, gaunt and weary looking, his tunic sleeve empty of an arm. "Papa, you should be in bed."

Tobiah frowned, and waved a hand in the air. "Nay, I have rested enough. 'Tis time I get back to living."

Zailia rushed to her father's side. "Let me help you to a chair."

Tobiah shooed her. "I am able to do that for myself, daughter."

She placed her hands on her hips. "And how is it you are able?"

Tobiah made his way to a chair and sat down. "Wysteria came by a day ago, while you were at the castle, and left me a healing potion to drink."

Zailia frowned. "You said you did not believe her potions could help."

Tobiah shrugged. "I had nothing to lose by trying." He smiled. "So here I be; a tad weak, but definitely on the mend."

Zailia hugged her father. "This pleases me so much, Papa. To see you up and about again is all that I have hoped for."

Tobiah patted his daughter's arm affectionately. "What is in the vial, Zailia?"

She backed away quickly. "'Tis nothing, Papa."

Tobiah arched a brow. "I will ask one more time, daughter. What is in the vial?"

Zailia slipped the small vessel back into her pocket and walked over to the fireplace. "Let me give you a bowl of stew," she said, changing the subject. "I have been simmering it all day."

"Zailia!" Tobiah snapped.

Zailia spun around. "Please, Papa, leave it be."

"Nay, I will not." He gave her a stern look. "Now, daughter, we are both too old for me to turn you over my knee. But I am still your father and you will respect me as such." He cast his gaze to her apron pocket. "What is in the vial?"

Zailia licked her dry lips. "'Tis poison."

Tobiah arched a brow. "Poison, huh?"

Zailia gave a taut nod.

"Where did you get poison, daughter?"

Zailia pulled the cylinder from her pocket and placed it on the table. "'Tis Devora's."

Tobiah retrieved the tiny container and rolled it over in his hand. "And why have you got it?"

Zailia moaned. "Papa, please do not make me tell you."

Tobiah glared at his daughter with authority. "Zailia Gabrella Finnley, I want a straight answer from you now."

Tears sprang to Zailia's eyes. "Remember I told you I went calling on Wysteria's guest?"

Tobiah nodded. "The young woman from Dublin...Meav is her name, right?"

"Aye, Meav O'Shay," Zailia added.

"And as I recall you enjoyed the lass, said you two had things in common," Tobiah added.

"'Tis true, we do...and I like her just fine, Papa...but..."

Tobiah narrowed his eyes. "But what, Zailia?"

Zailia's voice broke with emotion. "I have to poison her."

Tobiah arched a brow. "Please tell me my old ears have failed me."

"Your ears are fine, Papa."

Tobiah looked down at the vial he held. "What has Devora threatened you with now, daughter?"

"Your death," Zailia sobbed.

Tobiah chuckled sardonically. "Really, my land is not enough, eh?" He rolled the glass tube in his hand, then threw it across the room, smashing it to pieces against the wall. The deadly liquid flowed from the broken cylinder and ran into the cracks of the stone floor. "That is what I think of Devora's threats."

Zailia gasped. "Papa, what have you done?"

Tobiah leaned forward in his chair and lowered his voice. "You and I both know you could not harm a flea, Zailia, and would not have gone through with the plan."

Zailia covered her face with her hands. "'Tis true, 'tis true," she moaned.

"Then what recourse had you counted on?"

Zailia peeked at her father through parted fingers. "I

had notions at first of escaping...of us getting as far from Keronia as we could." Slowly she dropped her hands to her sides. "But Devora's spies are everywhere. She'd never let us leave."

"So what was your second notion?"

Zailia made her way to a chair and plopped down. "I was still contemplating that when you interrupted me."

Tobiah searched her face. "Why have you not come to me with this problem, daughter?"

Zailia cast her gaze elsewhere. "You have been so sick, Papa...losing your arm and...and...I just wanted to spare you from worrying about anything but getting well."

Tobiah reached over and placed a finger beneath Zailia's chin, turning her to look his way. "Aye, I have lost an arm, but not my mind. If you had come to me the moment Devora had threatened you, I would have worked out a solution."

Tears welled in Zailia's eyes. "What solution is there?"

"I have been a soldier all my life, daughter. Never would I be without a plan up my sleeve." Tobiah chuckled lightly. "Even if one of those sleeves is vacant of an arm."

Zailia leaned forward, eager to hear her father out. "Do tell, then."

Tobiah stroked the stubble on his chin. "You will have Meav here for tea as planned, in case the queen's spies are watching." He turned to look at the trap door in the corner of the kitchen and lowered his voice considerable. "Then after we will all go down below."

Zailia stared in disbelief at her father. Surely he has lost his mind. "That is your plan...for us to hide out in the root cellar?"

"Hush, daughter, not so loud," Tobiah warned, lowering his tone to a mere whisper. "'Tis not only a root cellar but also a tunnel to the Temple of Silah...where Devora and her cohorts can not follow."

Zailia frowned. "But there is no exit from that underground room."

Tobiah eyes twinkled. "Not that one can usually notice, but if you concentrate on the north wall, one will appear."

Zailia's eyes widened. "Why have I not been told of

this before?"

"'Twas for your safety I have kept quiet."

Zailia arched a brow. "You do not trust me?"

"'Tis not a case of trust, Zailia," Tobiah said softly.

"Then what, Papa?"

Tobiah affectionately squeezed his daughter's hand. "I would say I am much like you." He frowned. "Or is it you are much like me?" He shrugged. "Whatever the case may be, I did not want to worry you with anything more." He smiled warmly at his daughter. "'Tis not up to you to shoulder all the problems in this household, Zailia. I never wanted it this way."

"But the land...our home..."

"To hell with it all," Tobiah broke in. "'Tis not worth watching my daughter throw away her youth for."

Zailia looked around the tiny kitchen. "But 'tis the place where your father, and his father before him lived; where you and Mama started your lives together, had children, made your dreams come true. I thought it meant everything to you."

"Those things are in the past, daughter. What means the most to me now is you, your chance at happiness, love, and a family," Tobiah explained. He smiled warmly. "I want grandchildren to bounce on my knee before I die."

"But where will we live?" Zailia searched her father's face. "Surely we cannot stay forever in the temple."

Tobiah tweaked his daughter's nose, as he had done when she was a child. "We must take one step at a time and have patience."

"And why would you be privileged to have a secret passage to the temple?" Zailia probed.

Tobiah brought his mouth close to Zailia's ear. "Neteru, the high priestess, is your mother's sister."

Zailia gasped. "Something else I have not been told."

"No one on the island knew Neteru and your mother were related."

Zailia frowned. "But why...what is the reason for such secrecy?"

Tobiah sat back in his seat. "Neteru would then be vulnerable to Devora's wickedness if the knowledge she had family living on the island got out." Tobiah patted his daughter's hand reassuringly. "As it stands now the temple is off limits to Devora and remains a safe haven for all that dwell there."

Zailia sighed with relief. A giant weight had been lifted from her shoulders. No longer would she have to work for Devora; or fear each day that dawned. She stood and wrapped her arms around her father's wrinkled neck. "Thank you, Papa."

Tobiah squeezed her hand gently. "I want you to gather together a few belongs you cherish most, so after tea we can be on our way."

Zailia pulled back. "What about Meav?"

Tobiah looked up at his daughter. "She will have to come with us."

Zailia's face brightened. "She can become my sister...I always wanted a sister. Wait till you meet her, Papa. You will like her, I know you will."

For the first time in ages Tobiah saw the sparkle in his daughter's face that he so loved. "I am sure of it as well...now go and pack your things."

Zailia obeyed, hope reflecting in her eyes.

Tobiah stood and made his way to the window, looking out at the neglected garden, and remembering the days his lovely wife tended it with care. The memory of her took him a million miles away...so far were his thoughts that Tobiah failed to detect Devora's spy listening beneath the glass casement.

****

Rule had lain all night on the fur pile that was his bed, staring into space. When the morning sun filled the opening of the cave he looked around at the emptiness, void of warmth and human comfort. He felt a mixture of anger and disgust. How could he have been so blind? He should have listened to his first instincts and remained cautious of Meav. Why had he let his guard down? The answer to that question came quickly...he was taken by her. Aye, smitten like a young lad after his first kiss. The woman had bewitched him, made all his senses come alive. The ice encasing his heart had melted, he felt renewed, hopeful.

Rule laughed sardonically and sat up. Combing his fingers through his hair he battled the torment raging within. If he banished Meav he could never have her...and oh...how badly he wanted her. He still smelt her on his flesh, felt her touch. But if she stayed she would kill him.

"Am I not already dead?" he screamed, his deep voice echoing through the empty cave. "Do I not live in hell as 'tis?"

Burying his face in his hands Rule wept, pouring from his soul all the hurt and loneliness that was his life. The sorrow strangled him, the future looked dim, and his body ached for Meav.

'Twas the pangs of hunger rumbling in his belly that forced him to stand. In a matter of moments he would take on a feline form, and go out to hunt for his breakfast. From his jaws the blood would drip as he ripped apart the flesh of his prey. After his hunger was appeased he would slither back to the den to clean himself and sleep off his meal. 'Twas his fate each and every day, and would be for the rest of his time. Only when he was with Meav did he forget his present situation; felt like a real man and that his life in some respect had been returned. But he could never experience that wonderful feeling again. 'Twould disappear forever when he banished her.

Meav...gone forever from his world.

Rule shouted at the top of his lungs. "Damn...damn...damn it all!"

Chapter Thirteen

Rule's name came to Meav's lips so completely she could taste it. Had she really experienced his mind-drugging kisses; actually touched his tumescent manhood? Meav still felt the breath of passion between them, smelt his rich, musky scent. Even now, lying on her cot, his manly aroma played havoc with her senses.

She groaned, remembering the outcome of their meeting. The air between them had been thick with promise, until Rule misunderstood her intentions. She could still see his amber eyes burrowing into the core of her being, as he had refused to listen to the real reason she had come into his life.

"Banished...banished!" he had screamed.

His words pierced the heavy silence. Meav rolled onto her side, feeling the tears well in her eyes. Sorrow, mingled with her own anxiety, rose to strangle her. Pulling the blanket up over her head, she willed herself away from Keronia. She wished she had never set eyes upon Rule, or allowed him to stir her luminous with desire. Just the thought of him standing naked before her, stirred her loins...and yet she wanted rid of him...he wanted rid of her.

"'Tis all such a horrible mistake," she mumbled miserably.

"'Tisn't a mistake," Wysteria chirped, pulling the blanket off of Meav. "People come into your life when you need them...when they need you. This was supposed to happen."

Meav sat up quickly. "He believes me mother killed his mother, and at this point wants to banish me from the island."

Wysteria waved her hand casually over her head. "Oh, pish posh! You are not going anywhere, but to Zailia's for tea."

Meav's eyes widened. "Tea! Who can think of having

tea at a time like this? I mean...he might very well be on his way over here to set me afloat on a raft."

Wysteria ignored the outburst and reached down to unfasten the tiny white buttons on Meav's nightgown. "If you do not get bathed, dressed and have a bit of breakfast soon, you are going to be late for your first social invite."

Meav pushed Wysteria's hands away. "Did you hear anything I said?"

Wysteria placed her hands on her hips. "I heard every word, lass."

"And still you expect me to go about my day as planned...to have afternoon tea?"

Wysteria gave a taut nod.

Meav rose quickly from the cot. "I am beginning to believe all of you are insane on this island, and that I am just a pawn, as me mother was, to make the Prophecy...the glorious and sacred Prophecy come to pass. No one cared about her, and no one cares about me."

Wysteria suddenly reached out and slapped Meav squarely across the face. "That, child, is far from the truth."

Meav's mouth gaped open in shock, her hand going to her cheek. Slowly she rubbed away the sting.

"And if you ever say that again 'twill be your bare bottom that feels my wrath," Wysteria warned.

Tears slipped down Meav's face. "What am I to do, Wysteria?"

"Do you still trust me, lass?" Wysteria asked.

Meav nodded.

"Then strip off the nightwear, wash, dress, and start the day as planned." Affectionately Wysteria pushed aside a lock of hair from Meav's forehead. "Leave the rest to me."

****

Shell knelt beside the tub, lathering Devora with the heather scented soap. "Perhaps you should do away with Zailia's services altogether."

Devora closed her eyes, as Shell's large hand washed her back. "I have to admit 'tis more of a pleasure having you bathe me...but then who would guard my doors?"

Shell smiled. "Ah, but my dear queen, I have never stopped guarding your doors." He moved his hand around to the front of her body, rubbing the nipples of each breast with soapy fingers before traveling to the area between her thighs. "No one dares cross this opening," he whispered, penetrating her.

Devora moaned with pleasure and lay back, opening her legs wider.

Shell teased Devora's hidden fires, his own excitement mounting as he aroused the beautiful queen. Her moans of pleasure, her body trembling just before she climaxed, gave him great satisfaction.

Devora's burst of passion was interrupted by a loud knock at the door. Her serene face suddenly twisted with anger. "Who dares to disturb me now?"

Shell reluctantly stopped his foreplay and stood, making his way to the chamber door. "I will find out, my queen."

"And quickly, Shell," she snapped. "The water grows cold."

Wiping his hands on a towel, Shell opened the door and stepped into the hall.

****

Devora reached down and finished herself off, though her own touch was not as satisfying as Shell's. Fervently she worked until she became ripe for the release.

Shell returned just in time to see the end of her pleasure. He smirked. "You could not wait for me?"

Devora looked up into his steel, gray eyes. "I wait for no one." Suddenly she stood. "What was the interruption?"

Shell immediately reached for a towel and wrapped it around Devora. "Our spy had some news you will definitely find interesting."

Devora arched a brow. "Do tell."

Shell gently dried Devora as he explained what the scout overheard while hiding beneath Tobiah's window.

Devora seethed. "So the little twit plans to disobey me. And Neteru is Zailia's aunt, you say?"

Shell nodded.

Devora chuckled wickedly. "Well, now...this gets better and better at every turn."

"It does at that, Your Majesty," Shell agreed.

Devora threw her head back and laughed, the sinister ripple echoing throughout the room. "Oh, I love it!"

Shell joined in the devious mirth. "I have ordered two sentries to accompany me to Tobiah's cottage. All of them will be captured before they make it to the cellar."

Devora reached up and traced Shell's full lips with a long, red nail. "Too bad they will lose out on their afternoon tea." She leaned against Shell's hard chest. "And after our guests arrive, I have an order for you, Sentry."

Shell's eyes twinkled. "Your wish is my command, dear queen."

****

Ibrehem came upon the opening to Rule's cave. Drops of blood lined the path. Pity swelled Ibrehem's heart for his friend, knowing 'twas animal blood that spotted the ground and Rule must have just finished breakfast. If only there was a way Ibrehem could help Rule get back his life. Ibrehem remembered the times Rule fought beside him as a mighty and headstrong warrior. They battled in heat that nearly had them sweating blood; after celebrating their victory together over a cold mug of ale.

Shouts from within the cave brought Ibrehem back to the present and led him to draw his sword before entering the dismal den.

Rule frowned when he saw his friend armed and ready to do battle. "Is this how you come a calling on your comrades?"

Ibrehem inhaled the dampness. "I heard shouting, thought something was amiss."

"Something is amiss...my senses," Rule snapped.

Ibrehem gave one last look around the barren and crude dwelling before replacing the sword in the sheath at his waist. "Tell me something I do not already know, my lord."

Rule's frowned deepened. "I do not appreciate your humorous banter on this morn, my friend."

Ibrehem shrugged. "And what is different from this morn?"

Rule raked a hand threw his unruly hair. "This is the morn after the night I learned she would betray me."

Ibrehem blinked baffled. "Who would betray you, my lord?"

Rule gritted his teeth. "Meav O'Shay."

Ibrehem's voice rose with surprise. "Wysteria's guest?"

"Aye, one in the same...the sweet and tantalizing beauty with the flaming hair and sultry mouth has managed to...to..." Rule stammered.

"Surge your desires, it sounds," Ibrehem interjected smugly.

Rule gave Ibrehem a black layered look. "She has managed to infuriate me...to bewitch me, and finally she plans to kill me."

Ibrehem folded his arms across his chest. "What is this nonsense you speak?"

Rules mouth set in annoyance. "'Tis true, my friend. Meav O'Shay has come to finish what her mother started." His rage mounted in his voice. "And she must be banished from this island, just as her mother was."

Ibrehem frowned confused. "Who is her mother?"

Rule ground the words out between his teeth. "Her mother is Meridith, the woman who killed my mother...sister of Devora."

"And the sister of Wysteria as well," Ibrehem quickly reminded him. "That fact makes all the difference in the world, I would say, my lord."

Rule glared at his friend. "Explain yourself."

Ibrehem arched a brow. "Do you really think Wysteria would harbor and care for anyone who would harm a hair on your head? She has been like a mother to you since you were a wee lad, and has proven her loyalty."

"Perhaps Wysteria does not know what the maiden has planned?"

Ibrehem chuckled sardonically. "Wysteria...not know? Good heavens, man, the woman knows everything."

"Aye, you are right about that, Ibrehem," Rule reluctantly agreed.

Ibrehem smiled. "Of course I am right, and if you calm yourself you will see how absurd you are being."

Rule scowled. "*Letuna.*"

"Nay, I am not finished," Ibrehem countered, feeling his own anger toward his friend's stubbornness mount. He sat down hard on Rule's bed of pelts. "How have you come by this information?"

"It came to me in a vision quest...our thoughts merged and...then we...then I..." Rule paused.

Ibrehem smirked. "I can imagine much more than your minds met. Am I right, my lord?"

Rule scowled. "And then I learned of her plan," he concluded.

"So in the vision quest the two of you shared she confessed her plot to kill you."

"Nay, not in so many words," Rule murmured satirically.

Ibrehem studied his friend's face. "I do not understand, my lord."

Rule spoke with bitterness. "I did not give her the chance to explain."

Ibrehem shook his head. "Your heart is that of a lion, but your brain is that of a bird's."

"I am not amused by the comparison, Ibrehem."

"Only a bird-brain would base such a serious charge on something you did not fully hear in a vision quest, my lord."

Rule narrowed his eyes. "As a warrior you should know a vision quest is just as precise as realty, sometimes more."

"True," Ibrehem agreed. "But only when you listen, when you open your heart and mind to what is playing out before you. If you did not give the lass a chance to speak..."

Rule interrupted harshly. "I did not need to hear what I already knew."

Ibrehem arched a brow. "Knew or surmised, my lord?"

"Well I...I..." Rule stammered.

"And after you accused Meav, did you allow her to defend herself?" Ibrehem challenged.

Rule hung his head.

"Ah, that is what I thought." Ibrehem stood and made his way to Rule. "What first gave you the mind set Meav wanted your demise?"

Rule raised his eyes to met Ibrehem's and explained about the birth mark and Meav's admission that Meridith was her mother. "Meridith tried to kill my mother, and my father banished her from Keronia...sent her off on a raft to die at sea. But she did not die. Instead she landed on the shores of Ireland, fell in love and had a family."

Ibrehem frowned. "And now you believe Meridith's has sent her daughter to finish the job?"

Rule's voice hardened. "Aye, it makes sense...revenge eats at the heart of all humans."

Ibrehem folded his arms across his chest. "How does it make sense, my lord? The girl was ship wrecked to these shores; she did not come armed with military."

Rule stared at his friend in silence.

Ibrehem grabbed Rule by the arm. "We must go to Wysteria's cottage where you can confront Meav face to face; listen to her explanation. Then, after learning all the facts, you will make a decision as to what must be done."

Rule pulled his arm away. "Nay."

Ibrehem set his hands on his hips. "Aye...'tis the way of a worthy man." Ibrehem searched Rule's face. "Last I knew you still had your honor, my lord...unless Devora has managed to take that from you as well."

Rule sighed heavily. "Nay, I still have that to my credit."

"Then do the right thing," Ibrehem said flatly.

"Aye, the right thing," Rule repeated softly.

Ibrehem made his way to the cave's opening, then stepped aside and bowed politely. "After you, my lord."

****

Zailia's steps felt light, even had a bit of a bounce to them, now that so much had been lifted from her shoulders. As she made her way to Wysteria's cottage to pick up Meav for afternoon tea, she thought of all the promise that lay ahead. With the sanctity of the temple to shield her and her father, Zailia would no longer be forced to serve the evil Queen Devora. The days of bathing the witch's cold, white flesh, being humiliated and taking her abuse, were over. Zailia could finally plan her own life...perhaps there would even be a chance at love...with Ibrehem.

She closed her eyes and lifted her face to the sun. A gentle breeze spread the warmth over her cheeks, as the thought of her handsome warrior seeped through her heart. Suddenly she felt giddy...as a young girl should. All along Zailia had been smitten with Ibrehem Chancelor. Fighting the feeling at times became unbearable. But she had no choice. If Zailia drew attention to her affiliation with Ibrehem, Devora would have used it against her. Getting Ibrehem involved in her problems would have set him up for harm as well. Keeping him at bay was for his own safety. But now...now...

Wysteria opened the door before Zailia had a chance to knock. "'Tis such a fine day for two friends to enjoy."

Pulled from her thoughts of Ibrehem, Zailia hesitated with a response.

Wysteria chuckled lightly. "And an even finer day for a daydream, I see."

Zailia blushed. "Aye, 'tis."

Wysteria opened the door wider, welcoming her guest inside. "I think I can guess who the daydream might be about."

Zailia's blush deepened.

Wysteria laughed heartily. "Your secret is safe with me, lass."

It was then that Meav entered the cottage from the garden. Zailia admired the pale, yellow sundress her new friend wore. The white lace that trimmed the scooped neckline and short sleeve cuffs were as delicate as a spider's web. "You look so beautiful."

Meav glanced down at the full skirt and smoothed the material. "'Tis a lovely dress, at that."

"'Tis you that make it lovely, Meav," Zailia said.

Meav smiled and raised her eyes to meet her friend's. "Thank you, Zailia."

"And I have made a lovely batch of peach wafers for you two to munch on with your tea," Wysteria said, handing the basket filled with the delicious smelling cookies to Meav. "Enjoy your afternoon, and I will be by before dark to fetch you."

The walk to Tobiah's cottage, though pleasant, was a bit awkward. Without Wysteria around to promote conversation, the girls remained silent.

Meav's thoughts were occupied with Rule...and what had transpired between them in the vision quest. His anger had disturbed her greatly, and the thought of banishment preyed heavily on her mind. She did not want to leave Keronia, or Rule; and wished for a chance to show him her loyalty...her love. 'Twas the first time Meav admitted to herself the feelings she had for Rule...how the sight of him naked disturbed her even more than his anger; but in a good way...in a way that filled her like never before. Saints preserve us...if he could evoke such passions within her mind, what could he do in the flesh?

Zailia finally mustered the courage to speak. "Have you ever fallen in love, Meav?"

Meav gasped and covered her mouth with her hand. Had Zailia read her thoughts? On this island you never knew what ability someone had.

Zailia giggled. "Ah, me too."

The two broke out in laughter, as young women did when they talked about love.

Zailia moved close to Meav's ear and whispered. "My man is Ibrehem Chancelor, though I have not told him yet."

Meav had never met Ibrehem, but she had heard his praises sung by Wysteria. "I am happy for you, Zailia."

Zailia looped her arm through Meav's. "Now tell me yours."

Meav hesitated. She could not really call Rule *her man*...especially when he wanted to rid himself of her.

"Oh, do tell," Zailia begged. "I promise not to breathe a word to a soul."

Meav sighed. "For a wee bit of time I had thought...hoped...it would be Rule. But..."

"But...what?" Zailia probed.

"'Twas all in my own head," Meav said.

"Perhaps it could come true if you told him how you felt." Zailia suggested.

Meav frowned. "I would sooner die than ever confess my feelings."

Zailia's eyes widened. "Why is that?"

Meav sighed again. "Because Rule thinks..." she paused. "He does not trust women."

Zailia's eyes saddened. "'Tis Devora's doings...every hurtful and evil thing that takes place on Keronia has her mark on it. She twists and tortures other people's lives; robs them of hope and happiness. You must not blame Rule, he has been through a lot because of that witch."

Meav searched Zailia's face. "You sound as though you know first hand."

"I do." Zailia pulled her arm free from Meav's. "There is something I need to tell you, and when I am through, I cannot blame you if you never want to set eyes on me again." Zailia looked deep into Meav's eyes. "But first I must know...are you a forgiving person, Meav O'Shay?"

Zailia's words set Meav's heart pounding. "I am almost afraid to answer that."

Zailia's voice shook. "Hopefully after today, neither of us will ever be afraid again."

Meav arched a brow. "I like to think I am forgiving."

Zailia squared her shoulders. "Then I would say soon you will know for sure, because I have a confession to make."

Meav inhaled sharply. "Speak, Zailia...I am listening."

As Zailia shared the disturbing events that led to her seeking her out as a friend, Meav's face saddened.

"I want you to know," Zailia quickly added, "that I could never have really harmed you." She sighed. "But I was so torn at what to do. It meant my father's life." She wrung her hands nervously. "Can you ever forgive me, Meav?"

Meav remained silent, tightening her grip on the basket of goodies she carried. Keronia sure had a strange way of welcoming new guests. Rule was ready to banish her, and Zailia had entertained thoughts of poisoning her. If anyone ever had a reason to worry or fear...and not feel wanted, 'twas Meav.

Zailia bit her bottom lip. "Please, say something, Meav."

"I cannot hold it against you, Zailia. As you said, you were torn." Meav's face clouded with uneasiness. "You are forgiven, but what happens now?"

Zailia shoulders relaxed. "My father has taken control of the situation." She looked around with caution, lowered her voice to a mere whisper and explained Tobiah's plan.

Meav thought of her own father. He was strong and handsome; always there for his daughters as well. Maybe if she had been as loyal to her family, they would be alive today. "You are blessed to still have a father."

Zailia's eyes saddened. Slowly she reached out and took Meav's hand. "I am so sorry for all that you have lost, but perhaps we could be your family now." She smiled warmly. "I have always wanted a sister."

Meav nodded. "And I lost the two I had." She looked down at the basket Wysteria filled with cookies. "Saints preserve us...what about Wysteria? She plans on fetching me before dark."

"My father will find a way to get word to her about our plan." Zailia squeezed Meav's hand affectionately. "Then from this time on, united as a family, we will put our fears and hurts behind us...find closure with our losses and move forward with the hope of good things to come."

Meav frowned. "Do you believe there are good things to come, Zailia?"

Zailia's answer came without hesitation. "Aye, Meav, I do...I truly do."

****

Titiana stretched her tiny, naked form and yawned. The woven shelter of her cocoon had offered her warmth throughout the chill of the night, but now the sweltering sun made the cozy refuge unbearable. Spreading her wings she made her way out of the cocoon and to a giant palm tree. Standing beneath a leaf she lifted her face to catch the dripping dew. Each morning Titiana washed herself this way, starting her day with the morning's mist glistening upon her cheeks. But on this morning the foliage was dry.

Titiana frowned. Never in all the years she lived on Keronia had the island been deprived of the dawn's veil. She reached up and shook the leaf...no droplets fell. She shook it harder...nothing. Titiana grew concerned.

Just as she was about to fly away to find her sister Gila and question her about the abnormality of this new day, Titiana smelt the musty odor of a treog. Quickly turning around she spotted the tree dweller, his beady, black eyes staring rudely.

The treog crossed his arms over his chest. "What do you do here, pixie?"

Titiana's frown deepened. "What I do every

morn...bathe."

"But 'tis not morn," the treog snapped. "'Tis noon."

Titiana's eyes widened. "Noon?"

"Aye...can you not tell?" the treog quipped. "The sun is high, the dew is dry...'tis noon, silly fairie."

Titiana gasped. "Nay, it cannot be?"

"Well, 'tis...and comes each and every day at this time," the treog retorted with a scowl.

Titiana brought her hand to her forehead. "I have to be somewhere else at noon."

"Well, you are not somewhere else...you are here...trying to bathe under a dry leaf," the treog commented.

"But I am not supposed to be here," Titiana moaned.

"But you are," the treog countered.

You could never get a straight answer from a treog. To them everything has a double meaning and appears simultaneously black and white, ugly and beautiful, or right and wrong.

Titiana was becoming vexed by the snippy tree inhabitant and could feel her temper rise. "I know where I am, you misshapen little creature...but I should not be."

The treog lifted his thin upper lip into a snarl. "Then stop wasting time telling me and go where you are supposed to be."

Angered, Titiana spread her wings and left without another word to the annoying being. As fast as she could, which was not as fast on an empty stomach, Titiana flew to Tobiah's cottage.

Peeking through the slits of the shutters Titiana saw Meav and Zailia sitting down to tea. Just as Meav was about to raise the cup to her lips, Titiana burst through the open window and flew straight for Meav; knocking the cup from her hand. The pretty china mug crashed to the floor...shattering into a million tiny pieces. Titiana lay dazed not far away. Zailia jumped to her feet. "Good heavens, was that a bird?"

Meav looked around in the direction of the broken cup and spotted Titiana lying flat on her belly. "Nay, not a bird...'tis Titiana." Quickly she rose from her chair and went to the tiny fairie's aid. Gently Meav scooped the pixie up into her hands, fearful Titiana was badly injured.

"Is she hurt?" Zailia inquired, moving to stand beside Meav.

Meav carefully set Titiana down on the table and rubbed her belly with the tip of a finger. "Titiana, can you hear me?"

Titiana shook her head, golden curls flopping in her eyes. "Aye...aye, I can," she stammered.

Meav gently felt around Titiana's body. "Does it hurt anywhere I am touching?"

"Nay," Titiana muttered.

"Can you move your arms and legs?" Zailia asked concerned.

Titiana straightened her legs, and raised her arms above her head. "Aye, all is fine."

"I am glad you are not hurt, but now you have some explaining to do." Zailia placed her hands on her hips. "What on earth has gotten into you, crashing through folk's windows?"

Slowly Titiana sat up. "'Tis because of what you have done that I am here."

Zailia's eyes widened. "What have I done?"

Titiana cast a quick glance at Meav. "You know...what Devora ordered you do to Meav."

Zailia gasped. "You know about that?"

Titiana nodded. "I was on the window ledge, listening."

Tears welled in Meav's eyes at the thought the little pixie cared so much for her. "Why, Titiana, you tried to save my life."

"I did save your life...I stopped you from drinking the poisoned tea," Titiana boasted.

Meav gently reached out and stroked the pixie's head, suddenly feeling a new found affection for this littlest hero. "Zailia could not bring herself to carry out Devora's orders."

"We have another plan, Titiana," Zailia said. "That will free us from Devora from this day on."

Titiana's face brightened. "And I have taken care of that too."

Zailia frowned. "I am afraid I do not understand what you mean?"

"The blue flowers...in the dungeon...they are all gone.

All the pixies banned together and wilted them. They are dead...shriveled to nothing...and soon Devora will be too," Titiana said.

Zailia shook her head confused. "I still do not understand what you are talking about."

Titiana stood on wobbly legs. "The flowers...the blue flowers...they..." Her words were interrupted by the cottage door opening with a bang.

In walked three armed sentries.

Meav's heart fell to her toes. The man leading the others curled his lips into a sardonic smile and bowed politely. "Good afternoon ladies, enjoying your tea?"

Zailia shrieked and quickly grabbed Meav by the hand.

"Now, now, is that any way to greet company?" He said, making his way toward the women.

"I do not remember inviting you into my home, Shell," Tobiah snapped.

Meav turned to see Zailia's father enter the kitchen.

"Papa," was all Zailia managed to mutter.

"Take Meav to your room, Zailia," Tobiah ordered. "I will handle this."

Shell threw his head back and laughed. "You think so, old man?"

Zailia cringed and Meav instantly read her friend's thoughts. Tobiah was no match for these men...no doubt sent by the evil Devora.

"Go Zailia, and take Meav with you," Tobiah again demanded of his daughter.

Shell drew his sword. "No one leaves this room."

The sentry's voice was absolutely emotionless and it chilled Meav down to her bones.

Tobiah gave Shell a hostile glare. "I do not take orders from you."

A tense silence enveloped the room.

Zailia squeezed Meav's hand.

Meav squeezed Zailia's hand in return, glimpsing the fear etched on her friend's face. 'Twas all her fault their lives were in jeopardy. "'Tis me Devora wants, is that not so?" she said in a shaky voice.

Shell measured Meav with a cool, appraising look. "Aye, 'tis, lass."

Meav freed her hand from Zailia's grip and stepped forward. "Then let us be on our way and leave these good people alone."

Shell was impressed at the maiden's bravado, the way she squared her shoulders and defiantly raised her chin. Slowly he replaced his sword in its sheath and studied her freely. For an instant his glance softened as he took in her innocence...her beauty.

"You are not going anywhere, Meav," Tobiah said.

Shell transferred his gaze to the old man. "Wrong, Tobiah...my orders are from the queen. All of you are under arrest and will be imprisoned for your crime."

Tobiah stiffened. "And what crime is that, Sentry?"

Shell's eyes bore into Tobiah's. "Treason...all of you have plotted to betray the crown."

Tobiah answered in the same cool tone. "And you have proof of this accusation?"

"Aye," Shell said firmly. "Your plan was overheard by a..."

"Overheard, how?" Tobiah said.

Shell answered with the voice of authority. "It matters not how...the fact is your plan was discovered and you are now under arrest." He turned to the sentries that had accompanied him. "Seize them."

Zailia ran to her father. "Nay!"

Tobiah stood strong, pushing his daughter behind him.

One sentry grabbed Tobiah by the neck and shoved him to the floor. He forced Tobiah's arm behind his back and tied his wrist to his belt with a rope. When the sentry was sure the knot was secure, he yanked Tobiah to his feet, prodding the elderly man with the tip if his sword as he paraded him out the door.

The second sentry walked over to Zailia and moved her to stand against the wall. Then he tied her hands behind her back and marched her out of the cottage behind her father.

Shell moved toward Meav. "Your turn, lass." When he spoke again his words were almost tender. "'Twill be much easier for you if you do not struggle."

Meav drew a deep breath and forbade herself to tremble. She tossed her hair across her shoulders in a gesture of defiance. "You can go to hell."

Shell forced his lips to part in a curved, stiff smile. "I have already been there and back, lass." In one fluid motion he spun Meav around and bent her over the table, then bound her hands behind her with a piece of rope that hung from his belt. Taking a fist full of her hair, he bent her head back. "We must not keep the queen waiting."

Titiana flew at Shell's eyes. "Leave her alone."

Shell backhanded Titiana and the pixie landed on the table beside.

Meav's heart sank. "Titiana, Titiana!"

The little fairie shook her head to clear it and slowly stood. "I am fine," she said softly.

"Then go...warn Wysteria," Meav whispered.

Titiana frowned confused.

"Just do as I say...Wysteria will know what to do...then...find Rule," she quickly added.

Titiana stood and spread her wings. Before Shell could do her further harm, she flew high to the ceiling, then out the window.

Shell grabbed Meav by the shoulders and turned her around to face him. "Rule cannot save you."

Meav met his eyes without flinching. "You will see."

"Nay, you will see." Shell gave her a push ahead of him. "After you, lass." He watched her walk out the door, head held high and with unhurried steps. Every curve of her body spoke insolence. Shell smiled to himself. He had the distinct feeling Devora was finally going to meet her match.

Chapter Fourteen

Zailia was growing increasingly worried for her father. The trek through the woods to the castle was one she took often when she came home to visit, but Tobiah had not walked much in almost a year. Since he had lost an arm, he had been in and out of bed with infections and congestion. His eating habits were poor, and he had become quite frail.

Zailia watched in horror as Carson, Devora's most brutal sentry, dragged Tobiah along beside him. The large guard's strides were long and quick, way too fast for an old, ailing man to keep up with. Tobiah had already collapsed twice and looked as though he might for a third time. Zailia had heard stories about Carson, his tactics with prisoners and his appetite for the unusual. He enjoyed his position, taking Devora's orders one-step beyond for his own pleasure. Carson fancied the bazaar, and he was now in charge of Tobiah.

Zailia looked over at the sentry guarding her. She knew him as Wesley, a pleasant man about her age. He smiled often at her while she worked around the castle. Several times he had struck up conversation. All in all, Zailia had no quarrel with him and knew he was only doing his job, fearing retribution from Devora if he disobeyed. She had heard Wesley question Shell on orders, and felt he had a conscience. Perhaps he would listen to her plea for her father.

"Sir, please," Zailia began in a shaky voice. "Could you suggest being the one to guard my father?"

Wesley searched the young woman's face. Worry and fear filled her eyes. Instantly he took pity on her, but how was he going to convince Carson to trade prisoners? The man was a hard-nose, liked roughing up the men, then...

Wesley swallowed hard, knowing full well what was in store for the old man at the hands of Carson. "I...I..."

"Please," Zailia begged. "We both know what Carson

is capable of."

Wesley arched a brow. "And you would inflict his ways on yourself, lass?"

"Aye, if it meant sparing my father," Zailia said.

Wesley was not happy with the thought of putting this beautiful young woman in the hands of such a beast, but he understood her concern for her father. He gave Zailia a taut nod. "Let me see what I can do."

Tears filled Zailia's eyes. "I thank you a thousand times."

Wesley cleared his throat. "Hey, Carson," he called out.

"Do not trouble me," Carson snapped, not bothering to turn Wesley's way. He yanked on Tobiah's rope and laughed when the old man grimaced in pain. "Can you not see I am working?"

"I thought perhaps you would enjoy a change of scenery...this pretty lass for that old codger," Wesley said.

Carson turned briefly to look at Zailia. "She is a might easier on the eyes."

"She is easier to walk with too, will not keep falling as the old man does," Wesley added.

Carson looked at his charge, then back at Zailia. "I am getting sick of picking this bag of bones up from the ground every few feet."

"Then let me take gramps and you take the bitch," Wesley said.

Carson smiled. "Deal," he finally agreed.

As soon as the prisoners were switched, Wesley allowed Tobiah to lean on him and slowed the pace.

Zailia's eyes silently thanked Wesley.

Carson wasted no time in making himself familiar with his new prisoner. He pulled Zailia close and reached behind her to cup her shapely buttocks. "I like this already."

Zailia could feel the heat rise to her face. Flushing with a mixture of humiliation and anger, she kept her pace with her disgusting captor as well as her silence. Her father had not noticed Carson's violation, and Zailia wanted to keep it that way. If Tobiah thought his daughter had been compromised, he would come to her defense. It could very well mean his life.

Meav saw Carson fondle Zailia and fury lit her eyes. "Your guardsman is a swine," she retorted.

Shell chuckled lightly. "Nay, he is a man."

Meav's vehemence almost choked her. "I hardly think his actions make him a *man*."

Shell glowered at her. "No one asked you for your thoughts."

Meav gave Shell a hostile glare. "Demand that he stop."

Shell arched a brow. "You are in no position to give me orders, lass." His lips curved into a sardonic smile. "In fact, I might follow his lead."

"I am not Zailia. I will not stand for it," Meav countered icily.

Shell's face reddened with rage. "You will not have a choice."

Meav reacted angrily to the challenge in his voice. "Then I see clearly, sir, that you are one of those warriors that shame the name with your lack of honor."

Her accusing words stabbed the air, and for a reason Shell could not explain, disturbed him. Why did he suddenly care what *she* thought? His eyes blazed down into hers. Not once did she cower, but instead boldly met his rage with her own. With head held high, back erect, she dealt with the unspeakable fate that awaited her like a soldier would. Her honor put his to shame...and Shell felt the disgrace seep to his very core.

He almost felt compelled to explain to her how it had been. He was a *warrior*, in every sense of the word...honor bound and all; but he was made to follow orders. If not, he himself would hang in chains. And because he could not be the soldier he had been taught to be, he decided to make the best of his fate and take his pleasure from the beautiful and exotic queen that he served. Every time he took Devora, made her weak and vulnerable for his touch, he won his self-esteem back. Shell knew that he had stopped caring what others thought of him a long time ago...until now.

Shell's voice was harsh, raw. "Carson."

"Aye, sir," Carson answered.

"Enough with the girl...save it for later," Shell snapped.

"Aye, sir," Carson repeated.

Shell turned his attention back to Meav. "And not another word out of you."

Meav wanted to scratch his eyes out, kick him, and scream in his face. The man infuriated her. No one should have the right to persecute or hurt another. The whole situation brought Hollister McGreary and his tactics to mind. McGreary's evilness killed her family. These rogues were no better.

Meav tightened her jaw. She knew if she did not hold her tongue things would only be worse. So instead of blurting out the words circling her thoughts, she imposed an iron control on herself; kept her mouth shut and her eyes straight ahead. With each step she prayed Titiana would find Rule...and that, in spite of their last meeting, he would keep the words he promised her on the first day they met...*You are safe now; I will never allow anyone to hurt you.*

****

"Are you going to stand there, eyeing the door knocker all day...or knock? I am not getting any younger waiting for you to decide," Ibrehem teased.

"I have little tolerance at this point for your mockery," Rule snapped. "A lot is at stake here, I want to be sure of what to say."

Ibrehem slapped his companion playfully on the back. "Well, well, the ole' lad has a measure of sense after all."

Rule's brows drew together in an angry frown. "And I should have never allowed you to come along."

Ibrehem chuckled lightly. "Without my council you would be sending the lass adrift right now."

Rule's mouth twisted into a threat. "I still might if her explanation does not please me."

Ibrehem threw his head back and laughed heartily. "You are full of what a bull shoots out his arse, my friend."

"Go kiss an orkly," Rule retorted.

The door flew open and Wysteria stood, with hands on hips. "I should have guessed it would be the two of you making a commotion on my stoop."

Ibrehem pushed his way in front of Rule and politely

took Wysteria's hand. "Dear healer, how beautiful you are today."

Wysteria's eyes narrowed. "You are incorrigible, Ibrehem."

Rule rolled his eyes heavenward. "I can think of another word."

"'Tis true," Ibrehem continued. "You grow more beautiful with each day."

Wysteria gave Ibrehem a playful slap on the arm. "'Tis far from the truth, but I will not argue with you."

"And that will only encourage him," Rule mumbled.

Wysteria ignored the remark and pulled Ibrehem into the cottage. "I just finished making a batch of egg plant soup." She narrowed her eyes. "I do not imagine I could interest you in a bowl?"

Ibrehem's mouth watered. "Imagine away."

Wysteria motioned for Ibrehem to take a seat at the table.

"Must you always eat when you come here?" Rule scowled, his own stomach craving the soup he was unable to eat in man form.

Ibrehem smiled smugly. "Far be it from me to deprive this lovely lady a chance to fill my belly."

Wysteria filled a bowl with the egg plant soup and placed it before Ibrehem, than she turned her attention toward Rule. "Why have you come?"

"I want to speak with Meav," Rule said.

"About what?" Wysteria probed.

A muscle quivered at Rule's jaw. "That is none of your business."

Wysteria crossed her arms over her chest. "Everything that goes on beneath my roof is my business."

Rule could feel his anger mount. "Well, I say this time tisn't."

Wysteria raised her chin defiantly. "And I say this time is no different than any other."

"'Tis comforting to know the two of you never change," Ibrehem said through spoonfuls of soup.

Rule turned to look at his friend. "And much wind pours from your mouth even when you are filling it."

Wysteria poked Rule in the chest. "Why do you want Meav?"

Rule glowered. "Keep your bony fingers off me, old woman."

"I will give you bony fingers...all five of them...right across your bare bottom," Wysteria threatened.

Ibrehem choked on his soup.

Wysteria pointed a finger at Ibrehem. "And do not think I cannot take you on as well."

Ibrehem raised his hands in surrender, stifling a smile. "I have no doubt, dear healer."

Wysteria glared back at Rule. "If you have come here to frighten that young woman, you can just leave now."

Rule arched a brow. "Then she has told you..."

"About your threat of banishment?" Wysteria said. "Aye, she has told me. And I am here to tell you I will not allow it."

Rule's face reddened. "She has come to finish what Meridith started."

"And what was that?" Wysteria challenged.

"Meridith killed my mother, and Meav has come to kill me," Rule explained.

"Is that what you really believe?" Wysteria said.

"Aye, 'tis," Rule stated flatly.

"Then you have grizzle for brains," Wysteria snapped.

"I could have told you that," Ibrehem chimed in.

Both of them glared at Ibrehem and simultaneously told him to *shut his mouth*.

"Fine...I will just sit here and eat my soup without another word," Ibrehem muttered.

"Or have it dumped over your head," Rule warned.

Wysteria pointed to a chair. "Sit, Rule, and tell me why you believe Meridith killed your mother."

Rule hesitated.

"Sit!" Wysteria demanded sharply.

Rule roughly pulled out a chair from the table and plopped down; folding his arms across his chest. "I have come to speak to Meav." He craned his neck to look out the back window. "Is she out on the terrace?"

"Nay, Meav is having tea with Zailia, so you are stuck talking to me," Wysteria said.

Rule stood. "I will just go to Tobiah's cottage and have this out with Meav there."

157

Wysteria reached out and grabbed Rule by the front of the tunic. "You will not!" She again pointed to the chair. "Sit!"

Reluctantly he obeyed.

Wysteria took a deep, calming breath before she asked the question again. "Now, why do you believe Meridith killed your mother?"

Rule shut his eyes, reaching deep within and pulled to the surface the memory of the day his mother had died. He could see himself as a small boy walking into his mother's room. Oneida lie still and pale upon the bed. "He stood over her...my father...weeping as she lay lifeless." Slowly Rule had reached out to caress her hand, only to quickly jerk away. "Her flesh was ice cold to the touch."

"Who else was in the room," Wysteria queried.

Rule's mouth curled with disdain. "Devora."

He could see her as clear as if she stood before him now...her hand lovingly stroking his father's arm and consoling him. *"Tis Meridith who has done this...this is all her fault,"* Devora had said.

Rule's eyes shot open. "Devora accused Meridith for Mother's death...and my father agreed."

"Your father agreed because Devora bewitched him," Wysteria clarified. "You are a man now, Rule. You understand the wiles of a woman."

"Aye, I do," he mumbled, remembering Meav's soft touch during the vision quest they had shared, and all that her touch had made him feel.

"Devora is beautiful, clever, and a witch. The combination is deadly. So you can understand why your father had believed what she told him," Wysteria concluded.

Rule frowned. "Then who *did* kill my mother?"

"Oneida had been very ill, but 'twas Devora who helped her breath her last," Wysteria said.

Rule suddenly felt weak in the face of his anger. "Devora," he whispered.

"Aye, so she could have your father for herself and become queen." Gently Wysteria touched Rule's arm. "I knew what she had done and had tried to tell the king. But he would not listen. Instead he blamed Meridith and had her sent adrift to die naked at sea. Shortly after

Devora convinced Stefan I was no longer needed to care for you and had me banished from the castle."

"Then she contrived for me to be sent away to school," Rule added.

"Aye, and in that way she had the king all to herself...no witnesses present to see how she slowly poisoned him each day. And when you returned home and confronted her with Stefan's death, she put a spell on you," Wysteria finished.

Rule covered his face with his hands. "How could I have been so blind?"

Wysteria tenderly stroked his head. "'Twas not your fault, my lord. You were just a wee lad, who admired and looked up to your father. You would have believed anything he told you."

Rule looked up at Wysteria with moist eyes. "Then Meridith was innocent?"

Wysteria nodded slowly. "Meridith would never hurt or betray her queen. She loved Oneida with all her heart."

Rule nearly choked on his words. "And Meav...what about Meav...how does she fit into all this?"

Wysteria looked deep into Rule's sad eyes. "Meav is here to fulfill the Prophecy."

Rule's heart pounded in his chest. "What Prophecy?"

Wysteria made her way to a cupboard and pulled from the shelf the medicine book made of cornhusks and palm leaves. She walked back to the table and placed the old volume in front of Rule. "This spell journal was left to me by my grandfather. Within the pages of this book the Prophecy of Keronia is written."

Rule ran a finger over the worn cover. "You and Devora shared the same grandfather. She would also know of the Prophecy."

"Nay, only I can read the ancient script." Wysteria opened the book and carefully turned several of the yellowed pages before stopping. Clearing her throat, she began to read the foreign handwriting: *"Constella Lo glowena timenta coupla*...a star shall shine on the hour of their meeting for all is not doomed, dear Keronians."

Rule quickly interrupted. "This...this thing that has happened to me...to my family...was foretold?"

"Aye, many years ago," Wysteria said. She returned

to her reading. "The one who steps upon the crescent moon, with hair like fire and eyes like the sea will arrive in the night; tattered and worn, hungry and scared..."

Again Rule interrupted. "Meav...the Prophecy is describing Meav...she steps upon the crescent moon...'tis the birthmark beneath her right foot. And she has hair like fire and eyes like the sea." He swallowed hard. "The rest...how she arrived, how she looked when I found her...it all fits."

"Read on dear healer," Ibrehem urged.

Wysteria continued to read. "...and she will be innocent of her own powers; of the blood that runs through her veins. Only she...with the same blood as the evil one...can undo what the evil one has done."

"The same blood...the evil one..." Rule's mouth twisted with anger. "Devora," he spat.

"Aye, Devora," Wysteria repeated softly. She searched Rule's tormented face. "There is more, my lord."

Rule gave a taut nod. "Continue reading."

Wysteria translated further. "Only she...with love of her own accord and that of a true heart...can save the Highest Son."

Rule closed his eyes in agony. "'Tis with her love she will save me...only I have pushed her away with my mistrust. I have given her no reason to have a true heart for the Highest Son."

"If you give me a chance to complete the Prophecy you will see all is not lost," Wysteria said.

Rule opened his eyes slowly. "Finish then."

"Only His Majesty's love from his own accord in return will then break the curse and Keronia will be rid of the one with the evil heart. Elders of the isle, teach the fire-haired maiden well, how to use the gifts of her ancestors. In turn, she will save your rule," Wysteria concluded.

Rule felt his heart jump within. "I, in turn, must love her of my own accord?"

"Aye, you must," Wysteria said.

"Do you, my lord?" Ibrehem questioned eagerly.

Rule sat silent for a moment, his thoughts returning to the time they shared the vision quest. Never had his heart felt so complete, so happy. "Aye, I do," he finally admitted.

Ibrehem smiled broadly. "Well, then...half the battle is already won."

Rule pointed to the foreign script. "The powers spoken of...the gifts of her ancestors...what is that about?"

"As an elder of the isle I have been mentoring Meav as to what lies deep within her spirit...teaching her to overcome her sorrows and pull from them courage," Wysteria explained. "She blames herself for her family's death, thinks of herself as a coward because she fled her homeland and left her folks to die."

"And you as an elder can help her find her power, restore her bravery?" Rule said.

Wysteria nodded. "She slowly has come to grips with what happened in Dublin, and is eager to see the Prophecy fulfilled. 'Tis the reason I took her to the temple, and 'tis why she met you in the vision quest...to find the strength and ability to save you."

Rule combed his fingers through his hair. "And I blocked her attempt by mistrusting her motives and threatening to banish her from Keronia."

Wysteria folded her arms across her chest. "Well, your actions did not help your cause, but for what 'tis worth, I believe Meav has fallen in love with you in spite of your pigheadedness."

Ibrehem stifled a laugh.

"Did she speak of her feelings for me?" Rule asked hopefully.

"Nay, not in so many words," Wysteria said.

"Then how do you know she has fallen in love with me?" Rule demanded.

Wysteria arched a brow. "Trust me on this one."

Rule stood suddenly and walked over to the window, looking out at the cobblestone terrace where he first spoke to Meav. Even then, in those first moments, she had stirred his senses, filled him with desire and hope. Was he to lose, not only the chance to rid himself of the curse, but also happiness...and the opportunity to finally experience the love and passion he nightly craved? "I must hear how you have come to your conclusions."

Wysteria joined him by the window. "'Tis your lack of trust that has gotten you where you are now, my lord."

Rule frowned. "Tell me what you know, old woman."

Wysteria shook her head. "Will you never learn?"

"Speak," Rule demanded.

"After the vision quest Meav could not sleep. I heard her weeping, calling out your name."

Rule's frown deepened. "Perhaps she just feared I would carry out my threat."

"Aye...that could be the case...but then I would have seen fear in her eyes, not hurt. The crestfallen expression on that young girl's face was that of a woman in love who believed she had lost the chance to win her man's heart," Wysteria said.

Rule quickly turned to look at the elder. "Never have you led me astray, dare I hope you speak the truth?"

Ibrehem stood and made his way to the pair. "There is always a way to find out for yourself, my lord." He playfully slapped Rule on the back. "You did come here to talk to Meav...I would say sticking to that plan of action would be your first wise move."

"Ibrehem is right," Wysteria chimed in. "I am to fetch Meav at Tobiah's before dark...you go in my place. In that way you can talk with her on the stroll back here."

Rule shook his head. "She might believe I have hunted her down to banish her."

"Then I will come along," Ibrehem offered.

Rule turned to look at his friend. "Aye, to charm the pants off her, no doubt."

Ibrehem threw his head back and laughed. "Possessive of her already, huh?" He slapped Rule on the back again. "Not to worry, my lord. 'Tis Zailia I wish to charm, not your Meav. I will only be along to soften your arrival, than I will stay behind to talk to my own woman about the future." Ibrehem turned to Wysteria. "There is still some time until dark...perhaps I can talk you into filling a second bowl of soup before we journey to Tobiah's cottage?"

At that moment Titiana flew through the window, landing clumsily on the sill. "You will not find Meav at Tobiah's," she said breathlessly. "In fact, you will not find Zailia, or Tobiah as well. They are all gone!"

Rule suddenly felt a cold chill creep down his spine. He moved forward and scooped up the pixie into the palm of his hand. "Gone...gone where?"

"To the castle," Titiana said with a shaky voice. "Devora's guards have captured them...captured them all!"

Chapter Fifteen

Rule could feel his stomach churn. "Are you sure of what you are saying?"

Titiana sucked in her breath. "I am quite sure, my lord. With my own two eyes I watched the sentry, Shell, and two other guards bind their hands and march them to a doom I do not want to think about."

"Damnation!" Rule shouted, placing the pixie down on the table. "Again Devora's evil prevails." He turned toward Ibrehem. "This time she must be stopped."

Ibrehem made his way to the door. "I will round up the men and together we will devise a rescue plan."

Rule followed. "Aye, I am right behind you."

Ibrehem halted Rule with a raised hand. "'Tis not wise for you to attempt coming along, my lord."

Rule's frown deeply creased his brow. "And why is that, my friend?"

Ibrehem nervously moistened his lips. "The curse...your life."

"Have you not heard anything Wysteria has said?" Rule snapped. "My love for Meav, and her love for me has dissolved the spell."

Wysteria smiled. "Then you trust my words...believe Meav's heart is yours?"

"Aye, dear healer, I do," Rule answered in a softer tone.

"But we cannot be sure...you have not spoken to Meav as of yet," Ibrehem protested. "And you suddenly falling down dead 'tisn't something I am willing to chance."

"But I am willing to chance it," Rule countered. "Besides, if I have to live without Meav in my life, I would rather be dead."

"My lord, will you not listen to reason?" Ibrehem pleaded.

"Ibrehem, can anything stop you at this moment from

164

running to Zailia's aid?" Rule asked.

"Nay, nothing," Ibrehem admitted.

"Then there is nothing more to discuss." Rule rushed to the door and threw it open. "Come...we have wasted enough time as 'tis."

Ibrehem nodded in agreement. "I am at your heels, my lord."

As soon as Wysteria closed the door behind them she went to her spell book. Turning to Titiana, who still sat in wide-eyed fright on the table, Wysteria spoke with certainty. "This time my sister will reckon with a force she did not expect, the power of love. But it never hurts to have reinforcement."

Titiana slowly stood on wobbly legs. "What is your plan, dear healer?"

Wysteria turned the pages of the book. "I will conjure up a protection spell, one that will guard and guide Rule and his men to victory."

Titiana moved closer to Wysteria. "How can I help?"

"The spell calls for Pixie Powder," Wysteria said. "Will you share some of yours for the cause?"

Titiana smiled broadly. "Aye, dear healer...all that you need."

****

Neteru had summoned her apprentices. As they stood before her with silent patience, the high priestess chose her words carefully. "The day I have been dreading has arrived. The young maiden Meav, Tobiah and Zailia have all been taken by Devora."

One apprentice gasped. "The witch has found out then, that two are related to you?"

Neteru nodded sadly. "I am sure of it."

The other apprentice swallowed hard. "How have you come by this news?"

"Wysteria sent Titiana with a message," Neteru said.

The apprentice's eyes widened with horror.

Neteru felt her heart beating rapidly within her chest. "I knew things were not as they should be...I heard it in the wind, smelt it in the air. Titiana just confirmed what I had already felt." She squared her shoulders. "We must help Rule now...the time has come for him to fulfill what is his destiny."

"How can we help Rule, priestess?" one apprentice asked.

Neteru extended a hand to each woman. "Come with me and I will show you."

****

The commotion in the great hall had brought Devora from her chamber. Standing at the top of the staircase she gazed down at the prisoners. "Well, well, my guests have arrived."

Meav turned to look up the stairs at Devora. "What do you want with us, Devora?"

Devora was taken aback by her first sight of the maiden with the fiery curls. There was only one other that had such hair, and eyes as blue as the sea...Meridith.

"Nay...it cannot be," Devora whispered to herself. Slowly her shaky legs took her down the carpeted steps until she stood before Meav. "Do my eyes deceive me?"

Meav moved closer to Devora. "What is it you think you see?"

Devora swallowed hard. "Meridith...is it you?"

Meav defiantly raised her chin. "Nay, not Meridith, but I have been told often I bear a striking resemblance to her."

Devora's knees gave out from under her. Quickly she sat down on a step. "How...how can that be?"

Meav glared down at her evil aunt. "Meridith is me mother."

Devora looked up at Meav. "Meridith...is...alive?"

Meav's eyes clouded with hatred. "Nay, she died in childbirth."

Devora stood, her mouth twisting with annoyance. "Why have you come to Keronia?"

"'Twas the winds of fate that brought me...to undo what you have done," Meav said. "Shocking sometimes how things have a way of coming back."

Devora's face reddened with her rage. "And you think you can avenge your mother?"

Meav squared her shoulders. "Aye."

Devora threw her head back and laughed. "Then you will die trying." She turned to Carson. "Take them to the torture chamber and chain them to the wall."

Carson's eyes grew wide with wicked delight. "Do you

want them stripped and beaten, Your Majesty?"

Meav stood boldly in front of her evil aunt.

"Nay," Devora finally said. "I want the pleasure of cracking the whip this time. Leave them clothed, but douse them with cold water." She laughed wickedly. "I want their flesh cooled to the bone for the heating to come." She glared back at Meav. "Let the rats have their fun with them for now."

Carson bowed. "As you wish, my queen."

Shell waited until the two guards had taken the prisoners away before he moved to Devora's side. Tenderly he took her hand, turning it over and kissing the palm. "You are trembling." He searched her face. "What troubles you?"

Devora looked away. "Go...leave me...I am tired and need rest."

Shell cupped her chin, forcing her to look at him. "I will not be so easily dismissed."

Devora's eyes blazed with anger. "Could it be you would like to join my guests?"

The muscles at Shell's jaw throbbed. "Who is Meridith?"

"None of this is any of your business," Devora snapped.

Shell pulled her close, both hands buried in the thickness of her dark hair. "What is my business?"

She moistened her lips slowly. "To guard this keep, and on the nights I request your presence, to please my flesh."

Shell's left brow raised a fraction. "Aha, let me get this straight...'tis my business to caress your rosy tits...suck them, bite them...until they are round and hard."

Devora squirmed in his arms. "Let me go."

"Then lay you upon the bed, spread you wide and lick you, play with you, penetrate you," he whispered in her ear.

Devora could feel her loins grow wet. "Stop it!"

Shell dug his fingers into her scalp. "But to ask why 'tis you look as though you have seen a ghost...is not my business?"

Devora gritted her teeth. "I order you to remove your

167

hands from my hair."

Shell arched a brow. "As you wish, my queen." His hands traveled down her back and to her buttocks. He squeezed each rounded cheek. "Is that more to your liking?"

Devora stared wordlessly into his eyes, her heart pounding. He was so disturbing to her in every way...and he knew it. "Release me immediately."

He tightened his hold. "Nay...not until you tell—"

"There is nothing to tell," she said.

Shell moved his face closer. "Who is Meridith?"

Even though her anger raged, Devora could not deny the spark of excitement she felt as his fingers caressed her backside. "Meridith is...was...my sister."

Shell's voice held a huskier tone. "And what happened to her?"

"She killed Queen Oneida and the king banished her from the island," Devora lied.

Shell moved his eyes boldly over her face. "I overheard the young maiden say Meridith was her mother?"

Devora spoke with light bitterness. "You overheard correct."

"Is this why you fear her?"

Devora frowned. "I fear no one, do you understand...no one." She placed her hands upon the sentry's muscular chest and pushed away. "Now, I demand you free me this moment."

Shell smiled sardonically. "Very well." He released his hold. "You do not look well; perhaps you should get some rest before you pay a visit to your guests."

Devora quickly grabbed for the banister to keep from falling backward. "I am fine, never felt better...and by sunset I will have thoroughly enjoyed eliminating Keronia of them all."

"Until tonight then." Shell bowed politely. "Have a good afternoon, Your Majesty."

Devora watched him leave, her stomach tied in knots, her hands shaking, and a sudden fatigue filling her. Slowly she made her way back up to her chamber.

Once inside the confines of her room she made her way to the mirror. With the tip of a finger Devora traced the thin blue veins that had suddenly lined her neck. Dark circles were etched beneath her eyes. Shell was right, she did look tired.

Quickly she went to the wardrobe and unlocked the secret compartment. Because Shell had been with her most of the morning, she had not been able to take a sip of the *youth elixir;* putting it off for later.

Devora pulled out the velvet pouch and removed the vial, then closed her eyes and drank the sweet flavored potion, allowing its healing properties to slip down her throat...make her young again. She would definitely have to brew more of the cherished treasure...the bottle was nearly empty.

****

Zailia's garments, cold and wet, clung to her flesh. She sat shackled to the wall, with hands bound above her head. The tight restraints cut through her wrists. The chains hung low, close to the stone floor, so she was unable to stand. This made the soaked clothes feel even colder. Turning her head to the left, she could see her father. Chained by his one arm, Tobiah sat trembling, his eyes shut, his face contorted with pain.

"Papa," she choked out. "Can you hear me?"

Tobiah coughed and wheezed for several seconds before he could answer his daughter. "Aye...I can."

"'Tis so cold...I fear for you...Papa." She stuck her leg out, her toes just able to reach his leg. Up and down she ran her foot. "If I could just warm you."

Slowly Tobiah turned to look at her, a mixture of sadness and fear clouding his eyes. "It matters not what Devora has in store for me...but to think of even one hair on your head harmed..."

"Being wet and cold like this is not good for you, Papa."

"Zailia, I am a warrior. 'Twould take more than this to kill me," he tried to reassure her.

Zailia knew this was not true. Her father had been ailing for months and the treatment he now endured would definitely harm him. With resentment in her heart she glared over at Meav. "This is all your fault."

"Zailia, hush," Tobiah snapped.

Zailia met her father's red-rimmed eyes. "I will not

hush...all this has something to do with her...and her mother, Meridith." Zailia pulled her legs beneath her. "I overheard her conversation with Devora." Again Zailia looked over at Meav. "Why is Devora so concerned about your mother?"

Meav's wet hair clung to her eyes and mouth. Tossing her head from side to side she managed to clear her view. "Me mother is Devora's sister...the very sister she accused of killing the previous queen. Truth be told, Oneida died by Devora's hand."

Zailia narrowed her eyes. "So Devora thinks you have come to avenge your mother's death?"

"Aye...and I have...along with saving Rule and the rest of Keronia."

Zailia laughed sardonically. "And how do you propose on doing that?"

Tobiah rested his head back against the wall. "Have faith, daughter. Remember the legend of the leprechaun?"

Zailia's heart skipped a beat. "Aye...I do."

Meav frowned. "I know nothing of the legend."

Tobiah cleared his throat and quickly explained the tale to Meav. When finished he turned his eyes to Zailia. "And 'tis our fault, not Meav's, that we are chained to these walls."

Zailia frowned. "How is it our fault?"

"I spoke of the legend not long ago to you and Ibrehem...Devora's spies are everywhere. I have no doubt in my mind one of them overheard the tale, as well as our plan to escape to the temple, and retold all they learned to the queen. Devora, knowing she inherited the throne by her diabolical ways, began to fear Meav; thus using you to plot Meav's death." Tobiah sighed. "We owe her an apology."

Zailia turned sad eyes toward Meav. "I am sorry, Meav.

"There is no apology needed...we are in this together," Meav said.

Zailia's eyes grew teary. "What will happen to us now?"

"I sent Titiana for Rule...he will come...I know he will," Meav said.

Zailia tried to wiggle her fingers, but they were

numb. "Rule will die if he comes anywhere near the castle, 'tis the way of Devora's curse."

Meav stayed silent. She was not sure of the leprechaun fable, but she was certain of the Prophecy. Love will break the curse...her love of her own accord for Rule and his love for her. *But did he love her?* In truth, he had thought she had come to kill him and wanted her banished from Keronia. Meav bit her bottom lip. Would her love be enough to keep Rule alive? It had to be, for his sake...for their sake...for Keronia.

"Rule will come, and he will not die," Meav blurted out. She would not let him die.

Zailia shivered. "I pray you are right."

Meav took a deep breath...so did she!

****

Rule sent Ibrehem to gather the men while he took a moment to sit silently in his cave to meditate. Before warring, a warrior had to ready himself...clear his mind and focus only on the details of the battle. One quick swipe of the enemy's sword could be the end. A soldier had to be careful, alert, and his every move precise if he was to ride the fight to victory.

Rule closed his eyes and took a cleansing breath. 'Twasn't easy to rid his mind of the image of Meav at Devora's mercy, but essential if he was to save her. It had been so long since he was in combat...held a sword...led a mission.

"You will do fine, strong warrior," came a soft voice.

Rule quickly opened his eyes to see Neteru and the two apprentices standing before him...holding in their arms weapons and armor.

Neteru nodded to each of her helpers, and simultaneously the women placed the items at Rule's feet.

Rule looked down at the military garb, then up at the priestess. "How have you come by these things?"

Neteru smiled warmly. "They belonged to your great, great-grandfather, Thaddeus Ruleton." Neteru folded her hands before her. "Your mother, before her death, summoned me one night and asked me to save for you the gear that had been passed down in her family from generation to generation. She knew one day you would wage a battle that would save Keronia."

Rule's eyes widened. "She, too, knew what was to come?"

"Aye, 'twas her gift," Neteru said. She reached out a hand to Rule. "Now stand, brave soldier, and let us dress you for combat."

The apprentices slipped off Rule's linen tunic, replacing it with one made out of thick leather. Next, his sandals were removed and leather boots were placed upon his feet. A pair of steel greaves, made with an articulated knee piece for extra protection, was fashioned over the boots to protect his lower legs.

The steel vam braces were nicely formed and lined with leather. The women strapped the arm guards onto his inner arm, accompanied by a pair of mail gauntlets. They were cupped with steel all around the cuffs to protect his hands, wrists, and lower arms from sword slashes or draw cuts.

Neteru strapped on the leather Baldric across Rule's massive chest, the sheath for a sword hanging behind his right shoulder. "Your mother is with you now, my lord. Her spirit will guide and protect you."

Rule admired the armor he was being dressed in, feeling close to his mother and all those that wore the suit into previous battles. "I feel her within me," he whispered.

Neteru first handed Rule the Schiavona. The basket protecting his hand and wrist was made of steel, and the *cat's head* pommel of brass. It was fitted with a double-edged blade made for utilizing the cut as the main combat tactic.

Neteru brought Rules attention to the pearl encrusted handle. "Each pearl honors the tears of battle," she explained. "And many were shed, for those who died; for those who were saved."

Next the priestess gave Rule a domed buckler. It was smaller than a full sized shield and easier to use, enabling the warrior to move around quickly. The leather straps attached to the dome allowed for easy handling.

"A swordsman armed with a Schiavona and buckler is hard to stand against," Neteru said.

One of the apprentices placed upon Rule's head the leather war helmet. "Go with caution, my lord," she whispered.

172

Rule's eyes blazed with the supremacy he felt surging through him. "'Tis power I need, woman...only power."

Neteru frowned. "At this moment I see your stubbornness as being more of a challenge than the fight ahead, Rule."

Rule instantly bowed his head. "Forgive me, Priestess."

"A warrior to be proud of is one who knows humility," Neteru warned.

"I will remember," Rule said softly.

Neteru nodded tautly. "Now, one last thing...a silver ear cuff; the mark of a Keronian warrior." She placed the silver band around Rule's ear and stood back. "'Tis complete. May our Divine Maker be with you."

Just as silently as the three women arrived, they were gone.

Rule stood tall in his war garments. He had not tasted the uncertainties of war in a long time. The smell of death was in the air. Which one of them would fall this day? Rule heard the war cry of his comrades, and made his way out of the cave.

Rule smiled at his men. They stood ready to follow his command, armed with daggers, battle axes and rapiers hanging from leather axe holders and frogs belted around their waists.

Ibrehem stood at the head of the unit; his leather belt adorned with steel hardware was angled properly on his hips and sheathed his Schiavona. He eyed Rule's garb with astonishment. "How is it you are dressed in this armor?"

"Neteru had saved it for me...'twas my great, great-grandfather's," Rule quickly explained.

Ibrehem threw down Rule's old war equipment that he had brought for his leader to wear. "Then you will not need these." He bowed. "My lord, we listen sharply to your strategy and respectfully for your command."

Rule pulled his Schiavona from his sheath and raised it high. "Death to our foe!"

The men raised their weapons and answered in unison. "We will follow you to death and beyond!"

"To the castle!" Rule commanded.

****

Devora waited for Carson, her legs felt weak, and her eyes blurry. What had come over her? Grant the fact she had taken the youth potion later in the day than usual, but she had done the same a few times before and had never become ill. Why was she suddenly experiencing such effects now?

"Meridith," she whispered. Aye...it made sense...Meridith's daughter was in the castle...the blood of her sister had poisoned Devora's surroundings...cursed the air she breathed.

The instant Carson knocked on the queen's door, it flew open. He bowed respectively. "You called for me, my queen?"

"I want the red-haired woman brought to me immediately," Devora hissed.

Carson bowed again. "As you wish, Your Majesty." He turned to leave, and then hesitated.

Devora frowned. "Have I not made myself clear?"

Carson's eyes twinkled mischievously. "I thought you wanted to whip them yourself."

"I have decided to first interrogate the wench before beating her," Devora said.

"And what of the others, my queen?"

Devora casually waved a hand in the air. "Do what you like with them."

Carson's toothless grin spread across his face. "Aye, my queen."

****

The door creaked open and three sentries walked into the torture chamber. Meav recognized Carson and Wesley, but not the third.

"Bring the one with the fiery hair to the queen," Carson demanded of Wesley.

Wesley made his way to Meav, unlocked her wrists from the wall's shackles, then tied her hands behind her back.

Fear gripped Meav. "What about the others?" she whispered to the young sentry.

Wesley's eyes saddened. "They are to remain with Carson."

Meav gasped. "Nay."

Wesley quickly placed a finger over Meav's lips.

174

"There is nothing you can do for them." He pulled Meav to her feet.

Her knees buckled and she fell against the young guard.

Wesley caught her, and walked her out of the chamber.

Looking up into his eyes Meav pleaded. "Please, you have to help them."

Wesley quickly turned away. "I cannot."

Meav mustered her strength and pulled away from him. "Nay, I will not leave them."

"Please do not force me to hurt you, lass," Wesley said, grabbing Meav by the arm and dragging her with him to the queen's chamber. "There is nothing either of us can do for your friends." He tightened his grip. "Be concerned with your own fate."

"How can you stand by and not do something to help them?"

"What am I but one lone man among many?" Wesley said. "If I spoke my mind, tried to stop them, all I would manage to do is join the prisoners."

****

Carson leered down at Zailia. "After our walk to the castle, I have been thinking about you...wondering what you look like beneath your clothes." He wiped a hand across his moist mouth. "I think I have a craving for something different today."

Tobiah saw the blood drain from his daughter's face. "Leave her alone, you mangy dog," he choked out, despising the condition of his aged body more at this moment than ever before. In his youth he had been a formidable warrior. With one blow he could have felled the rogue that now threatened his daughter.

Carson's tone was mocking. "Well, how heartwarming...daddy is worried for his little girl."

"What do you want done with the old man?" one of the sentries asked.

"Strip and beat him," Carson commanded.

"Nay...please...I beg of you," Zailia cried.

Carson's laugh rippled through the underground chamber. "Oh, you will be begging me, but not for your father's sake." He unlocked Zailia's hands and roughly

175

tied them behind her before dragging her by the hair out the door.

"Where...where are you taking her?" Tobiah asked, before his chest tightened and he was consumed by a coughing fit.

Carson turned around, a devilish glint in his eyes. "To the rack, where she will first be spread naked for my pleasure, then stretched to death."

Tobiah lurched forward. "Nay...nay! You stinking son of a bitch!"

The third sentry reached for the club hanging from his waist belt and struck Tobiah over the head.

Zailia screaming his name was the last thing Tobiah heard before losing consciousness.

Chapter Sixteen

Wesley tied Meav to a chair and left her in the room with Devora. Hatred seethed from Meav's soul. "You are me mother's sister, yet you are nothing like her."

Devora's ruby lips curled in disdain. "And glad I am of that." She turned away and poured herself a glass of brandy. "Meridith...sweet, innocent, Meridith," her tone was mocking. "Everyone loved her, all the men admired her. And Oneida favored her."

Meav spoke curtly. "Is that why you hated her?"

Devora turned to face her niece. "'Twas part of it...the other part was that with my sister's tender care, Oneida would have probably lived on for many more years." She moved closer to Meav. "Rule would then have been too old to send away."

Meav narrowed her eyes. "And of course he would have watched out for his father's interests."

"True...and the throne would then have been lost to me." Devora said.

Meav forced her voice to remain calm. "So, instead you lost your soul and anything else that might have made you human."

Devora threw her head back and laughed. "And what is so wonderful about being human?" She glared at her niece. "Humans grow old, and die."

Meav lifted her chin, meeting Devora's icy gaze. "You are already dead...your black heart is rotting now within you."

Again Devora's laugh rippled through the room. "You know nothing of what you speak."

"I know about the Prophecy and what fate awaits you, Devora."

Devora's voice rose in surprise. "What Prophecy?"

"The one in Wysteria's spell book, given to her by her grandfather...and it tells of me coming to the isle." Meav squared her shoulders. "Little did you know that your evil ways were what made the predictions come to pass." Meav smirked. "And here, all along you thought you were in control."

Devora gritted her teeth. "I am in control."

Meav answered in a rush of words. "Nay, you are nothing but a pawn...used by fate to bring the true power into command."

Devora clenched her fists to her sides. "Rule...you speak of Rule?"

"Aye, he is the rightful heir to the throne."

Devora's vexation fueled the venom in her voice. "Rule will die if he comes anywhere near this castle."

"You could not be more wrong," Meav stated firmly.

Devora's eyes blazed. "How dare you contradict the throne."

"'Tis the truth...Rule will not die. Your spell has been broken, and he is on his way to rip you to shreds."

Devora features twisted with anger. "Rule will not make it out of the jungle, because nothing can break the curse."

"Aye, there is one thing," Meav responded sharply.

"Wesley," Devora screeched.

Immediately the door opened. "Aye, my queen."

"Take this little bitch to the torture chamber and have Carson split her in half, than feed her remains to the wild dogs."

Wesley pulled Meav to her feet.

"Love, Devora." The conviction of her words filled Meav with assurance and renewed hope. She felt Rule nearby and knew he would come. "'Tis the power of love that has broken the spell and there is nothing you can do about it."

"Get her out of here," Devora screamed.

"Me true love for Rule and his for me," Meav went on as Wesley dragged her to the door. "'Tis more powerful than any of your black magic."

Devora blocked her ears with the palms of her hands. "Nay...'tis not true."

"And the love I have for Rule cannot die with me own death...because true love transcends throughout all dimensions. Killing me will not stop Rule from killing you and everyone else in this castle," Meav shouted. "Your reign is through, Devora!"

Wesley forced her out into the hall.

Devora ran to the door and slammed it shut.

Wesley put his hand over Meav's mouth and dragged her into a nearby room. "Hush, lass, do you crave a death wish?'

Meav squirmed in his grasp.

"Listen, I think I can help you," he whispered. "Will you keep your mouth silent if I remove my hand?"

Meav nodded.

Wesley slowly took his hand away from her mouth and spun her around to look at him. "I overheard your conversation with the queen. This Prophecy...'tis true?"

Meav looked deep into the young sentry's eyes. "Aye, 'tis."

"Then Rule and his military are on their way?" Wesley said.

"They are, and they will overtake this castle. Devora and all that did her evil will perish."

Wesley licked his lips. "I am not one of her evil men."

Meav smiled warmly. "I know you are not. I saw how you tried to help Zailia on the way here."

"I only wish I could have done more," Wesley admitted.

"If you help us now, sir, Rule will spare your life...I will see to it that he does."

Wesley nodded. "I will bring you to the torture chamber through the outside exit...should any of the other sentries we meet on the way question me, I will tell them Devora ordered you be tied and stretched. 'Tis a torment she has inflicted before, so the guards should not stop us."

Meav shuttered. "Then what?"

"Then I will untie your hands and you must run...run for your life," Wesley instructed.

Meav frowned. "What about Zailia and Tobiah?"

Wesley sighed. "I will do what I can to help them...if 'tis not already too late."

Meav had run before for the sake of her own hide, and regretted leaving her family behind to suffer the consequences. She would not take the coward's way out again. "Nay, I will not leave them behind."

Wesley ran a hand through his hair. "I cannot

guarantee I can save them, but at least you will be safe."

Meav stubbornly stuck out her chin. "I will not leave them."

Wesley sighed, exasperated. Quickly he turned her around and unbound her hands." I know a quick and secret way to where the others are being held."

Meav turned to face him, laying a hand on his arm. "Thank you, sir. Your bravery will not go forgotten."

"Neither will yours, lass," he said, leading the way to the torture chamber.

****

Devora's body trembled all over, her legs felt weak. Slowly she stretched out her hands in front of her and examined them. Her fingers began to look gnarled, her red nails splitting.

"Nay, this cannot be," she whispered, panic rising to choke her. Only one sip of the elixir was usually needed daily. Meav's presence must somehow be stopping the magic. Perhaps another swig would help, than she would be her vibrant self again and could summon Shell to prepare the men for battle.

Devora hurried to where she kept the youth potion and quickly pulled the glass vial from its velvet pouch. Only a drop remained.

Devora rushed through the chamber and into the adjoining room. Reaching up, she pulled at the candle sconce, thus opening the wall revealing two secret staircases. One led to the garden and the other to the west end of the dungeon, where her precious blue flowers grew.

With trembling hands she lit the first wall torch and carefully descended the stairs. The joints in her knees and hips throbbed with pain. She wished the passageway was not so steep and narrow, as her vision suddenly did not seem as acute. Reaching the room where her herbs grew, Devora gasped in horror. Not one of the flowers bloomed. All of them lay wilted, their beautiful petals a soggy brown instead of bright blue.

"Nay...nay!" she shrieked, collapsing to her knees. With trembling hands she picked up one of the dead herbs and crushed it to her lips. Desperately she tried to siphon from the withered petals the nectar of life. The bitter taste stung her tongue. She coughed and gagged, spitting out the remnants.

Crawling on hands and knees, Devora combed the entire length of the dungeon floor, hoping to find a few good plants to boil down into a potion. But none remained.

"Oh, my poor babies," she wailed. "What has happened to you...what will happen to me?"

Devora began to shake at the fearful image of her cat, many years ago, dying of old age in a short time. The animal had turned to bones, and then to dust, right before her eyes.

A chill, black silence surrounded her. Was this how 'twould end...down in a dungeon with the rats?"

"Nay, not here," she whispered. With the last shred of energy she could muster, Devora crawled to the stairs and made her way back to her chamber. As she climbed onto the bed she felt her bladder release...soaking through her beautiful gown and onto the satin sheets. Immediately a horrible stench filled the room.

Pain gnawed at her chest...her breathing labored. She could not feel her arms and legs, close her mouth or her eyes. The evil she had lived flashed before her, overshadowing the good she once was...the childhood she once cherished with Wysteria and Meridith.

"Shell...Shell," she choked out hoarsely.

It was then that Shell appeared, standing over the bed with his eyes widened in horror as to what he saw. "Devora...what is happening."

She could not let him know the truth...the one thing in her life that brought her real happiness, she could not lose now. "'Tis Meav's doings," she lied. "She put a spell on me...believes I had something to do with her mother's banishment." She placed a withered hand on his arm. "And she has led Rule to believe the same. He is on his way to storm the castle."

"I will ready the men for battle," Shell said, making his way to the door.

"Nay, do not leave me," Devora sobbed.

Shell fell on his knees beside the bed. "What then would you have me do?"

"We must leave here...immediately. Take me down the stairs to the garden, we can escape through there and you can bring me to your village in the Jabri Valley. The Shaman...he can help me."

Shell nodded. "Aye, he could counteract the spell; I have seen him do that for others."

Devora felt herself grow weaker. She knew there had been no spell cast upon her, but perhaps the Shaman knew of the little blue flowers. "Hurry, Shell, there is not much time."

Shell quickly removed her wet clothes and dressed her in a long, white nightgown that covered her withering body. Wrapping her fragile form in a quilt he carried her down the hidden staircase and out into the garden.

****

Rule and his men crouched at the edge of the jungle, surveying the castle. Every minute he was made to wait brought him physical pain. But to try and get into the fortress before dark lessened his chances of a victory. Striking at night was always a wiser move.

Rule knew a way to get into the palace through the garden. The secret staircase led right to a room that adjoined the queen's chamber. Devora would be the first to be run through with his sword. Once he had watched her breathe her last breath, he and the men would infiltrate the rest of the keep and take Devora's sentries unexpectedly. His only prayer was that he was not too late to save Meav and the others.

Ibrehem knelt beside Rule. "As my eyes set on the invisible line that ends the jungle, I cannot help but fear I will see my life-long friend and fighting companion die with a step across that border." He sighed heavily. "Can you not let me and the others win this battle for you, my lord?"

Rule turned to look into the concerned eyes of his one and only true friend. "You already know what my answer is to that, Ibrehem."

"Aye, my lord," Ibrehem said resigned, quickly casting a glance toward the castle. "You fully trust her love for you, then?"

Rule followed his gaze, looking out at the place where he had grown up...where he ran and played with his dog Sabre; laughed with his parents and slept in his own bed. He was tired of hiding, tired of living life as a half man, half beast. "Aye, I do."

Ibrehem nodded. "I am happy for you, my lord. And will be right beside you throughout this night."

Rule reached over and patted Ibrehem on the shoulder. "I never doubted you would be anywhere else." He cleared the emotion from his throat. "And I expect you to stand beside me as my witness when I wed the fire-haired maiden."

Ibrehem turned to look back at Rule and swallowed hard. "And I expect the same when I wed my Zailia."

Rule laughed softly. "'Tis about time."

Ibrehem smiled. "What irony is this...that you would trust a woman under such circumstances?" He looked again at the castle. "How much longer now, my lord?"

Rule raised his eyes to the pinkish sky, the last shreds of day coming to a rest. "Tell the men we move in one hour."

Chapter Seventeen

Meav held tightly to Wesley's hand as he led her through the dark corridor and down the steep staircase. Upon nearing the last step Meav heard Zailia scream.

She pulled free from Wesley grasp and rushed toward her friend's voice.

Wesley quickly reached out and pulled her back. "You barging ahead will only spoil the plan to rescue them," he whispered in her ear.

Meav took a deep breath to still her nerves. "What plan do you have, sir?"

"To begin with you must stay out of sight. If Carson or the others see you, hands unbound and walking freely by my side, they will certainly question my loyalty. Then we will all be prisoners," he explained in a low tone. "There must not be a shred of suspicion on their part or else we will all die."

Meav gave a taut nod.

Wesley removed the small dagger hanging from his belt and handed it to Meav.

She looked down at the weapon, turning it over slowly in her trembling hand.

Wesley gently pushed a strand of hair from her face. "Can you bring yourself to use it, lass?"

Meav swallowed hard. "Never have I ever thought of taking a life...not even an animal's." Her grandmamma had tried to teach her to kill a hen for the evening meal. But she would always run away and hide; not even after the poor creature's neck had been broken could she stay and watch it being plucked and butchered. How would she be able to lay this dagger deep into human flesh?

Wesley placed a finger beneath her chin and raised her gaze to his. "I will need your help, lass."

Meav's voice cracked. "I...do not know if I..."

Wesley took her firmly by the shoulders. "'Tis horrid to watch a man breathe his last breath; more so, even,

184

when his life has been snuffed out by the actions of your own hand. This I know to be true from my years of being a soldier. And it never comes easy. But if we are to save your friends a choice has to be made. I cannot do this alone." He shook her lightly. "Are you with me, lass?"

Meav's heart pounded in her ears. "Aye, sir." Quickly she swallowed the nausea rising to choke her. "I am with you...all the way."

****

Pain washed over Zailia's body in hot waves. With hands bound above her head; feet tied and spread apart, she was at the mercy of Carson...Devora's mad man. With each turn of the grind, the rack stretched her flesh over her bones.

Carson's eyes shone with his excitement. He smiled, drool moistening his chin. He moved to the head of the rack and looked down at his victim. "Those big, brown eyes are full of pain and fear." He lowered his face to Zailia's. "I suppose 'tis time for a little pleasure."

Zailia quickly turned her face away from her captor's sour breath.

Carson roughly grabbed her head, returning her gaze upon him. "I have been watching those full tits, stretching and spreading as your arms are pulled, and I am thinking 'tis about time I do a wee bit of investigating...as to how pink the nipples are, how hard, how sweet."

Zailia's breath seemed to have solidified in her throat. "Please...do not do this."

Carson's laugh rumbled deep. "I told you that you would no longer be begging for your father's sake."

With a pang Zailia realized her father had to be near death by now. The thought filled her with sorrow and she could not control the spasmodic trembling within her. "All of you be damned."

"Damned we are for sure," Carson repeated in a husky voice. He removed his dagger from his belt and held it to Zailia's neck. "Let the games begin," he said, cutting loose a button at the neckline of her cotton blouse. "'Tis a game, 'tis. One little button, then another," he said, popping off the second round fastener. "Till the delicious bounty lies in full view of my eyes."

"Having fun, Carson?" Wesley said, entering the

chamber.

Carson glared up at Wesley. "Well, now, I was about to...till you interrupted."

"Sorry, but our dear queen wants a word with you," Wesley said.

Carson twisted his mouth in anger. "Now...this very moment?"

"Aye, that was her orders."

Carson let out a disgusting breath and replaced his dagger in his belt sheath. "'Twas her orders to do as I wish with this bitch and her father...and 'tis what I am doing."

Wesley shrugged. "Well, orders have changed, and if I were you I would not give her any reason to re-direct her venom elsewhere."

Carson nodded in agreement. "Aye, like on me."

"Exactly," Wesley agreed.

Carson looked back down at Zailia. "Sorry, my sweet...will have to leave you here alone for a wee bit while I answer the call of duty." He roughly squeezed her breasts. "Do not miss me too much." He threw his head back and laughed.

Wesley waited until Carson's back was to him before pulling his sword from its sheath and raising it to run the bastard through.

The sound of a weapon being drawn alerted Carson. In one fluid motion he turned on the younger sentry and blocked the attack. With his bare, muscular arms he overpowered Wesley and pushed him down onto the stone floor.

Wesley strained against the brute guardsman, his arms trembling as he tried to hold him off. Together they wrestled with the sword, until Carson's right hand became free and the massive fingers curled into a fist, slamming into Wesley's jaw.

Over and over Carson pummeled Wesley, the younger man's blood staining his knuckles.

Wesley's body went limp.

"Get up, Wesley," Zailia shouted. She knew her only chance lied in Wesley's help.

Carson raised his fist for the kill, but was stopped cold.

Meav drove the dagger deep into Carson's back.

Carson turned slowly around to face her.

Meav covered her mouth with her hands and backed away.

With heavy steps Carson came nearer and nearer.

Zailia screamed again at Wesley. "Get up...get up...help her!"

Wesley shook his head and slowly sat up.

Zailia pulled at her restraints, her heart pounding within the walls of her chest. "He will kill her...help her!"

Meav looked around for something to throw, and found a broken brick. Quickly she bent down to retrieve it, and aimed it at Carson's head.

The giant of a man swayed backwards, but did not lose his footing. Again he came at Meav.

Meav looked for something else to hurl at the sentry as she continued to back away from him. 'Twas then she tripped on a chain link and stumbled.

Carson had his advantage. He lunged forward, landing on top of her...trapping Meav with his massive body, and forcing her arms above her head. "Thought you could stop ole' Carson, hey?" He laughed wickedly. "'Twould take much more than what you have got."

"How about this, Carson." Wesley ran the swine through with his sword. After dragging the large sentry off of Meav, he helped her to her feet. "Are you alright?"

Meav looked up at Wesley's bloodied face. "Are you?"

Wesley wiped his mouth with his sleeve. "Aye."

Meav rushed to Zailia and began to release the holding pin to slacken the ropes. "Thank heavens we got here in time."

Zailia shuddered inwardly. "My father, Meav...do you know what has happened to him?"

"Nay," Meav said, her trembling fingers trying to untie a rope from around Zailia's wrist. "We came to your aid first."

Zailia's stomach clenched in knots. "Then hurry...please...we must find him."

Wesley pulled his dagger from Carson's back, and wiped the blood on the dead man's pant leg. He made his way to Zailia and cut through the ropes. Gently he lifted her from the rack and placed her on her feet.

187

Zailia leaned against him, her legs weak; head spinning.

"Take a moment to steady yourself, lass," Wesley warned.

"I have not a moment to waste, sir," Zailia said.

"You are no good to your father like this," Meav added.

"I have to get to him," she protested, but sat down on the stone floor for a moment to regroup.

Meav looked over at Carson's body and her face paled. She sat down quickly beside Zailia. "Saints preserve us, I have helped in taking a life."

Wesley knelt down before her. "And have saved two others, lass."

Zailia reached over and squeezed her friend's arm. "You are very brave, Meav."

Meav swallowed hard. "I do not feel brave."

Wesley placed a hand on Meav's shoulder. "Ah, but you are, lass. And I need you to stay brave." Wesley looked over at Zailia. "You as well, if we are to help your father."

Zailia nodded and stood. "I am ready." She looked down at Meav, and extended a hand. "Are you, my friend?"

Meav stood. "Ready as I will ever be."

Zailia smiled weakly. "We will both be heroes."

Wesley handed Meav the dagger, and stole Carson's blade for Zailia. "But you are women."

"No where is it written only men can be heroes," Meav said, following Wesley out the door.

****

Rule stepped over the borderline, no longer was he in the safe haven of the jungle. For a long moment he stood, looking up at the dusky sky, waiting to see if he would die.

He did not.

He felt jubilation in spite of the battle that lay ahead of him. The curse had been lifted, Meav's love for him and his for her had dissolved Devora's spell.

His men stood silent behind him, all holding their breaths, hoping against hope for his life to be spared. Slowly Rule turned to face them. With outstretched arms

188

he smiled broadly at the loyal bunch. "'Tis over, the curse is gone."

Silently the men raised their swords above their heads in celebrative cheer.

Ibrehem made his way beside Rule. Brushing a tear from his eye, he slapped his friend on the shoulder. "Welcome back, my lord."

Rule inhaled sharply, letting his first moment of freedom wash over him before he commanded his army into battle. "'Tis good to be back." He looked out amongst the others, and gave them all an encouraging smile. "We will be victorious on this day, and all that belongs to us will once more be ours."

Again the men raised their weapons in a quiet salute.

Rule pointed to the soldiers to his left. "You ten take the front side of the castle; make your way through the entrance. You will work your way up, and meet me in the queen's chamber." He looked over at Ibrehem. "You, my friend will come with me...as well as Bulwark, Olin and Ustin. We will enter the castle through the garden and up the secret staircase. That route will take us to the queen's chamber." He narrowed his eyes. "Take no prisoners."

"What about the rest of us, my lord?" one soldier asked.

"I will have you remaining men surround the perimeter of the castle, in case anyone tries to escape," Rule instructed.

"Aye, my lord," the rest of the men agreed simultaneously.

Rule raised his sword. "May our Divine Maker be with you all...now *charge!*"

****

Zailia cringed, listening to her father's moans. After each crack of the whip, Wesley had to tighten his hold on her arm to keep her from hastening to his aid. "It would be a deadly mistake to leave my side, lass," he cautioned.

He pointed to a secluded corner of the corridor. "The two of you hide there until I come for you," Wesley whispered before making his way into the torture room where Tobiah was being kept.

As he entered the damp chamber, he nearly heaved from the sight of the poor old man's back...bloodied and ripped apart by the beating he was receiving at the hands of Devora's guardsman, Kent. Like Carson, Kent enjoyed doling out punishment. Wesley watched the sentry's face contort with pleasure each time he brought the whip down upon Tobiah's flesh.

"Do you not think he has had enough?" Wesley said coming around to Kent's left side.

"Not if he is still breathing," Kent said, raising the whip another time and cracking it across the old man's back. He briefly glanced at Wesley and frowned. "What the hell happened to your face?"

Wesley wiped his bloody mouth with the back of a hand. "I had a little disagreement with Carson."

Kent struck Tobiah again with the whip. "Yeah, I have had my share of fights with the bugger as well."

Wesley held his rage as he watched Tobiah's body swing back and forth from the impact. "The queen has ordered us all to assemble in the great room, so you will have to finish your duties here, later."

Kent threw down the whip in disgust. "That woman does not know what she wants. With every whim she has we are all made to jump."

Wesley looked around the room. "Best you keep your opinion of our dear queen to yourself. These walls have ears...you never know who is listening." Wesley pointed to Tobiah. "Least you end up like him."

"Aye, 'tis the truth, comrade...and I thank you for keeping my head for me," Kent remarked, his tone somewhat appreciative. He looked over at Tobiah. "No matter, this one will surely have breathed his last by the time I return."

Wesley hoped the sentry was wrong, but truth be told, Tobiah had been badly beaten already; there was not much life left in the aged man. He instantly took pity on the prisoner, and his sweet-faced daughter. The maiden had reminded him of Becka, Wesley's own intended. How he missed her, and his home in the mountains on the family goat farm. If not for the steep tax Devora had laid upon the place, Wesley would be working beside his father now, instead of as an indentured soldier trying to save his land.

Kent made his way toward the door. "'Tis always

something around here, a man's work is never done."

Wesley followed him, feeding into the sentry's gripe. "'Tis long hours for sure you put in Kent, longest of us all, I believe."

"Aye, you said the truth, my friend," Kent agreed.

"After the assembly, why not let me dispose of the old man's remains," Wesley offered.

Kent turned to face Wesley. "I would like that, thought later I might have a chance to steal a few moments with Lorna, the lass who helps the cook. She hardly ever has time off as well." Kent smiled. "Been seducing the wench for quite some time now. Tonight just might be the night I have my way with her." His smile broadened. "A pretty little thing, she is, with ample bosoms and a real yearning for my looks."

Wesley patted the sentry on the shoulder. "Then go...have your chance with the lass...I will take care of the old man."

Kent smiled. "I am beholden to you." He waived his hand aside. "After you."

Wesley shook his head. "I have a few more sentries to notify about the assembly, but you go on ahead. No sense making the queen mad, single you out and keep you from leaving to be with your sweetie."

Kent frowned. "And it would be just my luck too."

Wesley pushed the guard out the door. "Then off with you, man."

As soon as Wesley saw Kent descend the stairway, he went for Zailia and Meav.

The three rushed to Tobiah's side.

Zailia gasped in horror at the sight of her father's bloody body hanging lifeless from one arm. Falling down on her knees she steadied the old man's legs. "Hurry and cut him lose, Wesley."

With trembling hands Wesley severed the rope around Tobiah's wrist and the three of them gently lowered him to the floor.

"Ah me, he is barely breathing," Meav said

Zailia's tears slipped down her cheeks. "We have got to get him out of here."

"Help me hoist him upon my shoulders," Wesley said.

It was then that Kent returned. "Forgot my whip..."

his words stuck in his throat when he spied the women. Frowning, he scratched his head. "Hey what is going on here?" Suddenly he realized what he was witnessing. He reached for his sword and pulled it free from its sheath. "Halt...all of you...in the name of the queen!"

Chapter Eighteen

Rule led the way, Ibrehem behind him; followed by the other three men. Their silent march led them to the garden wall. Not daring to enter through the gate, the soldiers scaled the six foot stone barrier, quickly making their way to the secret entrance.

"There are two staircases beyond this door," Rule explained. "One leads up to the queen's chamber, the other down to the dungeon." He turned to Olin and Ustin. "You two will take the stairs down and have a look at the situation there. If that is where Tobiah and the women are being kept prisoner, I want you to free them and get them out through the way we have entered."

"And if they are not there, my lord?" questioned Ustin.

"Then take the stairs upward and join us with the fight there," Rule commanded.

Both soldiers nodded in agreement.

Rule's eyes narrowed. "And remember...take no prisoners. I want Devora and her men wiped clean from my castle."

"Aye," the men answered in unison.

Rule reached up and placed his fingers around the halo of the decorative angel that adorned the outer wall. With one twist a small opening appeared just below the tiny statue. Rule crouched low and entered the passage. Once inside he drew his sword and made his way up the stairs. Ibrehem and Bulwark followed, readying their weapons, and the last two made their way down to the dungeon.

"The wall torches are lit, this leads me to believe this passage has recently been used," Rule said.

Ibrehem frowned. "Are you thinking what I am, my lord?"

"If you are thinking Devora has fled...then aye," Rule said.

Ibrehem's frown deepened. "But how...how would she know..."

Rule could feel his rage mount. "She is a witch, my friend...probably felt my presence in her evil bones."

"But as far as she is concerned," Ibrehem went on, "she believes her curse would render you dead if you dared to leave the jungle."

A sickening thought struck Rule. "Then she has learned of the Prophecy and her men are ready and waiting for us."

"The only one who could have told her is..." Ibrehem swallowed the rest of his words.

"...Meav," Rule finished for him. He inhaled sharply. "And she would not have revealed that information unless she knew she was about to die."

It was then that the other two men came up from below.

"Nothing in the dungeon but a bunch of dried up flowers," Ustin reported.

"Tons of them are littering the floor," Olin added.

"They could have been taken to the torture chamber," Rule said, hoping against all odds that Meav still lived.

"Can we get there from here, my lord," Bulwark asked.

"Nay...not through here," Rule said, coming to the landing. "Have your weapons ready, men, and brace yourselves against the wall. On the other side of this partition we might have much to contend with."

Reaching out he pulled down on a sconce and the wall in front of him opened. To Rule's surprise, no one waited. Cautiously he entered the room that was once his father's study. Cherry wood bookcases lined the walls, the shelves holding stacks of books Stefan had loved to read. A large writing table sat in the corner. Rule remembered the nights his father sat at the desk, engrossed in the volumes of history, many times reading aloud to Rule about battles and victories.

Guardedly, with his sword and shield drawn, Rule continued through the adjoining area and into the Queen's chamber.

The room was empty...and filled with a stench that could turn the strongest stomach.

The men instantly covered their noses with their hand and began to gag.

"What is that smell?" Ibrehem said.

"Stinks like piss," Bulwark choked.

"Nay...'tis more like death and rot," Olin added, turning away and heaving.

Rule walked over to the queen's bed. With the tip of his sword he pierced the wet dress that lay upon the soaked satin sheets and raised it for the men to see. "'Tis Devora's gown."

"Looks to me like she was scared right out of it," Ustin remarked.

"Where could she have gone?" Olin said.

Rule flicked the material off his sword and let it drop back onto the bed. "I have no answer to that, Olin. But as much as I want Devora dead, I cannot take the time to search for the witch now. My main concern is for Meav and the others."

"If Devora knew enough to flee, why then were her men not waiting for us?" Ibrehem said.

"'Tis what 'tis, my friend...Devora betrayed her own men. Cared only about her own hide and left them here to fight and die," Rule concluded. "Fortunately for us she did. We still have the element of surprise on our side."

'Twas then that a commotion could be heard below.

"The others have stormed the main floor," Rule said. "Let us secure this level and meet them...from the great hall we can make our way down to the torture chamber."

With that Rule swung open the door and made his way out into the corridor. There, he encountered two sentries. Plunging forward he raised his sword and ran through the first soldier with a force he had not expected. The weapon and shield seemed to have a power all its own.

Ibrehem finished off the second man.

Olin saw a third sentry come from the opposite direction, and with lightening speed felled the man with his rapier before he could reach Rule.

Bulwark eliminated two more as he descended the stairs to the great hall.

With blades clicking, Rule's men fought bravely, wiping out Devora's army with a vengeance Rule had never seen before. This war was personal, their victory essential.

With each enemy he dropped, Rule felt the supremacy of the weapons he used. Stronger he became, feeling an invisible wall of protection surrounding him. He sensed the spirits of his ancestors and the heart of his mother close by, and it gave him the courage to walk into the thick of the battle with confidence.

Only when Ibrehem shouted, "We are victorious...all are slain," did Rule lower his blade. Looking amid the dead bodies that littered the floor of the great room, Rule silently fumed. Devora's high sentry, the one called Shell, was not among the men. 'Twas then he knew who helped Devora escape. Shell had left his men, left his military post to safely escort the queen from the castle. The thought of the two fleeing from a fate they both deserved angered Rule.

"Come, my lord," Ibrehem called, breaking through Rule's thoughts, "to the torture chamber."

Rule quickly shook the rage from his heart and made his way down the stairs. Again he led his men; weapon raised and ready to deal with the sentries that might be below. Ready for them...but not for what might have happened to Meav and the others. With this thought most forward in his mind, Rule inhaled sharply and willed himself to meet his enemy with the power that had gotten him this far.

"Charge!" Rule commanded over his shoulder and took the set of steps two at a time. He was met with opposition halfway down the stairway, and again he felled each foe with the same authority. His men backed him, their bravery unyielding. All of Devora's men went down, breathing their last on a blood-washed floor.

'Twas the sound of Meav's scream that for an instant stopped Rule's heart. He bolted into action, quickly running down the corridor and to the room where the shouts came. With one sweep of his eyes he took in the scene before him. In one corner Meav and Zailia sat on the floor, Zailia holding Tobiah's limp and bloody body in her arms. In the center of the chamber two sentries were engaged in a sword fight.

Ibrehem arched a brow. "What do you make of this,

my lord? Devora's men cannot even tolerate each other. Should we lct them finish their dual and take the winner?"

Rule glanced again at Tobiah...the old man was in bad shape and needed to be tended to. "Nay, there is no time."

Rule and Ibrehem leaped into the fight, each one taking on a sentry.

Ibrehem swiftly overpowered the taller sentry. The man fell to the floor and gasped his last.

Rule was about to end the other's life when Meav screamed..."Nay, do not harm him, milord!" She lunged ahead and grabbed for Rule's arm. "Spare him...he is a friend!"

Rule slowly lowered his arm but held his shield between them. "He is one of Devora's men."

"Aye, he is, but he was helping us escape," Meav quickly explained. She tightened her grip on Rule's arm. "Without him we would be dead by now."

Wesley dropped his sword and raised his hands above his head. "I mean you no harm, my lord."

Rule lowered his shield and backed away. He looked down at Meav, his eyes glistening with relief that she was alive. Dropping his shield and sword to the ground he embraced her and lifted her off her feet. "Lass, this moment I prayed for."

Meav wrapped her arms around Rule's neck. "As well as I, milord.

Rule captured her mouth and kissed her with urgency. When she responded to his bold display of affection, a surge of heat coursed through every fiber of his being.

Ibrehem ran to Zailia, who by now was crying and rocking her father's battered body in her arms. Gently, he released her hold.

Rule motioned for Bulwark and Olin to take Tobiah.

Ibrehem pulled Zailia into his arms and showered her face with kisses. She did not resist, burying her face in Ibrehem's neck and holding him tight.

"'Tis over now, lass. All of Devora's men are dead." Rule called out to her, tightening his hold on Meav.

"'Tis true, Zailia," Ibrehem reassured her. "No one

will ever hurt you again and I will never leave your side."

"He is dying, Ibrehem," Zailia sobbed. "My father is dying."

****

Rule wasted no time in having Wysteria brought to the castle. She came bustling into the great hall, a satchel hanging from her arm filled with herbs and potions. Quickly she was ushered up to the king's chambers, where Tobiah had been brought. There she administered healing to the old sentry. Zailia and Meav helped. The three women worked the entire night to bring Tobiah from death's door.

As the sun shone through the window, Meav woke to find herself sleeping on a quilt that had been spread on the floor beside the large, canopied bed. Slowly she stood, finding Zailia resting at the foot of the bed and Wysteria asleep in a chair by the fire.

Meav reached forward and gently felt Tobiah's forehead. The fever had broken. This was a good sign. She smiled, relieved, and arranged the coverlet around the old man's shoulders. On tiptoe she made her way to the door as quietly as she could, opened the squeaky portal and made her way down to the great hall.

Along the labyrinthine maze of stone corridors she took in the splendor of the castle, admiring the rich tapestries hanging on the wall, and the beautiful, large, stained glass windows that allowed the morning's light to fill the interior. It seemed she and the other women were not the only ones working throughout the night. The dead bodies had been removed and the floors were washed clean from the blood.

Meav, directed by men's voices, found the great hall. Slowly she entered the room, finding Rule and his men sitting at a long table, eating and drinking, and talking about their victory.

Meav watched Rule take a bite of the meat. He seemed to savor it as he chewed, his eyes closing slightly with pleasure. Meav was delighted his curse had been broken, happy for him, that he was finally home. She smiled to herself. *'Tis the first cooked meal he has had in a decade.*

She decided not to bother him, and instead find her

way to the kitchen for her own breakfast. Just as she was about to turn and leave, he called her name.

Rule stood and made his way toward her. "Nay, my lady, do not leave me to eat my first civilized meal without your presence."

Meav raised her hand, gesturing to the men gathered around the table. "I do not want to interrupt, milord."

"You are not, my lady...anyway; I was just about to come upstairs to fetch you. I would much rather gaze upon your face across the table then some of these burly mates." He enclosed his hand around hers, and pulled her along with him to the table. "How is Tobiah doing?"

She sat in a chair he pulled out for her. "The fever has broken, and he is resting comfortably."

Rule sat beside her and raised his mug. "To Tobiah."

The other men around the table raised their mugs as well, cheering the old man's name in unison.

A young woman several years older than Meav sauntered up to the table. Her light brown hair hung in a braid down her back, and her large brown eyes twinkled. Placing a pitcher of goat's milk on the table, she smiled at Meav.

Meav reluctantly returned the smile. There was something about the lass that did not set right with Meav, though she could not pinpoint what it was. Perhaps 'twas because the young woman's smile looked forced...stiff, the merriment not quite reaching her eyes. Meav sighed, maybe 'twas just that she was tired, felt dirty, awkward, and very hungry.

"And now, down to business," Rule said. He turned to Bulwark and Ibrehem. "I want the passage leading from the garden to the queen's chamber blocked off. With Shell and Devora still around, I dare not take the chance of them secretly being able to enter the castle."

Both Bulwark and Ibrehem nodded in agreement.

The young girl took her time pouring the milk in a mug for Meav, listening all the while to what the men were saying.

Meav felt uneasy. She shifted in her seat, silently wishing Rule would not be as cavalier as to what his plans were in front of the maiden.

Rule directed his next words to Wesley. "And you, my

new found friend, I will knight."

Wesley shifted in his seat. "There is no need for that, my lord."

Rule frowned. "Then how else can I repay you for saving my lady and the others?"

Wesley met Rule's gaze. "By granting me permission to leave. I would like to go home, to my family."

Rule sat back in his seat. "Where have you family, soldier?"

"The mountain region," Wesley explained, "where my folks have a goat farm. To spare them losing the property, I worked for Devora." He sighed. "Now that she is gone, I would ask you lift the remaining tax. Then I would like to return to my home." A small smile curved his lips. "And to my own love, Becka, who waits patiently for me."

Rule nodded. "What you ask is done, Wesley."

Wesley beamed. "Thank you a thousand times, my lord."

"I only wish for you to stay till after my coronation ceremony, and join the feast that will follow," Rule said.

Wesley tipped his head politely. "It would be an honor to see you crowned."

Meav had been watching the young woman carefully, as she fussed over filling Meav's plate. She smiled again at Meav. "Would you be wanting anything more, my lady?"

Meav looked at the food that filled her dish. "Nay, all I could want is here."

"After your meal, then, I will be glad to help you bathe," the girl whispered.

Meav blushed, suddenly humiliated at the way she must look...and smell, but she did not need this slip of a girl to call it to her attention. "I do not think I need anyone to help me bathe."

Rule overheard the women's conversation. "'Tis the way of it, my lady. Lorna will be your handmaiden now, and will help you do whatever 'tis you women do."

Meav looked around the table. The other men had now stopped stuffing their mouths and were also listening. Meav's blush deepened. "I am no one special, milord. In fact, I should be helping in the kitchen...so much company...'tis only right I lend Lorna a hand."

"Oh...nay, my lady," Lorna gasped. "'Tis not your place."

Meav frowned, looking over at Rule. "I do not understand."

"Your place is with me, Meav...I am soon to be king, and you will be my queen."

Meav swallowed hard to clear the buzzing sound that now grew louder in her ears. "Queen...me a queen?" she mumbled. 'Twas then her arms and legs grew numb...then everything went black.

When she opened her eyes she was in a small room. 'Twas furnished with just a bed, a nightstand with a washbasin on top and a writing table by the large window. Before the crackling fire stood a large tub...ready and waiting for her. She looked over to find Rule sitting at the edge of the bed, his amber eyes showing his concern.

Gently he removed the damp cloth from her forehead and dipped it into the basin, squeezing it before he replaced on her brow. "What in thunder happened to you, lass?"

Meav touched her hand to her head. What had happened? She closed her eyes, slowly recalling the events of the morning. Queen...he said she would be his queen. Meav opened her eyes wide. "Me...a queen?"

He chuckled lightly. "Aye, 'tis what you will be after we are wed."

She could feel herself going out again, the arms, legs, all tingling. Nay...she must stay focused...the man mentioned marriage. She took a deep breath. "Have I accepted your proposal, milord?"

Rule cast his eyes down. "Forgive me, my lady...I just assumed...the Prophecy and all...that if you loved me enough to break the curse, you loved me enough to want to marry me."

Meav reached out and gently stroked Rule's face. "Do you love me enough, milord, to want to marry me? Or are you asking out of honor and duty."

Rule looked deep into her eyes. "There is much honor in my asking, my lady, but 'tis not out of duty." He reached for her hand, turned it over, and tenderly kissed her palm. "I love you, Meav O'Shay...I have since the moment I set eyes on you, though I was too stubborn to admit it." He placed her hand over his heart and held it there. "I want to wake every morning with you in my arms, and go to sleep every evening with you by my side. I want to make wee ones from our love, and grow old with you."

Meav drowned in the tenderness of his gaze, and her heart danced with excitement. "Oh, milord," she whispered breathlessly, spreading her fingers out over his masculine chest.

"Oh, my lady," he countered in the same manor.

Meav suddenly found herself completely conscious of his virile appeal. Her palm burned where he had kissed. Mercy, the very air around her felt charged with an energy she could not explain.

His hand slipped up her arm, pulling her into his embrace. He whispered into her hair. "Can you forgive me, Meav for the way I acted...for the way I mistrusted you?"

She put her arms around his neck and buried her face in his throat.

His grip tightened. "You have unlocked my heart and soul, lass, made me human again...and I can only hope that in time you might love me as I do you."

Meav pulled back, drowning in the pool of his eyes. They glistened with tears. "I do love you, Rule. I love you with all that is in me."

Rule face burst with joy. "Then you accept my proposal?"

Meav felt her own happy tears spill over and slip down her cheeks. "Aye, milord, I accept."

****

Zailia awakened with his gentle touch upon her back. She stirred, pushing a golden curl from her eyes.

Ibrehem smiled down at her. "Come downstairs for breakfast, lass."

Zailia sat up and quickly looked over at her father. "I dare not leave him."

Ibrehem stroked her face. The softness of her flesh soothed the tips of his fingers. "Wysteria sits only a few feet away, by the fire. She will heed his call should he wake."

Zailia moved to sit at the edge of the bed. "I want to

be here when he opens his eyes."

Ibrehem nodded in agreement. "Then I will have something brought up here for you to eat...and for Wysteria as well."

She smiled warmly. "Thank you, Ibrehem." She reached out and touched his hand. "But you need not worry about us any further. Papa and I will be fine now."

Ibrehem knelt before her and buried his face in her lap. "Zailia, please, do not push me away again. Let me take care of you."

She buried her hands in his thick hair. "I have taken care of myself for so long, I do not know how to let someone else do it for me."

He raised his face to hers. "Then you take care of me."

She looked deep into his eyes. "I do not understand...in what way could you need me?"

Ibrehem nervously cleared his throat. Right now, this slip of a woman had him on his knees, and if what he was about to say drove her away...he would come undone. "In every way, lass," he began, his voice shakier than he had liked. "I find my life incomplete, lonely, and empty without you."

Zailia blinked baffled. "You could have any lass you want."

He placed both hands at the base of her spine. "I do not want any lass, Zailia, I want you."

She raised her chin defiantly. "Only because you pity me...feel some sort of honor toward my father." Tears welled in her eyes. "I do not want to spend my life with a man who feels sorry for me."

He spoke in a suffocated whisper. "Is that what you think...that I feel sorry for you?"

Zailia gave him a taut nod, than lowered her eyes.

Ibrehem raised her chin. "Look at me lass."

She resisted.

He cupped her face with his hands and brought her gaze to meet his. "I want you to look deep into my eyes when I tell you this, Zailia...so you will see I say it with all truth and sincerity."

Her voice trembled when she spoke. "I am listening."

He gently rubbed a thumb over her lips. "I love you,

Zailia...there is no question about it. I want you for my wife and I will not have you denying me...us...the happiness I know we can have if you will just give me the chance to prove it to you."

The tears now slipped down her cheeks. "You love me?"

Ibrehem chuckled lightly. "Aye, lass, I do, with every fiber of my being."

"Really and truly?"

"Really and truly." Gently he tucked a strand of blonde hair behind her ear. "Now I would know, lass, if you could love me."

"I have always loved you, Ibrehem Chancelor."

He stood, pulling her up with him and covered her lips with his.

His tongue explored the recesses of her mouth, sending shivers of desire through him. Raising his lips from hers he gazed into her soft, brown eyes. "Will you marry me, lass?"

She melted in his embrace. "I will, Ibrehem Chancelor...I will."

Tobiah cleared his throat with authority. "'Tis bloody well about time."

Chapter Nineteen

Devora lay on the worn out cot in the tiny hut. Every bone in her body felt exposed. Her nightgown, though the material was light, chafed her flesh. Pain gripped her each time she breathed. Slowly she looked around the shabby dwelling, her eyes stopping on Shell and an elderly man sitting on a rug beside a fire pit. She groaned.

Immediately Shell went to her, kneeling beside the straw filled bed. Taking her fragile hand in his, he forced a smile. "Well, now, 'tis about time you decided to join us."

"What is this place?" she choked.

"'Tis the Shaman's hut in the Jabri Valley...I have taken you home...to my home, Devora."

Devora cast her gaze to the old man, long white beard hanging from his chin, skin tanned and creased like old leather. "I need to speak to him...alone," she added, turning to look back at Shell.

Shell nodded in agreement. Reluctantly he motioned for the Shaman, then stood and left the hut.

The old medicine man knelt beside the dying woman, gave her a toothless smile. "I am Cumbezzer," he said, sprinkling powder over the top of her head.

"Can you help reverse this...this spell," Devora whispered, pain shooting through her body with each word.

Cumbezzer's watery gray eyes looked deep into Devora's. "You and I both know this is no spell."

Devora forced the words from her throat. "Blue flowers...I drank a potion made from the blue flowers growing in the castle dungeon."

Cumbezzer's face fell. "Flowers that grow in darkness, that make old turn to young?"

Devora's eyes widened. "Aye...you know of this herb?"

Cumbezzer nodded. "Grows in a cave not far from here."

Devora placed a hand on the old man's arm. "You

must pluck them quickly and bring me the blooms."

Cumbezzer shook his head.

Devora's mouth twisted with her pain. "I will die without them."

Cumbezzer narrowed his eyes. "Then you will die."

"Nay," Devora gasped. "You must help me."

Cumbezzer shook his head again. "I cannot...to open the cave, remove the flowers, would mean sudden death to all in the Jabri Valley."

Devora dug her nails into the old man's flesh. "No one would have to know about the flowers but you and I...not even Shell."

Cumbezzer shook his head harder. "No can do...flower evil, herb of the devil." He sprinkled the powder on Devora's head. "You sleep now, death come easy when you sleep."

Tears welled in Devora's eyes and slipped down her bony cheeks. "I do not want to die," she sobbed, remembering the horrid way her cat Gotham had expired from lack of the youth brew. "Nay...do not want...to die..." her voice trailed off, her eyelids grew heavy. And then she saw all the colors of the spring melt together in her mind's eye. The smiles and laughter she shared with Meridith and Wysteria...her mother and father. She felt joy at healing a little rabbit, sorrow when she could not help a tiny bird. 'Twas all still there, deep inside of her; waiting for her to find her way back to the goodness life held...and now, when it was too late she finally had.

I'm sorry, she heard her heart cry. *For all the wrong I did, for all the hate and evil*, she sobbed. But there was no one that could hear her. She thought of Shell. He loved her in spite of what she was, what she had become. How different could things have been if they met in the right way...loved with pure intent. Devora would never know this and it hurt worse than the pain that now enveloped her body. She tried to open her eyes, see Shell's handsome face one more time...even now, on her death bed, she longed for his kisses, to feel him inside of her. And with that thought the pain ceased, the sadness lifted, she felt her body floating...floating...away.

Shell watched Devora take her last breath, and to his horror, her body slowly dissolved right before his eyes.

There was nothing left of her but dust.

He fell to the ground and wept, vowing he would avenge his lady queen. The red-haired maiden had put a spell on his woman that caused her death. Shell could not let the bitch live on when his own love was gone.

Forcing himself to focus on what had to be done Shell stood; wrapped Devora's remains in a blanket and carried them outside. The Shaman began to chant as Shell set the blanket on fire. Together they watched it burn.

Cumbezzer picked up a handful of dirt and sprinkled it over the ashes. "She is gone, and you must go now too."

Shell nodded, turning away and walking to his father's home. He needed the wisdom and comfort of his family...to feel the love and acceptance...and their help in ending Meav's life.

****

Lord have mercy, her new handmaiden was drying her between the thighs, and a tad rough at that. Meav covered herself awkwardly with a towel and moved to sit on the bed. Again a disturbing feeling about Lorna surfaced. She shivered.

"Cannot be having you catch a chill now, my lady," Lorna advised. "Let me finish drying you."

"I am dry enough, Lorna."

"So sorry, my lady. A scullery maid by trade I am...not schooled in the fine ways, or how to assist a queen." Her eyes widened. "But give me a chance, I beg of you. 'Tis agony, 'tis to spend my life rotting below, scrubbing pots till my fingers shred." She bowed politely. "Real happy and grateful I am to have this chance to better my position and serve you." She searched Meav's face. "And sorry I am if I have spoken out of turn or hurt you in any way. I must remember I am not scrubbing pots."

Meav forced a smile. "'Tis not your fault, Lorna," she lied. 'Twas best she played along, acted like she suspected nothing. But the next chance Meav had she would speak to Rule about her feelings toward the handmaiden. "I am a farmer's daughter, brought up in a humble but loving home, and I am not used to being helped with me bath." Meav sighed. "The whole thing is rather strange to me...I have been bathing and dressing meself since I learned to walk...why would I need help now?"

"'Tis because you are royalty, my lady. Doing for yourself is a thing of the past." Lorna explained.

Meav shrugged. "'Tis just...new ways take time to get used to."

"Aye, but 'tis best you do, my lady," Lorna said, extending a hand. "Now off with the towel so I can rub on the oil. And then I will open the trunk and get you dressed pretty for your betrothed."

Meav cast a quick glance at the trunk in the corner. Rule had Bulwark fetch it from Wysteria's cottage last eve when he brought Wysteria to Tobiah's aid.

"Such beautiful garments inside," Lorna went on.

"Aye," Meav agreed, not quite liking Lorna being able to rummage through the chest's contents. "They are very precious things that belonged to Rule's mother."

"And now they are yours, my lady. Come," Lorna coaxed, moving closer to the bed.

Meav stood, reluctantly dropping the towel to the floor. She closed her eyes while Lorna rubbed the oil on her neck, across her shoulders, and down her back. Though the girl's message felt good upon her flesh, Meav still could not relax. What was it about Lorna that bothered her...what indeed?

****

Shell smelled trouble. As he took the road from the Shaman's hut to his father's dwelling, he had not seen one Humbler at work. Jabri Valley was maintained by the Humblers, short in stature but strong in muscle. Hard working, indentured servants that made life easier for the higher ups...the aristocratic Jabrians, like Shell's family. Humblers worked the fields, toiled and brought to fruition all of the valley's wealth. They lacked reason, stumbled with words and common sense, and therefore feared fighting for their freedom. 'Twas easy for Jabrians to oppress the Humblers...they just kept Humbler children from learning the things Jabrian children learned. In this way the Humblers remained slaves, happy only for a morsel of food and a dry place to sleep.

Shell opened the large oak door to his family's home. At this hour, the Humbler women would usually be bustling around, doing the wash and scrubbing the floors.

But the house was quiet.

Shell made his way to the garden. No Humbler men worked the fields or chopped wood. Instead, Shell found his father trying to lift the ax and his mother on her hands and knees, picking vegetables.

"What goes on here?" Shell shouted.

Magna raised her sun burnt face, a smile spreading her lips when she spotted her son. Quickly she stood, and ran into his arms. "My boy," she sobbed. "'Tis the happiest I have been in months." She pulled back to look at him. "Are you hungry, how was your journey, how long can you stay?"

"Let the boy have a word, mother," Kinnely chastised his wife, dropping the ax and making his way toward his son.

Shell looked from one to the other. How he had missed them. His mother, wiping her tears with the end of her apron, looked worn. Her green-gray eyes feasted on him, her chubby face gleaming with a mother's love. And his father, gray-haired and gray-bearded, shook his hand with a slighter grip than Shell remembered.

"What goes on here? Why are not the Humblers doing the work?" Shell probed.

Kinnely meandered over to a chair and set his plump self down. "They are gone. Every last one of them...the ungrateful idiots."

Shell frowned. "Gone? Gone where?"

"Back to the mountain region, their ancestral home," Magna added.

Shell stared at his mother, baffled. "I always thought Jabri Valley was where they originated from."

Kinnely grunted. "Were you asleep in history class, son?" The older man sighed heavily. "Humblers were captured centuries ago by Jabrians and brought to the valley to work. The lot of them was so dumb; they would have died if left to their own devices." He hammered at his chest. "Why we saved their lives, we did, teaching them to plant and harvest, build homes and hunt for food. And what thanks have we gotten for all our trouble?"

Shell's eyes widened in astonishment. "But how did they rise above the Jabrian Elders?"

Magna's mouth puckered with her annoyance. "Oh,

'twas not their own doings." She shook her head. "Mercy nay...they could not free themselves from seaweed."

Shell's voice was harsh with frustration. "Then who did free them?"

"Stefan's military," Kinnely snapped. "The whole troop of the blooming buggers, led by Ibrehem Chancelor, marched in here about a moon ago, fought for the Humbler's freedom, and won."

Magna nodded in agreement. "And now they are gone...back to their homeland in the mountains."

Shell stiffened. "Why did you not send word to me and my sentries?"

Kinnely stroked his beard. "None of us could get through the pass, son. The military had every road blocked. Must have been planning the attack for a long time, they knew every in and out of the valley." He sighed exasperated. "If only our castaway had arrived a few nights sooner."

Shell moved closer to his father. "What castaway?"

"The one that survived the ship wreck," Magna said. "Took him in, we did. He helps with the labor in place of his food and lodging."

Shell frowned. "What good would one, half drowned man do against a whole army?"

Kinnely yawned and stretched his arms above his head. "'Twas not so much him, but what was in the crate he came a floating on that would have helped us, son."

Shell combed his fingers through his hair. "And what might that be, Father?"

"Something called firearms, son...and a whole lot of something else called gun powder...the thing what makes the firearms deadly. If we had these weapons when Stefan's men attacked, we would have easily won the fight and the Humblers would still be here doing the work."

"Why, we were just speaking about you," Magna exclaimed.

Shell turned around to find a tall, thin man with a balding head and round, black eyes standing in the door frame.

"This is my son, Shell," Magna gleamed with pride.

The man extended his hand to Shell. "I have heard so much about you, lad, I feel like I already know you."

Shell shook the man's hand. "I am sorry, sir, I did not catch your name."

The man smiled, exposing a gold tooth. "'Tis McGreary, lad...Hollister McGreary."

Chapter Twenty

Shell narrowed his eyes. "Ship wrecked you say?"

Hollister's expression became serious. "Aye, and the only survivor."

Shell's mouth curved into an unconscious smile that soon widened to consume his entire face. "What would you say if I told you that another *did* survive...a young woman."

Hollister jumped on the soldier's words. "One with fiery red hair and eyes of blue?"

"Aye, that be the one," Shell confirmed.

Hollister eagerly moved forward, his mouth twisting upward. "Then I should want to find her immediately."

Shell raised his hand. "One moment, sir...I would know first what the lass is to you?"

"She is me wife," Hollister lied, seeing a way to recapture Meav. No one here needed to know the little bitch tried to escape from his proposal or that he had murdered her family. When his informants learned she took refuge on the *Sea Dragon,* Hollister followed. Having many friends aboard the British ship, he was able to board the vessel. For many days he searched while out to sea, but never found her. He then angrily assumed his contacts were wrong.

"And why were you both on the ship," Shell probed.

Hollister's voice cracked. "We had just been married in Dublin, and on our wedding trip."

Magna clapped her hands with delight. "What a joyous day for you, Mr. McGreary. Your bride is alive and my Shell was the one to bring the good news."

Hollister dipped his head politely. "Aye, dear lady, a fine day 'tis."

Shell placed a hand on Hollister's shoulder. "Mr. McGreary, I have much to tell you." He motioned to the path that led from the back of the house to the water. "After you."

The two walked in silence, each taking a moment to ponder what they learned.

Hollister's casual strides masked his excitement. If Meav thought she would escape him, she was sadly mistaken. Playing the loving husband, anxious to be reunited with his wife, would make the young soldier lead him right to her. He faked concern. "Where is she? Is she well?"

"She has been captured by Rule Thornton, a warrior in Stefan's army," Shell lied. "He has killed the queen, taken over the throne and claims your wife for his own."

Hollister's eyes bulged with his rage. "Then we need to gather the men of this valley and unite for battle. Stefan's army has done a great injustice to the folks here by liberating the Humblers...and now they have kidnapped me wife." He stopped walking and looked Shell square in the face. "I have firearms...and will teach you how to use them. Together we can conquer these rogues."

Shell saw a plan developing that would work exactly to his liking. Let Hollister McGreary believe that Shell was helping to reunite him with his wife. After Hollister and Meav were together, Shell would kill them both. The Jabrians could then use McGreary's firearms to kill Rule and his men, opening the throne for Shell. He smiled to himself...aye, he would be king.

Shell spoke with deceptive calm. "I still have a contact within the castle walls. I know where she goes each night to bathe. I believe she would help...deliver your wife right into our hands."

Hollister's eyes gleamed. "And once we have brought Meav safely back here, we can return with the village men, armed with me weapons, and will take the castle."

Shell extended his hand to seal the deal. "'Tis a glorious plan...we will all be victorious."

A slow smile spread across Hollister's face. "Aye, gloriously victorious."

****

Lorna inhaled the night jasmine, a light breeze played with the tendrils of hair that framed her face. She looked content coming to the tiny secluded spot by the river to bathe.

Loreli watched the young woman strip off all her

213

clothes, stretch her arms above her head and do a little dance. This one loved being naked...fully enjoyed freeing herself from the worn garments she wore.

The mer-woman had watched the young woman's bathing ritual many nights, and took much pleasure in the way the earth-bound's full breasts had bounced as she frolicked to and fro beside the water's edge.

Loreli could wait no longer. Tonight she would claim the maiden, pull her down into the depths of a mermaid's world and own her. Slowly she submerged herself into the black waters, silently swimming closer and closer to the water's edge, waiting for her chance to spring forth and capture her prey. But she sensed another human lurking nearby, and instead lay still beneath the water.

Looking up at the moon, Lorna rubbed her nipples; her mind thought back to the nights her beloved pleased her, teased her, seduced her...then left her panting for more.

Never had she allowed Uri Kent to enter her. A scullery maid she might be, but smart enough to know that when you give the goods away too soon, you are left with a heavy belly and no man to care for you. She had seen it many times, her own mother had fallen prey to such a situation...left to raise Lorna without a father. Perhaps Lorna would have been destined to do more than scrub pots, had she had an ample dowry...one only a father could provide.

But she did not care anymore, she was resourceful all on her own...smart, held her wits in many circumstances and was doing something to better herself already. Her new position as the next queen's handmaiden would bring her closer to the new king. When Rule tired of his wife's charms, as husbands always do, she would be ready and willing to warm his bed. Then she would use him; steal from him his riches...and take revenge for the way Rule and his men took Uri Kent's life.

Lorna stepped to the river's edge and reached down for a handful of water. She splashed herself several times, becoming acclimated to its chill. It refreshed her hot flesh, cooled her desires.

But Lorna's contentment did not last, as suddenly she felt a presence. Instinctively she crossed her arms over her breasts and was just about to run, when a hand was slapped over her mouth and an arm around her throat. Sheer black terror washed over her.

Shell brought his lips close to Lorna's ear. "'Tis me, Shell...Devora's sentry."

Lorna tried to wiggle free from his hold.

"I will not harm you," Shell went on, his arm tightening around her throat like a vice. "I come to you tonight with a very interesting proposition...one that might be the answer to all your dreams."

Lorna relaxed, dropping her arms lower on her breasts. She was always open to those kinds of proposals.

"If I remove my hand from your mouth, do I have your word you will not make a sound?" Shell said.

Lorna nodded.

Shell released her and took a seat on a nearby rock. Raking his eyes down her naked body, he smiled. "Such beauty belongs garbed in fine garments fit for a queen." He reached over and picked up her worn, discarded dress. "Not rags like this."

Lorna ripped her dress from his grasp and quickly slipped it over her head. "Where is Devora? All the word around the castle is that you and she escaped together."

Shell's mouth twisted. "She is dead. Meav put a curse on her, and Devora died last eve."

Lorna glared at him. "Good...she was an evil woman."

Shell eyes filled with rage, but he stayed silent.

"You left your post and did not care about your men." She gritted her teeth. "Uri Kent died defending the crown."

Shell stood and moved closer. Slowly he traced her lips with his finger. "I had no choice, lass...and if I could somehow do it over again I would be standing by my men. But all the arguments in the world will not bring those who died back to us. We can only take peace in getting our revenge and live on."

Lorna found her heart racing. "What kind of revenge?"

Shell's mouth twisted with a slow grin. "The kind that would make me king and you handsomely rewarded."

Lorna leaned forward, placing her hands on his muscular chest. "Now that Devora is gone, how about me being queen?"

Shell arched a brow. "You drive a hard bargain, lass."

She smiled sardonically. "I have to look out for my own."

Shell's hand moved to her breasts. "Have you a chance to befriend Meav?"

Lorna had not felt the touch of a man in nights, and her body ached for such caresses. "I have been made her handmaiden."

Shell playfully pinched a hardened nipple. "Well, now...what could be more perfect?" He slowly roamed his hand down her belly, to the hem of her dress. Raising it, his fingers found the juncture of her thighs. "Your skin is so soft, Lorna. You deserve to bathe in a tub filled with warm, scented water. And after, I will rub oil all over you." He gently parted her V and found her hidden fires.

Lorna moaned with pleasure, opening her legs wider. His touch sent spasms throughout her body. "What is your plan?" she asked breathlessly.

He continued to tease her slippery nub with the tip of his finger. "Bring Meav to this very place by the river for three afternoons. Let the first outing be the day after the morrow. Then bring her again a few days later...then a day after that. Pack a lunch, pick flowers, and talk as women do. Gain her confidence"

Lorna closed her eyes with the ecstasy of her climax mounting, her legs becoming weak with the pleasure. She leaned against Shell's muscular chest. "Then what?"

Shell abruptly stopped his bold advances and stepped back. "That is all, lass...leave the rest to me."

Lorna's eyes flew open, frustrated with how he left her moist, hot desires unappeased. "Rule is not a fool," she snapped, feeling a little like a fool herself. "He would never let his woman out of his sight with you and Devora still unanswered for."

Shell frowned. "You have a point."

Lorna angrily smoothed her dress down over her thighs. "Your plan will never work, and you can forget the garden passage. I heard with my own ears Rule order his men to seal it shut."

Shell's eyebrows quirked questioningly. "Do you have access to sleeping herbs?"

"Aye, I know where they are kept."

Shell's voice was almost an affront to the silence that surrounded them. "And I know that Rule's man Bulwark is a glutton...not able to resist any morsel of food that is handed his way. Convince Meav she needs a bit of sun."

"And what do I do when Rule objects to the two of us going off alone?"

Shell smiled. "That is when you suggest that Bulwark come along to guard the two of you. Pack him a meal as well, but on the third day hand him a piece of freshly baked raisin bread laced with the sleeping herbs." He chuckled lightly. "The buffoon will never know what hit him."

Lorna laughed wickedly. "And then what?"

Shell moved toward her, again tracing her full lips. "As I said, lass, leave the rest to me."

Loreli raised her head out of the water...just for a moment...permitting herself a withering stare at the two humans outlined by the moon's light. To her surprise anger rippled along her spine. Why should she care what happened to the earth creatures? She never particularly liked Rule. Tracing with her finger the scar on her arm, she remembered the day the panther ripped Meav from her grasp. Perhaps Rule did not matter, but she wanted no harm to come to the red-haired maiden. The mermaid had saved the girl from the shipwreck for her own pleasures and would not lose her to the two standing here tonight. Taking a deep breath, Loreli dove deep into the water and swam away...knowing that she should...nay...that she *would* have to find some way to warn Meav.

****

Meav watched Lorna in the reflection of the dressing table's mirror. Her new handmaiden was readying her for Zailia's nuptials and took pains in rolling into large curls each long strand of Meav's tresses, then securing them atop her head. Never had she worn her hair in such a fashion. There was little need for such elegance in Dublin, when your day was only spent cleaning the barn or feeding the chickens.

Meav fingered the lace that trimmed the sloping neckline of the cream colored dress she wore. The

217

expensive material felt like a soft cloud enveloping her flesh. "This gown is as elegant as a wedding dress." She frowned. "I should wear another. 'Tis Zailia's day to shine."

Lorna looked into Meav's eyes through the mirror. "But this is the gown my lord instructed I help to dress you in." She bit her bottom lip. "'Tis trouble you will be bringing down on my head should you change into another."

Meav certainly did not want Lorna to get in to trouble because of her. She sighed heavily. "Not to fear, Lorna, I will stay wearing the gown."

"And 'tis a fine one at that, my lady." Lorna stood back and admired her handiwork. "As well as the way you look with your hair up." She gently stroked Meav's neck. "A fine and delicate neck you have, long and slender like a beautiful swan. 'Tis no wonder my lord is so taken with you." Lorna frowned. "But such a lovely neck needs adornment."

Meav held up a finger and made her way to the trunk. In a hidden pocket she pulled out a small, black box. Turning toward Lorna, Meav slowly opened the box.

Lorna's eyes bulged.

Resting in the folds of soft, black velvet material was an opal stone cut to fit into a teardrop setting. The gem was framed in gold and hung from a serpentine link chain.

Reaching for the pendent, Lorna removed it from its box. "Let me help you put it on, my lady."

Meav nodded, turning her back to the handmaiden.

Lorna fastened the clasp, then turned Meav back around. Her eyes filled with envy. "Such beauty."

"Does it do me well?" Meav asked.

Lorna motioned to the mirror. "Have a look for yourself."

Meav walked to the looking glass and took an audible breath. The pendent lay perfectly around her neck, settling just right above her cleavage. In awe, she traced the beautiful jewel with the tip of her finger.

Lorna clapped her hands together in delight. "The perfect finishing touch, do you not agree?"

"Aye, perfect," Meav whispered. "But this was Rule's

mother's. Perhaps I should just replace..." she hesitated. Nay, not a chance in the world would she leave this beautiful piece of jewelry unguarded. "Perhaps I should return it to Rule."

Lorna frowned. "The chest was given to you, so all that is in it is yours."

"Aye...that is true, but this is so...so splendid and such a personal keepsake. I truly do not think Rule meant for me to..."

"You will take his breath away," Lorna interjected. She placed a hand on Meav's shoulder. "Keep it on, my lady."

Meav nodded slowly and smoothed down her full skirt with trembling hands. Would she ever get used to all the changes in her life...and Lord have mercy...how would she ever get used to being a queen?

****

"Meya pulma sonata te," Rule whispered in her ear, taking her hand and helping her down the last two steps.

His nearness made Meav's senses spin. "What did you just say to me?"

"My heart sings to thee," he translated, caressing her with his eyes.

Meav sucked in her breath, as she searched the inherent strength of his face, the amber eyes, and the handsome warmth of his smile. She admired the way his white shirt and black vest clung to his muscular chest. Shiny black boots came to his knees, black breeches fitting snugly around his thighs. A delicious shudder heated Meav's body as the scent of musk and leather permeated her senses.

Rule touched the pendent around her neck, his finger brushing against the velvety mounds peaking above her neckline. A golden wave of passion washed over him, arousing his desires. Slowly he moved his hand to cup her chin and looked deep into her eyes. "My mother would be pleased you wore it...I am pleased you wore it," he added quickly. Then, "I am pleased you are mine."

Meav moistened her lips with the tip of her tongue. "I am too."

By thunder, if he did not watch himself he would be taking the lass on the stairway, dueling that dainty tongue with his own, slipping her gown off her shoulders and freeing the fullness he so slightly glimpsed above her décolletage. The heat emanated from her body and Rule wanted...nay, needed to bury himself deep within the warmth.

'Twas Ibrehem's hand Rule felt upon his shoulder. "I recognize the look in your eyes, my lord...'tis one I have had many times for Zailia...no doubt fueled by the same thoughts." Ibrehem cleared his throat. "We best be getting to the temple." He smiled, a glint of anticipation glowing in his eyes for what the night ahead held for him. "Where my own bride awaits."

****

Zailia wore her mother's wedding dress of light pink organza, fashioned with an empire waist.

"How I wish my mother could be present on this special day," she confided to Meav.

"Do you not feel her love and spirit in the temple?" Meav questioned.

"Aye, I do at that, as well as seeing her love in the face of the high priestess, Neteru, her sister," Zailia admitted.

Meav watched as Tobiah took Zailia's right. Ibrehem was on her left, ready to accept her hand from Tobiah. Meav could not remember a day she had seen Zailia happier...or more beautiful. She looked like a princess.

Her friend's sweet face was illuminated by love and candlelight. Meav smiled through her tears as Neteru read the wedding blessing, pronouncing Ibrehem and Zailia husband and wife. After kissing, hugging and wishing the bride and groom a happy life, Meav watched the two depart for their private night.

She knew where the two were headed. Ibrehem would now take his bride to the mansion behind the castle, a dwelling given to the highest man in command of the king's army...the position Rule had bestowed upon him only the night before. All day the castle's staff had cleaned and prepared the estate for Ibrehem to take his bride to, and Meav thought he could not get there fast enough.

'Twas the warmth of Rule's hand upon hers that broke her thoughts. Slowly he led her to the altar of love.

Taking a stick, and igniting it from a candle already burning, he lit another candle. Then he handed the stick to Meav for her to do the same. "Will you marry me, Meav O'Shay?"

"Aye, Rule Thornton, I will," she whispered.

Lifting her hand, Rule brought it to his lips, gently kissing the top. "Now, my lady...will you marry me now?"

Meav suddenly knew why Rule had asked her to wear the beautiful cream-colored gown. Looking around the romantic little chapel, cassia and sandalwood scented incense burning and candles lit, the sacredness of the moment swelled her heart. Meav decided 'twould be exactly the right time to pledge her love and life to Rule. Sadly, her folks would not be sharing in this moment, but Meav had made peace with all that had happened and knew her family would want her to move on and be happy.

She smiled up at him...her heart filling with joy and love for the handsome warrior standing beside her. "Aye, milord...I will marry you now."

****

The king's chamber was a large suite where a stone terrace awaited through double doors. The candles burning on the mantle cast soft flickers of light on the wide bed, draped with deep blue brocade hangings and covered with silky sheets. The lush pillows were piled invitingly against the cherry wood headboard. A crackling peat fire laid with sheaves of fragrant jasmine added to the ambiance of the room. Meav's feet sunk luxuriously into the oriental carpet that covered the floor. Awed by the rich tapestries that lined a far wall, she moved to get a better look.

Rule's heart swelled with love and pride for his young wife. After the private wedding ceremony in the temple he escorted her to a dinner in the great hall set for just the two of them. There, by candlelight, they ate, laughed and had a chance to talk. Then he took her hand and led her to his chamber, the one he would share with her from this day forth.

Rule poured them each a goblet of wine. Looking up, he saw Meav standing by the terrace doors, her slim body silhouetted by the moonlight. "'Tis a beautiful sight."

"Aye, 'tis," she said softly, admiring the wall hanging. She was thankful Rule had chosen the king's chambers for them instead of the queen's. He also promised her she would never have to spend a night in the room where Devora once slept.

"I meant you," he said, making his way to her side and handing her a goblet.

When Meav took the wine their fingers brushed lightly. The mere touch of his hand sent a warm shiver through her. She raised the chalice to her lips and took a sip of the wine, still conscious of where his warm flesh touched hers.

Rule drank in her beauty, his eyes studying her, memorizing her. Never did he want to forget her. Slowly he cast his gaze to her neck. "The pendent enhances the curve of your velvety throat. And I cannot help but wonder if 'tis as smooth as a sweet expensive brandy?" He took the goblet from her and set it with his upon a nearby table. Returning, he pulled her close. "Me thinks I shall taste you, now, for myself and see if 'tis just as delicious." He brought his mouth to her neck, and gently licked her there, making circles with his tongue around the pendant and down to the creamy expanse of her full breasts.

Meav responded breathlessly. "Ah, me."

Looping his fingers in her dress, he slipped it off her shoulders and down to her waist. Taking a full breast into his mouth, he suckled her.

Meav arched against his mouth. Her nipple, already erect, swelled even more as he nipped and teased.

Her response aroused him, his phallus unyielding and ready. Rule slipped her dress down passed her hips, than out from beneath each one of her dainty slippered feet. Standing, he cast the gown to one side. She stood before him naked, except for the adornment of the tear shaped opal around her neck.

A twinkle of moonlight caught her eye as he gazed into hers. His body throbbed to life, making it perfectly aware of what he could do...what he would do on this night, their wedding eve.

Rules loins tightened as he began to learn her, touching her where elbow joined the upper arm, where shoulder meets the neck, down to where her breasts rounded out at the sides. Lifting the full mounds, he traced the crease beneath, cupping their heaviness in his palms and gently squeezing.

Warmth coiled low in her abdomen, her body quivering under his passionate exploration. "Mercy," was her husky response.

"No mercy," he whispered, sweeping her off her feet and placing her on the rich velvet of the coverlet.

Meav watched him slowly remove his own clothes, giving her the chance to feast her eyes on every inch of his body. When her gaze caught upon the size of his rod, her eyes widened. "Saints preserve us...nay, me. That will never fit."

Rule chuckled lightly and lay down beside her. Gently he stroked her belly. "Ah, but 'twill, my love." His languorous strokes moved to caress her inner thigh. Separating the walls of her valley, he found her mound of desire and flicked it back and forth, his finger becoming wet with the dew of her yearning.

Meav lifted her hips.

Rule smiled and pleasured her throbbing bloom more deeply.

Meav gasped, parted her thighs and arched her back. With eyes closed she gave in to the magical moment, the wonderful sensuality. She welcomed the glorious sensation to disperse through every facet of her being, taking her consciousness like a drug. Reaching for his tanned chest, she pushed her fingers through his hairs, and tweaked a nipple.

Rule's own breath became heated and raspy as his finger strummed her bud faster, the scent of her female arousal filling the room.

As her climax mounted and exploded within her, Meav's hand roamed to his turgid shaft. Wrapping her fingers around his erection, she felt it pulse, branding her palm with the heat of his desire.

Rule groaned deep in his throat and moved atop her, slowly pushing the tip of his throbbing manhood into her moist warmth.

Meav inhaled sharply when he gently pushed past her hidden pearl, breaking the covering. But the pain was quickly taken over by the pleasure that shuddered through her.

"You are mine, now, my lady." His last words were smothered on her lips. *"Amin tialo."*

His kiss sang through Meav's veins. She moaned with pleasure, burying her fingers in his thick hair. He was stiff and unbending within the walls of her womanhood and she opened herself wider to accommodate his size.

Rule was entirely inside of her now, his need quickening his rhythm. A surge of passion swept him along when she closed around him. He could hold on no longer. His wet warmth burst from him, the nectar of his love spilling into her, filling her insides.

They lay entwined, the aftermath of their lovemaking leaving them sedated.

He kissed the back of her neck. *"Quest sill*...sleep well, my lady."

"What does *amin...amin...*"

"Amin tialo," he finished her sentence.

"Aye, what does it mean?"

He tightened his embrace. "I love you."

"Amin tialo too," she whispered before falling asleep.

Chapter Twenty-One

The whole situation reminded Lorna of a stray cat she had once found. The animal hid beneath the porch of the tiny cottage she shared as a child with her mother. Each day Lorna would set out food for it, never forgetting to replace the empty dish with one filled. And so it went for days, until the cat had decided to stick its nose out and become friendly.

Now Lorna felt she was doing the same in front of Rule's chamber door. Three times a day she replaced an empty food tray with a new one. She had learned from Cook that Rule and Meav were married in the temple and did not want to be disturbed. But that was three days ago! How on earth could they go at it for so long?

She bit her bottom lip, wondering when the pair would come out. Already too much time had passed for Lorna to be able to do exactly as Shell instructed. And if Meav did not emerge from the chamber by the morrow, the final plan would not take shape. Lorna could not afford for that to happen. Having Shell in command of things was the only way she would prosper, in finances and in her station at the castle.

Sighing heavily she placed a dinner tray in front of the door and retrieved the one she had brought up earlier for lunch. Their appetites certainly had not waned...not a morsel of food remained. Curiosity getting the best of her, Lorna placed an ear to the thick oak door. Closing her eyes she strained to hear what was happening on the other side.

Wesley had his suspicions about Lorna. Any lass, whose head had been turned by Uri Kent, needed watching. Coming up ever so softly behind her, and leaning close to her ear he whispered. "Something wrong, lass?"

Startled, Lorna screeched and threw the tray she had been holding in the air. Dishes tumbled down around them and shattered.

Face flushed, she turned and glared at Wesley. "Merciful heavens! Why on earth are you sneaking up on me?" She quickly looked around the corridor at the broken dishes. "Now I am certainly going to catch the devil from Cook, and be held responsible for all the damage. Not to mention the fact that glass might have splattered on the new tray, and I will have to bring up fresh food."

Rule's voice came thundering from within the locked room. "What goes on out there?"

"All is fine, my lord," Lorna lied. "I just dropped the tray. A new one will be brought up immediately." She narrowed her eyes at Wesley and bent to clean up the mess.

Wesley knelt to help her. "I am sorry...I certainly did not mean to provoke such havoc." He placed a broken cup on the tray. "I am sorry," he repeated. "I just found it odd that you were...well, lurking at..."

Lorna grabbed the old tray and stood with a huff. "Lurking," she interrupted quickly. "Is that what it looked like to you?" She straightened her skirt, annoyed.

Wesley reached for the new dinner tray and stood. "Aye, lass, it did."

"'Twas concern. Heavens, they have been in that room for days," she scowled. "Has it not crossed anyone's mind that...well, perhaps they could have the fever?"

Wesley threw his head back and laughed heartily. "Oh, they have the fever all right, but not the kind that needs worrying about." He looked down at the tray she held. "And since they are partaking quite well in nourishment, I do not see a reason for concern."

Lorna raised a defiant chin and marched to the head of the stairs. "I trust you will bring Cook the tainted tray?"

"Aye," Wesley agreed. "'Twould only be right since I caused the problem."

She turned back to look at him before descending the stairs. "And you should bring up a new dinner tray as well?"

Wesley grunted, following her downstairs. "Aye, that too."

****

Meav had been sound asleep when the noise outside the door exploded her dreams. She saw Rule jump from the bed and reach for the sword leaning up against the fireplace.

Meav rubbed the slumber from her eyes. "What is wrong, milord?"

Amusement flickered in his eyes as they met hers. "'Twould seem Lorna dropped our dinner."

She sat up abruptly. "'Tis dinner time already?"

She watched him walk naked across the room, the strength in his thighs working with each purposeful step. God, he was grand...velvety bronzed skin stretched over muscle, shoulders broad, arms powerful. A delightful shiver of wanting ran through her as he replaced the sword and dropped down next to her on the bed.

Rule stretched out, reaching over to caress her back. "Aye, comes everyday at this time."

She rolled into his embrace. "Just how many days have passed?"

Rule shrugged. "My count is three."

Meav's eyes widened. "Three! We have been...been..." she stammered. The things he had done to her, and she had to him, the various positions, and the heated passion, came flooding into her thoughts. Her voice rose. "It has been three days?"

Rule chuckled lightly. "Aye, lass, three glorious days." He smiled devilishly. "Shall we try for three more?"

Her cheeks turned crimson. "Saints preserve us, what will everyone think?"

He reached out and tweaked a rosy nipple. "They will think you are completely and utterly in love with your husband." He cupped the full breast. "And that he is totally and wholeheartedly in love with you as well."

Meav eyes softened dreamily. "I am, you know, completely and utterly in love with you." She stroked his chest, her hand roaming down his abdomen and to the engorged member between his thighs. Smiling, she could not remember in the last three days when his manhood had not been swollen.

Rule tightened his arm around her and closed his eyes.

Meav wrapped her fingers around his hardened

shaft, her thoughts going back to the vision quest they shared...and the first time she touched Rule. Reality was so much more wonderful than what had transpired in their minds.

He inhaled sharply as her light touch massaged his yard with painfully teasing strokes.

As she caressed the length of him he grew longer and more solid, the tip of his erection wet and oozing. She then scooted down and placed her warm lips around the rock hard shaft.

Rule's eyes shot open. "By thunder, lass, you will cause me to spill my seed right here and now," he said, reaching down for her and pulling her up from beneath her arms. Gently he placed her beside him. Rolling her onto her stomach, Rule pushed aside the long strands of her hair and trailed scorching kisses down her neck. Slowly his tongue followed the curve of her spine, stopping at the swell of her buttocks. Separating the firm, twin mounds, he lapped at the opening.

Meav felt her toes curl. His laving was evoking sensations through her body that drove her wild. When the tip of his tongue entered her, she moaned with pleasure. Her flesh tingled, her heart raced. Mercy, she felt weightless. Hot...wet...and like she could float to the clouds...but glad she could not...happier to stay put and feel the moist pressure of his tongue.

The scent of their sexuality filled the room, threatening whatever control he had. In an instant Rule placed a knee on the bed and flipped Meav onto her back. His gaze fixed hungrily on her lips. "'Tis a wonderful ache that needs appeasing."

Meav sucked in a hissing breath as he consumed her mouth, claiming her with hot glides of his tongue; deep erotic slides into the supple recesses. Her tongue dueled with his; circling and darting, tasting him.

Rule growled soft and low as he closed his teeth around her lower lip and pulled, then suckled. Tasting and touching her drove him wilder than when he roamed the jungle as an animal.

Leaving her mouth, he kissed a path down her neck. Meav lifted her chin; the heady scent of her own personal musk increasing his hunger for her.

Her skin was warm and smooth. Rule felt his loins grow hard with desire. Lowering his head to one full breast, he wrapped his lips around the aureole. It puckered and grew in his mouth.

His breath fanned over her skin, soft and warm, as he brought his mouth down around the other breast. Gently he drew the nipple into his mouth. The rake of his teeth across the taut nub sent currents of desire through her.

Rule licked his way to her muff, savoring the pearly hardness hidden deep, circling with his tongue. Then nipping at her privities with his teeth, he pulled the slippery bud into his mouth.

Meav inhaled sharply, entering the realm of rapture. Not only did the man make love to her body, but her soul as well. Raking her fingers through his hair, she parted her thighs.

He delved the depths of her sexuality and lapped at her hidden treasure, almost spending himself when he flicked his tongue over her swollen tissue.

Meav convulsed as he teased her mercilessly. Her bud quivered with each slow, lazy stroke. She cried out for him to go faster, harder.

But Rule savored wanting her, lost in an erotic haze he continued to gently tease her swollen labia, inserting his tongue into her intimate recesses until her silken inner walls contracted.

His hot, rigid erection cradled against her mound. With slow, rhythmic thrusts he entered her slick passage before the last shudder of passion died away. Rubbing back and forth against her feminine spot, he spread her creamy warmth on him...all over her.

Smelling the essence of her heat and the scent of their lovemaking drove him to his brink. With volcanic spurts Rule exploded inside of her, taking them both to the zenith of ecstasy.

Exhausted, they held each other, slipping into a lover's slumber. It was the sound of their dinner tray being returned that finally aroused them.

Rule slipped on a robe and made his way to the door. Upon opening the heavy portal, he spied Wesley sneaking away down the corridor. He frowned. Had his men somehow been turned into servants while he hid away in his chamber with his bride?

He shut the door behind him and placed the tray on the table. "Most peculiar," he commented, pouring them each a goblet of wine.

Meav found her robe and slipped it on. Hungrily she eyed the plates of smoke salmon, pork and various cheeses. "What is?"

Rule popped a piece of cheese into his mouth. "That Wesley would be bringing us our dinner instead of Lorna."

Meav sipped her wine. "I have been meaning to talk to you about Lorna." She sat down and filled a plate with slabs of pork.

Rule also sat and dove into the food. "Why is that, my lady?"

Meav tasted the succulent meat and rolled her eyes heavenward. "There is something about her that troubles me."

Rule speared a piece of salmon with a fork and stopped mid-way to his mouth. "Has she done something to warrant your suspicions?"

"Not that one would notice, but..." She tilted her head sideways. "How well do you know Lorna, milord?"

Rule sat back in his chair. "Just before I was sent away to school, Lorna's mother came into Devora's employ as a seamstress. Lorna was only a young child at the time, perhaps five or six. She played with the cook's children while her mother fashioned Devora's gowns." He narrowed his eyes. "Come to think of it, she did not play well with the others."

Meav leaned forward in her chair. "What do you mean?"

Rule frowned. "Just that she was sweet around the adults, but selfish and pushy with the children. I caught her many times teasing them, taking their toys and making them cry."

Meav reached for a piece of cheese. "I knew she was not as genuinely sweet as she acted."

Rule's frown deepened. "And being around Devora's influence certainly could not have helped her to behave better." He stroked his stubble-shadowed chin thoughtfully. "I will have a talk with Wesley about her.

He has been here throughout the years Lorna was growing up."

"Good idea," Meav agreed, taking another sip of the wine.

Rule cast her a devilish smile. "You know what else I think would be a good idea?"

Meav shook her head.

"That after I ravage this meal, I ravage you."

Meav returned his smile with a mischievous one of her own. "I think that is an excellent idea indeed."

****

Lorna was relieved when the chamber door opened and her services were once again needed. Her eye caught a glimpse of the blood stain on the sheet. Meav blushed and quickly covered the it with the quilt.

Lorna cleared her throat and engaged herself in fixing Meav's hair. "When I am done with braiding, I will send someone up to put fresh linens on the bed, my lady."

"I would appreciate that, Lorna," Meav said, her blush deepening.

"I believe you would also appreciate inhaling the beautiful floral scents filling the air on this magnificent warm day, instead of what circulates in this stuffy castle." Lorna forced a sweet smile. If she did not get Meav to the river today, her plans with Shell would be ruined. As 'twas she would only manage to get to the river twice instead of three times, as originally planned. "A wee bit of sun would put some color into your face, my lady."

Meav frowned. Goodness, what was Lorna thinking? Three days with Rule, doing things she did not dream two bodies could do, had left a permanent flush on her face.

"I can pack a lunch and we can eat down by the river...pick berries for pie making," Lorna went on.

"As much as that sounds wonderful, Lorna, I have to help me husband organize the coronation ceremony and ball. Anyway, Rule would never go along with just the two of us going alone."

"We could take Bulwark along...I will pack him a lunch as well." Lorna forced a giggle. "Have you not noticed how the man likes to eat?"

Meav laughed lightly. "Aye, 'tis true. Bulwark does like his food." She looked at the handmaiden through the mirror. "Your idea does sound like fun. Back in Dublin I loved to pick berries." Meav sighed. "I will talk to Rule. Perhaps we can have a picnic in a few days."

Lorna bit her bottom lip nervously. "Can we plan it for the day after the morrow, then? I will bake raisin bread."

Meav nodded reluctantly, feeling apprehensive as to why Lorna was acting so anxious about this outing. "Aye, the day after the morrow," she finally agreed.

Lorna breathed a sigh of relief and finished braiding Meav's hair.

****

Wesley stood silently, hands behind his back, in front of the large cherry wood writing desk. Rule sealed the last bit of correspondence and looked up. "Your quick response to my summons is appreciated."

Wesley inclined his head respectively. "I am at your service, my lord."

Rule pushed back his chair and stood, going over to a large set of windows and looking out at the courtyard below. "I will get right to the point."

"'Tis always a good thing to do, my lord."

Rule turned to face him, and motioned for Wesley to sit. "What can you tell me about Lorna?"

"Personally," he began, pausing for a moment. "I do not trust her."

Rule moved to his desk and sat down. "Why."

"She was involved with a sentry by the name of Uri Kent." Wesley frowned. "Devora's guards were blood hungry rogues, but the two that were the worst was Uri Kent and Hugh Carson." Wesley sat back in his seat. "They went beyond despicable to the bazaar." His eyes clouded with remorse. "It pains me now to realize what I kept my mouth shut over the things they did just to save my own hide. I will forever be ashamed for being such a coward."

"You were but one man, caught in a situation you had no control over," Rule said. "I thank you everyday for the final stand you did take. Without you my wife and the others would be dead." Rule's insides shuddered at the thought. "Forgive yourself, Wesley. 'Tis time to move on." He crossed his arms over his chest. "What more can you tell me about Lorna?"

Wesley met Rule's gaze. "The wench is sneaky. Just yesterday I caught her with her ear to your chamber door."

"Did she know you caught her?"

Wesley nodded. "Scared the hell out of her too."

Rule smirked. "Could that be the reason she dropped my dinner tray?"

Wesley chuckled lightly. "Aye."

"And why you returned with a new tray?"

Wesley's eyes widened. "You saw me?"

Rule nodded. "Thought my soldiers had decided to go domestic."

Wesley laughed harder. "The chit blamed me for the accident, said I startled her into dropping the tray. So, to keep the peace..."

"You agreed to bring up a new one," Rule concluded.

"Aye, my lord, 'twas the way of it."

Rule stood, went to a table in the corner and poured them each a brandy. "I have made a grave error in appointing Lorna handmaiden to my wife." He handed Wesley a glass. "But to take the position from her now, without being able to state a good cause, would be unwise." He reclaimed his seat. "Yet, to wait for her to do something harmful or disrespectful to Meav is not something I will allow either."

Wesley frowned. "What measures are there to take then?"

"Very cautionary ones, to be sure," Rule countered. He took a sip of the brandy, savoring the way the sweet liquor warmed his throat. "While you still reside with us, Wesley, your duty will be to watch every move Lorna makes. You are more accustomed to where she goes, what she does, who she likes and dislikes, than any of the other men." Rule twirled the glass between his palms. "Do not let her out of your sight, and report anything, no matter how minuscule it might seem, to me."

Wesley nodded in agreement. "When would you have me start, my lord?"

Rule downed the last of the brandy. "Immediately."

****

Mercy, the work ahead! Meav sighed as she looked

over the guest list for the coronation ceremony and dinner-ball to follow. Though her grandmamma had schooled her well in the task of cooking and baking, it still had been on a small scale; just for a household of five. The dinner planned for the coming festivities had a count of two hundred or more. It surprised her that there were even that many living on the island.

The food preparation was not her only concern. The castle was in bad need of a good cleaning. And even though Devora bought rugs, table and wall coverings of great value and quality, she did not take care of them properly. Meav had been told by the help that the prior queen had tired of a certain decor so quickly, cleaning it was rarely necessary. This meant the tapestries and small carpets had to be rolled up and brought outside to be beaten, floors scrubbed, and walls washed. Fresh table coverings and doilies had to be cleaned and pressed so they looked crisp for the quests.

The staff was another challenge. Living under Devora's reign for so long left them cautious and suspicious of Meav's nature, especially when they learned she was Devora's niece. She had to gain their loyalty and trust. Everyday she approached the servants with a smile and a kind word, hoping they would soon see she was nothing like Devora. She held their children, laughed at their jokes, gave positive praise and was supportive to their suggestions. In time she believed their hearts would come to favor her. In order to speed their approval of her Meav also worked side by side with them; and 'twas now why she found herself on hands and knees scrubbing the castle's foyer floor.

Pushing a strand of hair from her face, Meav sighed. Why had she chosen to clean the floor that received the most traffic? With people constantly coming in and out, her job would never end. 'Twas Lorna's indignant gasp that stilled Meav's hand from rinsing a slab of stone.

"Heaven help you, my lady. This work is not fit for a queen."

Sitting back on her knees, Meav looked up at her handmaiden. "Fit or not, it has to be done. With so much cleaning and baking, and so little time left, an extra hand was needed." Meav quickly took notice of the fact that

Lorna did not offer to help, in spite of being appalled at her new queen scrubbing a floor.

"You are pale, need some fresh air," Lorna advised.

Meav frowned. Again the comment about being pale, and both times Meav had been flushed with color. First from Rule's ardor and now from the vigorous way she was washing the floor.

"Remember your promise, my lady."

Meav nodded. "'Twas for tomorrow, but there is so much to do right now, Lorna, I have not the time for such a luxury."

Again Lorna grew anxious, biting her bottom lip nervously as she had done before. "For your own health, my lady, I cannot take no for an answer. I will make sure Bulwark is available to escort us, and then I will bake raisin bread and pack a few baskets for the berries we will pick. We can dangle our feet in the river and feel the sun on our faces."

Though Lorna was annoying with her constant badgering, Meav's back and arms ached and truthfully, a picnic by the river was beginning to sound quite nice. She sighed. "Fine, Lorna." She forced a smile. "I am looking forward to it all."

Lorna clapped her hands with delight. "I am as well, my lady...I am as well."

****

Another day dawned...another day of frenzied commotion, of women cleaning and preparing every nook and cranny of the castle...and another day of following Lorna about. Wesley wished the coronation would come and go quickly so he could go home to the mountains...once again able to be with his sweet Becka.

Delicious aromas from the kitchen filled the air, and brought the men in from the outdoors to sample a piece of this and that. Wesley was one of those men, his mouth watering for a taste of the raisin bread that now sat cooling on a nearby tabletop. He had followed Lorna into the kitchen and while she wrapped sweet meats in a cloth, he stole a large piece of the bread with his fingers and plopped it into his mouth. Closing his eyes he savored the way it melted on his tongue. Just when he was about to help himself to another delicious taste, Lorna turned from her task and shouted a protest.

In one fluid motion she was beside Wesley, rescuing the raisin bread from another one of his attacks. Her face screwed into a horrible scowl, and her eyes blazed with hatred. "This is for Bulwark."

"Bulwark!" Wesley barked. "Why does he get the entire raisin bread to himself?"

Lorna narrowed her eyes. "Have you ever seen the way the man eats? I fear perhaps one might not be enough."

'Twas the truth. Bulwark could make this one loaf disappear in an instant. "But why does he rank you baking anything for him at all?" Wesley argued.

Lorna turned her nose up smugly. "He has agreed to escort me and my lady to a picnic by the river later this day, and in appreciation I have baked him the bread." Again she narrowed her eyes at him. "If you want more, there are two other loaves in the cupboard that stands beside Cook's wash basin."

If Wesley was to keep Lorna in his sight at all times he had to know exactly where she would be. Nonchalantly he probed. "And where by the river are you ladies going?"

Lorna frowned. "That is none of your business." She brought the loaf to where her other picnic food sat, then turned with her hands on her hips. "And stop following me about."

Wesley feigned innocence. "I am doing nothing of the sort."

"Aye, you are," Lorna snapped. "And I want to know why."

Wesley stifled a yawn. Why was he suddenly feeling so tired? "Perhaps I find you fetching."

"Perhaps I find you a liar," Lorna retorted in response.

He blinked his eyes to keep them focused. "Now, why would you say such a thing, lass?"

She stomped back to his side. "I have worked in this castle for nearly eleven years. Daily I smiled at you, hoping one day you might smile back. Never in that time did you so much as look my way. 'Twas then Uri caught my eye, and I washed you from my mind." She folded her arms across her chest. "So you will have to forgive me now for not believing what you say."

Wesley's lids felt heavy. He stifled another yawn. Heaven above, what was wrong with him?

"You do not look so good," Lorna commented. "Perhaps you should return to your quarters and lie down?"

He shook his head to clear it. "I was fine before I..."

"Before what?"

He almost said *before I took a piece of the raisin bread,* but hindsight made him swallow his words. 'Twas then he realized what was happening and why he suddenly felt so tired. "I thank you for your concern, lass." He bowed politely. "Excuse me now while I take your good advice and rest a bit before my nightly duties."

Lorna waited for him leave the kitchen before she made her way upstairs.

Wesley hid in the shadows, listening to her climb the steps. When he knew Lorna had reached the top, he made his way back into the kitchen. As fast as his sudden weariness would allow, he opened the cupboard and reached for one of the loaves of raisin bread; removed the cloth, broke off a large piece and ate it. There was a subtle difference in taste from the first loaf. 'Twas then he knew for certain Bulwark's bread had been tainted with sleeping herbs.

Quickly Wesley exchanged the bad loaf with the good, then fighting his fatigue, he made his way to find Rule.

****

Loreli hid behind a rock. She had come to this side of the river every day since she heard the humans talking of their plan. She was sure this was the day Shell would return. How she had hoped she could warn Meav, but the chance had not presented itself. Now, the mer-woman worried for the fiery-haired maiden and knew there was only one other plan of action to take.

Throwing back her head Loreli screeched the siren's song. The eerie sound carried on the wind and was swallowed by the trees. Her call would then be passed on to the others. 'Twould not be long before help would arrive.

Chapter Twenty-Two

Meav stood very straight, and completely still while Bulwark's sister pinned up the last bit of material on the hem of the dress. The new coronation ball gown was made of organza and lace, had a fitted bodice and scooped neckline that accentuated Meav's bosom. The light aqua color, a striking contrast to her hair and eye color, was Meav's favorite. She was very pleased with Grendel's work, marveling over the way the seamstress took such pains in making sure each stitch was perfect.

Meav liked Bulwark's sister; she even talked to Grendel during the fittings about replacing Lorna. The seamstress...a sweet-faced blonde, somewhat stocky like her brother...was very enthusiastic about the idea and hoped to be placed in the new position soon.

Too soon was not soon enough for Meav. Daily she was becoming more uncomfortable with Lorna. The handmaiden had an obsession with going out and getting the sun. Meav loved the outdoors; after all she was a farmer's daughter and had to be out in the elements daily to do the chores. But there was a time and place for all things. The last few days everyone in the castle was trying to get ready for the coronation ball and dinner. 'Twas an important and sacred ceremony...planning it took precedence over romping by a river to pick berries.

When Meav spotted Lorna at the door she secretly cringed, knowing full well why the woman had a frown upon her face and was biting her lower lip nervously. Meav was late for their picnic. "I am just about through here, Lorna."

Wringing her hands in front of her, Lorna gave a taut nod. "I just do not want the sun to go down or our food to grow cold, my lady."

Grendel straightened out the hem and stood. "We are finished here, my lady. Go enjoy your picnic."

The two women helped Meav off with the beautiful

evening gown and into a bright green linen dress. The soft, cool material was perfect for a summer day's outing.

Meav turned to Grendel. "Why not join us?"

It appeared to Meav that Lorna held her breath as she waited for Grendel's answer.

Grendel picked up the ball gown. "I must finish with your gown, my lady."

"Another time, then," Meav offered.

Grendel nodded in agreement.

Lorna sighed relieved. "Bulwark waits below, my lady, by the garden doors."

Grendel giggled. "How did you get my brother to join you two on your ladies outing?"

Meav smiled. "I believe Lorna bribed him with food."

"Ah, that would do it," Grendel said. "The man does love to eat."

Lorna just smiled.

****

Meav had to admit, the day was beautiful. Birds sang, a light breeze blew, and the sun was bright. Bulwark's scowl lessened as he ate the food Lorna packed for him. With one eye on his small feast and another on Meav, he seemed quite content.

After filling a basket with berries, Meav slipped off her shoes and waded into the river. She sat on a rock, propping the basket beside her, and ate the luscious fruit while she wiggled her toes in the cool water. A deep peace filled her, but her contentment was not to last long.

Fear gripped her heart when a hand gripped her ankle. Meav looked down to find Loreli's eyes peering through a veil of water.

Loreli slowly rose from the river, the large rock shielding her from the other's view. "Good afternoon, my lady."

Meav's eyes widened in horror as the memory of the last time they met flooded her thoughts.

"Do not be afraid," Loreli whispered. "I can no longer claim you...you belong to Rule now." She released her grip on Meav's ankle and pointed to the basket. "I have always wished I could taste those."

Meav, dread still racing through her body, reached for a few berries and with a trembling hand dropped them

239

into Loreli's waiting palm. Clearing her throat she attempted to speak. "You have never tasted—" instantly she clipped her sentence, feeling foolish for asking such a question. Of course the mermaid had never tasted berries, how would she have gotten to the bush?

Loreli closed her eyes and savored the sweet, juicy nectar. "'Tis good." Opening them again, she smiled. "I knew they would be."

Meav reached for more and gave them to Loreli. "I owe you a thank you."

Loreli's eyes brightened. "For what, my lady?"

"For saving me life."

Loreli chuckled lightly. "Ah, but I had my own selfish reasons for keeping you alive...I wanted you for myself, to live beneath the sea where the air is right for humans. Then you would be my companion...my family. And my life would not be so...so lonely."

Meav's heart went out to the beautiful sea nymph. "We can still be friends."

Loreli narrowed her eyes. "How can that be? You live on land, I live in the water."

"I can come to the river now and then to visit you. We can talk, sing, and tell stories to one another." Meav relaxed and bent nearer to the mermaid. "I would love to hear all about your world beneath the sea, and in turn I will tell you about me life in Dublin." Meav smiled. "I can bring you berries and many other delicious fruits that grow out of your reach, so you can taste them all."

Loreli returned the smile. "You would do all this for me?"

"Aye, that I would. 'Twould be me pleasure."

Loreli's expression turned to one of joy...and then in an instant clouded with fear. "As much as I wish for this moment to last, my lady, you must leave the river and hurry back to the safety of your husband."

Meav frowned. "I do not understand?"

"You are in grave danger here," Loreli said. "Go, quickly, back to the castle."

Meav felt a chill run down her spine. Grabbing her basket she stood and turned to run. But instead of fleeing as the mermaid had advised, Meav stood shocked at the sight of Devora's sentry standing before her. She looked quickly around for Bulwark, and when she spotted him lying on the ground, she screamed and ran to him. Looking for wounds, Meav spoke softly. "Nay, Bulwark, you cannot be dead."

Shell made his way to her side with two long strides. "He only sleeps...for now, my lady."

Meav looked up at Shell and frowned. "Why does he sleep?"

Lorna moved near. "I baked sleeping herbs in the bread," she boasted.

Meav stood and lunged for Lorna. "You little witch. I knew you could not be trusted."

Shell roughly grabbed Meav by the arm and pulled her around to face the sneer on his face. "Lorna was carrying out my orders."

Meav stiffened. "Take your hands off me."

Shell snickered. "I think not, my lady." He bent his head down and stared deep into her eyes. "There is a score to even, and a crown to recapture."

Meav tried to pull free from his grasp. "Rule is, and always has been the rightful king."

Shell's lips thinned with his anger. "He has not been crowned yet."

"But he will be in a matter of days and there is not a thing Devora can do about it."

Shell's eyes clouded with hate. "Devora is dead."

Meav's eyes widened. "How did she die?"

Shell dug his nails into Meav's arm. "You know exactly how...'twas your curse that did her in."

"Nay, there was no curse."

Shell's eyes filled with rage. "Only a spell could make a person die as she did." He pulled Meav against him. "Her body dissolved into dust."

Meav met his gaze. "I tell you there was no curse."

"You lie," Shell spat. "And now you must pay."

"Nay, she speaks the truth," a wee voice said.

Shell looked up to find Titiana sitting on the branch of a nearby tree.

"Go...quickly...warn Rule," Meav shouted.

Shell pulled a dagger from his belt and held it to Meav's throat. "If she leaves that branch I will slit your throat."

"Meav did not kill Devora," Titiana called out.

Shell gritted his teeth. "How would you know?"

"Because 'twas I who killed her," Titiana stated flatly.

Shell threw his head back and laughed. "And how could one little fairie do such a deed?"

"She had help," another wee voice added.

Shell turned, taking Meav with him...holding her tight against his chest and pressing the dagger under her chin. "So, you two wee ones expect me to believe you could harm even a hair on Devora's head?"

"Not just us two," Gyla said.

"But all of us put together," Titiana concluded. She whistled and in an instant the tree was filled with pixies sitting upon every branch. "And we did not have to touch one hair on her head." Titiana smiled with pride. "We just peed on her flowers."

Shell frowned. "What flowers?"

"The blue ones that grew in the dungeon...the ones Devora brewed to make the youth potion," Titiana explained. "'Twas because we pixies peed on the blooms and wilted them that Devora could not remake the brew. That is why she died. Without drinking the potion every two days Devora faced growing old...withering away to dust." Titiana spread her wings and flew to a lower branch. "So, you can release Meav. She had nothing to do with Devora's death."

The muscles at Shell's jaw twitched. "All that has happened is because of her. The day she stepped foot on Keronia she brought trouble to the crown, and now she must pay...you all must pay. Within a day's time the Jabrians will seek their revenge for what Rule's army has done to their village and will strike with weapons far greater than swords and daggers." Shell pushed the knife against Meav's throat. "But for now, 'tis my pleasure to see Meav breathe her..."

Shell never finished his words because Bulwark rose to his feet from behind and with one slice, as though he were cutting through butter with a hot knife, slit Shell's throat with the dagger.

Shell's blood splattered all over the side of Meav's face and hair, soaking her dress. As he fell to the ground, he took her down with him.

Lorna, who luckily was looking up into the trees at the pixie's, didn't see Bulwark rise. Hearing a *thud* behind her, she spun around. Her eyes went round with shock as she saw the blood pour form Shell's throat. Clutching her own throat with her hand, she screamed.

Bulwark reached for Meav and pulled her to her feet.

'Twas then Lorna regained her wits enough to lunge at Meav.

Bulwark stepped in front of Meav and shielded her with his body. He raised the bloody dagger. "I have never killed a woman," he warned Lorna, "but if you take one more step I will be forced to spill your blood as well."

"As I will yours, for I have a deadly weapon aimed at your head. Drop your dagger and turn around slowly," the voice grated harshly.

The tone was like an echo from an empty tomb, and one Meav recognized. Her thoughts prickled with warning as she spun around to face him. Icy fear twisted around her heart, and panic welled in her throat. Swamped with confusion, her eyes locked with those of the enemy's.

Meav could hardly lift her voice above a whisper. "Hollister McGreary...but how?" The fearful images of this very man burning her farm and murdering her family flashed before her eyes.

Hollister sneered. "Did you think I would let you get away, love? I followed you that night you fled Dublin, boarded the *Sea Dragon* and survived the wreck...just as you did. We are the only two alive." A wicked grin curled his mouth. "Do you not find that amazing. I believe it must be fate. Our destiny is to be together."

Bulwark slowly turned to face Hollister, measuring him with hatred.

Hollister quickly appraised Shell's lifeless body, then returned his attention to Bulwark. "I would like to thank you for disposing of *that* nuisance for me." He arched a bushy brow. "The idiot really believed he would challenge the crown using me weapons to rise to victory." His glanced again at Meav. "Not even a smile, love?" he asked with deceptive calm. "And here I thought you would be overjoyed to see me."

Bulwark's face twisted with contempt. "How do you

know this rogue, my lady?"

Meav's voice was unsteady. "'Tis a long story, Bulwark."

Hollister's tone was heavy with sarcasm. "Can it be, me precious Meav, you have neglected to mention me to your new friends?" Hollister's eyes raked over Bulwark in disgust. "I am her betrothed."

"And I am her husband," boomed a voice from behind a hedge plant.

'Twas then Meav's world shook, as her warrior husband's power burst forth from the bushes. Ibrehem and Wesley followed close behind.

Hollister was thrown to the ground with such force his lungs exploded a loud grunt; the gun flew out of his hand.

Rule's large fist came down across Hollister's jaw.

Hollister threw a punch to the side of Rule's head.

'Twas then Rule picked the scoundrel up, held him high over his head and tossed him like a rag doll into the air.

Hollister came down head first on a rock, splitting his skull. Blood poured from his mouth, the beady eyes glazed over...he was dead.

Meav rushed to Rule's side.

Gathering her into his arms, Rule held his wife tight, blocking her view of Hollister's and Shell's bodies. "'Tis over, my lady."

"Not quite," Lorna screeched.

All of them turned to find Lorna holding Hollister's gun in her trembling hands. The barrel was aimed at Meav. Her finger fumbled for the trigger, though she had no idea how the weapon worked. "I...I watched the man...saw how he held this...this..."

"'Tis a gun," Meav said. "You do not know what you are doing."

"I believe I only need to pull on this latch," Lorna went on in a shaky voice, placing her finger on the trigger.

"Nay, Lorna, do not touch the lever." Meav warned. "That is a very deadly weapon."

"Good, then it will get the job done," Lorna retorted sharply.

Rule pushed Meav behind him. "Put the weapon

down, Lorna."

"Nay," she screamed. "All of you must die."

Meav pushed her way forward. "Please, put the gun down."

Rule took a step in front of Meav and moved closer to Lorna. "Lass...I demand you drop the weapon, *seda*!"

"Nay, I will not. At this moment I stand strong, for the memory and honor of Uri Kent," she sobbed, her finger fumbling with the trigger.

"Nay, Lorna!" Meav screamed.

Lorna was ready to shoot, when a buzz of little bodies knocked her off balance, causing her to drop the gun. Many little hands beat at her head and face, pulled her hair, and ripped her clothes. Tiny mouths bit her earlobes, neck and nose.

Lorna began to scream as she swatted the horde of pixies. When her attempt at stopping them failed, she ran to the river. Deeper and deeper she waded into the water to free herself from the angry fairies.

'Twas then that Loreli sprung from her hiding place, grabbed Lorna around the waist and claimed her.

The last thing they all heard was Lorna's shrill, petrified scream as she disappeared beneath the water.

Chapter Twenty-Three

Meav's dress was completely ruined...stained with Shell's blood.

Gently Grendel removed the garment from Meav's trembling form.

"Toss it into the fire," Meav bitterly instructed of her new handmaiden.

Both women stood silent before the fireplace and watched the beautiful linen dress burn.

Grendel's soft words broke the silence. "Let me help you wash, my lady." She led Meav to the basin of warm water and with tender strokes washed her clean of the blood that had stained her flesh.

Meav continued to stare at the flames. "Where is Rule, Grendel?"

Grendel knew Meav was suffering from shock. Softly she spoke, slowly removing the rest of Meav's clothes. "He is with his men in the great hall, my lady."

Meav looked around the bedchamber, casting a glance out the window. "Already it is dusk? I do not remember the day passing, or walking up the stairs to this room."

"Your husband carried you up them, my lady." Grendel washed Meav's face. "You were near faint, pale as an Elwin's hair and weak as a newborn babe."

Tears welled in Meav's eyes. "I was?"

"Aye, 'tis true, my lady. And your husband," Grendel went on, as she redressed Meav in a clean dress, "set you upon the bed, stroked your face and talked ever so sweetly to you."

Meav swallowed hard. "My memory is a blur. What did he say?"

Grendel tenderly dampened the ends of Meav's hair with a cloth, washing the strands splattered with blood. "Why, my lord told you that you were his love, that you need not ever worry again because no one would ever hurt

246

you...he would make sure of that."

Meav's lips curved into a tentative smile. "Aye, he did make sure." She reached for Grendel's hand. "Twice now he kept his word."

"And he will always keep that promise to you, my lady," Grendel assured her. "All one needs to do is look into his eyes when he is looking at you to know you are his world, the very reason he breathes."

Tears slipped down Meav's face. "Aye, I feel the same towards him."

Grendel smiled warmly. "Then 'tis a match made in heaven."

"And by fate," Meav added.

Grendel took Meav by the hand, led her over to the dressing table chair and helped her sit. "Let me braid your hair now, my lady."

Meav frowned at her reflection. 'Tis still dirty...I am still dirty...his blood still feels like 'tis on me."

"Your husband has requested a bath for you, but first he asked I just get you cleaned up enough so he could speak to you about the...the...strange weapon that..."

Meav clenched her eyes shut. "That Hollister McGreary had," she finished the sentence.

"Aye, my lady...do you think you are ready?"

Opening her eyes, Meav chuckled nervously. "If I wait for when I am ready, Grendel, we will all be old. Right now I do not know if I can bring meself to put one foot in front of the other in order to go where Rule is." She frowned. "Nor if I have the courage to ever leave this room."

Gently Grendel rubbed Meav's trembling hand, pity rising in her heart for the new lady of the castle. "Shall I tell him you will not be joining him?"

Meav shook her head and straightened her shoulders. "Nay, Grendel. I will go to me husband and help him with whatever he asks."

****

Rule was standing by the window, looking out at the courtyard when Meav entered the great hall. Ibrehem and Bulwark stood by the fireplace. Wesley, Olin and Ustin were seated around the large table. In the center was Hollister McGreary's gun.

247

All three men stood when they spotted Meav.

Rule rushed to her side, took her hand and led her over to a chair. Kneeling down in front of her, he tenderly stroked her cheek. "I know you are still in a state of shock over what has happened...and I would not ask this of you, my lady, if it were not of immense importance."

Meav nodded. "What do you want to know, Rule?"

He stood, reached for the gun and held it out to Meav. "Show me how to use this weapon."

Meav ran her finger over the handle's scroll and border engraving, around the ivory grip and down the ten inch barrel. Suddenly she jerked her hand away...remembering who it once belonged to.

Rule reached out and enclosed her trembling hand in his. "I know this is not easy for you, my love...but if I do not know how this weapon works...in what way it is deadly, I cannot guard against it."

Meav took a deep breath. "I remember this gun well," she began. She wet her lips nervously. "Once, when Hollister came to me farm," she paused, glancing into her husband's amber eyes. They hardened with the mention of the evil man's name. "He showed me this gun." Meav felt a chill run through her. Standing, she made her way to the large fireplace and warmed her hands. Keronia was warm by day, but after the sun set the climate changed. A chill breeze from the ocean left the island damp. Meav felt it now throughout her very bones. Or was it still the fear of coming face to face with her family's murderer that left her trembling?

Rule followed, standing silently beside her, but reached out and gave her arm an affectionate squeeze.

She glanced at the gun in his hand. "That is a dueling pistol. In my country they are all the fashion of the upper class, a statement of wealth."

Rule arched a brow. "That villain considered himself to be of high station?"

"Aye," she said softly.

Rule frowned. "Why was McGreary showing this gun to you?"

"He wanted me to know 'twould be used if I fancied another."

Rule's frown deepened. "Then this is not for

warring?"

"Nay, 'tis for challenge...but 'tis still very deadly."
Meav pointed to the artillery's nose. "Even just loading
the gun powder into the barrel wrong can cause an
explosion."

Ibrehem moved closer, holding a crescent shaped
vessel made of ebony wood. A silver stopper closed the
opening at the top and a long piece of leather was
attached to each side. "I found this draped over
McGreary's shoulder."

"'Tis a powder horn," Meav explained. "It holds the
black gun powder."

"And what about these two pouches?" Ibrehem
questioned.

Meav pointed to the larger pouch. "This one holds the
balls and wadding...the other the caps."

Ibrehem frowned. "These things are used to make the
gun work?"

"Aye," Meav said.

Rule took her by the hand and led her outside.

Meav had to run to keep up with his long strides.

The others followed close behind.

Once they were a safe distance from the castle, Rule
gripped the gun's handle. "Show me how to make it work."

Meav bit her bottom lip. "I am not all that certain I
can remember every detail. I have seen me father ready a
musket many times, but this gun is a wee bit different."
She frowned. "Should I forget just one detail, or do not
instruct you right..."

"This is how McGreary held it," Bulwark said,
reaching for the gun and demonstrating the grip.

"Careful," Meav choked out hoarsely. "The hammer is
fully cocked and the gun is loaded."

"Loaded...what do you mean by *loaded*," Rule asked
eagerly, taking the gun from Bulwark.

"Hollister was very proud of this firearm. 'Tis a fairly
new weapon, and not like the one me father used. This
firearm, I have heard, is called a percussion lock gun."
Meav reached over and pointed to the gun's hammer.
"When this lever is cocked back it cannot strike the cap
that is placed on this part here," she said, pointing to the
nipple of the gun. "Having the lever half-cocked means

the shooter is preparing to fire a shot, but when 'tis fully cocked, as 'tis now, then the weapon is ready to use and will go off just by pulling this lever down here," she said, pointing to the trigger. She sighed heavily. "I am surprised, having been handled so much, that it has not gone off already."

"So the caps are placed here?" Rule asked, indicating the gun's nipple.

"Aye, and the gunpowder and balls are shoved into the long part up front with the rod that is beneath this part here," she said, referring to the barrel. "The cloth wadding is then stuffed into the gun so the balls will not fall out. Then somehow, when the bottom lever is pulled back it snaps the top lever on the cap, and a connection is made through the channel of the gun that flames the gunpowder and shoots out the ball."

"And 'tis that ball that kills," Rule concluded.

"Aye...rips apart the flesh. More times than not the wound is fatal."

Bulwark suddenly looked green. "And that scoundrel had this thing pointed at my head."

Rule arched a brow. "Then you can only get one shot for each ball?"

"Aye, 'tis how it works," Meav agreed. "Then you must do the whole loading process over if you want it to work again."

His eyes widened. "By thunder, a man's life would be at the mercy of how fast he could reload his gun."

"But one shot goes a great distance," Meav explained.

"So, with your foe far from you there is time to reload," Rule said.

Meav nodded. "And after you grasp the whole procedure it can be done fairly fast. But this gun is not used in battle. There are much bigger ones called muskets that can shoot farther. A musket is what me father used."

Bulwark grunted. "Give me a sword and dagger any day."

The muscles at Rule's jaw tightened. "Do you know if the muskets were aboard the ship?"

"Aye, they were...I hid down in the hull, and there were many crates packed with guns and ammunition," Meav said.

Rule's muscles tensed. "Teach me how to use this, my lady."

She took a deep breath, wishing this day to be over. "Place the handle of the gun securely in the palm of your hand, and spread your feet far apart for balance." Meav watched as his hips, tapering to long, muscular legs, braced his stand. She reached over and lifted his arm. "Now aim the nose of the gun at that tree over there," she instructed, pointing to a tree in the distance The lines of concentration deepened along the brows and under his eyes. "Now pull the bottom lever."

A blast sounded from the weapon. Rule was thrown back a bit, but caught himself. White smoke blew from the barrel, filling the air. It made them all cough and the explosion made their ears ring.

Bulwark ran to inspect the target thirty feet away. He stuck his finger in the hole that now marred the trunk and felt for the ball. 'Twas lodged deep. His heart sank at the thought of the Jabrians having their hands on weapons like this, only larger. He turned and shouted to Rule. "My lord, we are in for some trouble...big trouble."

****

Meav's stomach rumbled with her hunger. She had not eaten since she broke the morning fast, yet she could not manage to swallow one morsel of the delicious meal now set before her. Quietly she pushed the food around on her plate and listened to Rule instructing his men on what strategy to use while fighting the Jabrians...'twas hardly dinner talk, and did naught to increase her appetite.

Hollister and Shell's dead bodies lying bleeding on the ground, was etched in her mind. Aye, they were bad men, and deserved what they had gotten, but the truth be told...it all was a ghastly way to keep the peace.

And now her husband had to lead his men into another battle, one with villagers that may not have a warrior's skill, but did have weapons of a far greater destruction. Her stomach lurched with each plan the men hatched; hiding in the trees with bows and arrows...such danger, behind bushes with swords and daggers...such odds. Good Lord in heaven 'twas no wonder she feared for all their lives...but especially for Rule's. What would she do if anything happened to him? The thought of losing her husband was just too much for her.

She felt tired and dirty, still not having the bath she had been promised. By the time she had finished instructing Rule and the others on how to load and reload the gun, dinner was ready. Her ears still rang from their practice shots, making her head throb along with her other wretchedness.

Meav stood and pushed back her chair. With a quick glance at Rule, she ran from the great hall and up to their chamber. Once she had closed the large oak door behind her, she slid to the floor and wept.

She was losing everything in her life that she loved...her family in Dublin, her home, and now mayhap her husband.

"You are all I have left, Rule," she sobbed. "Do not leave me too."

****

The look on his wife's face, a mixture of fear and worry, had wrenched his heart. Scowling to himself, Rule realized he was wrong to talk in front of her. She had gone through enough today, things no gentle woman should see. How stupid and insensitive of him to allow her to listen in on the warring plans.

He quickly drained his mug of the ale and stood. "We leave at midnight," Rule said to Ibrehem. "Make sure all the men are gathered by the river an hour before."

"Aye, my lord," Ibrehem responded.

"For now, you go to Zailia." Rule looked around the table. "All of you go to your homes and spend the last hours of this day with those you love."

All the men nodded in agreement.

Rule addressed Wesley. "You will stay and guard the castle, along with five other men. Ibrehem will appoint the soldiers who will remain here with you."

Wesley squared his shoulders. "Aye, my lord."

Rule tipped his head politely. "Excuse me now while I go and comfort my wife." Or should he have said, *while she comforts me*?

Rule found Meav sitting on the window seat, looking out at the night.

"Meav," he said softly.

She turned, wiped the moisture from her face, and forced a smile. "Have I finally got you all to meself?"

He smiled in return. "Aye, lass...this time is all ours."

'Twas then a knock came at the door, and Rule moved to open it.

Two servants dragged in the large tub. Three women behind them carried pails of water.

Silently Meav watched from her seat at the basin being filled.

When the task was finished, Rule thanked them and bid all a good evening. Making his way to his wife, he held out a hand. "Your bath awaits, my lady."

She fell into his embrace, her arms wrapping around his neck, fingers entwined with the hairs at his nape. "Do not go, milord. Stay here with me, 'tis not necessary for the king to accompany his men into battle."

Rule pulled back and traced the full curve of her lips. "I cannot ask them to do what I would not."

"Aye, you can," she said earnestly. "They will understand. You are the king of this island, you have a wife and..."

He silenced her lips with the tip of his finger. "Hush, my sweet. 'Tis the way of it, and I must do as I feel is right and honorable." He kissed her eyes, then her nose. "Do not spoil the time we have with talk," he whispered against her mouth before he fully consumed it.

Meav leaned into him, hungrily returning his kiss, all the while feeling the tears scratching the back of her throat.

Rule broke away and began to unlace the bodice of her dress. "Let me wash your velvet flesh, memorize every inch of you."

Meav could feel the agony rise to choke her. Did her husband fear he would not return as well? Would this night be the final memory of their lovemaking that she would have?

A sob caught in her throat. She grabbed his hands and stilled them. "I cannot live on without you, Rule. You must come back to me...you must."

Again he hushed her words, only this time with a kiss. Pulling back to look at her, he smiled. "You must trust me, Meav...my judgment and my skills. I have no

253

intention of lying in a quiet grave when I have such a beautiful wife waiting in my bed."

"Death comes unintentionally," she choked, fighting the tears that threatened to spill from her eyes.

"I am most cautious," he stated softly.

"But is caution enough, milord?"

Rule slipped her dress down over her shoulders. The beautiful twin mounds spilled free. Gently he rubbed a rosy peak with his thumb. "No more talk, wife."

"Rule..." she began.

He arched a brow and looked deep into the aqua of her eyes. "I need this time, Meav...to love you...to be loved by you. Please do not let your fear rob us of this night."

Meav nodded slowly. "Love me then."

After stripping her of the rest of her clothing, he picked her up into his arms. Carrying her over to the tub, he gently placed her into the warm water. Quickly he disrobed from his own clothes and joined her.

Meav watched as he stretched out a long, muscular arm and with lean fingers reached for a cake of soap from a nearby table. He lathered the bar in his hands, and then began to bathe her. First he took her right hand, and washed between each finger. Than he moved to her wrist, up her arm, to her shoulder, and down across her chest. He lingered there, his palm resting just above her heart. Its rapid beat she was sure vibrated against his hand. When he cupped her breasts and circled her nipples with slippery fingers, heat pooled within her. Gasping she looked into his eyes and became lost in the heat of his gaze.

Passion rushed straight to his loins as he splayed his fingers across her slim belly, than moved down to the lush triangle between her thighs. Spreading her downy fleece, Rule teased her bud with slow strokes. Beneath the water his rod grew painfully erect. "You are so beautiful, my love."

Meav fastened her gaze full upon his swollen yard. Reaching out, she encircled him with her fingers and matched his lazy caress.

Rule smiled, teasing her petal faster. With frenzied strokes he rubbed back and forth. She trembled and spread her thighs.

Shards of desire swept through him when she tightened her hold, slipping her fingers up and down his shaft fervently.

Rule filled his palms with water and rinsed her flesh, before he snared her in his arms and stood. He kissed the naked slope of her shoulder, than bent his head to a succulent, ripe peak; sucking on one coral center and then the other.

In those dizzying seconds his mouth consumed her, Meav allowed all her worries and fears to lift from her thoughts. 'Twas her body that became her master and she could not...would not...fight the delicious sensations washing through her. Everything else fell away, and in her world there was just the two of them. Nothing else mattered now but being one with her husband, feeling him buried deep inside of her...so far inside that he could touch her heart; her very soul. He would become the essence of her core.

Pulling back to look at her, he smiled. "I love you with every fiber of my being."

"And I you, milord," she whispered, wrapping her arms around his neck.

Rule exited from the tub, taking her with him. Slowly he dried every inch of her body with a soft towel. When he was finished he stood while she dried him as well.

He turned toward her, his finger trailing along the line of her jaw, than he captured her chin. Gently he tilted her face so her gaze would meet his. "Do you even know how happy you have made me, lass?"

Meav did not answer, but instead helped herself to his lips. With fierce ecstasy she ran her tongue over his teeth, probed the warm recesses of his mouth, and sucked on his bottom lip.

Rule growled deep in his throat, picked Meav up into his arms and carried her to the bed. Lying down beside her, he smiled. "You are mine, Meav Thornton...all mine."

There was so much feeling in his burnt-whiskey eyes, Meav's heart melted. Tracing the curve of his lips, she returned the smile. "Forever and ever, my love."

"Forever and beyond," he whispered before reclaiming her lips. He loved her soft mouth, warm and moist. Good heavens, he would never have enough of the

Roberta C. M. DeCaprio

splendor he now tasted.

Kissing her sent shivers of desire racing through him, as his tongue probed the soft folds of her mouth. She amalgamated her own lips to his; hard and demanding she returned his kiss with reckless abandon.

He groaned with pleasure and crushed her to him, drinking in her sweetness. As he roused her passion, his own grew stronger. Breaking from her lips he placed kisses along her throat, down her neck, to the creamy orbs. Taking a roseate peak into his mouth, he caressed the swollen nipple with his tongue.

Meav arched into him, calling out his name in a breathless whisper.

Lower his mouth probed, until he was buried deep in the heat of her, laving the hidden font of her womb.

Meav's wreathing body made it definitely clear to him that she wanted more of the sweet torment. Her impatience grew to explosive proportions, making her cry out his name louder.

By thunder, her response sent spirals of electricity through his loins. He rose above her with trembling arms and penetrated her with his jutting male desire. In and out he slipped, slowly at first...then faster and harder at her urgent demands. The way her body curved, wiggled, arched against his made him burn inside.

A moan of ecstasy slipped through her lips, as her desire soared higher. She cried out with her release, her passion exploding.

The turbulence of her fervor and a downpour of sensations swirled around him like a hot tide, raging through both of them. His raw act of possession vibrated through his body like liquid fire, bursting forth the love from his loins. He flowed into her like warm honey.

He rolled off her and lie beside her, a protective arm pulling her close.

She melted into the curve of his body, their world just filled with the two of them.

And together they succumbed to the numbed sleep of the satisfied lover.

****

At the hour of ten, Rule slowly rose from the bed. Quietly he slipped on his breeches and shirt. Though he

256

wished to hear her sweet voice bid him goodbye, he chose not to wake her. Her fear and sorrow would only wrench his heart. Leaving her then would be a worse hell than it was already.

He picked up his boots and tip-toed to her side of the bed, looking down at his beautiful queen; a small hand tucked under her chin, long, dark lashes fanned out over freckled cheeks. Rule's mouth went dry and his heart thumped against his ribs. Squeezing his eyes shut, he silently called to the heavens for a safe return...for the chance to live his life with her...to love her each and every day...to have a family.

"Meya pulma tearina timenta coupla...my heart will weep until I see you again," he whispered, planting a gentle kiss upon her lips. Then he turned and silently left the room.

****

Meav woke with a start. In the darkness she reached for Rule, but he was gone. Hot tears slipped down her cheeks. She buried her face in his pillow and inhaled his scent; the clean citrus of the soap, the musky smell of their lovemaking. Sweet Mother of God how her heart gnawed with pain.

Meav pulled back the coverlet and swung her feet off the bed. Finding her robe and slippers she downed them and made her way to the window. The courtyard below was silent; all was asleep, except for the band of men led by Rule. They would hide in the jungle and wait for daylight...when the enemy would approach. Then they would fight to the death to protect what was theirs.

A knock came at the door, followed by Grendel's voice. "Are you awake, my lady?"

Meav turned to face the heavy oak portal. "Aye, Grendel, come in."

Zailia followed behind Grendel. "I am sorry, my lady...I needed to be with someone who would understand."

"'Twas how 'tis for me as well," Grendel admitted. "I have two to fret for, my brother, Tomas Bulwark and Victor Olin."

Meav smiled. "Olin, is it?"

Grendel nodded. "Victor asked me to marry him last

eve."

Meav crossed the room and embraced Grendel. "I am so very happy for you."

Zailia moved to place a hand on Grendel's shoulder. "I am as well, Grendel."

Grendel pulled back and looked deep into Meav's eyes. "What will we do if they do not..."

"Hush, Grendel," Meav broke in softly. "We cannot think that way."

Zailia's eyes filled with tears. "How can we not?"

Meav took a deep breath to still her own fear. "What we will not do is spend this night cringing in fear." She squared her shoulders. "We will help them instead."

Grendel frowned. "How can we help them?"

"When me grandmamma worried for a loved one, she prayed for their protection." Meav took each woman by the hand and led them before the fireplace. "We will sit in a circle, hold hands and pray till the men return."

Grendel's frown deepened. "How do you pray?"

Meav sat cross-legged in front of the fire. "By just talking to the Heavenly Father."

Zailia sat down beside her. "We can do that...just start talking to the Divine Maker."

"Aye, we can," Meav assured her. "Me grandmamma did it daily."

Grendel sat down on the other side of Meav. "And you believe this prayer thing will work."

"Aye, I do," Meav said, taking each woman's hand in hers.

"How certain are you?" Zailia questioned.

"As certain as I am that without heavenly intervention, our men are walking unprotected straight into hell," Meav said. "And we have nothing to lose by trying, now do we?"

Both women shook their heads.

"Then close your eyes," Meav began, "bow your heads, and repeat after me."

Chapter Twenty-Four

Rule looked about at his men. Each had found a position and was ready for war; holding a sword and shield, axe, dagger, or bow with arrow. They were crude weapons, but rough tools that dealt hard, fatal blows. They were useful in slaying, even if they were not elegant...like the gun. Killing need not be elegantly done as long as 'tis done effectively, and in all truth, 'twas the skill of the man behind the weapon that made the difference. His perception, his force and energy...the speed and experience in using the battle gear he chose, was what mattered most in the end.

Ibrehem hid in the brush beside Rule. He searched his friend's somber eyes. "What crosses your mind, my lord?"

Rule sighed. "I was just thinking how precious each moment in time is...each opportunity, each season...each fragment of ability...even the responsibilities. Why do we take such things for granted, Ibrehem?"

Ibrehem shrugged. "'Tis man's way, my lord. We do not realize what we have until we stand to lose it."

"I do not want to lose any of what I now have, my friend." The muscles at Rule's jaw tightened. "'Tis why I am hoping our impulses are sharper than the devils that are united to rebel against us."

"Our force is many, and our foes are few," Ibrehem reminded him.

"But their weapons are greater," Rule countered.

"Perhaps that is true, but their skill is limited," Ibrehem stated. "When our militia marched into Jabri Valley to liberate the Humblers, the fight was like taking food from an ant. The Jabrians have let themselves grow weak. Their only source of power was in the way they demanded work from the Humblers. Without the backbone of their slaves, they are a lost civilization. I am surprised they have survived at all."

259

Rule thoughtfully rubbed his chin. "Your point is valid, and in our favor, if they are as inept at using the firearms as they are at working their land and building their village."

"I am sure this is the case," Ibrehem reassured.

Rule frowned. "But there is something else you are overlooking,"

"What, my lord?"

"We also do not know how long they have had to learn how to use the guns, and the skill of their teacher." Rule adjusted his sword belt. "With practice even a Jabrian can be a threat."

Ibrehem shivered with disgust. "Their teacher would be that rascal that came for Meav."

Rule gritted his teeth. "Aye, and he was a ruthless murderer, Ibrehem. His fighting tactics would match who he was."

Ibrehem's voice was almost grudging. "What then, my lord?"

Rule arched a brow. "Call upon your training, my friend...and remember well the warring decree."

Ibrehem nodded. "Never underestimate your enemy."

"Aye, and always be one step ahead by using the element of surprise. An elf can slay a giant if the giant is not expecting it," Rule added.

"'Tis good to have you again at my side, my lord," Ibrehem admitted.

Rule chuckled lightly. "As much as I am fond of you as well, dear friend, there is someone else I would much rather be with right now."

Ibrehem smiled. "Aye, my sentiments exactly.".

Rule returned the smile. "Thinking of Zailia, are you?"

"Aye, my lord. The last I left her, she was sleeping naked in my bed."

Rule sighed heavily. "As was my lady." A large raindrop splattered on Rule's head. He looked heavenward. "There is one other thing you should never underestimate during a battle."

"What might that be, my lord?"

Rule scowled. "The weather, Ibrehem...never, ever count on good weather."

****

Meav watched Zailia and Grendel as they slept on the blanket they all shared by the fire. Their golden tresses mingled. Even in sleep their faces showed the strain of their worry and concern. Her two dear friends held out as long as they could, each one reinforcing the other's spirit, but alas their lids grew too heavy to keep open. She was thankful for their company...and could have never gone through this night without them.

Quietly she stood and made her way over to the tub she had shared with Rule. Dipping her hand into the water, which had now cooled, she wiggled her fingers. Ripples swirled around the floating cake of soap, bouncing it up and down.

Meav unbraided her hair, than reached for the bar, and tipping her head forward she began to wash. Vigorously she lathered and scrubbed her scalp, washing from each long strand the remains of the day. As she rinsed the grime free, her spirits lifted and were renewed...making her feel she had shed the hate that had hurt her.

As she dried her hair with a fresh towel, Meav felt a surge of freedom. Hollister McGreary was dead, so were Shell and Devora. All their wickedness had only led to their demise. No longer could they harm anyone, take what was not theirs, and taint the earth with their dark power.

After braiding her wet locks, Meav slipped on a dress and shoes. Quietly she left the bedroom chamber, making her way downstairs and to a room that opened off the great hall.

The solar, as the room was called, by day was bright with the sun's light. Its large windows and glassed doors overlooked the garden. The room was quiet and dark now, as the wee morning silence enveloped the Keep.

She sat down upon the window seat and looked out at the pink hues of the approaching dawn rising above the distant mountains. Since the beginning of time women sat vigil for their men to return from war—waiting, praying, hoping to spot their love's familiar face amongst the others marching home.

And when they did not...

Meav swallowed hard and blanched at the thought.

A light, drizzling rain was wetting the earth, droplets pelting the leaves like constant tears...like her tears, which now slipped silently down her cheeks. She wiped them with the backs of her hands and rose from the seat.

Passing through the great hall on her way back to her chamber, she stopped to watch the flames dance in the large stone fireplace. The hearth had been cleaned...every inch of the castle had been scrubbed, polished, and food prepared for the coronation the day after tomorrow.

She glanced around at the potted citrus trees that had been placed about the room, as well as the other foliage and decorative flowers. Slowly she walked over to where two thrones had been placed on the dais; one for the king, the other for his queen.

Meav sat in Rule's throne, caressing the ornate carvings on the arms with the tip of her finger. She snuggled her bottom down deep into the red velvet cushion; 'twas soft and inviting, especially to one who had not slept. Meav's fatigue finally claimed her against her will. Resting her head back on the plush pillow she closed her eyes and fell asleep.

****

"I see them, my lord...the enemy approaches," Olin warned from his vantage point. "I count about thirty...maybe a few more."

Rule saluted Olin, who sat high in a tree with his bow and arrow ready. Strapping on his helmet, Rule turned to Ibrehem. "Are the snares all in place?"

"Aye, my lord."

Rule gave a taut nod of approval. "And the men all prepared?"

"Aye, to that as well, my lord."

Rule squared his shoulders. "And what of you, are you ready, my friend?"

"As ready as I will ever be, my lord." Ibrehem slipped his blade from its sheath.

"Then it begins." Rule grabbed his shield and raised his sword. "Death to our foe."

Rule and his men waited until the Jabrians came closer before they used their warring tactics. The first twenty men captured were either caught in the snares and left to hang by the ankle, or were shot with arrows. Those that took up the rear, after witnessing their comrade's demise, began firing the muskets.

'Twas then Rule, Ibrehem, Bulwark and several other soldiers rushed from their hiding places and challenged the Jabrians with swords and daggers.

Silver blades clashed against flesh and firearms. Many of the Jabrians, never having fought before, just dropped their weapons and ran away. 'Twas then that Rule's men confiscated the abandoned guns and turned them on the enemy.

Bulwark, his attention on slitting a foe's throat, failed to notice another that came up behind, intending to fire the musket at his head.

Olin, seeing his friend in danger, aimed his arrow and shot the enemy through the back. The Jabrian fell at Bulwark's feet.

'Twas then Bulwark noticed his would be assassin. Looking up at the tree branch where Olin sat, he smiled. "I thank you, mate."

Olin saluted. "Cannot be making Grendel cry for her brother, now can I?" He smiled broadly. "I promised her I would watch your back."

Bulwark saluted in return. "I made her the same promise."

Ibrehem felled three Jabrians with their own weapons.

Rule also reached for a gun and opened fire on the enemy.

Between the Jabrians that ran like cowards and those lying dead, the only ones left were the ones hanging by their ankles from the snares.

"And what shall we do with this bunch of buffoons, my lord," Bulwark questioned.

Rule scrutinized the group of ten. Most were lads in their teens. So frightened were they, that some had wet themselves. Throwing his head back, Rule laughed heartily. "Send the whelps back to their mothers."

Bulwark nodded, than motioned to the soldiers sitting in the trees to help him.

One by one the Jabrians were freed from the snares.

With their hands tied behind their backs and their soiled breeches pulled down around their ankles, the humiliated lads waddled away.

Olin arched a brow. "I have heard wild bores love tender flesh."

Bulwark cupped a hand over his manhood. "Ack, the thought makes me cringe."

Olin began to chuckle. "Not as much as they will when they walk into their village half naked."

Bulwark slapped his friend on the back. "I would have rather fallen in battle then to face such humiliation."

"Aye, my thoughts as well, my friend," Olin countered.

Rule arched a brow. "I believe our work is through here. So whenever you two are done with your antics, we can leave."

The men nodded and together they confiscated all the guns, pouches and powder horns of ammunition from the dead men.

Rule looked around, accessing the spoils of war. He sighed heavily. It was never a pretty site, even for the victor.

Then suddenly the quiet battlefield was broken by the blast of a gun...the lone shot broke the silence, taking them all by surprise.

Rule felt like he had been struck by lightening. White heat coursed through his body...his eyes widened and he gasped for air. Slowly he pivoted on trembling legs to find an elderly man peering from the bushes with a musket in his hands.

"That was for my son, Shell," the old man spat.

Bulwark took aim and shot the Jabrian clean between the eyes.

Rule's world spun, he stumbled, and then hit the ground hard

Ibrehem ran to Rule's side and cradled his head in his hands.

Rule looked up into his friend's agonized face. "Take me to Meav," he choked before everything went black.

****

Meav's eyes shot open. The searing pain made her bolt upright in her seat. Clutching her chest she rose from

Rule's throne and staggered to the stairs.

"My lady, what is it?" Wesley said, coming from behind and taking her arm.

Meav turned, feeling the blood drain from her face. "Rule," was all she whispered.

'Twas then that Wesley caught her before she collapsed to the floor.

Chapter Twenty-Five

Both Grendel and Zailia stood at the top of the stairs and screamed in unison.

Zailia was the first to reach Wesley's side. "Merciful heavens, what happened?"

Wesley scooped Meav in his arms and carried her up the stairs. "I do not know, lass...I just came in from standing guard on the night shift and saw my lady stumbling to the stairs."

Grendel ran ahead to open the chamber door. "Poor thing is so distraught," she said over her shoulder. "Has neither eaten or slept."

Wesley placed Meav gently down on the bed, his heart going out to the beautiful young woman.

Zailia ran to fetch a compress. "We should have stayed awake with her."

Grendel covered Meav with a blanket. "I think she is still suffering from shock over what happened yesterday by the river."

Zailia returned with a damp cloth and sat at the edge of the bed. Gently she placed the compress on Meav's forehead. "She fears for Rule's life."

Wesley nodded in agreement. "'Tis the way of it, I believe. Just before she collapsed she whispered his name." He thought of his own sweet, Becka. Could she be fretting in the same way for him? The idea that he had caused his love such pain filled him with guilt and sorrow. As soon as he could leave for home he would, and straight into Becka's arms; never to venture far again.

Zailia pushed a copper tendril from Meav's cheek. "Meav, Meav, can you hear me?" She gently caressed Meav's face. "Oh, may the Devine help us all. My own heart aches as well, with the thought of Ibrehem surrounded by danger. Heaven forbid he should never return."

Meav stirred, blinking her eyes into focus, looking up

at the three of them, there faces etched with concern. "Why are all of you staring at me like that?"

"You collapsed, my lady," Wesley explained. "Thankfully I caught you before you hit the floor."

Meav closed her eyes, searching her thoughts for some recollection. As her mind cleared, the dreaded feeling that something had happened to Rule once more surfaced. Her eyes shot open. "I felt him...his pain...I know something horrible has happened to my husband."

Zailia took Meav's hand. "'Tis natural you would feel such a way. I also fear for Ibrehem."

"And I for my brother and Victor," Grendel added. "This has truly been a torturous night for us all."

"Your husband is a wise man, my lady, who calculates every obstacle that might crop up," Wesley comforted. "He does not tread blindly into any circumstance, and is fully aware of the dangers and mishaps of war. Never would he take unnecessary chances."

Meav sat up, for an instant the room spun. She shook her head to clear it. "How do you know this, Wesley, when you have never fought beside him."

Wesley moved to stand by the window, gazing out. The season's earthy hues decorated the land, and a new day began. What would it bring? "'Tis true I have not been with him in battle, but I have witnessed his caution."

"When," Meav probed.

"Rule came to me with his suspicions about Lorna...asked I follow her about the castle. 'Twas how I discovered she spiked Bulwark's bread with sleeping herbs." Wesley looked back at Meav. "When I warned him of Lorna's actions, he immediately devised a plan for...."

"...for Bulwark to fake his slumber and for the rest of you to hide in the bushes," Meav finished his sentence.

Wesley nodded. "So you see, my lady, nothing gets past your husband."

Meav bit her bottom lip nervously. "But I felt it...I could almost..."

Wesley turned again to glance out the window. "They are here, my lady."

Zailia stood and rushed to the casement. "'Tis true, my lady."

267

Meav ripped aside the blanket and bounded off the bed. In her haste, the room tilted and spun. She reached for the bedpost to steady herself.

Grendel ran to her aid. "It might be best if you remain in bed, my lady."

Meav swallowed hard. "Nay, I will greet my husband upon his return from battle, as a wife should." Taking a deep breath she slowly made her way to the door and down the stairs.

Once out by the castle's path, Meav stood with outward calm waiting for the band of soldiers to round the corner, but inside her heart slammed against her chest.

Ibrehem was the first to appear.

Zailia let out a cry of relief and ran to him, throwing herself into his arms, and smothering his face with kisses.

Meav frowned, panic rising to choke her. Why did Rule not lead his men?

Then there came Bulwark and Olin. Grendel's feet took flight as she ran to her brother and betrothed, tears of joy falling from her eyes as she hugged each warrior.

Meav pressed her lips together, daring not to blink an eye. If she did, she knew her tears would fall in torrents. Where was Rule? She squared her shoulders and stretched on tiptoe, not wanting to miss her husband's face. Surely he had to be next?

But he was not.

Instead Ustin and several others marched passed, worn and sweaty.

Meav shifted uncomfortably, trying to be patient and brave...aye, she would be brave, like Rule. She lifted her chin and stood tall to greet her husband. He was probably taking up the rear, thinking of his men at all times and watching their backs.

'Twas then she spotted him...not marching but being carried by four soldiers on a stretcher of woven palm leaves.

Fear numbed her and her mouth was dry with dread. Swallowing hard the sickly knot lodged deep in her throat, Meav ran to him.

The bearers gently placed the stretcher on the ground.

Meav knelt in the damp earth. "Nay, tell me this is

not so," she choked, pushing dark strands of hair from his forehead. "Rule," her voice broke. Her fingers trembled as she stroked his handsome face.

Ibrehem came down on one knee beside her. "He was shot in the back and has lost a lot of blood, my lady."

"Rule," she sobbed. "Please, milord, do not leave me." She took his hand in hers and brought it to her lips. "Someone find Wysteria." She looked over at Ibrehem. "Fetch her now...and hurry!"

Ibrehem turned to Ustin. "Go, find the healer."

Ustin nodded and quickly departed.

"You promised me you would come back to me, milord," Meav whispered close to his ear. "You cannot break your word, my love. I won't let you."

Her sweet voice filled with anguish penetrated Rule's pain. His eyes fluttered open and were met by his wife's terrified gaze.

Meav's tears fell from her eyes, dropping softly onto Rule's lips.

He licked the moisture with a slow swipe of his tongue. "Your tears are salty," he whispered.

"Oh, Rule," she gasped, caressing the line of his jaw. "Wysteria is on her way, she will help you."

He grimaced with pain. "Meav," he said hoarsely. "I want you to listen to me."

Meav traced the outline of his mouth. "Hush, save your strength."

Even now, with pain enveloping his entire body, her soft touch brought him comfort. "Nay, I need you to listen."

She nodded. Shards of pain and fear shone in her eyes. "I am listening."

Rule cleared his throat. "You, my queen, must lead this kingdom in my place."

"Nay, I will not...'tis you who will lead this isle," she protested through her tears.

"I am so sorry, my lady," he whispered, his own eyes growing moist.

"There is nothing to be sorry for, milord...you will get well and be king and we will live together forever and ever," she babbled hysterically.

Rule, with his last ounce of strength squeezed her

hand. "'Tis not to be for us, love, and I need your promise..."

"Nay, if I do not promise, you cannot go," she interjected. Quickly she looked around. "Where is Wysteria...what is taking her so long?"

Rule gasped for breath. "Her herbs cannot help this time, Meav."

She turned back to gaze into his eyes. "Aye, they can," she sobbed. "They have to."

"*Levena*...do you promise?" he choked.

Meav's tears slipped down her face. "This is not how 'tis supposed to be, milord...The Prophecy says I am to save you...Keronia's Rule." ·

He smiled weakly. "And you have saved their rule, my lady...Devora is gone."

"Nay, that is not how I thought..." her words caught in her throat...but 'twas how the words were written. Fear gripped her heart like a vice. All this time she thought she was destined to save him, but 'twas Keronia's rule not Rule himself that was meant to be saved. All of them were just pawns...Meav's mother included...for what was foretold hundreds of years ago. Their lives did not matter. They were just players in a story, and now the curtain closed. Suddenly resentment filled her heart. The whole thing...all their efforts had turned out to be a cruel joke.

"Do I have your promise, Meav," he whispered, hanging on to the last thread of life.

She looked deep into his eyes. "Aye, you have my promise."

"Ibrehem," Rule choked.

Ibrehem leaned forward. "I am here, my lord."

Rule began to shiver, his body growing cold and numb. "I leave you first in command. Never let harm come to my queen."

Ibrehem blinked back his tears. "I will guard her with my life, my lord."

Both Grendel and Zailia could be heard sobbing.

"*Do wa goncha*," Rule whispered.

Meav turned to Ibrehem. "What...what did he just say?"

Ibrehem inhaled sharply. "That he is entering the silence."

"Nay, Rule...stay with me...please, milord, stay with me," Meav begged.

Zailia moved forward, placing a hand on Ibrehem's shoulder and leaning down beside Meav. "You taught me how to pray for Ibrehem's safety, and my prayers have been answered. Now I am here, my lady, for you."

"I do not need prayers, because Rule is going to be fine," Meav said. She caressed Rule's face. "You are going to be fine, milord," she repeated.

"Meav, *Amin tialo*," Rule whispered. "Do you remember those words?"

"Aye, I do...you proclaimed them after the first time you made love to me."

"Never forget them," Rule choked.

"I love you too, milord...forever."

Rule forced his eyes shut...sparing her the sight of them staring blankly. A lone tear slipped from the corner. He felt Meav catch the drop with the tip of her finger.

Faintly he heard her voice for the last time. "I taste your sorrow, milord, as you did mine. Your tears are salty too."

His hand relaxed in hers, his heart slowed, peace enclosed around him, and then there was nothing.

Chapter Twenty-Six

Meav's anguish was so acute she actually felt physical pain. Throwing herself on top of his body, she wept her heart out.

'Twas over...Rule was gone.

"Come, my lady," Ibrehem said softly. Gently he reached for Meav's arm. "There is naught to be done now."

Meav smothered Rule's quiet and serene face with tender kisses.

Again Ibrehem tried to coax her from Rule's side. "Come, my lady."

Meav's mind raced. 'Twas Rule who should govern Keronia, not her. If only she could...

Meav stiffened, remembering the legend of Hugo Pierre Quinn. Hope resounded. Quickly she bolted to her feet shouting. "I can...I can!"

Ibrehem stood with a frown. "What can you do, my lady?"

She turned and grabbed Ibrehem by the front of his tunic. "I can take his place."

Ibrehem placed a comforting arm around her shoulders. "Aye, 'twas your promise to him...to rule Keronia in his place. And I will help you, my lady."

"Nay, I mean, I can take his place in death," Meav said. "Do you not remember the legend of the warrior god, Hugo Pierre Quinn? Centuries ago he granted a maiden the ability to take her dying love's place."

Ibrehem frowned. "I remember, my lady, but 'twas just that...only a legend."

"But surely there are some truths to legends...how else would there be a river of orange?" Meav argued.

Ibrehem shook his head and looked down at Rule's lifeless body. "'Tis in life you will carry on his wishes."

Meav shrugged Ibrehem's hands off her. "Nay, my husband can return and rule Keronia himself."

Ibrehem turned to his wife. "Zailia, help her to

understand."

Zailia frowned. "She is beyond consoling right now, husband. Can you not see?"

"'Tis exactly why we need to get her away from Rule's body and into the castle," Ibrehem advised.

Zailia sighed heavily. "If 'twas me in her place, I would seek every way to change things, as well. Anyway, what harm can it do to let her try?"

"This is madness," Ibrehem scowled. "We are only prolonging the inevitable." He turned to Meav. "Please do not make me take you by force, my lady."

"But I can do this...I can!" Meav shrieked, backing away. Quickly she looked heavenward, raising her hands above her head. "If you can see me, hear me, I beseech you with all my heart. I ask to take his place." When nothing happened she threw her head back and closed her eyes. "Do you hear?" she called out, her words echoing through the wind. "I ask to take his place!"

Ibrehem moved toward Meav with an outstretched hand. "My lady, please come with..."

But his words caught in his throat when the sky blackened and the earth trembled.

Everyone froze where they stood.

"See, 'tis true, 'tis true," Meav exclaimed.

'Twas then a dead calm spread over the island. The deafening silence was dropped like a veil over Keronia; not a bird sang or a breeze stirred.

Meav inhaled sharply.. "I am ready...take me now...take me instead."

In an instant a blinding bolt of white light exploded.

Meav shielded her eyes and fell to her knees beside her husband's body. Gently she bestowed one last kiss upon his lips "Live well, my love," she whispered.

Her body felt as light as air and she began to float higher and higher to the heavens.

The clouds parted and the figure of a woman came forth.

Meav was awed by the majestic sight.

"I am so proud of you, and how you saved my people," the familiar voice said softly.

A warm feeling bathed Meav's heart. "Mama?"

"Aye, my little girl, 'tis I for sure," Meridith said.

"Oh, Mama, I have missed you so much," Meav exclaimed, running with outstretched arms.

"Stay put, Meav," Meridith warned, halting her daughter with a raised hand. "Your time is not yet done."

"Meav frowned. "'Tis done...I have taken Rule's place."

"Nay, love," Meridith said softly. "You have much to do yet."

"But if I return than Rule dies...I cannot live without him, Mama."

Meridith tilted her head sideways. "Do you trust me, Meav?"

"Aye, you know I do."

"Then go back." Meridith smiled. "When 'tis your time we will meet again. I will come myself to guide you, and all of us will be together."

Meav watched her mother return to the clouds. "I love you, Mama."

"I love you too, Meav."

And then, Meridith was gone.

****

When Wysteria entered the scene she expected to find Rule in need of her ministrations. Instead she found Meav face down in the dirt; bleeding from a deep wound in her back. And Rule screamed. The agonized howl that came forth from the deepest part of his heart brought chills down her spine and time back to the island...

He leapt from the stretcher and gathered Meav into his arms. "How has this happened?" Rule bellowed in agony. In wide-eyed terror he turned to look at Wysteria. "One moment I am floating to a place white and quiet, free from the pain, out of my cold carcass. And then suddenly I am ripped from the heavenly cocoon and forced back into my body...only my flesh now is healed of the gaping wound in my back and my strength has returned in bounds. Slowly I open my eyes to see..." he looked at Meav in his arms. "I do not understand."

Wysteria knew exactly what had happened. Pride welled in her heart for the bravery of her sister's child. She came forward. "She took your place, my lord."

Rule crushed his wife's body to his chest. "Nay...nay!" Throwing his head back to the heavens he howled again, like an animal in pain. "Undo this...*seda*! Bring her back!" Then bending his head, he wept, his tears wetting the copper curls that framed Meav's tranquil face.

The sound...the sorrow unfolding paralyzed all that watched.

Wysteria ran to his side. "Hurry...'tis of the essence that you bring her to the river."

Rule, for the first time in his entire life, did not question the crone. With Meav tight against his chest, he ran to the river's edge and walked into the water without hesitation.

Wysteria followed close behind, her own heart beating rapidly against her chest. "Quickly...submerge her."

Rule obeyed, falling to his knees to allow the water to wash over Meav.

The river was still, like layers of a mirror...its smooth lacquer flowing across the pebbles lying below as the blood from Meav's wound mixed with the sun's light, coloring the water a deeper orange than before.

Loreli rose from the water to face Rule, her translucent eyes held a purposeful sheen.

Rule gritted his teeth and pulled Meav closer to his chest. "She is mine. You will not claim her."

Loreli moved closer. "I have not come to claim her."

Rule's mouth thinned. "Then why have you come?"

Loreli smiled warmly. "She is my friend. I have come to save her...as I did many months ago." Slowly the mermaid reached out and placed her hand on Meav's heart; then brought her lips to gently meet Meav's, breathing life back into her lungs.

Meav stirred, feeling the cool lap of water against her breast. Slowly her eyes opened to the heavenly vision before her. Was this now an angel, taking up where her mother had left off? Perhaps Meav had not yet made it back to her body? Where ever she was, the beauty of the moment made her gasp.

Loreli's golden hair shone in the sun like a halo around her head. Kind, opal eyes filled with tenderness gazed deep into Meav's. "Welcome back, my lady," she said smiling, then turned and swam away.

'Twas then Meav looked up into the tiger-gold of her

husband's eyes. Her face instantly brightened, her voice rose with her elation. "Rule...Rule!" She wrapped her arms around his neck and kissed his tear-stained eyes. "Saints preserve us, you are alive!"

****

How Meav's heart could rise from the depths of despair to the height of happiness in one day was beyond comprehension. All she knew was that sitting before the mirror, admiring her coronation ball gown, and watching Grendel weave tiny pearls in her hair was enough to make her know she was truly blessed.

"Aqua is your color, my lady," Grendel commented.

Meav smiled warmly, smoothing down the organza skirt. "You have done a beautiful job on this gown, Grendel. Never, anywhere is there one so grand."

Grendel blushed. "I thank you, my lady." She straightened out a bit of lace on Meav's sleeve. "I am just happy all has turned out so well."

Meav sighed. "'Twas all quite frightening there for awhile and me sorrow was so tremendous. Never did I think I would ever feel the joy that now fills me heart."

Grendel squeezed Meav's hand affectionately. "Oh, my lady, you deserve the best of all things to come. Keronia is forever grateful for you, how you saved Rule and all of us from Devora's reign." Grendel wiped a tear from her eye. "I wish for you a long and happy life with your king."

****

He waited for her at the bottom of the staircase, his muscular chest filling the white linen shirt, and the red cape flowing from his broad shoulders made him look even more like a hero. His tight black breeches complemented the long lean legs. Meav felt her cheeks burn at the thought of touching his burly hardness.

Meav took the hand Rule extended and walked proudly beside him into the great hall.

All eyes turned as they entered. Gasps of awe and pride filled the room.

Rule felt like a peacock puffed up with pride. His beautiful wife had brought him such love and glory...as well as restoring his being. Never in his fondest dreams did he think he would kiss a hero, but that is what Meav was. And Rule would spend the rest of his life making her happy, filling her days with love and nights with passion.

Even now, his loins ached for her warmth. He wanted to uncoil the fiery curls laced with pearls, and caress her delicate, oval face. The musk-rose flush on her ivory cheekbones made Rule's heart skip a beat. Perhaps she was thinking the same thing? His anticipation rose as his yearnings grew for their time alone, when he could plant hot kisses all over her rosy mouth and down her creamy throat.

****

Neteru waited on the dais, her golden robe adorned with wisps of silver trim, a beautiful gold tiara on her head. To Meav she looked like a heavenly apparition she had seen once in the scene of a chapel's stained glass window.

As they approached her, the high priestess bowed respectively, then held her arms high above her head and addressed all those gathered. "We come together on this glorious day to crown a king and queen." She looked heavenward. "May their reign be blessed with long life, love, happiness and may they sire many heirs."

All the people cheered.

Neteru placed on hand on Meav's shoulder and another on Rule's. "Please kneel."

Rule helped Meav to her knees and quickly knelt beside her.

Neteru then handed Rule a box.

He arched a questioning brow.

"Your mother's ring," Neteru whispered. "She gave it to me to keep safe, along with the armor, the royal batons and crowns."

Meav watched Rule's long, lean fingers open the lid and pull from the small package a gold ring, encrusted with rubies and sapphires.

"Claim your queen," Neteru said.

Rule reached for Meav's hand and slipping the ring onto her finger, gave his oath. "I, Rule Thornton of Keronia, before all these witnesses claim you, Meav O'Shay Thornton, as my wife and queen; to reign with me for all the days of my life...and should I depart before you, I hereby bestow onto you my duties as ruler of these here isles of Keronia. From our loving union may there be many heirs, who when the time comes, will sit on the throne and govern with honor and loyalty, and carry on for generations the Thornton dynasty."

Neteru turned her eyes to Meav. "Do you accept all he has pledged?"

Meav looked deep into her husband's amber eyes, so thankful to be able to see their glimmer, feel their warmth. "Aye, I accept all he vows."

"And will you, Meav O'Shay Thornton," Neteru began, "stand by and honor your king, nurture his seed, and be the mother of future generations?"

"Aye, I will...with all me heart," Meav answered.

Neteru handed them each a gold baton, engraved at the tip with the Thornton crest. Then she placed a gold crown inlaid with rubies and diamonds on Rule's head. "I crown you King Rule Thornton. Long live the king!"

All those present cheered in unison, "Long live the king."

Then Neteru placed a gold crown, much daintier and inlaid with pearls and diamonds, on Meav's head. "I crown you Queen Meav Thornton. Long live the queen!"

"Long live the queen," everyone cheered.

Neteru smiled. "Now rise."

Rule reached for Meav's hand and they both stood.

Neteru bowed. "Your Majesty, 'tis time for you to face your subjects."

When Rule and Meav turned to look upon all their guests, the room filled with applause.

After a few moments of cheer and congratulations, Rule raised his hand for silence. "I will now hold court...as I call your names please come to the foot of the throne." Offering Meav his hand, he escorted her to her seat and then took the one beside her.

Meav looked out at the sea of faces, their eyes twinkling and smiles wide. Then she turned to look at Rule and her heart lurched with pride at the way he sat so regal upon his throne. His thick, dark hair hung to his shoulders, his profile spoke of power and ageless strength of character. When he turned to look at her, his face melted into a buttery smile that nearly took her breath away.

One by one Rule's men approached the throne. Standing, he placed his sword upon their shoulders and knighted each of them, including Wesley.

After the last had been honored, Meav leaned toward her husband. "I have honors to bestow as well, milord."

Rule tipped his head graciously. "Carry on, my lady."

Meav stood.

The room went still.

Nervously she cleared her throat. "In Ireland, me homeland, those who have fought bravely for the crown receive a medal of honor." She looked over at her husband and reached for his hand, then turned back to the guests. "Would you all come with me to the river, please?"

Without hesitation Rule did as she asked, the others following in a procession behind them.

Meav stopped at the river's edge, and called for Grendel.

With her cheeks the shade of crimson Grendel quickly made her way to her queen, bowed, and handed her a pouch.

Meav opened the pouch and pulled out two tiny shells. A leather cord was threaded through a hole made at the top of each shell. "Titiana and Gyla, me pixie warriors, will you please come forth?"

The fairie sisters flew to Meav and landed on her arm.

Meav smiled down at the two. "With great honor, I bestow upon you each this medal of honor, for your brave service and loyalty to the crown." She slipped a necklace over each fairie's head. "And Gyla," she whispered. "If you ever spank Titiana again, you will deal with me. Do I make meself clear?"

Gyla nodded with wide eyes.

Rule stifled a smile.

Meav raised her gaze and smiled at the rest of the pixie clan sitting in the trees. "I have not forgotten you, me brave troop. Titiana and Gyla will now lead you all to the back solar terrace, where you will find a cake waiting for your eating pleasure."

In an instant dozens of little flapping wings took flight.

Meav then pulled from the pouch another shell,

fashioned in the same way on a leather cord, and walked over to the river's edge.

Everyone's eyes widened when Loreli's face surfaced from beneath the orange water. Meav placed the medal around the mermaid's neck. "I thank you for saving me life."

Loreli inclined her head respectfully and quickly swam away.

Meav turned to Rule and smiled. "I am finished here, milord."

Rule beamed with pride and took her hand. "Then let the feast begin."

And what a feast it was...duck soup, coconut and shrimp salad, black bread, all sorts of cheeses and fruits, wine, ale, and several sweet delicacies to melt in one's mouth.

There was music and dancing, laughter and story telling, all ages coming together and having fun.

Rule poured Ibrehem another glass of ale. "It has been a long time since this island has been so merry, my friend."

Ibrehem took a swig of the brew. "Aye, too long." He bowed respectively to Rule. "Thanks to you, sire, all is as it should be."

"Nay, Ibrehem," Rule said, looking over at his wife who laughed and talked an arms length away with Zailia. "Thanks to Meav."

Ibrehem raised his goblet. "Then to our queen."

Rule lifted his glass as well. "Aye, to our queen...my queen...my beautiful, brave, queen."

****

Meav looked out her chamber window. The sun was preparing to kiss the earth goodnight, the guests were gone and the Keep was quiet. She closed her eyes when she felt Rule come up from behind her, brushing aside the hair from her neck.

Gently he bestowed a kiss upon her shoulder. "What thoughts occupy you, my lady?"

She turned to face him. "I saw her, Rule."

He smoothed her hair from her face. "Who did you see, love?"

Meav caressed his cheek with the back of her hand.

"Me mother...when I took your place, me body rose to heaven. 'Twas there, from the clouds she came forth. And she spoke to me."

He wrapped his arms around her and pulled her protectively close. "What did she say?"

Meav rested her head on his shoulder. "She told me I had much to do yet, and I had to return."

Rule wrapped a curl around his finger and brought it to his lips. "'Tis true, you are needed here."

She pulled back to look at him. "At first I protested."

He arched a brow. "An obstinate child to the end, eh love?"

Meav frowned. "I thought if I returned, you would die again."

"I am glad your mother convinced you otherwise," he said, kissing her furrowed brow.

"She asked me if I trusted her, and when I said that I did, she bid me farewell, and said when 'twas me time she would be waiting to guide me," Meav explained.

Rule kissed her nose. "And that will not happen for a very long time, my lady." He looked down into her azure eyes. "I plan on us having a full and happy life, filled with laughter, children, love and passion." He cast her a mischievous smile. "And I intend to start right now."

She wrapped her arms around his neck, her fingers entwining with the strands of hair. "*Amin tialo*," she whispered.

Gently he kissed her lips. "I love you too, Meav," he said tenderly, his heart full of love. "Meav...my beautiful, Meav...even your name is dear to me."

She giggled. "How is that so?"

He smiled warmly. "Because when a man loves a woman, as much as I do you, calling out her name is even different...an experience that leaves him awed. The way the sound comes forth from my tongue is so moving it fills me with acceptance and care...and love."

"Me name sounds so...so beautiful and cherished when you say it. Aye, 'tis safe forming in your mouth and rolling off your tongue, Rule," she whispered; as she was in his arms, his life, and in his heart.

Epilogue

One year later...July, 1831.

Meav emerged from the bed, enveloped herself in the fine, silk robe, and went to the window. Affectionately she caressed her swollen belly as she looked out at a full moon exploding behind a thread of silvery gray clouds.

In only a month's time she would give birth to Rule's child. She could not believe how the time had sped by...already she had lived on the island a year.

And so much had changed since those first days she found herself marooned on Keronia.

Ibrehem and Zailia lived in the mansion behind the castle and were expecting their first child any day now. Tobiah also lodged at the mansion. Rule had appointed the wise old warrior to a position teaching new recruits wanting to serve the crown. Tobiah took charge of their young minds, educating their reasoning abilities while Ibrehem coached their fighting skills.

Victor Olin and Grendel married six months ago, and were housed in the east wing of the castle. Grendel still served as Meav's seamstress and handmaiden, but also became a trusted friend and confidant.

Tomas Bulwark married Cook's daughter, Hannah. They lived in the west wing of the castle. Because Hannah was so good with children—helped her own mother wean three of her siblings—Rule appointed her royal nanny. Now, Hannah waited anxiously for the big day to arrive so she could begin her job.

Cook, ready soon to retire, had begun to train her second eldest daughter, Magdalena in the castle's food preparation. Magdalena had caught Phillip Ustin's eyes and now the two were betrothed. After their nuptials, they would share the west wing with Bulwark and Hannah.

Meav hoped she would regain her girlish figure by

September, so she could attend the wedding garbed in a new gown that would do her husband proud.

Wysteria still maintained her tiny cottage, healing everyone on the island. But as of late she also resided at the castle...staying close to Zailia and Meav until their babies were born.

Titiana and Gyla were royal informants. Because of their ability to fly all over the island, they were able to watch Keronia from an aerial view. They kept their ears and eyes open to what went on and about the island, reporting their findings once a week.

Loreli had become a dear friend. Meav taught the mermaid how to braid hair and sing Irish songs, all the while munching on the island's produce. Loreli never mentioned Lorna and Meav never asked.

Brian Wesley went back to his family in the mountain region and married his childhood sweetheart, Becka. A few months ago the two paid the castle a visit to announce they too were expecting a new addition to their family. Wesley taught the Humblers to be warriors, and the gentle giants stood guard at the Jabri Valley border...ready to defend the crown.

Meav sighed, raising her hair off her shoulders and inhaling the floral scents carried upon the gentle breeze that now flowed through the window. Hearing her husband stir in bed, she adoringly glanced his way and smiled. How she loved him, her love growing with each passing day.

Rule frowned when he reached out for his wife and discovered her side of the bed empty. Concerned, he rose and lit a candle. Instantly the honey glow cast a romantic radiance to the room.

Rule lifted his gaze. 'Twas by the window he spotted her; the moon's light silhouetting her form beneath the robe's whisper light material. Her body, in the full bloom of motherhood, caught his breath. Rule's heart leaped and filled with gratitude for this moment. Pride welled within, love overflowed. Never in his life had he been so happy or content.

"Sorry if I woke you," she said, reaching to massage her spine. Slowly she kneaded the ache with gentle fingers.

He made his way to her and engulfed her in his arms. "Baby kicking again?"

"Aye, like a soldier on a march," she said, snuggling into his embrace.

Rule chuckled lightly. "My son, the warrior hero."

She peered up at him. "Or mayhap a daughter."

He kissed the slope of her shoulder. "And if she is anything like her mother she will be a brave one."

Meav hid a yawn with the back of her hand. "I just wish it would happen soon."

Rule kissed the top of her head. "You poor lass, you are exhausted."

"And swollen, and clumsy, and..."

"...Beautiful," he added.

Meav arched a brow. "If only that were true."

Rule smiled. "'Tis, my lady...there is nothing more beautiful to a man than his wife carrying his babe beneath her heart." His touch was light, tender, as he stroked her arm, and then snared her hand. "Come back to bed and I will give you a backrub."

Meav rolled her eyes heavenward. "Ah me, how can I resist such an offer?"

One last time she gazed out at the night...the breeze gently stirred the palm trees; the moon a beacon in the dark sky.

And, in the distance, Loreli, the island's beautiful water lady, bathed herself in the lunar glow; on a rock by the river...

A river of orange.

Roberta C.M. DeCaprio has been writing for over twenty-five years, winning awards for her poetry. She is a member of The International Women's Writing Guild and Romance Writers of America, holding the position of Newsletter Editor of her local group from 2002 to 2004. Currently she is an Assistant Editor for Independence Today newspaper (a national publication dedicated to the needs and rights of the disabled). Having a walking impairment since birth, Roberta knows first hand the challenges of living with a disability. She has authored two books to date: Coma Coast, a paranormal romantic suspense, and the sequel The Vanity, a paranormal romantic thriller, both published by Wings Press. She is the creator of The Word Merchants Society, an online support site for writers.

To visit TWMS, log on to:
www.timesunion.com/communities.thewordmerchantssoci ety and get plugged in to helpful writing tips. Roberta is a mother and grandmother of two who shares her upstate New York home with her artist husband and many beloved pets.

You can visit her site at www.robertadecaprio.com and her Blog at: www.tagworld.com/Roberta8150

www.ingramcontent.com/pod-product-compliance
Lightning Source LLC
Chambersburg PA
CBHW070839250626
47159CB00003B/843